Death
Before Dawn

A Guardian's Diary Part II

Amelia Hutchins

Death Before Dawn

A Guardian's Diary Series Part II

ISBN: 978-0-9970055-4
Cover Art Design: Vera DC Digital Art & Photography
Cover Art Illustrations: Vera DC Digital Art & Photography

Edited and Formatting: E & F Indie Services
Copy Editor: Gina Tobin

Published by: Amelia Hutchins
Published in (United States of America)
10 9 8 7 6 5 4 3 2 1

Dedication

Thank you so much to the fans who spend countless hours supporting authors with their precious time and reviews. For understanding that we are merely human, and sometimes, it takes a lot longer than we expected for a story to play out in our heads. The characters don't always play along when I want them to, and more often than not, they won't talk loud enough for me to hear until they are ready to be written.

To Gina, who has been with me from the start of this journey, and hopefully for a very long time to come.

To my husband, who spent countless nights without me in bed, for understanding that sometimes these assholes inside my head never shut up! For the dinners you cooked, and the rooms you cleaned to help me be able to spend the time on this book. I love you. You are my world, and yeah, those little monsters we created are also a huge part of it. I love them mostly when they're behaving. The others times, I'm not sure who they belong to.

To the team who helps me through each and every book with hours of dedication. The Minions, who pimp the shit out of these books. You ladies rock my world.

Dedication (Cont'd)

To the beta team and editors who always help out no matter how much shit you got going on in the real world, thank you.

To the bloggers, you run the book world. Thank you for everything you ladies do!

To the authors who paved the way so that little authors like me could make it? Thank you too!

Also by Amelia Hutchins

The Fae Chronicles

Fighting Destiny

Taunting Destiny

Escaping Destiny

Seducing Destiny

The Elite Guards

A Demon's Dark Embrace

A Guardian's Diary

Darkest Before Dawn

Death Before Dawn

Monsters Series

Playing with Monsters

Death
Before Dawn

Warning

This book is not suitable for anyone under the age of eighteen. This book is intended for those who enjoy dark humor, and a wild ride. There is adult language and scene's that may leave you tying up your partner and making him or her, very happy. This book is a series, but has a happy for now ending. There are no zombies in this book, but should my imagination place a few in the next book, do not worry, I will kill them off shortly. Not intended for anyone who doesn't enjoy being taken for plot turning, panty soaking, and edge of your seat wild ride.

Death
Before Dawn

Chapter One

My eyes took in the savagery of the killings. Someone had enjoyed it; they'd tied up the men, women, and children and took their time torturing and mutilating them. It was disgusting; knowing that these people had survived the Rh Viridae virus and still ended up this way shook my confidence.

"And you say we're animals," Jaeden said, his face a mask of disgust as he took in the small remains that hadn't been spared. "Someone slaughtered these people for fun."

Fun.

I reached down and picked up a small, tattered, brown bear that was missing an arm, the fluff escaping from the opening. Grayson was out here with our psychotic mother, being exposed to monsters like this. I placed the bear next to the little girl, who had died curled up beside her mother's corpse. She had a gaping head wound, probably from a violent blow to the head. It looked as if the little girl had tried to run to her mother, and had been beaten viciously for it.

People no longer died from the virus; now they died from others who had survived the sickness. Deaths caused by the sick, twisted, lawless world that the virus had left us with.

"Emma, lass," Lachlan chided when I wiped at the tears that filled my eyes as I wondered how my brother was doing. It was an endless loop of worries running through my mind that I couldn't stop. No matter how much I tried, I couldn't.

"I'm okay," I mumbled, and turned to give him a small smile, which was the biggest one I could manage. I'd seen a lot of shit in the trek down south, but this? This was once a town that somehow was filled with people who had banded together and had obviously managed to work collectively to survive. This new world was harsh, and seemed to have no regard for human life.

"Nae, ye are nae okay," he argued in his soft Scottish burr.

"Lachlan, this sucks. Finding an entire town of survivors, super cool. Finding that they'd been killed just a few hours before we arrived? Not cool at all," I growled as I felt the sense of someone watching me again. I'd felt that sensation a lot lately; as if someone was following my progress as I made my way south. I hadn't mentioned it to the others, only because they hadn't seemed to sense it, and if I couldn't find the source of the sensations, it was doubtful that they could. "I want their fucking heads," I snapped harshly. "And I want their hearts, just to show them they should have used them here."

"That's my girl," Jaeden announced as we stood among the carnage.

"Not your girl," I grumbled. I hadn't been, not for a while now. I'd been watching him feed from the women that Shamus had brought with him, camp followers as Jaeden called them. They were much-needed walking blood-bags that gave him goo-goo eyes all day long. I'd heard him with one, and that one had been enough.

A few days after we had passed through Boise, Idaho, Shamus and his portable buffet joined up with us. He was supposed to have dropped Astrid off with the elders; instead, she was here and seemed to be leading the women and giving me her best bitch-face whenever Shamus or Jaeden weren't looking.

Along with their arrival, came Shamus's warning: The elders had forbidden Jaeden or any of the other vampires from feeding from me. They'd decided that since none of them knew much about my kind, and no one knew if feeding from me could hurt or affect the vampires in some sort of voodoo way, that it was best not to do it.

We'd been traveling for almost a month now, and Jaeden and I hadn't had sex since those few stolen moments after my father's funeral. I missed the closeness that he and I once had together, but I didn't feel like I could be myself with him anymore. It was a problem, a big one. I wanted him daily. I knew what he could give me, but at night, I sought the safety of my hammock that hung high in the trees instead of snuggling up with him and taking what he offered me.

I may not be human any longer, but the instincts my father had instilled were still inside of me. I still carried my bug-out pack, still wore a mask when I went into the woods alone; it was a part of how I survived. With the group, I allowed myself to let my guard down, knowing they'd protect me, but I stuck to my instincts when I went out alone. There was also the fact that I was being watched, and followed. I'd begun to suspect it was a lone Sentinel following me, since no one else seemed to be aware of it. Had it been human, the others would have already been aware of his presence. There weren't many beings that could get close to me without bringing the attention of the vampires and wolves to their presence.

There was also the fact that I could feel him, as if we were connected. I knew when he got too close, because my heart went into overdrive, and my senses went up, heightened, as if his powers helped mine somehow.

I needed to figure out how to actually use the powers that I kept triggering accidentally; to be able to use them when I needed them. I was willing to bet the Sentinel trailing me knew exactly how to trigger his powers, and I needed to figure out why he was stalking me.

“I’m going to look for herbs,” I stated, my heart already beginning to accelerate. Jaeden had assumed it was just another one of my ‘panic attacks’, as he dubbed my escalation of fight-or-flight instinct when the Sentinel was near, but he kept his secrets, and I had mine.

“Lass, ye dinna need tae,” Lachlan said, but I ignored him as I equipped my pack, checked the bow, and made sure I had enough ammo. I’d brought guns with me, and heavy ammo that had slowed us down—or them, rather. I thought I was doing pretty damn well until Shamus pointed out how slow I was moving.

“I’ll be fine. I need mint and ginseng, and as far as I can tell, no one else is gathering new things,” I pointed out as he examined cans of food.

Jaeden handed him a can of dog food. “Dog chow, or do you prefer kibble?” he offered with a smile, and I frowned. They’d gotten a lot closer again, cracking jokes, and even though it was a nice change from the name calling, it still got on my nerves.

“Nae, but if ye have a bit o’ wolves bane, ye be telling me, aye mon?” he laughed, and his men followed suit.

They were laughing. In the midst of a town full of innocent victims, they were laughing. It was one of the things that got to me; their off-the-wall comments. As if the world hadn’t gone to hell in a handbasket. I ignored their curious looks as I walked into the woods, knowing they'd still be pillaging the town when I came back.

Once I was alone, I slipped the mask on and looked towards where I felt the Sentinel. He knew I looked for him, and yet he never let me get close enough to catch a glimpse of him. I could smell him; his masculine scent lingered, giving away that he'd once filled the space in this general area. It wasn't cologne or aftershave, just the earthy scent of a man who cared enough about hygiene to bathe, which was rare these days.

I unclicked the chest buckle from my pack, making it easier to breathe as I entered the heavily wooded area. I walked blindly, not bothering to look for herbs until I was a good mile or so into the woods. Once I had put enough distance between myself and the others, I pulled off my pack, as well as the mask, and dropped to my knees in the middle of a small clearing.

I sobbed for a few moments, hating the weakness, but unable to stop it as the faces of the slaughtered fluttered through my mind. Babies. They'd killed helpless babies! Small children, innocent lives had been lost. It seemed surreal. Like some nightmare I couldn't wake up from, but it wasn't. It had happened. It was real. Grayson was out there with fucking monsters disguised as humans. My mother wouldn't protect him if she thought him useless; she'd let him loose in the world with those vile creatures.

I wiped at my eyes, collecting my thoughts and my mind before I got back up to my feet and paused. My heart was beating painfully fast, my stomach felt knotted, and I was trembling. The Sentinel was inches from me; even now I could smell his earthy scent. It was stronger than I'd ever sensed before. Male.

I'd been distracted by grief, and he'd used it to sneak up on me. I stood still, unsure of how to handle it. I had a sinking feeling that if I turned around, he'd use that inhuman speed to disappear. I remained still until I felt the heat of his body against my back. I could feel him, as if we were connected somehow. He exuded power. Raw, uncut power that slithered seductively over my exposed flesh. I hadn't dressed for the woods; my arms were bare, and the tank top I wore was soaked through with sweat from hours of hiking up to the town. Sweat beaded on my brow, and my breathing was labored from the tempo of my heart.

Still, I didn't move. My instincts were to run, to get as far away from him as possible. To go back to the safety of the group, and yet I remained frozen in place, while my hands and body trembled with fear of the unknown. Had I miscalculated something? Was he here to kill me? Easy enough to do, with how careless I'd been.

I heard the sound of a blade leaving a holster; the soft noise was loud in the clearing as he stepped even closer to me. I felt my palms sweating with the anxiety of my thoughts.

"Do it," I whispered breathlessly.

He paused.

Had I expected something? Evil laughter or something like it? Okay, I totally did. I could see his shadow. He was taller than me, and his head tilted at an angle, as if he was trying to see me better. It was a weird thing for a murderer to do, right? I expected the dagger to find a home in my back. I heard him moving away from me and watched his shadow as he found my pack and, if I was right, he'd just put something inside of it. A bomb? With my luck, it would have been. He made his way back to me. His feet made no sound, which explained why I hadn't heard him while I'd been blabbering like an idiot, crying my eyes out.

Once again, I could feel him next to my back, inches away from me. No sound, still. I wanted to turn around; see who it was that had been following me for the last month, watching me. I didn't move. I felt his power as he got closer to my body, less than an inch away from me. My body reacted, my skin prickling with the awareness of his proximity.

I winced as I felt the dull edge of his blade as he ran it over the skin at the nape of my neck. Gloved fingers fluttered over my flesh, and relief washed through me. I moaned softly as the tension I'd felt left my body. I felt him tense behind me, his fingers slowly retracing the path they'd just taken. I wanted to spin around, see who the fuck was touching me, but he moved like the other Sentinel had. I'd felt him close before, and the moment I'd turned around, he'd been gone, which was why I hadn't tried to do it this time around. I felt a slight tug on my hair, listened as a piece of my ponytail was cut, and growled low in my chest. My hair was too long;

it hadn't been cut since before the virus outbreak. It wasn't blonde, but it wasn't red either. It was in between, strawberry blonde, with a few occasional sections of burgundy from Cayla, who was obsessed with my hair lately. Burgundy was safer than the other hues of the rainbow she'd wanted to color it.

Minutes passed since I heard the knife return to its sheath, heard him removing his gloves and still, no noise other than the sound of leather sliding over skin. He didn't speak to me; he simply stood behind me, waiting for something.

At once I was yanked against him. The knife I'd thought he'd put away was dull; the side of it pressed against my carotid artery, and I was flat against his chest. He was dressed in some sort of armor; I could feel it through the skimpy tank top I wore. I should have been panicking, or screaming…something! I did nothing.

"You've been watching me, why?" I asked, my words coming out as a soft whimper.

His other hand slid to my thigh, slowly examining the exact spot where I'd been hurt last week, which was now fully healed. He touched me with a shaking hand, ripped the cargo pants open to reveal the healed flesh. I cried out softly, which seemed to make him pause. His nose touched my hair, inhaling my scent like I was some exotic creature. When his nose brushed against my ear, I inhaled the clean smell of his breath. His nose touched my neck and I trembled against the sensation the connection created. He placed a soft kiss against my neck, touching my quickening pulse with his lips as he lowered the blade, sheathed it, then continued to hold me in place. I'd given him control, and I hadn't even meant to. I could feel the muscles that his armor should have protected, muscles that no longer had armor over them. I realized he was testing me. He was seeing if I would struggle against him.

"You're like me, right? That's why I feel you?" I questioned. I sure as hell hoped I didn't feel like this every time I encountered a Sentinel. It felt like I was being attacked internally by a pack of wild butterflies. My heart was threatening to break my ribs; to break free from the cage that held it. Worse, his touch was turning me on! I was in need of some serious mental help, or at least an evaluation.

If he felt the same thing, he ignored it. He ignored me, lifting my shirt and brushing his fingers against my midsection. Shit, was he seriously skipping the first few bases and going for a homerun already? His hand touched me softly, like I was the rarest porcelain doll left in existence. As if he was afraid he'd break me. Shit.

"Um, you should at least buy me a drink before you try to steal home base, right?" I squeaked, and throaty masculine laughter hummed against my ear. I expelled the breath I'd been holding, relaxed into his hold, and wondered why I wasn't losing my shit at being felt up in the middle of a forest by a total stranger.

I was doing exactly that. I was standing in a forest, being fondled by a guy that I knew nothing about. I was allowing it to happen, but what was worse was I responded to his touch! The slightest pressure was creating a reaction from my body. Not just any response either, a fucking hurricane of sensations that I wasn't sure I liked. Yet, I felt safe. I shouldn't. I knew nothing about him. He could be the one who slaughtered the people back in the town, yet here I was, alone with him.

"Soon, Emma, very soon," he whispered against my ear. He kissed my neck softly, and I felt the earth moving around me. My world spun, time stopped, and even the butterfly that was inches away from me stopped flying mid-air.

Then time started back up again. I dropped to my knees as my shaking legs refused to support me any longer, and remained there until I finally heard someone else coming.

"Emma, where are ye, lass?" Lachlan called; his heavy feet hit the ground with a reassuring thump as he jumped over one of the many downed trees. "Shite, Emma, I been…Emma?" he asked, coming to me and picking up my gear as he made it to where I was on my knees in the small clearing. "Are ye alright?" he demanded as he kneeled on the grass with me.

"I don't know," I replied in a hushed tone, my legs still useless beneath me. I looked around, trying to see through the trees whether or not he was still close to us, but my body had returned to normal; he'd left the vicinity. "I think he's like me, a Sentinel," I continued. Lachlan cussed, and looked me over for wounds. "He didn't do anything." Okay, he totally did things. He'd made me feel vulnerable, and yet the way he touched me had made everything feminine inside of me stand up and take detailed notes about him, not that I could see him. What the hell was wrong with me?

He'd cut my fucking hair!

"Who, Emma?" he asked, watching my face. "Emma," his tone grew hard. "How long?"

"How long what?" I asked.

"How long has this mon been following ye, lass?" he demanded.

"Since we left Newport, I think. I don't know," I admitted. "I didn't know what it was at first; I mean, I thought it was anxiety at leaving home, leaving Addy behind. Then, a few weeks ago, I noticed it again, and it continued to worsen. My heart races, and my body… it gets heated, weird, like it senses him. It's hard to put into words what I feel when he's close. Look, don't tell anyone. He doesn't want to hurt me; if he did, he's had more than enough chances to do so. He's like me, Lachlan. I know he is. I can feel it. He can use his powers and I need him to teach me. I need to know how to use them to be useful."

"Ye are useful, lass," he laughed and hugged me tightly. "I'll be holding yer secret, but do nae expect me tae like it, okay? If he gets tae close, ye will tell me."

I relaxed a bit and nodded against his shoulder.

My eyes shifted to my pack that was zipped up, and I remembered that I'd seen his shadow bend over to place something inside of it. I swallowed, doubting it was a stick of dynamite or a bomb.

We hiked back to the group slowly, noting that they'd remained in the town, as planned, to scavenge anything useful.

"We'll camp closer to the creek, get some fresh water, and bathe before moving on in the morning," Jaeden remarked once he was closer to me, as his eyes vacillated between myself and Lachlan. I ignored it, considering his dinner was busy swishing her hips as she made her way to him. She wasn't beautiful, but she was sexy in the ways a man looked for in a woman. Plus, unlike some of the others, she bathed.

"I could use some fresh water," I said, pushing past the group, who stared at me as though they expected me to start collecting and burning the dead. I would have liked to have helped, and Lord knew these people deserved it, but I didn't have time to do it properly. I also wanted to get away from the carnage before I had another breakdown like I did in the forest.

"Bury the children," Shamus ordered without emotion, his eyes on me as he spoke. "The creek is less than a mile from here. We can at least bury the small ones."

"Thanks, Shamus," I whispered barely above a breath, knowing he'd hear it.

"Don't thank me; Cayla wouldn't let me leave them like this," he admitted.

No, his crazy woman-child, who was mentally unstable, would have trekked back here and done it herself. That was, if she didn't bring one of the smaller babies with her as her newest doll, which she'd done once already. Cayla had been turned vampire with a hellish head wound. It made her crazy on most days, but once you got used to it and her ghostly friend Nery, who apparently only she and I could see, she was pretty cool.

I missed the shelter. The water there was warm if you got to it before the others. Out here? Ice cold creek water, which occasionally had dead bodies floating in it the closer we got to the small towns. I didn't care; clean was clean. Once we'd reached the campsite, I made haste to the creek, because I knew that, within moments, the other girls would swarm the water, hoping to end up with one of the men for the night. Me, I just wanted sleep and the dreams of home and Grayson that came with it.

I pulled off my pack, looking around the area, where a small pool of rocks seemed to create a deeper pool than the other sections I'd explored. I unzipped the pack and dug through it. Inside the bag was a bar of chocolate and an iPod, which I knew hadn't been there before. I pushed them back into the pack as I looked around furtively for the Sentinel, while pulling clean clothes out of the pack and setting them on the rock beside the creek. I slowly stripped off my dirty clothing and threw them at the water's edge along with everything else I needed to get clean.

I slipped into the water and sat down enough that I was semi-hidden in it. I knew the moment Jaeden made his way through the brush and into the small clearing, his eyes watching me as he approached, then sat on the rock as he gave me his back. It was something he'd started doing after the first time he found me alone and unguarded while bathing. Since that day, he would join me, although silently.

"Long day," he commented, and I frowned.

"Rough day," I agreed.

"Emma," he whispered as he turned towards me, and his eyes skimmed the water before rising back to my face.

"Jaeden." I wondered if he was about to try it again. He did it every few days, attempted to mend the wedge between us. Ever since he'd left me on that lonely road near the Ark, he'd ruined me. It had taken weeks to get up off the ground, to get my motivation back, and right now I couldn't handle his little overtures. At any given moment, he could be called away by those who controlled him, and it wasn't something I wanted to deal with. I couldn't. Lachlan was my rock; he was with me not because we'd been together, but because he wanted to be.

Jaeden made me feel shit I wasn't sure I wanted to feel, rocked my world and a few other things, but he was also bound by the elders and had to go where they told him to. Like now, he'd sold me on this trip so I could look for my brother, but the more I listened, the more I realized that the true reason for the trip was so that he and Shamus could look for their maker and several of the elders who had been taken. I was actually just along for the ride, as were Lachlan and his men, who were looking for Lachlan's father. I wondered how much Jaeden would deviate from his mission to find his maker in order to help me find my brother. I had a feeling that if push came to shove, I would be on my own unless Lachlan and his wolves decided to remain with me.

"You are stubborn," he exhaled and rubbed his face as Valarie sauntered into the clearing, her eyes darting from me to him, and back to me. She didn't like me, we both knew it, and so did he. She was his dinner; I was his first choice for dessert, and based on the way he was looking at me, he wanted to have dessert first.

"Am I?" I whispered softly as I waded away and grabbed the shampoo and conditioner, quickly using them as I washed up, and tried not to pay attention to his eyes that I knew were taking in my naked body. It wasn't as if he hadn't seen it before. Hell, he was the first and only man who'd ever touched it, but there was just too much between us, and I was dealing with too much mentally already.

"You are." He stood up and stripped out of his shirt, uncaring that he had an audience.

"I'm not done," I protested as I watched his

magnificent body with a hunger I couldn't wish away. I missed it, his touch, and the demanding kiss that always curled my toes.

"Duly noted, Valkyrie." He kicked off his boots and undid his jeans as we women watched him. I watched her reaction to his body and wondered if I looked as lost as she did when I took in the contours of his male perfection.

It wasn't until Valarie started to strip that I hurriedly finished up and excused myself, much to his disappointment. I wasn't up to watching her ogle him, or feeding him.

"Emma…" he growled.

"Valarie is here, Jaeden. *Bon appétit*, you look hungry," I murmured as I gave them my back and quickly dressed.

Once I was finished, I hurried through the camp and set up my hammock high in the trees. It gave me an advantage, allowing me to see miles from the camp which was nestled beneath it, but occasionally smoke would be bothersome, as the wolves cooked whatever they'd caught or scrounged to eat.

I placed my bag beside me and pulled out the iPod, slipping the earbuds into my ears, and smiling as soft music poured through them. Marvin Gaye's *Let's Get It On* played, and although it was pretty random, it made me grin. I had loved music before the virus hit, and the rarity of music and finding anything with enough power available to play it with was near to impossible anymore. I closed my eyes, allowed myself a moment to finish the song before I took the ear buds out, set them on my chest, and went to sleep.

Chapter Two

Over the next two days, we covered at least twenty miles, which, considering we were traveling for the most part through the mountains, and on old country roads, wasn't much. We occasionally came to a small town and cleared it of anything usable we could find. There were never enough supplies. Somehow, there were always signs that someone had been through it just before us, along with fresh bodies. As if we were following someone without knowing it.

We'd come across a little town today, one with a quaint barn at the edge of town that Shamus and Cayla had been obsessed with. Apparently, the guy had tried his hand at farming once and failed miserably. Shamus had been born sometime during the early ages and had done a lot of stuff, based on the endless stories he told. Most of it didn't make any sense to me. He'd gone from silent and watching me, to trying to lure me into conversation with every mile we covered.

As Cayla climbed around, exploring the barn, Nery slowly materialized next to me and stood quietly for a few moments as we watched Shamus and Cayla explore. He shoved his hands in his barely substantial pockets and fidgeted, as if he was uncomfortable with what he wanted to say. After a few strained minutes, he softly muttered, "Things are changing for you soon, Guardian." He looked at Jaeden in the distance and back to me with a resigned, sad look on his pale features. "Death is coming for you."

I gave him a long, sideways look, and finally grinned.

"If you haven't noticed, ghost boy, he's been coming for me for a while and there's sort of a rumor going around that I'm part of the immortal crew now, so I don't think he's after me this time."

"He is death for all, Sentinels and Vampires alike. He will come for you soon, and when he does, you need to let him take you. If you truly care for those here, you'll allow it to happen," he said softly. He shook his head with a soft frown, as a chill raced up my spine. I had to take a deep breath before I could speak.

"Are you speaking literally or metaphorically?"

"Both, Guardian." With a small, enigmatic smile, he turned from me and glided to the barn and Cayla, leaving me to wonder what the heck he'd meant.

I looked behind me to the farmhouse that was part of the same property as the barn. I took a few steps until I was inside of it. As my eyes adjusted to the dark interior, I took in the family pictures of those who had previously lived here. Framed photos of two children, a boy and a girl with wide cheeky grins, seemed to blanket the walls. As I padded slowly down the hall and into the living room, examining the pictures, I saw that the girl was always smiling, her eyes lit up from within. The boy, the older child, was always watching her in the pictures. As if he was afraid to take his eyes from his little sister; I knew that look. The one that said he took care of his little sister; it reminded me of the pictures of me. I'd hardly ever smiled, and when I had, it was at Grayson for doing something, sometimes just something mundane.

"Figured ye be aboot," Lachlan said as he followed me into the room, the pockets of his green army pants filled to bursting with snacks. You'd think the guy had a sweet tooth, but apparently, wolves needed a shit ton of sugar because they burned some major calories shifting to wolf form. "We are heading oot, lass," he added when I didn't look away from the pictures. "They looked happy enough." He ambled further into the room, his eyes taking in the pictures, along with the decomposing bodies that lay on the sofa, as if the father, mother, and children hugged each other one last time and passed.

"So happy they sat here and died together, waiting for help that never came," I whispered through the sudden pain in my heart. Every day it felt as if I failed Grayson, and every day he got further away. Lachlan had spent a long time in Grayson's room, learning his scent. We'd been lucky and caught a few whiffs of it here and there, enough to let us know that we were on the right path. Both Lachlan and Cian had said it was strangely faint, which worried me. However, we were flying blind, so those little whiffs were the best hope we had right now.

"Ye can nae do this," he said as he got closer to me, his green eyes zeroing in on mine. "They're nae ye, Lass, and ye are nae them. Grayson is alive, ye ken? We just got tae find him, and we will. Aye?"

"We will, because losing him isn't an option for me." I gave one last lingering glance at the photos, then turned and left the house. I was losing hope. I was with the best chance I had at finding him, but what if our mother had brainwashed him? Or worse, he blamed me for not saving Dad? I didn't even know if he wanted to be found, but I had no plans of ever giving up. He was the only family I had left, and Addy was barely holding her shit together. If we lost him, I wasn't sure she'd be okay. Maybe eventually, but she'd lost everyone she cared about without even getting to say goodbye. Her parents had never called, and her brother had probably died with his unit across the damn ocean, or maybe on his way back.

I stepped outside the house and pulled out the small device Jaeden had given me, then hit call and listened as static turned into an excited Addy.

"You got him?" she chirped excitedly.

"No, not yet," I replied, trying to hide the melancholy I felt at seeing the brother and sister curled with their parents, dead. "Holding down thc fort?" I asked, knowing she'd distract me. It's what she did, talked endlessly, and after she would finish with her mile-a-minute ramble, I'd hand the little phone off to Jaeden, and a little while later he'd return it fully charged. I didn't ask how, I just accepted it and moved on.

"You've been gone so long," she complained. "I have no one to bitch to, and the vampires? They are all up in everyone's business, taking blood samples—which, let's just say it, fucking weird, right? They're asking for birthdates, weight; shit, one even tried to actually weigh me. Like brought me the scale," she snickered. "Like I was getting on that thing; it's not that I've gained weight, I'm just I'm allergic to those things."

"They're taking blood samples?" I murmured. My eyes locked with Lachlan, who I knew was listening to the entire call no matter how much he tried to pretend he wasn't. "Why?"

"I didn't ask why, but they've been on a tear for a bit," she admitted. "We got a few more in the shelter, Jaeden and Shamus apparently sent them here."

"Awesome," I groaned. "Any other things I should know about?"

"Cat and the baby are doing awesome, little thing's off the breast-bottle, and Emma, remind me not to breastfeed. That shit looks painful. In fact, remind me to not get pregnant at all. Grab all the birth control you can get your mitts on, please."

"Will do. Hey, Addy, I need to go. It looks like we're heading out." I watched Jaeden follow the others, who were crossing the street leading into town. "Love you; I'll call back tomorrow and check in."

"Emma, seriously, please be safe out there. I have the shelter under control," she whispered and made a kissing noise.

"I'm always safe; besides, I'm running around with vampires and werewolves. I'll be okay."

I hung up and started towards Jaeden, my mind racing, wondering what the hell his vampires were up to at the shelter. Taking blood samples? Really?

"What the fuck, Jaeden," I demanded. "Why are the vampires you left behind taking blood samples? Those are my people!"

"Calm down," he said, his turquoise eyes skimming my face, and he smiled. "It's not what you think it is."

"Really? Because to me, it looks like someone is setting up a fucking menu with humans being the main course. My humans," I snapped.

"Lachlan," Jaeden's voice was tense, and I turned and watched as Lachlan and he had some silent dispute before Lachlan nodded and walked away from us. Great…

"Are you done yet?" Jaeden asked before looking around quickly, then picked me up and moved us further into town and towards an alley, away from those who were watching us.

"No, and put me down!" I snapped.

"No," he growled as he shoved me against a building and his mouth hovered dangerously close to mine. I shook my head, preparing to tell him off, but he kissed me. I moaned against it, hating that I kissed him back. My legs touched the ground as he released me and started pulling at my clothing. I stopped him and stepped away; regret filled my eyes, but I couldn't lead him on.

"I can't do this," I mumbled as I turned, and left him standing between the buildings.

"Can't do what? Can't admit what you feel?" he snapped, and I turned on him.

"I can't do this with you," I growled. "I can't be who I need to be with you. You left me—*you* left *me*. If those people who you answer to told you right this minute to leave me here, you would! You'd have to. Us? It's too complicated."

"There's nothing complicated about it," he replied angrily. "I want you; you want me. There's nothing fucking complicated about it!"

"No? How about the fact that you need to feed from someone else, or that she orgasms every fucking time you feed, and I have to hear it! Every. *Fucking.* Time!" I shouted, uncaring that my voice was increasing in volume and people could probably hear us arguing. "Feed from me, Jaeden, right here, right now," I challenged, knowing he couldn't. Knowing he would never go against whatever Shamus and the elders told him to do. Not that he wouldn't want to go against them. Part of the problem was his tie to his master; the compulsion to follow his master's and the elders' orders. Then there was the failsafe that I'd recently found out about. If a vampire managed to disobey or find a way around the compulsion, they were summarily put to death, as if they were defective or something.

"Emma," he growled as his fangs extended, and his eyes flashed red. Even knowing what I did, hope still washed through me, but he shook his head, retracted his fangs, and stepped away from me.

"Didn't think so, Jaeden," I murmured as I adjusted my bag and hurried back to the group, ignoring the angry eyes of the other vampires, who didn't look happy that I'd tried to make him break away from the elders' decree or whatever fucked up shit they had to follow.

I felt his anger, and theirs. I didn't care; I'd made my point. He wasn't safe anymore. He wouldn't and couldn't choose me when it mattered, and I couldn't count on him as long as he followed some ageless vampire cult that held his life in their hands. I couldn't force him to choose, so letting him go seemed the only way to be sure he wasn't tempted, while protecting myself in the process.

Yes, it was painful, but in the end, it protected us both.

"That was harsh, lass, even if he deserved it," Lachlan commented, falling into step beside me. My heart hurt, but my pride was still intact.

"We're toxic together. He can't be with me as I need him to be, and I can't be strong with him. I need to be strong right now, Lachlan. It's the one thing holding me together. If those people told him to pick up and leave, he would. I can't let emotions lead me; my father taught me better than that."

"Yer da, Emma, he'd want ye tae be happy, no?" he asked.

"He'd want me to be strong. He'd want me to save my brother at any cost. He'd probably tell me to pull my head out of my ass where Jaeden is concerned. He taught me to go to war with my mind, not my body. With Jaeden, it is war with him, and it's not with my mind," I pointed out.

"Emma…"

Shots rang out, and Lachlan stared at me, his body stiff as he looked down at his chest, where blood was blooming across his white shirt. I screamed for help, but everyone was scrambling to figure out where the shots had come from. Instinctively, I reached out to catch Lachlan, which, by the way, holding up about two hundred pounds of werewolf wasn't exactly an easy thing to do.

"Lachlan, stay with me," I pleaded as I helped him walk to the buildings for cover against the unseen shooter.

"Emma, run," he growled, as he began to shift into wolf form.

"Lachlan, you were shot, stop changing!" I demanded, knowing his wolf would be stronger than his current form, but also that he'd be stuck in wolf form if he was too weak to change back. He ignored me and tried to speak as his face contorted with the change, and his clothing ripped away from his body. "Dammit!" I snapped as I pulled out one of my small handguns and checked the chamber and clip to be sure they were full.

"Emma." Jaeden's voice was filled with worry as he slid in beside me, his eyes assessing me for wounds, then they snapped to Lachlan, who was mid-change; apparently wounded wolves didn't change as easily. "Lachlan, we think there's multiple shooters, be careful," he warned.

"Are you expecting an answer?" I asked, incredulous as the change was now complete. What was Lachlan supposed to say, *woof*? He growled once, and then struggled up, whining as he limped to where the rest of his pack was waiting, all in wolf form.

"Stay down! Whoever it is, they used fucking silver bullets," Jaeden explained, his eyes locking with mine as he grabbed me, protecting me as we used the wall for cover and made it to the next set of structures.

“I am wearing Kevlar,” I whispered, hoping he would let go of me. He didn’t; he used his body as a shield until we could hide in one of the buildings, and the other vampires filed in behind us. Once inside, he let go.

“Three have been shot, one wolf, two vampires,” Shamus rambled as he pushed one of the girls to where a vampire was laid out on the ground, having been carried in by Bjorn. I locked eyes with the girl, who knew exactly what was going to happen. No fear; in fact, she looked happy that she’d been chosen.

She was shoved to her knees, and she pushed her hair away from her neck, only the barest of moments before the vampire savagely bit into her. She moaned, smiling as he sucked noisily from her throat. Nausea swirled inside of me as she started fondling herself, right in front of everyone. She didn’t care, or seem to object as he gulped greedily, which would probably leave her on the brink of dying if he wasn’t stopped. I knew the pleasure of the bite, but only from Jaeden, who had done it during sex.

“How many of the girls were hit?” I asked, watching as Jaeden shifted uncomfortably. Yeah, that’s what I thought. Mortal lives meant nothing to this group. Not because they actually thought about it like that, but because when it came down to it, their own people meant more to them.

“A few,” Jaeden said carefully.

"Where are they?" I countered smoothly, wondering if they'd been left outside to die.

"Sven is changing one over; the others were killed instantly."

"This wasn't someone defending their turf," I hissed, sending a silent prayer for the girls who'd been killed. "There's also the problem of silver bullets. They know what you are." That was a huge freaking problem. "Where did the wolves go?" I wondered why the pack had fled into the woods instead of staying with us.

"When the alpha is wounded, the pack will go wherever they think they can protect him best. Obviously, they didn't feel he would be safe packed into a room full of vampires," Shamus responded, his eyes blood-red as he watched the girl, who'd gone limp.

I raised an eyebrow when no one seemed in a hurry to stop the drinking binge. "You want to stop him?" I pointed at the spectacle on the floor. "He'll kill her." I felt my face flood with anger as they just stood around, watching. "I said stop him," I growled angrily as the vampires turned to look at me. "She's no good to you dead."

"She knew what he needed. She refused to allow another to aid in his healing. She's his woman." Jaeden's face was an unreadable mask. "Some care to understand our way of life more than others." He turned his head to me with an accusing look.

"So, the way I understand it is, all of you are

choosing to let her die. Maybe it's better not to care, than to choose to become a supplement, seeing that they're a disposable commodity," I countered as I took off my pack, set it on the ground, and pulled the AR-15 out of its case, which wasn't ideal for long-range shots, but the scope would at least allow me to see into the woods to find the sniper.

"It's not that easy, Emma." Frustration laced Jaeden's words as I pushed my way past the despicable sight and headed towards the stairs, hoping for a loftier perch to search the woods. "Would you just stop and listen to me?" he demanded as he grabbed my arm painfully. I stopped, turned and looked at him coldly.

"Let me go, Jaeden," I said evenly, surprised I'd managed to keep my anger in check.

"Never." His voice was barely audible over the noise of the room. A bullet exploded through the window, hitting another vampire who'd been staring out of it, and he hit the ground hard.

"Get away from the windows," I shouted as I ripped my arm away from Jaeden's grasp and ran up the stairs and down the hallway, until I found the door with access to the roof. I ignored Jaeden who followed close on my heels, or tried to.

I crouched low and combat-crawled towards one of the large, protruding vents, and brought the gun up to butt it against my arm; I closed one eye as I peered through the scope with the other. I caught the sight of a muzzle flash and tried to focus on it, but whoever was shooting was doing so from a gunny suit or heavy camouflage, one that the shooter must have spent a lot of time in to be sure it blended in with the terrain.

"Human, I think," I muttered to myself as I looked through the scope, taking in the area around him. There was a truck a few paces away from the guy, and other people were there, rifles in hand, but it was difficult to see from this distance. They were blurry at best; the AR-15's scope wasn't meant to see at this great of a distance.

"What's that?" Jaeden whispered, pointing to somewhere closer to us, about a mile outside of the small town. "I smell blood."

"Maybe from the girl being drained downstairs?" I snapped, unable to stop myself because I hated it. I hated that he fed from another, I hated that it gave her pleasure when he did it. I also hated their blatant disregard for human lives.

"Stop it, now," he growled. "There," his finger indicated the spot, and I looked through the scope.

"What…children?" There were two of them, along with three women? All of them were covered in blood that ran from fresh wounds. "Jaeden…" I whispered as I watched them dodge bullets. "They're being hunted."

I looked away from the scope to focus on him, but he was gone. I looked around briefly before looking back through the scope, watching as he rushed to where the women and children were hidden. Fucking hell, he was making his way towards them, and a heavily armed male was moving in the same direction. I butted the gun against my shoulder and released the safety.

The moment the guy spotted Jaeden and lifted his gun, I took the shot, watching as it sailed through the guy's forehead, and he fell backwards. I directed the scope back to Jaeden, who was looking directly at me. My ears rang from the noise the gun made when firing, but I refused to stop protecting him as he made his way to the women and children.

Another shot, another body. I kept taking aim and firing, until a bullet tinged next to my head; shards of wood flew outward and I was forced to take cover. I peered around the other side, making sure my head was protected by the vent. Once my position was concealed, I looked through the scope once more.

I froze.

I'd assumed my heart was erratic because of the current situation, but just at the edge of the woods stood a man. One dressed in tactical gear, but unlike the others I'd shot, he wore black instead of camo and his gear looked more like all-over body armor. Cerulean blue eyes watched me, looking right at me. Most of his face was covered by a mask, but I didn't need to be told who I was looking at—I felt him. I let my finger hover over the trigger before I released it, and continued to look at him.

Although he wasn't quite as tall as Jaeden, he was still well over six foot in height, and the hair I could see peeking out from the mask looked dark, but it could have been a shadow distortion caused from a combination of the scope and the distance between us. As I watched him, he held up a strawberry blonde lock of hair and smelled it, never taking his eyes from mine.

"Soon, Emma," a male voice whispered inside my head, and I blinked in disbelief. Much like those other Sentinels on the day Grayson had been taken, he could talk inside my head.

"Soon what, asshole?" I muttered out loud.

As I watched him, I felt a bullet moving through the air for a split-second before it hit the barrel of the gun I held, sending me to all fours. The reverberation hurt, and it took effort to regain my balance and take cover. I picked the gun back up and peered through the scope in time to watch as Jaeden took down two assailants easily, retrieved the women and children, and ushered them to the safety of the buildings that skirted town.

I shifted the scope to where the Sentinel was, but he was gone. I heard shots ringing out in the hills and tried to peer through the scope again, and just as the ringing became unbearable, I saw a black blur take down the men who'd fired at me.

I smiled as he snapped a neck and turned to look directly at me before pointing at his eyes, and then me. I swallowed, wondering if he'd ever saved me before without me even knowing about it. It was possible; this world was a fucked-up place, and no one was being spared. No one.

Chapter THREE

The rescued women were giving details of the men who'd been hunting them as the vampires looked them over. To me, something about these women seemed off, but the vampires seemed okay with them, so I settled in and helped out bandaging up the newcomer's wounds with Jaeden. My mind wandered away from the task at hand as I wondered if Lachlan was okay. There had been no word from the wolves, and that bothered me.

I missed Lachlan; his humor and wisdom seemed to keep me balanced, and knowing he was out there, hurt, bothered me.

"Hold that," I told the woman I was working on as I moved her hand over the gauze I had placed over the stitches so I could secure it with medical tape. Her eyes were fixed on the men who milled around the room. "How old is she?" I asked, nodding towards the tiny girl who sat crying without any sign of stopping.

"Her? I don't know," she grunted indifferently, once again ignoring me.

"You don't know how old she is?" I sat back and removed my gloves.

"She's not mine," she hissed as she tried to move her arm. "Just one of the brats we picked up on our way."

"She's not from the town?" My eyes zeroed in on her pulse.

"Yeah, but she's not mine."

I looked at the children, and then at Jaeden, who was talking to one of the women he'd saved; she was staring at him like he hung the moon high in the sky, just for her. I shook my head mentally. I realized that the vampires needed to replace some members of their 'blood buffet' and would probably say or do whatever they could to suck up to these women. Literally. If the vampires got their way, then the women would be staying with them, trading blood and sex for protection. I sat back and stood up as I replaced the medical supplies in the duffle bag and headed to one of the couches to observe the room. I felt like an outsider, as if I didn't belong here.

"You don't," a sultry male voice whispered through my mind, and I mentally shrugged.

I didn't fit in anywhere, except at the shelter.

"With me. You belong with me," the voice growled in my head.

"No, don't think so," I whispered, wondering how the hell he was hearing my thoughts.

"Something wrong?" Raphael asked carefully, his eyes keen as he watched my reaction to his words. His eyes were a startling shade of blue, and with all of that thick, beautiful hair that brushed against his shoulders, he was guaranteed to have a bevy of blood-bags vying for his attention every time we broke for camp. That much I knew about him.

"No," I huffed, leaning my head back against the couch, which was as tattered as I felt.

"You always talk to yourself?" he mused as he sat too close to me, and placed his hand on my thigh.

"Yes; I'm also partial to biting limp flesh and other things that get too close," I replied easily, turning my head to look at him and then pointedly at his hand, which he removed as Jaeden made his way to us.

"No sign of the wolves, but I don't imagine they'd bring Lachlan too close to us if he's been seriously injured. We probably won't see him or them until he's finished healing."

"Great," I muttered and looked at the women, who watched us carefully. "They seem off." I wondered if it was just me who'd noticed it.

"If you watched an entire town being slaughtered, you'd be off, too," Jaeden said sharply, and I looked up at him. His eyes were on me, and then they slowly slid to my thigh, which Raphael had just released. "You can't expect everyone to deal with shit the way you do, Emma."

"No, but they took children into their group. Children which they seem to know nothing about, nor are they caring for them. Look at them, the one child is hurt, and not one of those women has moved a muscle to help or comfort her. She's been crying since you rescued them, you'd think they'd try to calm her," I pointed out.

"This is a new world, Emma, shit happens. Look at the shelter, its mismatched people, those who cling to each other for support. These women? They didn't have that. They saved those children; don't expect them to know shit about them."

"The massacre at that town happened days ago, Jaeden, are you telling me that they wouldn't have asked the children anything about who they were? Seems a little bit off, but if you want to defend their honor, by all means, continue."

"You're acting childish, Emma," he snapped.

"Maybe I am, but I would have at least asked them their names—you would have too."

The tick in his jaw hammered, and his eyes narrowed on me. "You're jealous."

"I am not jealous. I'm worried about the children. I'm worried about my hurt friend, but I am not jealous." I was. I'd seen the tender touch he'd used to reassure one of the women; I thought I'd heard them call her Jolene. I'd also watched her latch on to that hand, and her eyes filled with something I couldn't place, but whatever it was, it wasn't good. "I'm going out to try and find diapers," I mumbled as I stood up, noting that Jolene was heading towards us.

"You're not leaving this building, Emma," Jaeden ordered.

"I am, because they need clean clothing and the little ones need diapers. So yes, Jaeden, I am. I survived a long time on my own before I met you; I'm not some feeble little damsel who needs help. I'll be safe. Besides, Jolene needs you to calm her, I'm sure."

"Emma," he warned, but Jolene's hand touched his shoulder and I slipped out the door using the distraction to get away from him.

It boggled my mind how women like her had lived this long, while mothers had given their lives to protect their children. I was biased, I knew it; I hated that my own mother was a psycho-bitch, while others died saving their children. Mine? She'd had me shot.

Once I hit the main floor, I gazed out the window and crept towards the door slowly. The building was situated between two others, luckily with a door that opened into a well-covered alleyway.

"Going somewhere?" Bjorn asked.

"To get diapers and a few things for the children," I

replied, nodding as he grunted, but opened the door for me to slip through.

"Be careful, Emma," he rumbled.

I nodded and remained in the shadows of the buildings, knowing the black outfit I wore would allow me to blend in easily. I could feel my heart hammering and knew my stalker was close; I just couldn't pinpoint where he was. I made it three blocks from the small store we'd passed as we entered town, and was shoved back against a wall, with a gloved hand covering my mouth.

I began to struggle, but voices stopped me cold. My eyes locked with cerulean blue ones, and the earth seemed to spin around us. He pulled his eyes away from mine as he slowly walked me towards one of the many open building entryways.

Once inside, he carefully continued to push me back into the shadows as people passed the window. We were surrounded by empty boxes, but it gave us cover as one of the armed men entered the building, peering in as he did a sloppy sweep of it.

The Sentinel was pressed against me, and I could feel the heat radiating from his body. I couldn't tell what he really looked like, because he wore a mask that looked like it had part of a skull covering the lower half of his face and black armor covering the rest of his body. I looked to where the other man was searching through a few boxes and as I did, my hand touched his, which seemed to send a tremor through us both. I held my breath as I brought my eyes back to his.

"Don't move," his voice whispered inside my head.

I hadn't planned on it; the heat and mixture of emotions his body created against mine was holding me locked into place. I didn't even try to move or make a peep as I felt his hands wrapping around my hips as he slowly guided us further into the dark building. His movements were graceful, calculated. Together we made no sound as he walked us slowly to the opposite side of the room, where the intruder had already searched through the empty boxes.

"Wade," someone called from the doorway.

"It's empty," Wade shouted back as he strode across the room.

I remained still, not moving a muscle, not even after they had left the room, because the Sentinel was staring at me. His eyes were beautiful, captivating as the light from the midday sun hit them as we passed through a spot that allowed light into the building. He didn't release me either; instead, he seemed to be taking me in as I examined him. It wasn't until I caught the glint of a smile in his eyes, and his hands released my waist to capture my wrists and hold them above my head, that I worried. I didn't fight him, but I struggled to get distance from him. He had me at a disadvantage; the men outside were too close for me to be vocal, and struggling would make noise.

"You can't fight it, Emma," he whispered as the lower half of his mask seemed to melt away, exposing full lips that he used to kiss me.

I stopped struggling. Time stood still, pieces inside of me fit into place, and I moaned loudly against his mouth as emotions swept through me. My body grew pliant, allowing him to push me against the wall as he released my wrists and continued deepening the kiss until my lungs burned for oxygen.

When he finally pulled away from me, he looked as shocked as I was, but the lower half of his mask was back in place, and he turned his head before taking me to the floor hard. Voices exploded from the doorway, and he rolled us into the corner where boxes were scattered, making it a good hiding place.

I didn't make a peep, not even as he kissed me again, ignoring the fact that the room was being invaded by hostile forces. I could hear footsteps, could hear them discussing how best to approach a building. It didn't matter, nothing did. Flesh met mine as he tugged on the vest I wore, but the moment I heard scuffling, my mind returned.

I smelled blood, and I watched the man who hovered above me, his eyes smiling as if he knew some joke only he was privy to. Blearily, I wondered how he got that mask to do that partial melty-off-and-on thing, the way it did. He sat me up, and held up a finger, indicating to continue to be still for a moment. I sat on the floor, dazed by what I'd just allowed to happen. Then someone kicked the boxes, and I cried out as one sailed past my head.

"Dammit, Emma," Jaeden's voice was angry, and as I stood up, I found myself in the room with him, Shamus, and Bjorn, along with dead bodies on the floor. I looked around for the man who'd kissed me, but found no sign of him. "I told you it wasn't safe out here." He grabbed my arm and pulled me closer.

My eyes skimmed the corner, finding the black-armored Sentinel watching me carefully from the shadows with something dangerous in his eyes. A warning not to give away his position? How would I even explain him?

"Mine." The single word tore through my mind, and I flushed without being able to prevent it. As if he held some cosmic connection over my body and mind.

"Emma, what the fuck?" Jaeden demanded, moving his eyes to the corner, which was now empty. "Did you feel that?" he asked the others and then me; everyone shook their heads in reply. But I had felt it; it was the sensation my kind made when they disappeared. "Let's go, before more people come. We need to get the fuck out of this town."

"We need diapers and salve for the little girl," I argued.

"She'll be fine, but we won't be for long unless we get out of this death trap."

"What about Lachlan?" I asked as I allowed Jaeden to pull me with him, as he turned and looked at me. His eyes narrowed and he sniffed me, which I knew was his way of telling what I'd been up to. *Shit.*

"He'll find us, they're trackers," he growled. He continued to look me over. "If you needed to get off, all you had to do was tell me."

"Excuse me?" I countered.

"I know the smell your body makes when it needs to come, sweet girl. All you had to do was ask, and I would have scratched that itch. You didn't need to lie about going out for fucking diapers."

I glared. "If I have an itch, I'll scratch it myself," I seethed. How dare he say something like that in front of them!

"No, you won't," he smiled. "Let's go."

Chapter Four.

A few days had gone by since Lachlan had been shot. Not one moment had gone by where I didn't want to rush out into the woods and find him. I hadn't felt the Sentinel again either. I'd spent a lot of time trying to connect with him again, even going as far as wandering around in the woods by myself, hoping he'd take the bait. I needed to know what he knew about us. He could use his powers; I couldn't. There was also the strange reaction I'd felt when he kissed me.

Where Jaeden's kisses had tilted my world, mystery guy's kiss had flipped it over and sent me spinning out of control. He hadn't been rough, and maybe that was the difference. Maybe I was just imagining the reaction, trying to replace Jaeden in my world. I was such an idiot.

On my third day of searching for Lachlan (and the Sentinel), I found clues left by his pack. Clues that told me he was still in the area, and it gave me a little bit of comfort that he was still alive. I was sure if he'd died, Cian would have come to deliver the news, and he hadn't.

I was sick of listening to the girls giggling and men acting like children, as if the world was all right. It was part of the reason I preferred being away from camp. I'd made it a point to be away from the camp during the times that Jaeden fed, and so far, I'd done great at missing out on it. During my trips, I tended to find enough time to listen to the iPod left in my pack by my stalker. One of the playlists was titled 'mine,' which I was sure wasn't an accident. The second was titled 'bad day,' and the last was named 'slow seduction,' and all of them had songs that made me smile, or remember briefly how the world used to be. It was an escape from reality, and I enjoyed the brief respite it provided.

I'd found a few spots in the woods that were teaming with berries and herbs that kept me fairly busy, but after the fourth day of being stuck in the same camp while we waited for the men to heal, I had become increasingly impatient to get back on the road. Mostly because I was worried for Lachlan, but Shamus was also watching me like a hawk, and it was making me feel caged. Jaeden was keeping his distance, but he was never far from me, unless I left camp so he could feed.

His new camp follower, Jolene, was never far from him. Astrid had become the ruler of the feeders, keeping them clean and choosing meals for them based off what the men preferred. Astrid hadn't taken long to throw it in my face that Jaeden had lost interest in me, and while

I could have been a bitch and pointed out that I'd ended it, I hadn't. She'd grown bolder since the ambush, sensing the tension between myself and Jaeden. I wasn't an idiot. I could sense a few things on my own, like Jolene's lust for Jaeden; never mind her blatant lack of clothing, which, of course, was for his benefit. She was willing to do whatever it took to get him; I wasn't.

I was denying him the relief that I knew he preferred. He was a hot-blooded male, one who still wanted me. I remained strong in my stance, knowing that asking him to choose me over his elders' orders could potentially get him killed. I loved him enough to let him go, to let him be who and what he was. I could do this. I was cold, yes, but I was alert. I listened to the men around me. I paid attention. I wasn't stuck on stupid and batting my eyelashes like the others who wanted the pleasure the men could give.

It was nearing dusk when I accidentally wandered into the area of the camp that was full of the women who supplied the vampires with blood. I paused, pulled the earbuds out of my ears, and slipped the iPod into my pocket. They looked normal, like women you'd find at a barter fair up north, doing each other's hair, or helping to cook a meal. They had huge tents, ones that came down easily and went back up just the same. They were preparing for the night's revelry that was sure to go down. The men had been having some fairly wild evening parties since we'd stopped for the wounded to heal. They'd drink, talk about shit that had no bearing on what we were doing, and then rut like wild animals until the early morning hours.

"Lost?" Astrid called out, her cold blue eyes looking me over as if she wanted to suck the marrow from my bones, or kill me, probably both.

"No," I replied, already turning to leave. I didn't get very far; Jolene stepped into my path, and I rolled my eyes. "Let me pass," I ordered, but she shoved me hard. I righted myself and looked at her.

"Bitch thinks she's so much better than the rest of us," she sneered and slapped me. I hadn't thought she'd have the balls to, but with Astrid backing her up, I guess I should have expected it.

I tried backing up, but Astrid was a brick wall, barring my path. I swallowed down the urge to slap Jolene, knowing if my Sentinel strength kicked in, I'd either kill or seriously hurt her.

"You don't want to do this," I warned her, watching as her eyes darted to Astrid. Then, she balled her hands into fists and started hitting me before I could dodge her blows. As I started to defend myself, I caught Shamus watching the attack with a sly look on his face. Asshole.

I brought my hand up and punched her, knowing the moment Astrid joined in, I'd be outnumbered. Astrid grabbed my braided hair and yanked me off balance with her inhuman strength as Jolene continued punching me, slamming her fist into the side of my face. Astrid snarled as I hit Jolene back, fighting to gain my balance, which wasn't an easy feat with Astrid pulling on my braid like a handle and forcing me backwards.

Astrid caught my arm, twisting it behind my back at an angle that made panic seize me. I went into fight-or-flight mode, with no way to get away from them. I fought. I punched Jolene hard with the one arm I had use of, listening as cartilage and bone snapped while Astrid continued to twist my arm painfully. I heard more cartilage tearing as I punched Jolene in the nose, landing a solid hit. I continued hitting her until she staggered and started to fall, and then I turned on the vampire who held me. Astrid started wailing for help, the sound reverberating in my ears as she screeched.

My nose was shattered, my arm broken. I could feel it all; the blood that poured from my nose, my arm hanging at a weird angle, limp and useless. It burned with pain. Astrid had released me and stood beside Jolene and the other women who gathered to watch the fight. Jolene was on her feet, but she swayed from the blows I had landed.

"Fucking whore," Jolene screamed, her arm moving to wipe at the blood pouring from her nose. Vampires converged on us, alerted by the sounds of Astrid's screeching for help.

"Emma?" Jaeden's voice was dangerously soft, and I turned to look at him, knowing my face was a bruised, swollen mess from the blows I'd taken to it. "What the fuck?" he snapped, his eyes moving accusingly to Astrid.

"Emma started it," Shamus announced, and my eyes bugged out. "She attacked them. Astrid protected the women as I instructed her to do, should Emma become jealous of the new feeders. She made her feelings for Jolene apparent the other day, Jaeden, you heard it the same as I." He shook his head sadly as Jaeden looked at each of us with a slightly confused expression on his face. Almost as if he was torn as to whom he should believe. He knew Astrid was a liar, but Shamus?

"The fuck you say?" I snapped, wondering what the fuck was going on. I hadn't started this! I'd wandered into their camp, but I was trying to leave.

"Do not argue with me," Shamus growled, his eyes changing to red as his fangs slipped from his gums.

I watched as Astrid sidled to Jaeden, along with Jolene, who threw herself into his arms, uncaring that he didn't hug her back.

"She attacked them; I had to protect them." Astrid sounded so convincing, *I* almost believed her.

"She just started hitting me for no reason; she's jealous of what we share, this just proves it!" Jolene gushed.

"That's not what happened," I argued, apparently to deaf ears. I laughed as I put it together. They'd set me up, and it had all been to turn Jaeden against me. Why? I'd already ended the relationship. What was Shamus gaining from this?

"Go to the other side of camp, Emma, now," Jaeden ordered as he watched me with something cold in his eyes.

"I didn't do…"

"Go to the fucking camp now!" he shouted, and I straightened, hearing the anger in his tone. Directed at me. "I'll deal with you in a minute."

"Fuck you, you don't *deal* with me. I'm gone," I snapped back, flipping him off as I turned to retrieve my things. Screw them.

I made it five steps before Jaeden jerked on the arm that Astrid had twisted and broken. I spun around and glared at him. Tears burned my eyes; pain shot through me, almost sending me to my knees.

"You had no right to attack them," he growled.

"I didn't!" I shot back.

"Shamus has no reason to lie about it, Emma, and you've been brooding around the camp for days. We've all seen and noticed it. You are not above the others, and you have to follow the rules that have been set out, just like the rest of us. You don't get to attack someone just because you're jealous!" he shouted, and I lost it.

I threw a wild punch with my broken arm, crying out as the bone snapped more. I kicked out, fighting him as the crowd watched him dodge every jab and kick. He was backing me into the other side of the camp, away from the women. He grabbed my arm as I threw another punch, twisting my broken arm and shattering the bone of my wrist. I threw myself backwards, away from him, away from the pain and the gathering vampires. Normally, what he'd done wouldn't have hurt the wrist, but it was already weakened and cracked from his ex-wife twisting it.

I hit one of the trees hard as Astrid and Jolene cheered Jaeden on. I expelled a breath as tears welled in my eyes and I lifted my hands. The entire area went silent. I looked down at my hands and found a sharp tree limb protruding from my stomach.

"Emma," Jaeden whispered as he rushed forward to help me.

"Don't," I hissed coldly. "Don't touch me," I coughed, spattering him with blood as it began to dribble from my mouth and nose. I bent over, snapping the branch and falling to the ground. I crawled in silence to my bag, which lay beneath the hammock. I grabbed the bag, tore at my shirt until it gave, and ripped it from my body. I felt Jaeden's pain at what had happened, and I knew it hadn't been fully his fault. I'd thrown the punches, and he'd dodged them. I'd also thrown myself backwards because of the intensity of the pain, and I'd just happened to do it against a tree that had many of its lower branches sharpened. They were used to impale a fresh kill so that it could be skinned and gutted.

Once I was naked from the chest up, I tore the rest of the branch out, throwing up blood as my vision swam. I tossed it to the ground, fighting to remain awake and upright. I struggled as I unzipped my bag, pulling out the gauze I kept in it, and wrapped the gauze around my stomach where the wound was. I reached for the knife to cut the gauze and tied it off. I brought the knife up to my hair, and sliced through the braid, leaving it severed just below my ears in a crude fashion. They'd fucking held me with it, used it against me. I'd known for a while that it had to go. It was time.

"Emma," Jaeden growled as he watched me toss the hair to the ground. I turned my head, finding Shamus beside him, his hand restraining Jaeden from moving to me. "I can heal you," he whispered.

"No, you cannot," Shamus spat out. "I forbid it. She needs to be punished for attacking those weaker than her."

"No, you should keep listening to Shamus." I coughed out the words, feeling my body already beginning to heal itself. For me, it was the principle of the matter; I didn't want his blood running inside of me. I could heal on my own, away from him. I would leave them, find somewhere I was safe, and heal from the injuries. I could hear him arguing with Shamus, but I knew this was one argument Jaeden wasn't going to win, and whatever Shamus said was law.

I looked up at the hammock that still hung high in the trees, and winced.

"I can put you in it," Jaeden offered.

"I-I need it down…" I hissed, barely able to get words out, as whatever my body did to heal began doing so. It burned. I was on fire. Tissue and muscles were reattaching. Bones were trying to reset, but I had no idea how long it would take to heal.

Raphael took the hammock down effortlessly, and I accepted it with one hand before setting it on the ground and pulling things out of my bag as I cradled the other arm close to my body. I stared briefly at the strawberry blonde hair that covered the bag and the ground, and then dismissed it. I pulled out holsters, weapons, my hoodie, and mask. Slipping a shirt over my naked breasts, I winced as the front of it blossomed with blood as the wound refused to heal. I slipped the harness on over my shoulders, tucked the weapons into place, and then pulled the hoodie over my body. Pushing the hood off, I slipped yet another harness into place and then ran my fingers through the thick black make-up, covering my eyes before slipping on the mask.

I pushed knives into the sides of my boots, and shoved a canteen of water into the bag along with the hammock, and zipped it up. I bit my lip hard enough that it tore the flesh as I hefted the pack onto my back. It took effort to make it to my feet; a gurgled cry escaped my parted lips as I clung to the tree for support to make it to my feet. I was going to find Lachlan, and then sleep until my body finished healing.

"No," Jaeden growled as it finally hit him that I was leaving. "Not alone, not like this!" His voice shook, but I was beyond caring. I turned to look at him, and whatever he had seen in my eyes stopped him cold. Maybe it was the death rattle in my chest, or maybe it was the betrayal I felt. Whatever it was, he stopped, dropped his hands, and shook his head.

"Let her go," Shamus hissed as Astrid slipped her hand into his and Jolene pushed her way closer to Jaeden. "I need the receiver for the Ark, Emma." He held his hand out expectantly, and there was something cold in his eyes.

Fine; Addy had orders. Orders I'd given her as a safeguard the day I left the Ark. If I didn't personally make contact within a three-day timeframe, she'd lock it down, and the wolves would guard them until I could get back to them. I'd started moving pieces together in case they'd planned a hostile takeover. The wolves were on our side; at least, I hoped they still were. Without Lachlan, it was hard to know what his people were doing.

I struggled painfully with the bag, wincing when Raphael got too close, and glared at him. He backed up, and my eyes focused on Jaeden's as I struggled to get one of the pockets unzipped. He silently pleaded for me to stay, even though Astrid and Jolene flanked him on both sides. I pulled out the phone-like device, then dropped it to the ground as my hand refused to hold it.

I turned and slowly but surely walked away from the group who watched me. I knew without needing to be told that Jaeden would come after me, especially once Shamus learned that the shelter was locked down, with his vampires on the outside. They may need blood to sustain their lifestyle, and to live, but they weren't using my people to do it.

I'd made it less than a mile before my legs gave out and I hit the ground. I'd searched for signs of the pack, or even the Sentinel, but it was useless. Delirium was setting in, and I couldn't force my eyes to remain open. I heard a twig snap and moaned in pain as strong arms lifted me and my face was pressed against something solid and warm. I mumbled when I heard a Scottish brogue, and gave up. I couldn't fight the darkness that was pulling me towards the abyss. It was seductive, the numbness it brought, divine.

"Jesus, lass, what the fuck did you do?" Cian's voice tried to break through, but my lungs were done. I'd used everything in my reserve just to put distance between me and the vampires. I allowed my face to press against his chest for warmth.

"We've got you, Emma, girl, you're going to be alright. Sleep, heal. You look like you need it more than Lachlan does right now," were the last words I heard as I sank into darkness's warm, welcoming embrace.

Chapter Five

I woke up to something warm and wet licking my face. I pushed it away, but it came back and continued licking. It stunk, and I hurt. I pushed it away a few more times before I opened my eyes to striking emerald ones that were filled with worry. He nuzzled me, and continued to do so until I tried to move my arm, only to scream as white pain tore through me. I looked down, and found my arm tied to some kind of stick, and my chest bare of clothing, the wound exposed to the crisp morning air.

"Lachlan," I whispered as my eyes tried to focus on the huge black wolf that lay beside me, whining as he watched me. His paw moved to my face and he continued to push at it, as if he worried I'd pass out at any moment.

"What the fuck happened, Emma?" Cian demanded, noting the through-and-through hole in my stomach. Cian's eyes lowered to my breasts and lowered even more as he reached beside him and pulled a wet cloth from a bowl and washed the wound. "Answer me girl, so he stops his insistent bitching in my head."

"You can talk to him?" I asked, watching as a small smile spread across his lips.

"Duh, Emma, he's the alpha. He wants to know how this happened, and where the fuck Jaeden was when it did. He vowed to protect you in Lachlan's absence."

"Hard to do when he had orders to do otherwise," I mumbled, wincing as he pushed against the wound.

"Elaborate, Emma," Cian continued as more wolves crowded into the crude cave we were in.

"Astrid and Shamus set me up. I walked into the feeder camp and one of the new girls we saved was with Astrid. God, I knew better than to go in there. I got lost in my head, wandered in, and she attacked me. She started hitting me, Astrid grabbed my hair from behind, and we started fighting big time. It got ugly, and then Jaeden showed up, Shamus told him he had seen everything, that I'd started it. I told Jaeden I wasn't willing to deal with it anymore. Shamus carried on until he got Jaeden angry at me, so I flipped him off, told him I was leaving. He followed me, grabbed my arm that Astrid broke, and I started fighting him. He didn't hit me, just dodged every blow I threw at him. He was getting me away from the women, but he grabbed my arm. I threw myself away from him, ended up stuck to a tree on one of the pikes that we were using to clean the animals with."

He winced and shook his head. "That explains the bark I just spent an hour digging out. I knew I liked you for a reason." Cian didn't have the accent that Lachlan had; his was almost as American as my own when he wanted it to be.

"Our people are safe," I stated, nodding to Lachlan, knowing he'd want to know that his people that he'd left with mine were alive and well. "Addy and Liam had orders from me to wait until the vampires went out, and then lock it down if they didn't hear from us for a few days. I haven't spoken to her in three as it stands. Tomorrow she'll lock them out as soon as they leave. Any that were left behind will meet up with a friendly boot out the door from Liam."

"That was smart, but by now they may have figured out how to get back in. I found a radio a few days ago, contacted Liam; he said the vampires were watching them, but other than that, no signs of any plans to take over the shelter. Shamus wouldn't hesitate to hunt you down if you cut them off from the Ark, Emma; he's as ruthless as they come."

"I noticed." I grimaced in pain and ignored his hand that had risen to rest on my breasts.

"Don't take this the wrong way, lass, but you have to go. In case he is hunting you, I won't allow them to get close to Lachlan in his current state. He's on the mend, but he's got a few more days of recovery to go. They had silver bullets; silver is a bitch to get out, even for someone as strong as he is."

"I understand." I'd known that if Lachlan wasn't healed yet, I would be sent away soon after I found them. I understood why it needed to be done. "How's he doing?" My hand absently found Lachlan and petted him while I ignored the other arm and the incessant itching that was from it healing.

"He's stubborn as hell, refused to rest until he knew you were safe. Now maybe he'll sleep. What's your plan, Emma?" he asked, ignoring the growling wolf who hadn't taken kindly to his taunt.

"Find Grayson," I said softly. "Rest, heal, and head out on my own, I guess. I have to find him, and I know I can't do that with Jaeden, not with Shamus gunning for me. He isn't on my side, that much I know for sure now. He wouldn't allow Jaeden to heal me; he ordered him not to."

"We noticed that he and Jaeden haven't always seen eye to eye. I figured their bromance was in danger with the way Jaeden was grasping on to you. Didn't know he'd do something like this. By the way, what the fuck happened to your nose?" he asked offhandedly.

"Got a nose job, what the fuck you think happened to it?" I snapped, pissed that she'd caught me off guard and that I'd been stupid and hesitated.

"You need a better surgeon," he snapped back. "I reset it while I worked on the rest of your injuries while you were passed out."

"I hesitated. I've never hesitated in combat in

my life, and I did. Jolene's human and I was afraid my powers would show up, and I'd hurt her; the last time Astrid tried to fuck with me, they kicked in, and I knocked that bitch's ass across the yard!" I laughed, which hurt like hell. If my powers had kicked in with Jolene, I could have killed her and lost Jaeden forever. It shouldn't have even crossed my mind. My father would be disappointed.

"I could see that after watching you take down the rogues, but your life was in danger, girl. When you're backed into a corner, claw and chew your way out of it even if you think your enemy is weaker," he said, and Lachlan's sudden barking made me jump and cry out in pain. "He says stay away from Shamus; he probably has orders to separate you from Jaeden. He's bound by the same laws, but he's also running on his own agenda. It wouldn't surprise us if he was aiming for a seat to become an elder so that he would be out of reach and above reproach."

"I get it," I mumbled. "He wants to be untouchable." My eyes grew heavy with the need to sleep.

"Rest, you look like you need it. I'll cover you up so Lachlan stops staring at your tits," he smiled, and used his shirt to cover me up, which caused Lachlan to growl and huff. It was funny, since he looked like a dog that had been denied his favorite chew toy.

My eyes closed and I felt the other wolves moving in, surrounding me and the alpha while we slept. I slept the sleep of the dead as I healed. When I awoke the next day, it was to Cian nudging me with his foot.

"Jaeden's out looking for you, so you'll need to head out soon. Are you healed enough to manage it?" he asked, and I heard distinct growling beside me. I slowly sat up, testing my body as Cian peeled the bandages and stick from my arm. My arm was weak, but I was able to move it without too much pain. My stomach was another situation. It hurt like hell, but then again, internal organs probably needed a lot of time to heal.

"I'm good. You'll find me once he's healed?" I was already digging through my bag for clean clothing.

"The moment he's healed enough, we'll find you. He said to head east, and then south again. Zigzag, no straight lines. We'll follow you, but we can't move as quickly as you will need to. Jaeden will slow them down, according to Lachlan. He won't be able to do it too much without Shamus figuring it out, though. Jaeden is the brains and the brawn, but he is blooded to his maker, which means he is Shamus's property until he finds him. Watch the woods around you for Cayla. She'll be Shamus's eyes. She won't like it, but she's bound to him, too. Stay alive until we can get to you." Cian handed me the bloody bandages. "Throw these somewhere, make sure it's not into water, or it will lose the blood scent; it should buy you some time."

"Okay, and if they catch me?" I hated that, with my stomach still on fire and in pain, it was a probability.

"Then we'll save you at the soonest moment we can

do it without endangering Lachlan. They won't kill you, remember that. They can't if they expect to get back inside the shelter. Last Lachlan heard, they'd collected enough supplies to last them a few more months. They're holding up; we are the ones falling apart right now. Think about you, not them. Liam won't let them starve; he'll hunt wild game before that happens."

"Thank God," I whispered.

"Lachlan says he hates your hair, but he understands why you did it. It kind of looks badass, in a sexy way," Cian grinned.

"He said it looks sexy?" I asked, disbelieving.

"No, I did," he replied easily as he sat back, handing me the harnesses. "They're slowed down by the humans they travel with. Use it to your advantage. If you feel them getting close, scream. If we are close enough, we will do what we can to help. Lachlan needs a few more days of healing before he'll be able to take human form. Unlike most of us, he's a born wolf. Takes him a while to regain his human form, and healing is simpler in this one for him."

"Tell him…"

"You tell him, he understands you."

"You were right; he broke my heart."

The wolf didn't gloat, or maybe he did and I just couldn't tell, but he scooted closer and licked my face a few times before he sat down in front of me.

"He says nae being stupid, lass, be the Emma who kens how tae survive."

"Did he also tell you to use a brogue?" I laughed, and Cian nodded. "I'm me; there's no part of that Emma left for now. I'm my father's daughter again. I will get through this; I have to. See you soon, wolf boy." I bent down to lean my face against Lachlan's furry muzzle.

"He says he's going to hold you to that, lass. He's a man, virile and ready to claim his mate, however stubborn she may be," he said, looking pointedly at me. "He says there's no boy left in him. He's his father's son. Born alpha to the pack, he's a survivor like you. Fate is tricky, you know, throwing this crew together at the end of the world. Like she knew what we needed."

Chapter Six

I was on my own, zigzagging through some pretty rough terrain. I'd had a few close encounters with the vampires, who didn't seem as hostile as I'd assumed they would be. I'd managed to get away because they didn't want to hurt me when they tried to capture me, and I'd used that against them. I was back to being me, the Emma before I'd allowed myself to be duped by hope that we didn't have to be alone. By trusting Jaeden, I'd brought in more problems.

I watched the stream of smoke from a fire, high in the mountain range, about five miles from where I stood on a jagged hillside that was filled with rocks. The terrain had begun to slowly change as we approached Utah.

I could hear muffled shouts, some catcalls, and something that sounded like it was screaming in pain. The latter was muffled and sent a chill up my spine. I slipped my mask into place, checked the weapons I carried, and unsnapped my bow from the pack, checking it carefully to be sure everything was in working order. Once I'd made it closer to the area of the fire, I climbed a tree, trying to get a better look at what was actually going on.

The problem with the aftermath of the virus was that people who were normally pretty decent became dangerous. They were desperate to survive, and with time moving on and food growing scarce, they'd turned into animals. Then there were those who enjoyed the animals they'd become as a result of the breakdown in society since the virus.

My father had never sugarcoated anything. He was brutally honest about what life would be like after the government was gone. People always complained about it, but the government kept order; it maintained a balance in the world that worked. It may not have always been correct, but it had kept humans somewhat safer from the animals we were now left with.

I could make out three men, but no sign of the person who was screaming. A tent was positioned a little ways back from the fire, which had something that smelled heavenly cooking in a Dutch oven. I shimmied down the tree, trying to decide if I should bypass it, or figure out where the crying and muffled sobs were coming from, because it sounded female, and there'd been no sign of one outside of the tent. My instincts told me to investigate, the same ones that had always been right before.

I set my bag down, unwilling to fight with the extra weight attached to me, as I was still recovering from the stomach wound. I untied the thin metal wire that I had threaded through the belt loops of my pants, knowing that I'd have to get close before I knew the situation, and stealth might be my best option. I checked the knives at my waist, hidden beneath the shirt I wore, and started to tie my hair up, only to remember that most of it was gone. I swallowed and crept closer to the camp, securing my mask as I entered.

"What the fuck," one of the guys said; he was older, mid-forties, with a potbelly stomach and beady eyes. He had a gun draped over his shoulder, and a lustful look in his eyes as he took in my figure.

"Mmm, new meat," one of the other guys catcalled, a younger, mid-twenties guy who had greasy hair and food stuck in his goatee. "Kind of skinny, though." He tilted his head to look me over slowly.

"Guys," another male called to them as he ducked out of the tent and looked at me. "Get her!" he snapped, and I smiled as I took in the blood and meat the man held in his hand. What the fuck?

"You don't want to do that," I murmured, watching as fatboy advanced on me, as if he thought to overpower me. He swung out, expecting me to be slower than he was, and I dodged it, effortlessly moving behind him as I pulled the wire taut between my hands and wrapped it around his neck, dropping my weight as his friends watched. Normally, choking someone took time, but with a wire thread, it sliced through his carotid and soft tissue on his neck, killing him the moment I dropped my weight to the ground.

I watched as he dropped, turning my eyes to the other two. The young guy moved swiftly, his hands darting out with blades I hadn't seen him pull. I danced around them, listening as the air whooshed with each swing he took; I pulled my own blade and took a swing, slicing through his arm and then slicing him open from stomach to chest, and watched as he hit the ground.

Once it was just me and the guy who'd emerged from the tent left, he whined like a bitch, begging and promising he could change his ways. I tied him up, using the wire to tie his wrists to the tree that was just at the edge of the camp. If he moved or tried to get away, he'd slit his own wrists. I made sure he knew it before I moved to the tent.

What I found inside made my hope for humanity die. I stumbled from the tent, striding with purpose as I pulled the knives from their sheaths and shook my head. Tears blinded my eyes, and I had to fight to keep from throwing what little food I'd eaten back up.

"You sick fuck!" I shouted through a sob that threatened to knock me to my knees; I was losing it. The little grasp of sanity that I still had was slowly slipping away. I felt like a monster. I wanted to slice him open, cut him to pieces, making sure he felt every fucking slice of the blade. "How could you!"

"I was starving to death! I'm a doctor; I'm valuable! You need me alive. If you get hurt, I can help you!" His cunning eyes seemed to search mine as he tried different tactics for what he thought might work best.

I pulled at my hair as I fought to not throw up. "If you're a doctor, then you took an oath! Do no harm! Why?" I sobbed, and shook my head as I wiped my mouth off, trying to keep myself from losing it.

He cried, shaking his head as he continued to beg and bargain for his worthless life. I left him there, tied to the tree, with only one option for escape: Suicide. I made my way back to the tent, my stomach churning with what I was going to have to do. This shit wasn't fair.

Once inside the tent, I pulled off my mask; sobs rocked my body as I struggled to contain them. The flap to the tent closed and the smell hit me. In the middle of it, laid out on display, was a woman who'd been badly mutilated. A propane lantern flickered, casting an eerie light on the macabre scene as her wild eyes looked at me. I shook my head; I couldn't fix this. There was no medical way to fix the damage they'd done.

She moaned with pain, and I felt hot tears burning in my eyes. They'd cut out her tongue to mute her screams and reduce the chance of attracting attention from miles away. The inside of her left thigh had been sliced open and cauterized after the meat had been taken; the other leg was gone from just below her knee. My eyes latched on to her thighs; tendons and ligaments had been removed and sutured with surgical precision. The ones you needed to…walk, or run away.

"Ell me," she moaned, and I lifted my eyes to her and shook my head.

"I can't heal this," I rasped through the constriction of my throat. I couldn't fix her legs; I didn't know how.

"Ell me!" she moaned again, trying to sit up, but her arms had been sliced open and sutured, just like her legs.

"I don't know what to do," I cried. All of the fatty flesh was gone, missing; she had other patches of skin all over her body that looked crudely sewn, as if they were trying to keep her alive as long as they could.

I sat back, my mind running scenarios because the one in my head just couldn't be right. They'd strategically cut pieces from her and had used her for pleasure, judging by the way her legs were draped open, and the doctor had come out of the tent with his pants undone when I had surprised them.

"Ell me," she sobbed as her fingers stretched at odd angles as she reached for me. Her words hit me like a ton of bricks. It knocked the wind out of me. I shook my head and left the tent, stumbling to get away from her. Once outside, I screamed with rage, pain, and the knowledge that I was going to go back in there to do as she asked.

"Pretty, isn't she?" The so-called 'doctor' sneered,

having lost his need to beg. He needed to brag more, admiring his handiwork. He wanted praise for the monstrous thing he'd done.

I fell to my knees as violent sobs tore through me. The level of fucked up shit they'd done to her was off the charts. I screamed with rage for every person who'd been assaulted from the start of the virus. Every inch of her body flashed through my mind on replay, and I doubled over and threw up. I heaved as tears ran down my face.

When I was done, I stood up. I turned and looked at him, really looked at him. He was laughing. His eyes were wild, and he laughed as I could hear the woman moaning from the tent, broken and dying from what they'd done to her. I reached into my boot, pulled out a knife and walked slowly to him.

"I could make you just as pretty," he laughed.

"Are there more like you?" I asked, needing to know. The three of them couldn't have killed the people in the towns alone, not with how many people we'd found dead.

"There are hundreds of us, maybe thousands; it's a new world. The ones who hunt will get the best pick. I'm needed," he cackled maniacally. "I can make them pretty, like her. Make them useful, live longer. They serve our needs, until they…don't. Then we find new ones." His voice trailed off dreamily.

I bent down low, looking up at him as he watched

me. "I don't have a medical degree like you must have, but then again, I don't intend on keeping you alive." I sliced under his thigh just above the knee where the ligaments were, enjoying the scream that tore from his lungs. I matched it to his other leg, making sure to miss the artery. I took a few steps to the fire, picked up the metal poker that was red-hot, turned back to him, and closed the wounds. I listened as screams ripped from his lungs until he passed out from the pain.

Once I was sure he wouldn't bleed to death, I stepped back to the fire, threw the poker down, and looked back at the flap opening that hid the evil that had been done to that poor woman behind it. I dropped to my knees, staring at the tent. I hadn't felt anything while I'd sliced him open. Just cold, as if I'd become some kind of monster. Maybe this world belonged to them now, the monsters. Maybe I had to become one to survive this world.

I fought to get to my feet as I slid the knife into its sheath and withdrew the 9mm. I entered the tent and sat down beside her, holding her hand as I looked at her. They'd torn her apart and sadistically abused her. She'd been their entertainment and dinner. I didn't want to live in a world where people could do this to someone. I didn't want my friends or family to live in it. It was sick. If these subhuman creatures were what was left of humanity, we were doomed.

She didn't moan again; she could see the tears streaming down my face as I looked at her. She wouldn't survive what had been done to her for much longer.

There was just no fucking way. She was broken; her arms were useless, and her legs would never allow her to carry weight again. If she even survived the infection that had probably already taken root in her body, she couldn't protect herself from anything, and I couldn't take her with me. There was no fucking way. I held her hand tighter as I brought the gun up and held it against her temple.

"You're sure? I can probably find help for you," I whispered, seeing the resolve in her eyes. She shook her head and yet I still hesitated. It wasn't like a mercy killing. She wasn't crazy or violent. She was a fucking victim. She didn't deserve this. I didn't deserve to carry this burden. She looked at me with tear-filled eyes. The poor woman was in her late thirties, fit, and looked as if she'd been in good health before she'd fallen into this mess. "I hope there's a heaven and hell, and I hope that when you get to heaven, you can sit in on judgement for those assholes. Know this: I killed them. They'll never do this to anyone else again." I pulled the trigger and flinched at the recoil of the gun. I'd lied. But it would be the truth, though, soon enough. I wasn't letting the butcher of a 'doctor' die quickly; he didn't deserve it.

I didn't cry. I forced myself to hold it together as I propelled myself backwards from the tent. The moment I was on my feet, I felt the muzzle of a gun against my temple. I expelled a shaky breath and allowed the tears to flow, because I couldn't hold them back. I turned to look at the man who held the gun, noting he was decked out in a United States National Guard uniform, full body armor and gear. He looked to be in his mid-twenties, maybe a little older.

"What happened here?" he demanded, and I let go of the sob I'd been holding and dropped to the ground, landing on my knees as I dry-heaved. There wasn't anything left in my stomach to come up. "Jesus," he said. As I retched, more of them converged into the camp. They all had uniforms on, all from the same unit. I hadn't even known we still had army or any type of military left.

"You find her?" a guy asked as he burst into the camp, only to stop cold when he saw the lifeless bodies, and then me, as I tried to pull myself together. "Is she here? Oh my God, that's the guy who took her! Where is she?"

"Don't let him inside the tent," I choked out, only to feel the gun as it rested against the back of my head. "It's bad."

"You smell that?" someone asked, removing the lid from the Dutch oven. I retched, violently.

"What the fuck is wrong with her?" the guy who was sniffing the pot asked.

"It's her," I whispered brokenly as I lifted my eyes to the first guy. They'd yet to remove the gun from my head, and I wasn't fighting them, why? Where was the fight, the will to live?

"What?" the guy asked, bending down to look at me. I had weapons everywhere, which he noted, and his friend began removing them. I didn't fight him. What was the point anyway? "What did you say?" he demanded, poking the gun harder against my temple.

"The food, it's her," I rasped, barely able to get the words out.

"The fuck you say," he mumbled. Just as he did, someone entered the tent, and as he shouted, I dry-heaved violently. "What the…Chad?" he asked, but his friend had seen what I had, and he'd put it together a lot faster. "Got her weapons?" he asked the guy behind me.

"She's a walking fucking arsenal," he complained, finding more as he pulled me to my feet and zip-tied my hands behind my back. "Look at this." He dropped more weapons into the pile.

"Is she here?" another guy snapped, which must have been the husband looking for the woman in the tent.

"Don't let him see her," I repeated as I was roughly pulled away from the tent and hauled towards one of the trees, and I felt the bite of a knife as the guy changed his mind about my hands being tied behind my back, and secured me to the tree. I sank to my knees, and looked away from the chaos.

As a man began screaming hysterically, I knew he'd discovered the remains. Instead of looking at the dead men who littered the camp, he rushed at me, kicking and hitting me. I didn't try to block it, which the others noted as they pulled him off of me. I was tied to a fucking tree.

I'd let it happen. Some fucking monster I was.

"You need to tell me what the fuck happened here," the soldier who'd held me at gunpoint ordered.

"Humanity died," I chuckled without any trace of humor. This was a fucking travesty.

"Did you help do that to her?" His gray eyes met and held mine. "Yes or no?" he demanded as he grabbed my throat.

My eyes darted to where children had just pushed through the bushes, and fresh tears filled my eyes.

"Did you find Mommy?" The little girl's eyes were filled with hope. "I want Mommy!" she sobbed uncontrollably. An older boy, who looked to be about thirteen, reached down and picked her up, comforting her.

"It's going to be okay, Sadie Mae, we'll find her."

"Stop them," I pleaded, tugging on my wrists as I watched them near the tent. "Don't worry about me, stop them!"

"Guys, come sit on the logs," he directed, and nodded as the other soldiers took positions in front of the tent; one of the National Guardsmen tried to comfort the woman's husband. His eyes slid back to mine as I watched the kids. "Do not even fucking think about it," he warned.

"Children have no place in this sick world," I whispered and turned my eyes back to his.

"You didn't do this to her, it's in your eyes," he murmured as he sat beside me, and rested against the other tree. "What's inside that tent?" He turned to look at me.

I didn't answer him. Instead, I closed my eyes as the one man started to scream again. Full grown men, soldiers, couldn't stomach what was inside that tent.

"I killed her," I whispered, turning to look at him. "I ended it."

Why I told him that, I didn't know. I felt the butt of his gun as it smashed against my face. When I woke, it was to the man staring at me, the woman's husband. Someone else was digging a hole, and the children cried silently.

"Why?" her husband demanded, and I knew the other soldiers listened.

"Because she was dying, and she asked me to do it," I said evenly. "They cut her legs, severing the tendons, and removed the ligaments so that she couldn't run. They cut her tongue out so that she couldn't scream, and they had been taking parts and pieces of her for supper. Her arms, and her legs, they were probably infected, seeing that this isn't the most sterile of places. I couldn't carry her. I couldn't save her," I expelled a shaky breath. "I ended it because she knew that she wouldn't survive, or hell, maybe she had me do it so that you didn't have to. I'm a stranger, no one. She was in pain; it was in her eyes. No one deserves that kind of torture, no one."

"You killed the men?" the first soldier asked, his eyes leveling me with a look of unease. "Little thing like you couldn't have done this alone."

"I was trained well," I replied. "I had the advantage because they underestimated me, just as you're doing now."

"He was fucking garroted," he snapped as he pointed to the fat man's corpse.

"Indeed, he was. He was sloppy, ill-trained. I wasn't. Is the National Guard running?" I asked, noting the way he stood; it was taught, ingrained into them right after they enlisted. It wasn't something a civilian would do when his gun was resting, and he held it correctly, too.

"Nah, it went down when the CDC did," he stated, his eyes on me as blood continued to ooze from my nose.

"We need to find food," another soldier stated, his eyes looking me over as if I was a wild animal he was afraid to get close to. "Kids are starving."

When the little girl whispered how hungry she was to the older boy, I groaned. I had food; MREs that tasted like shit, but it was nutrients. I didn't want to offer what I had and be left with nothing, and I didn't expect help anytime soon.

My eyes lowered to one of the guys' boots, which had his blood type on the back. I narrowed my eyes on it, and asked, "Why put it there?"

"Why put what, where?" the guy asked; according to his uniform, his last name was Bernard.

"Blood type, it's on the back of his boot," I replied.

"In war, they don't have time to look shit up. Just easier to look at the boots, ya know?" he answered as he crept closer. "Where you from?" he asked.

"Not around here," I answered. "Untie me."

"No can do, wild thing," he stated, sizing me up.

"Scared?" I asked, but his eyes didn't scream fear; they were looking at me as if he was impressed.

"No, just not as sloppy as these guys were," he smiled. "How's a wild thing like you survive out here alone?"

"Who said I was alone?" I smirked as a little blood trickled over my lip. He went to alert immediately. Searching the woods, another thing that was military training; not many knew the signals, but he did, telling the others with his fingers and hand, to watch their six; I knew what he was doing, my dad taught me.

"Where are your friends hiding, then?" he asked, not convinced I wasn't alone.

"Who says I have friends?" I smiled.

"Sass won't get you anywhere." He smiled back. "Johnson, see if you can reach the Ark, and tell them we're coming in one soul light, and get us the coordinates for it from here."

"The Ark?" I perked up, but his eyes snapped to mine and I knew, without needing to be told, he wasn't going to tell me anything. Good, because if he'd started blabbing details, I'd have told Addy to shut up on the cords.

"Ark this is NG1, you out there?" Johnson barked into the radio, which apparently was part of his backpack. Static. "Ark, this is Johnson from NG1, over."

"This is the Ark, copy," Addy's voice filtered through, overriding the static.

My heart leapt to my throat.

"Ark this is NG1, we lost a soul, coming in light, over," he said.

"Addy!" I screamed, and everyone turned to me.

"Emma?" she asked. "Emma? Is that Emma?"

"Addy, it's me. These assholes have me tied to a tree," I explained, watching as the 'doctor' I tied to the tree started to move. *Shit.* I'd almost forgotten about him, and they'd assumed he was dead.

"You motherfuckers caught Emma?" she asked in a shocked tone. "Hats off to that shit, but you better let her go."

"You know this girl?" the guy asked, his eyes holding mine as he continued to talk.

"Strawberry blonde, probably decked out in black and an arsenal of weapons, sound familiar?" Addy asked.

"Very," he mused, already moving towards me. "Tell me why I should let her go? We could just bring her to you. She's apparently dangerous."

"I'll give you one reason: You want in this shelter?" she asked.

"You know we do," he answered.

"She owns it, she runs it; piss her off, and I won't open these doors. Her father built it."

"No shit?" he asked, producing a knife and slicing through the plastic tie.

I stood up as I rubbed my wrists, nodding to the kids. "Take them away from here for a few minutes. I have a promise to keep. If any of you are squeamish, go with."

I didn't wait to see if they listened or left. I walked determinedly through the camp towards the pile of my weapons, swooped up a knife, and made my way to the guy who was coming around.

"What's she doing?" Addy asked. "Hey, what's she doing?"

"Plug your ears, Addy," I warned as I sliced down the guys arm, shoving my fingers into the tissue and ripping at the ligaments. "Where are the others like you?" I demanded.

"I'll never tell!" he screamed; his body shook and trembled in pain. "I'll die first!"

"You're right about that, asshole. Last chance," I warned. When he tried to spit at me, I sliced his other arm open, watching as he slit his wrist the moment he began struggling again in earnest. The skin stretched, and blood started pouring. I was covered in it. "She was a human being! How powerful are you now? Do you feel like a God? You did this to her! Worse. You did so much fucking worse." I slit him from sternum to his navel, and stepped back, turning away to find the men staring at me in open horror.

I could hear Addy's shuddering sob, and I wanted to hug her, to promise her I wasn't like him, but I'd crossed a line. He needed to be punished, to be put through what he'd done to her. He deserved so much more.

"Emma, what did you do?" Addy cried. "Who was that?"

"That was a monster," I whispered. "He reaped what he sowed, but not all of it. He deserved it. He deserved so much more, Addy."

"Mercy?" she asked.

"No, I have no mercy to give," I replied as I pulled

my canister of water out and poured it over my hands. "I gave all the mercy I had to his victim."

"Good kill?" she asked.

"No, never a good kill," I whispered as I fought for composure. "Everything good there?" I asked, needing to change the subject. The men watched me as if I was the monster, but the truth was, I'd wanted that asshole to suffer for what he'd done. I'd enjoyed his screams. Mostly, I enjoyed knowing he'd felt some of what he'd forced an innocent woman to endure.

"Um, so we asked about the other situation, with the blood? They're building a hospital, said ours is shit. Bringing in doctors, and wanted to be ready in case of an emergency situation."

"Shit," I whispered as I looked at the radio the guy held.

"Yeah, shit. It's all good, though, they were allowed back in when the truth came out, and we're doing well, Ems, we are running things smoothly, and you don't have to worry about us. You find Grayson, bring him home. I got this."

"I know you do," I replied as I looked at the kids, who were coming back into camp as one of the soldiers draped a tarp over the guy I'd slaughtered. "They've got little ones coming in with emotional baggage. Cat around?" I should have told her about what happened with Shamus, but if I did, her life could be in danger. I bit my tongue, refusing to chance it. When I got back to the Ark would be soon enough to tell her.

"Of course, all souls accounted for," she replied carefully. "Souls on your side?" she asked.

"I don't know, left the party. Lachlan got shot, he's wounded. He's healing, though, just needs some time. He's got his pack with him. Jaeden and his team; they were okay when I left them."

"I heard that you left them, but not why you left. He's called every fucking day, freaking out about you. He said you're giving him a merry ol' chase round the mountains," she snickered.

"He tell you what happened?" I asked.

"No, what happened?" she asked.

"It's a very long story which I'll tell you all about later, but I'm okay for now. I'll survive. These guys need directions; you got it?" I asked, but the radio had gone silent momentarily before she started talking to the other guy. "Addy, I'll find a way to talk to you later, I need to head out."

"Emma, be careful," she said.

"Always am," I quipped.

"Uh huh, that's why you got caught just now?" she countered.

"You think I would have been caught if I didn't want to be?" I asked, which caused the soldiers to look at me.

"Not in a million years; see, I knew it was something like that," she laughed. "Emma caught. That's a good one."

I swallowed. I did get caught, and I hadn't fought them. They could have been more cannibals. They could have just been horrible people.

"So, you run the Ark?" the guy asked as he followed me to where I'd hid my bag.

"I do, but not alone. My father built it. I have MREs for the kids, if they're hungry," I offered.

"I'm Cage," he said, offering his hand to me.

I shook it, and grabbed my bag, heading back to where the kids were. I emptied my pack of all the MREs, watching as Cage ordered one of his guys to empty the Dutch oven. The little girl cried silently as she watched her father fall apart next to the sheet-covered remains of her mother.

"Some sick shit," someone said, and I turned to look at him. "How did you find this place?"

"Found it because they were cooking, the fire was noticeable from a few miles away," I replied. I turned to Cage. "How you hear about the Ark?"

"An old man, he answered our call when we were stuck in Montana, but then we got another call that there was a family stuck, went to help them out. Figured we'd make it back before he did, never found him. Used the same radio signal, but got silence up until a few weeks ago. We have been heading there ever since."

I nodded. We'd changed channels; we did it every few weeks to be sure we weren't giving too much away while we looked for other survivors.

"He made it back home okay?" he queried.

"No, he was killed by some really nasty people," I whispered.

"Was he someone important?" he asked.

"He was my father," I replied, watching them take me in as I repacked my arsenal, as they called it, into my bag and different holsters. "You have to work at the Ark; it's not easy work, either. We all help because it makes it work; it's also mostly girls," I announced. The men smiled and I rolled my eyes. "The girls there have been through hell. Nothing like what happened here, but hell all the same. You hurt them, or try to; I'll rip out your heart, and if I'm not there to do the job, some of the guys living there will. Won't think twice about it, either," I said coldly. They flinched, because I'd shown them firsthand that I wasn't kidding.

"What are you doing this far away from home?" Cage asked, his eyes carefully watching my reaction.

"Those people who killed my father took my brother. I plan to get him back," I replied, unsure why I was comfortable with people I'd just met, but I was. Maybe it was the solitude of being alone after at least having the company of the wolves or vampires, and then nothing. I may not be the best with people, but I'd never done well with silence or being alone.

"We can help," he offered without hesitation.

"No, you can't," I replied. "Thanks for offering, but it's going to take an army to get that family to the Ark safely. He's in no shape to do it; they need you. I was trained from a very early age how to survive an apocalypse. I got this handled, and the Ark needs soldiers. How did you guys make it this far anyway?"

"We were in Montana stationed up in Helena, but when the sickness came, they built a fence around a quarantine area. No one got in or out; once everyone started to panic, chaos erupted. Loved ones just wanted to be together, but the guards, we were ordered to hold the perimeter at all costs. Wasn't right; we were ordered to shoot anyone who broke through the gate, and then on the last day, they ordered us to kill them all. All the people who were sick, trying to prevent the sickness from spreading, I guess. The virus dies with the host, so they figured to cut the losses and move on. We left then; none of us were willing to slaughter those inside the gates. I took my unit, and we made our way north, hiding in the woods and surviving. Eventually, we found a ranch, set up shop. The militia came, and we got in over our heads, so we took to the woods, easier to cut our losses and get on with things. Right when we figured we were done for, your dad answered our call."

"Cage, we got company," Johnson interrupted,

dropping to his knee to look through his scope.

I did the same, pulling my rifle up and looking through the scope just in time to catch sight of Jaeden and Bjorn as they traveled through the woods.

"They're here for me," I replied. Even though Addy was giving the other guardsman the directions, I felt better showing him the way to the Ark myself, so I pulled out my map and ignored the Vikings as they stopped, knowing I'd seen them. "Take out your map," I directed, as I unfolded mine and started mentally crossing off all of the reasons why I should go back to the caravan, versus reasons I should stay on my own. I pulled out my last Hershey's bar and looked at the kids, before moving closer to the little girl. "Hi," I murmured as I watched her brother pull her away from me.

"She's shy, been through a lot tonight," the kid offered, eyeing me carefully.

"I know she has, but I was about her age when my mother was…killed," I countered, hating that it was a lie now, but knowing exactly how the little girl felt. "Life isn't easy, that's for sure, and it's never fair, is it?" I talked to the kids as I pointed out the route for Cage. "It felt like the sky had fallen on me," I whispered, and watched as Cage raised his eyebrows along with the others as they absently listened to me. "You have to let her go, because she'd want you to. She loved you enough for you to remember it, right?"

"Yes," the little girl hiccupped. "But I want

Mommy."

"I know you do, but she's gone, and you're still here. It's not fair, nor is it right, but it's happened. We can't change it, but you can learn from it."

"You lost your mommy?" she asked with wide green eyes.

"I did, and I cried for a very long time. I blamed her, because she wasn't strong enough to come back to me. I felt like I'd never be able to breathe again, ever, but I did. I thought she chose to leave or that dying was her choice." My own mother *had* made a choice, she'd left me. "It wasn't, though, so you can be mad, but you can't stay sad or mad forever."

"Why not?"

"Because that kind of sadness or anger? It does things to the soul, and it holds hers here; you want her to be happy in heaven, right?"

"Yes," she rubbed her eyes with her small hands, and eyed the chocolate bar I held hungrily.

"Then let her find peace, and know if she could have stayed with you, she would have."

I set the chocolate down on the stump and finished giving the unit the coordinates to the Ark, along with notes on which towns to avoid with the kids, and where we'd had trouble crossing. With a quick round of goodbyes, I left the camp.

Chapter Seven

I plunged into the woods and put as much distance between myself and the camp as fast as I could, knowing Jaeden would follow me, and giving the humans time to cope with their loss as they prepared to follow my directions to the Pacific Northwest and the Ark. They'd seemed nice, but, more to the point, they had actually been in the National Guard, and they would be a welcome addition to the shelter if they made it there alive.

Slipping my pack back on, I winced at how light it felt. I'd left behind a lot of the MREs for the National Guard and those kids. I was still reeling from what had just happened; I couldn't get the woman's haunted eyes out of my mind. I couldn't imagine what she'd endured at the hands of those monsters, but what was worse was the knowledge that there were a lot more of those kinds of monsters out there.

I entered the little town I'd been heading to when I'd seen the smoke from the fire and paused. Jaeden was close; I could smell his earthy scent, and even though I didn't really want to see him, I needed him. I needed someone to hold me, to tell me this world wasn't as bad as it seemed to be. It would be a lie, but it was what I needed.

I waited, turning slowly as I felt him nearby. He was standing inches from me; his eyes looking me over for wounds, and he seemed to relax when he found that, other than a fat lip and sore nose, I hadn't sustained any in my last skirmish. I was covered in blood, but none of it was mine.

"Emma," he started, shaking his head as he geared up for an apology. I didn't give him a chance. I threw myself into his arms as sobs rocked my body. I cried unchecked, gushing about what had happened, and what I'd done. He held me through it, until I calmed myself enough that only tears remained. "I've got you; you're okay."

"No, no I'm not. I killed someone; I cut him up, brutally. I *liked* it. He did it to her; he cut her up, cut out her tongue, and ate pieces of her. I can't do this. I'm not strong enough." In what reality was this world worth saving if everyone started seeing each other as food? I was shaking; the tears wouldn't stop. I needed him to make the images go away. If only for a moment, I needed to stop seeing the monster I'd become while I killed one.

"It will go away, but what you did…it will always be a part of you. You know what you're capable of, what everyone else is capable of. You're strong, Emma, very strong. You're a born Valkyrie. You're the strongest woman I've ever known."

"Make me forget what I saw, what I did," I begged, and he smiled as he nodded to Bjorn, who watched us. Jaeden grabbed my hand, pulling me towards a dark house, which was the last house before the stores stretched out through the town.

He pushed open the door, looked inside and pulled me in behind him as he did a quick check of the house, revealing no living or dead inside. The moment he found clean blankets, he laid them down on the floor, and then he was stripping me, removing my pack and his, then our clothes. I let him, not caring that it would only be sex, or that he might think it meant more. I was being selfish, but I knew he'd make me forget the horror of the days I'd spent without him.

"I've missed this," he groaned as his mouth found mine in a hungry kiss. Jaeden's fingers slipped between my legs to ready my sex for his cock. He laid me down slowly, suckling my breasts as he pushed his fingers inside my tight heat. "Have you missed me?" I ignored his question as I claimed his mouth.

"No!" The Sentinel's voice screamed inside my head, and I stiffened. *"Emma, don't do this!"*

"Yes," I whispered, lifting my hips to meet his intrusive fingers. I enjoyed the hiss of air that left his lips as he pushed his massive cock against my wetness, then pushed inside without warning. I needed him rough, hard, violent even. My legs wrapped around him as he started to thrust inside me deeper. I cried out, digging my nails into flesh as I urged him to move faster.

"You'll pay for this, Emma," the voice threatened coldly with a sense of finality, as if it was a done deal. What the fuck was wrong with me?

"Come for me, Emma," Jaeden encouraged, needing me wet so that he could let loose. It was the first time we'd had sex since just after the funeral of my father. I'd kept my distance, kept him at arm's length. I would do it again, later, but right now I just needed contact. I needed to know that I wasn't alone.

There was still smoldering heat between us; that mindboggling connection that seemed to drive us to this mutual need. He hadn't pushed me too hard to be with him, and I was grateful, even though I had known he'd wanted it. My hands held his hair, holding his mouth against mine. I felt the presence of the other Sentinel in my mind, pacing, watching as I took Jaeden with vigorous determination to forget everything else. I was using him to forget; he was using me for the pent-up need he'd denied himself with the women he'd fed from.

He turned me over until I was on my stomach, and lifted my ass as he pushed inside, slapping my ass as he reached for my hair, only to stop as he took in the short, crude haircut which was growing back surprisingly fast. It almost reached my shoulders in just a few days, but it was a reminder of what had happened. His hands slipped lower and gripped my hips instead, and he continued to pummel me; flesh hitting flesh was the only sound inside the silent house.

He continued until I shattered around him. The earth spun, and the stars erupted as I cried out his name. His own release followed mine, and we collapsed in a pile of sweaty bodies and heavy breathing. We did this well, the mindless sex. It was outside the bedroom we struggled, where we had to face reality.

We lay on the floor for a while as I listened to the Sentinel's voice in my head that promised retribution. How did *he* know what *I* was doing, and who I was doing it with? It made my mind whirl with what it could mean, or maybe I'd imagined it? It had sounded real, as if he'd watched me and was upset about Jaeden and I having sex.

"Emma," Jaeden interrupted my thoughts as he rested his head in his hand as he stared down at me. "We're building a medical facility, that's why they asked for blood types."

"I know." I was already regretting that I'd given in to my baser needs. I was being selfish. It wasn't like me, and while he may not care that I'd used him to forget, I did. "This was a mistake," I murmured as I sat up and searched for my clothes.

"This wasn't a mistake," he countered. "You've talked to Addy?" His blue eyes filled with unease.

"Little while ago." I explained what had happened

before he'd found me.

"That couldn't have been easy," he said after a few moments of staring at me. "You took away the pain."

"Did I? Or did I kill someone because I was too weak to help her? She had kids, little ones. I should have been able to do more!" I slipped into my pants, carefully adding the knives as I watched Jaeden sit up, his eyes filled with a softness I didn't want or need. Yeah, I'd wanted him, but not this softness. I wanted him to look me in the eye and tell me that what I'd done was wrong, because it was.

"Emma…" he froze midsentence, his hand outstretched as if to grab me as I slipped my tank top over my head and smoothed it down.

I swallowed as my heart began to beat faster, painfully so. I turned to find the Sentinel there, inches from me with a wicked sword held at the ready, those beautiful eyes locked with mine but where they'd held heat before, they were cold. Ice cold. The blade swung, and I instinctively stepped in front of Jaeden, hearing the whistle of the blade as it sliced towards him. I shielded him from the blow meant to remove his head. I felt a slice of pain, and brought my hand up to touch my ear that had been nicked by the sword.

I turned, slowly rising as the Sentinel backed up, his sword held in front of him. I'd been wrong about him, dead wrong. I shook my head, watching as his eyes slowly slid over my body, the coldness in them sending a chill bone-deep inside of me.

"No," I whispered breathlessly, as I dropped my hand and prepared to fight for Jaeden.

"You're no better than your mother," the Sentinel gritted out, derision dripping from each word. "He's your enemy. *Our* enemy."

"He's not my enemy," I replied, inching closer to him, knowing I wouldn't win.

"No?" he laughed coldly.

"No."

"You keep giving him something that belongs to me, therefore, he dies," he sneered as he pushed his blade into a scabbard that rested on his back.

"And just what do you think is yours?" I asked coldly. I stepped closer to him, intending to attack. He'd been able to stop time, the same way I had, but where I could hold it for seconds, he held it effortlessly, and for an extended amount of time.

"You are mine," he answered heatedly, his eyes sliding over my body with a possessiveness that sent off warning bells.

"I'm not yours," I said, shaking my head.

"Yet."

"I'll never be yours. Not happening," I replied

coldly.

"You can tell yourself that all you want if it helps you sleep better, but you feel me, don't you?" he murmured as I kicked my foot out, trying to catch him off guard. He blocked it, as if he was clairvoyant. "The way your heart races when I get too close? Even now I can hear your heart hammering in my presence," he laughed coldly. "The only question you should be asking yourself is *when* will I take you and make you mine."

"Fucking try it, asshole," I snapped as I punched out, trying to catch him; but he allowed it, my fist connected with armor. I'd been wrong; he wasn't wearing tactical gear; he had actual armor that clung to him. "Ouch," I cried, pulling my hand against my chest as I danced away from him, keeping him away from Jaeden's frozen form in the process.

The Sentinel smiled, as if he'd known I would shatter my hand against it. He started towards me, the mask he wore shifting as if it were alive, and the lower half disappeared. I almost tripped over Jaeden, and changed tactics, rushing the Sentinel with my body and enjoying the gasp that stole from his lips as we collided hard.

My teeth chattered, my body screamed in pain, and his hands wrapped around me, taking us both to the floor with him on top. I struggled against him, wondering how long he could hold Jaeden frozen as he was. Minutes, hours, or indefinitely?

"Fuck him again, Emma, and I'll show you that not

even immortals can escape death. Next time, I won't let you save him," he growled, but he didn't let me go; he hovered over me, watching me as if he expected me to react.

He raised his hand, and one glove shimmered and melted away as he held me trapped with the weight of his body, and then he touched me. His eyes widened, his lips parted, and he shuddered with the mere contact. I felt hot tears slipping from my eyes as I considered just how fucked I was if he decided to rape me. Jaeden was frozen, unable to save me. I couldn't move, as if he had some power over me. Time had stopped, and he was touching my cheek, catching the tear that slipped free.

"I will kill you," I rasped through the thickness of my tongue as I watched him look down the length of me.

"You reek of his touch," he countered. His fingers slid over the soft flesh of my cheek and then over my lips as his eyes explored me. I wiggled to get away, and he groaned and closed his eyes.

What the fuck?

"I've waited lifetimes for you," he said softly as he moved to sit between my legs. I felt like I was being held to the floor, as if invisible hands were holding me down.

"Wait a few more," I said, and he smiled as if it was funny.

I felt myself being freed from whatever had held me and grabbed the knife I'd returned to its sheath just before he'd arrived. I brought it up, intending to bury it in his heart, but he was faster. He pulled me up and shoved me into the wall, causing the air to leave my lungs as he slammed against me, shattering the thin wall. His hand captured mine and gripped it painfully until the knife fell from my hand. The sound of it hitting the floor was loud; the deafening noise of our labored breathing filled the room.

His arm pushed against my chest and I cried out. He watched me as if he found me interesting, and it bothered me on so many levels. He didn't try to kiss me, and I knew he wanted to. I, on the other hand, had no intention of kissing him back this time.

"You kissed me last time we met, why?" I watched as his eyes slowly rose from my heaving bosom, and he smiled.

"Testing you, seeing if you survived it," he said cryptically. "Same as when I kissed the back of your neck; you know what they say about the third time being a charm."

"You think kissing can kill me?" I snorted as I kept him busy while I mentally tried to come up with something, anything, to get away from him.

His face turned hard, cold, and then emotionless. He stepped away so fast that I wasn't ready and landed on my hands and knees as he watched.

"I won't hesitate to kill him next time, or you. Stay away from him, understand?" he ordered, and I smiled coldly.

"I'm not yours, and you sure as hell don't get to decide who I'm with," I snapped, and watched as his eyes turned from icy cold, to heated with something I wasn't sure I wanted to see in his eyes. Possession.

"Yet," he laughed as something cold returned to his eyes, and he crouched down to look at me. "You stink, fix it," he growled, and I watched as his eyes changed back to cerulean blue and narrowed as he smiled. "Remember what I told you, because I don't give second warnings. Not even for you, *Mate*," he whispered before he disappeared—as in, vanished.

I expelled the air from my lungs as I watched Jaeden come back to life, his eyes snapped to where my ear was dripping blood from the cut of the Sentinel's sword.

"Emma, what the fuck just happened?" he demanded.

I couldn't answer. The word replayed in my mind. *Mate.*

Chapter Eight

Jaeden and Shamus watched me carefully as Bjorn was giving his detailed report, or to the point, what he could remember of the events that happened at the supposedly-vacant house. He hadn't heard or seen anything as I'd struggled with the Sentinel; to him, time had stopped just as it had for Jaeden. Bjorn had been instructed to watch over us, protect us. He hadn't had a chance once the Sentinel had shown up; hell, I didn't have a chance and I *was* a Sentinel.

One minute I'd been arguing with Jaeden, pulling away from him, and the next I'd been flinging myself in front of him as a human shield. He'd been *frozen*. I'd told them as little as possible about the Sentinel, unsure as to why I felt the need to protect the guy. He had an agenda, which was apparent now. I was no longer able to delude myself into thinking he was on our side, or assume he didn't plan to hurt me. He'd said as much.

He'd actually told me he'd kissed me to see if I

survived it. What the hell did that mean? Maybe he had some unknown power that had to deal with kissing, or maybe he'd lied to me. Either way, for the last few hours my heart hadn't stopped hammering, and this time, I didn't know if it was because he was near, or if it was my response to what he'd done. He'd materialized inside the house. I'd felt him, and it scared the shit out of me.

There was also the fact that he'd threatened Jaeden's life, and it wasn't an idle threat. He'd meant it. Jaeden had tried to hug me afterwards, and I'd pulled away from him. I'd been cold, mostly because I was terrified that if I allowed myself to seek the comfort his embrace afforded me, I'd want more. I wasn't willing to play games with his life. The Sentinel could freeze time, not for seconds, but longer than I'd ever seen before. He could teleport, hold me to the floor without lifting a finger, and he'd looked at me with a possessiveness that terrified me.

"Emma, welcome back," Shamus greeted coldly, his eyes searching my body for any signs of weakness from the wound. His eyes were hard, and anything but welcoming. "Jaeden has informed me of another Sentinel; he has become a problem for you, correct? It means we have one now too, no?" His eyes lowered to where my shirt was ripped.

"It's my problem, not yours."

"Emma." His eyes wandered up to hold mine as he scolded me as if I were a disobedient child. "You are my ward, therefore, my problem when you have one. We share an interest, a common home. I'm invested in the welfare of all those who reside in it."

Nice touch. He knew I'd had Addy kick his people out. He had no plans of admitting it in front of Jaeden, but he was aware I could do it at any time I chose to.

"Have you ever seen him before?" he asked, and I felt the subtle push of compulsion in his words.

"Yes, a few times. Once in the forest, when he cut off a lock of my hair, and then again during the ambush when he kissed me." I felt Jaeden's eyes as they watched me. Guilt washed through me, but then, I'd watched him with the feeders a few times, and it hadn't always been innocent touching. I wasn't an idiot, either; bloodlust could happen. Jaeden himself had taught me that, to prepare me in case it ever happened when I was near his kind.

There was also the little tidbit he'd imparted on our way back here: That Jolene was now directly under his protection. Not his choice, but it meant she was to sleep beside him when he was in camp. Where I could have been, had I not chosen to end things with him.

"Anything else? Did you fuck him as well?" Shamus wasn't asking, he was speculating. "Details, darling," he demanded.

"I'm not your darling, Shamus. I didn't sleep with him. The only man I've ever been with is Jaeden. The Sentinel kissed me. He is following me; it's not the other way around."

"Stay close to camp, Emma; no more nature walks. Since Jaeden was in charge of your care and is now otherwise occupied with his new female, Raphael will take over where you are concerned. Raphael's feeder is shared between him and Sven at the moment, and I'd rather not allow this…whatever he is, to get close to you again," Shamus said, making sure I knew Jaeden was with Jolene. Whatever, I had a feeling Shamus was, and had been, interfering between myself and Jaeden for a while now.

He'd fucked me over, and he'd set me up to take the fall. I wasn't under anyone's protection; if I had been, Astrid and Jolene would have been punished for what they'd done to me. It was their way, rules or whatever. It felt like Shamus was playing with matches, and I was left holding a paper heart, which was easily burned.

"Maybe you didn't hear me, or want to hear me. He froze Jaeden and Bjorn, easily. Bjorn didn't even realize he'd been in a precarious position until he was told otherwise."

"Look around you, Emma; we are fifty strong, and the wolves will soon return to us when the alpha is healed," he snapped. "You will do as I say, child."

"Or what?" I replied crisply. "I'm not bound by your laws or words as the others are. So exactly what will you do? Spank me? Tie me up?" I shivered as he smiled coldly, his eyes slowly moving down my body as if it was something he'd wanted to do for a while.

"Pray you never find out, little one," he mused as he stepped away, dismissing me.

"Emma," Jaeden called out when I turned to do the same. "We need to talk about what happened."

"No, Jaeden, we don't. I told you, it was a mistake."

"You need to listen to Shamus. I'm counting on you to behave."

"Don't," I ground out. "Don't count on me for anything. I'm drowning, and the last thing I want you to do is to drown with me." I turned away from him and started my search of the layout of this camp for a tree where I could hang my hammock.

Once I'd found it, I set it up and climbed back down the tree, then headed to the little area that was used to bathe in, my new sidekick tagging along. Raphael didn't have the same moral code that Jaeden had. Instead of giving me the gentlemanly courtesy of his back while I bathed, he lay in the grass a few feet from the water, chewing on a flower stem. His eyes skimmed the water as I sank my naked body beneath it.

"I can see the attraction, you've got a nice ass," he called, and I silently growled. I missed Lachlan; he was the one who I could trust myself to be around, and still be me. My body ached from being with Jaeden, as he'd tried to make up for lost time, but it wasn't his eyes I saw when I closed mine, it was the eyes of the Sentinel who attacked us.

I opened my eyes and heard laughter bubbling inside my head. He definitely had some kind of telepathic power and remote viewing capability, because he'd known the moment I was with Jaeden. It gave him an advantage, considering he had powers and I was fumbling with my own. So far, I had discovered all of my powers by accident and usually at moments of extreme duress or fear.

I left the water without care that Raphael was getting a front row view of my birthday suit. I wrapped a towel around me after I dried off and slipped into a soft pair of baby blue sweatpants and a white tank top that I'd taken from one of the stores we'd rummaged through on our trek south. I slipped a sweatshirt on over it, shivering as the wind picked up, chilly in the evening air.

"Damn, he's an idiot," Raphael whined, his eyes watching everything.

"I'm going to make your job easy tonight. I'm going to bed," I replied, ignoring his jibe, even though I had to agree with him. Jaeden was an idiot.

"You could sleep with me. Naked. It's preferable," he laughed.

"Hold your breath while I decide, hmm?" I asked, and then realized that I was talking to the undead, as in, he could probably hold his breath and be just fine.

"Actually, I just saw something walk by that I know

won't turn me down." He stared at something in the distance, towards the feeder camp. "Walk faster," he ordered, and I stiffened my spine.

As I arrived back at camp, I noted that there was a huge fire burning, and that the vampires had changed the layout of this camp from the last several. Instead of having the fire just outside the camp, or not having one at all, they had a huge bonfire. It was in the middle of the camp, and they were all gathered in the open, some partially clothed or missing clothes altogether. Some fed openly from the humans.

I sighed as I caught sight of Jaeden, who apparently thought he'd have more time before I returned. His demeanor was stiff, as was Jolene's. I caught and held his eyes before I shimmied up the tree, ignoring the debauchery going on right beneath it. I just wanted to forget the entire week.

It had been one thing after another, and my hope for humanity had hit an all-time low. Cannibalism. Just when I thought I'd seen enough with the rapes, brutal murders, and innocent lives lost, someone decided to tip the cup and throw in the sickest shit I'd ever encountered.

"You disappoint me," the voice said, and I closed my eyes.

"Get in line; my fucks have been given, I'm all out."

Throaty laughter filled my mind, and I swallowed hard. Had he heard me? Could he hear my thoughts?

"You're my woman, of course I can. I come for you soon…Be ready."

"You said mate earlier, I'm not your mate and if you come for me, I will fight you," I answered inside my mind.

"I'd expect no less," he murmured, and my heart hammered briefly, as if he was close and reminding me he could get to me anytime he wanted.

"Look around, asshole, army of vamps. I'm safe from you," I purred. I win!

"Indeed," he replied, and I felt my heart pounding again, until it reached a dangerous level, and then stopped as quickly as it had started.

What. The. Ever. Loving. Fuck!

Sleep came slowly; my mind whirled with thoughts of the guy who seemed hell-bent on driving me insane, and Jaeden, who was sitting with Jolene. She was beaming, he looked pissed; his eyes kept returning to my hammock, and every once in a while, I'd look down at him, regret filling me.

I needed to talk with him; he deserved that much. Shamus watched me as I watched Jaeden, noting the tension between us. Lachlan had once told me that Jaeden would break my heart, and he had. When he'd left to go find the elders, he'd left me in pieces. Now? Now I was numb, as if he'd broken me so badly, that I was still working on gathering back the pieces of my heart.

~~*

I opened my eyes, heavy from sleep, and smelled the rich scent of roses. I smiled, stretching out as much as the hammock would allow, and winced as something poked me. I blinked to clear the sleep and tried to bring into focus the splash of red beside my head. *Roses?*

I sat up, quickly sensing the increased tempo of my heart as I took in the multitude of roses that covered me and the hammock. I shifted a bit, sitting up even further as I looked around, and watched as the roses started to tumble to the ground. What the hell? I started pushing them off, until I found a note.

I win ~A was scrawled onto a thick piece of paper. It had a blood-red border, and the handwriting had a beautiful, masculine flair to it.

He'd gotten to me, and he'd made damn sure I knew it. It had to have taken him a few trips to bring in this many roses! I felt his eyes on me, my heart tripping over the rapid rhythm. I turned to the right and looked to the expansive cliff-side that bordered the valley we'd camped in. There, at the top of the cliff, he stood.

"Sweet baby Jesus," I whispered as I started pushing more of the roses off of me, as the vampires took note of them falling to the ground.

"Emma?" Jaeden called up, as Raphael started to stir. "What the fuck?" he demanded.

What the fuck, indeed; I wasn't safe. He wasn't safe. He'd entered a camp full of vampires and got to me while we were sleeping! I don't know what worried me more, that he'd done it without waking me up, and no one ever got the jump on me—prepper's daughter and all that—or that he'd done it right under the noses of the vampires who were supposed to be impossible to get past. Wasn't that what Shamus had said?

"Nothing can protect you from me, nothing. I'll be close, Emma," the voice purred victoriously inside my head.

Technically, he'd won that round. Hands down, couldn't talk my way out of that one.

"Game on, Asshole," I replied, using my imagination for what the A stood for.

Chapter Nine

Everyone was on edge; we'd passed more hairy and visually disturbing shit as the day passed. Human remains, charred cars along with what looked like traps meant to lure unsuspecting people to their deaths. Birds feasted on the dead, or more to the point, they feasted on what had been left on the bones. I'd suspected I wouldn't get off that easy; one case of cannibalism just wasn't enough.

It felt as if we'd been walking forever. Jaeden kept watching me when he thought I wasn't paying attention; his blood-bag had taken note of it as well. She was currently vying for his attention, pretending to be too tired to walk.

She did nothing except complain. I didn't complain, because I'd chosen this path. I knew it wouldn't be easy, but every treacherous step I took led me closer to finding Grayson. The blisters on my feet had been earned, the never-ending pain in my stomach—it was all worth it.

I touched my ear, wondering why it hadn't healed at all. Raphael had pointed out that, while it wasn't a deep cut, it still needed to be tended to. He'd done so, cleaning it, refusing to allow me to do it myself. Jaeden had watched the entire awkward situation. Raphael had tried not to touch me while trying to fix it. As if he was aware of the murderous looks Jaeden was throwing his way.

It burned my pride, probably because it was a reminder of how close to death I'd come. I'd been willing to die to protect him; that said something, right? I didn't want him to be hurt by whoever the masked guy was, who could obviously get as close as he wanted to get to me, as his show of roses had explicitly told me.

The vampires had been shaken by it, but then again, I figured he'd known they would be. He could have taken me then, why wait? Why the insult of showing me how easy it would be for him, but not following through?

"Emma," Jaeden said as he interrupted my thoughts. "This isn't my choice."

"No, I can see that, but I find it funny that Shamus decided to change the rules while I was gone." I continued to walk at a quickened pace. "Before I left, there was no 'protect her' rule, and the moment I come back, there is?"

"It's not safe this far south; we told you that. Those who survived the virus think the south is safer, no brutal winters, sun to grow food, basic tactics for survival.

They outnumber us here, so we are taking precautions."

"I see." I didn't, not really. I knew what was happening, even if he couldn't see it. Shamus was making damn sure we remained at odds. He was up to something, and while I needed to figure it out, Jaeden's words rang true. We were coming across settlements, ones that contained people who looked as if they'd experienced a lot a shit since the day of the virus. I'd started calling it B.V. and A.V. Before and after the virus.

Before the virus, these people had probably been happy, law abiding citizens, but after? No one was the same. People were either good or horrible. We'd just entered a town, one with no dead that could be obviously seen. It meant someone had gone through a lot of effort to clear the bodies to keep the town free of other diseases, and our group was walking into a trap, knowingly.

"I have asked to be given a new feeder," he offered, pulling me once again from my thoughts.

"Cool," I threw out flippantly and stopped in my tracks as a man walked out from behind a building with a semi-automatic rifle. "Saw that one coming," I mumbled.

"Turn around and walk right back out of this town," the man called out as he aimed the rifle at us.

"Can't do that," Shamus said smoothly, his eyes on the barrel of the gun.

The guy didn't realize he was aiming that thing at an immortal, but we all did. I wasn't sure if a vampire could die from a slug to the head, but with the way Shamus had been acting, I was willing to let it play out. After all, it was aimed at him, and not the rest of us.

"We don't need trouble," the guy continued.

"We don't intend to cause any," Shamus replied carefully. "We're just passing through. We don't intend to stay, but this is the only route that doesn't go through the passes."

"You're not from the army?" the guy asked, lowering the gun a smidge.

"What army?" Jaeden broke in and ended up with the gun turned on him.

This was getting old really quick.

"The Clarkston Army," the guy sneered, his hatred for the army apparent in his tone. "They take everything." He frowned. "Women, children, food and gas, pretty much everything that good people need to live."

"When was the last time they came through here?" Jaeden continued carefully, his posture at ease even with the gun aimed at him. If he was worried about being shot, he didn't show it.

"Few days ago," he offered, his gun finally lowering.

"And what did they take?" Shamus asked, and the man answered with a laundry list of things taken, both material and human. I ignored them, noting the men trying to keep out of sight that had weapons trained on us.

Jaeden took notice of them too; there were at least five that I could find on the tops of the buildings that lined the town. All were heavily armed. If they'd lost women as the man was saying, none of this made sense. Why hadn't they fought? Obviously they had weapons and were trained to use them.

"Just one night," Shamus offered, which pulled me from my thoughts.

I didn't trust the guy; his sad story said he'd either hidden while they'd taken his family, or he was spewing lies. I didn't want to judge him, because I'd seen my fair share of fucked up shit in this new world, but I would have died before I let some army run off with Addy.

"Fine, but only one night," the guy responded, offering no argument. I raised an eyebrow at how easily the guy had given in. It could have been as simple as Shamus had used compulsion, or something of that nature, but something about this situation was giving me the creeps and it was odd that the vampires weren't sensing the same thing. Perhaps they were, and were just too cocky-confident that they could overcome any treachery from the residents of the town.

I watched the vampires gather towards the front of

the group. The men on the buildings pulled away from the rooftops and made their way down the street to join in the masculine handshaking, as if they'd just played basketball and were showing good sportsmanship. I rolled my eyes and turned away from the group, heading back towards the buildings at the edge of town. I easily shook Raphael, who was distracted by the large group of men, and made it into the woods without being noticed.

I went a few yards into the woods before I climbed up a tree and started to prepare my hammock for sleep. There was no way in hell I was sleeping in a town with an army who stole women and children camped just a few towns over. The vampires seemed to assume they always had the upper hand. Being immortal had its perks, I'm sure, but I had no idea how my own immortality worked, as I had no clue as to all of the powers the Sentinels had, or their limitations. Like, if I took a bullet to the head, would it kill me? Or would it simply regrow my head, and if it did, would I be the same person? Brains were tricky already, who the hell knew if you could come back the same if you lost enough of the cells that made you who you were?

Once the hammock was set up, I climbed back down the tree and checked my bag, making a mental list of what I needed to collect. I'd been collecting herbs and other items along the way, just to make sure everyone remained healthy, since no one else thought it necessary to do so. We'd be entering desert terrain soon enough, and leaving the mountains.

No one seemed to notice my absence, and I doubted

they would while they fed and replenished the women. I watched them from the trees; Jaeden seemed to be concentrating on the newcomers, along with his ex-wife, who never seemed to be far from his side lately. Jolene stood with her, probably feeling like a third wheel.

Astrid seemed in her element, smiling and enticing the men, who looked upon her beauty with something akin to worship. Gag. The bitch was bat-shit crazy, and it was bone-deep; fuck, it was soul-deep. She'd messed with me, and I'd be damned if I let her do it again. I was sure she and Shamus had known I'd end up leaving the group if they fucked with me bad enough; what they didn't count on was me giving orders to the Ark before I'd left it.

I turned and left them, heading deeper into the woods without a backward glance as I started my search for mint, ginger, and anything else I could find before it got too dark out to see.

My mind wandered back to the Sentinel, who seemed to be stalking me. He'd told me I was his, and that he'd come for me. He'd been able to get past the vampires, which meant if he ever did come for me, I'd be fucked.

There was no way around it. He was faster than I was, he knew how to use his powers where I was newly immortal, and on top of that, I had no freaking clue what the hell I was. Sentinel, that's all I knew. I also had the ability to freeze time for mere seconds, and that only happened when I was in fight-or-flight mode, as Dad called it.

I didn't have time to take notes, or try to figure out how I had done it. I just did it. Now, when I wanted to, I couldn't, which meant I might as well slap a bow on my ass and accept the inevitable.

A branch broke beneath my foot and I paused, looking around the woods. Shit. I'd gotten lost in my head, and in doing so, I'd gone deeper than I intended to. I looked around at the moss on the forest floor and slowly lowered myself to it, moving it away from the herbs it shielded.

I picked a few jars of mushrooms, some moss, and the little ginger that I could find and looked up at the trees, noting which side the moss was growing on, observing it was on the north side, and finding my position. Dad had taught me that in the Northern Hemisphere, moss grew on the north side of the tree, and in the southern, it grew south. It was a damn good thing to know when lost in the woods.

It was dark by the time I made it back to the hammock, and the town was deathly silent. All lights were down, but then so was the electrical grid. I tilted my head, listening…Nothing. I stepped closer and saw a muzzle flash, and gunfire ripped through the night. I backed up, slowly at first, and faster with every step closer I took to the safety of the woods.

I could hear voices moving towards the hammock, and once I'd reached a safe distance, I stopped, taking shelter behind a giant pine tree.

"Where is she!?" Jolene's high-pitched whine rose in the now silent night.

"You sure she was even here?" the guy who'd aimed his gun at us when we'd first arrived said over her, huffing and puffing.

"Look up there, see?" She aimed a flashlight up towards my hammock. "That's where she sleeps, and she's not in it! I want her found, and I want that bitch alive. Jason will want to see her; she's not like the others. She's not a vampire; we need to figure out what she is, and how to kill her," she snapped.

"We got the vampires; all of them are down thanks to the holy water we slipped into the well. As soon as those bitches drank it and they fed from them, it went down pretty fucking smooth, Jo. We got an endless supply of food now. They regenerate, and we got their women for all the fun we'll need for a while. Jason won't be caring about some bitch. No matter what she is, she won't be a problem. We got an army."

I covered my mouth as a cry of outrage tried to escape. Vampires, an endless supply of food? Motherfuckers. What had I done to deserve this? Had I been some mass murderer of cute and fluffy animals in some other life and earned enough bad karma to flow into this one? Cannibals. It was a fucking army of cannibals?

"I want her! She fucked with me, put hands on me. Jason will want that bitch for that alone, I'm his favorite!" she whined.

"Every girl is his favorite, right up until new meat is found," he laughed, and so did someone else. There were at least four flashlight beams roving around my tree; God only knew how many assholes were in this group.

I looked around me, wondering how I planned to escape this mess. I wasn't leaving the vampires to their fate, even though for the briefest moment, I considered freeing everyone except Astrid. Not even I was that fucked up, that I would leave her among people who would consider her a delicacy on the table…blah.

"You sure there wasn't more of them?" he asked.

"Just some wolves, but I heard they got fucked up when we shot them up in the town. They split, so they won't be a problem; besides, we got silver bullets. They come sniffing 'round, we'll get them too, see how wolf tastes." She laughed, and I fought a bout of nausea.

It was official: This new world was hell, and there may not be any reason to try and save it anymore. Hate and greed ruled, hunger and need were the weapons of choice, and humans were the main course. Or, ya know, vampires. Like Jolene said, they regenerated and didn't die like humans.

I winced at the burning in my legs as I remained squatting behind the tree, listening as they removed my hammock—assholes—and headed back towards the town. Once I was sure I was alone, I suited up in full camo and pulled out the black face paint, and prepared to follow them back to see if I could figure out where they took the vampires. Army of one. Just freaking awesome.

Chapter Ten

I was able to find a hiding place that still had a great view of the town below. With the light of day, I had figured out that the townsfolk had moved the vampires and their blood-bags from where they'd been captured, and with some difficulty, I had tracked them to this town and had begun my reconnaissance.

The town was in a strategic location, over a mile or more on almost all three sides of the town, giving them the advantage of seeing any threat moving towards them. The only downfall was the heavily wooded hill behind the town, and that was where I was able to wedge myself fairly comfortably into a tree that was high enough to give me a great view, yet provided enough camouflage to hide behind.

It didn't take too much reasoning power to determine that this was the 'Clarkston Army' and they'd taken over a lot of towns; however, the town below me was definitely their home base. From what I could see of it, most of the town had probably been abandoned long before the spread of the virus. The town was large, larger than I had figured they would have been able to add on to with the limited supplies available these days. Maybe there was some sort of lumber yard or 'Building Supplies R Us' nearby. One thing that stood out as strange to me, were the boxes of canned food, sitting just inches from the gates…As if they were daring someone to try to take it.

From my vantage point, not only could I see the barely-disguised men with guns patrolling the town, I could also see cages of people. It turned my stomach, watching when people were removed from the cages and taken into the main building in the center of the town.

Right in front of the main building was a platform, one that had probably been used in the past for town officials, which had been turned into a different kind of spectacle these days. In the center of the platform, they'd built some kind of medieval device that currently had a vampire tied to a wooden post. As I watched, some sort of butcher was hacking slices of flesh from the vampire's thigh, much to the cheers of the sick and twisted crowd.

How they'd known they were vampires before their initial ambush was beyond me, but Jolene hadn't given anything away in her act. She'd been good; I'd give her that. I knew something was wrong and off about her from the beginning, but even in my wildest imaginings, I couldn't even think that she was bait for something like this.

A shout of agony ripped through the air, and my eyes slowly swept through the town, finding the source. Another vampire was being brought to the stage, and my stomach dropped as Raphael's proud form stumbled.

Holy water; they'd put it in the town's well, and had given it to the women who fed the vampires. In essence, poisoning them to a weakened state. Jaeden had always described vampirism as more of a virus, so the concept of holy water being a problem for them didn't make sense to me. Perhaps it was more of a reaction to the bacteria in the water than any kind of mystic holy properties that the water had, unless there really were supernatural properties to the virus that caused vampirism. After all, silver was an anti-microbial, so I could understand why the vampires and wolves were so allergic to it; so holy water having bacteria in it that could make them sick made perfect sense to me, and I would rather think it was bacteria that took them down rather than some holy hocus pocus.

Either way, it seemed to disorient the vampires, and the townspeople had taken measures for when the vampires snapped out of it by chaining them. Raphael struggled back to his feet as some asshole kicked him in the stomach, and he lunged, ripping the guy apart with his fangs as he took the asshole to the ground with his body weight alone. It looked like the vampires didn't need their hands to do serious damage. I watched with cold detachment as someone fired a shot at Raphael, making his body jerk with pain, and four more men crowded in to subdue him with the butts of their rifles.

My hands trembled with the need to kill them all. They weren't human; they were monsters. They shot and beat him while I had to sit on my hands, doing nothing. I needed a plan, and I couldn't just go in guns blazing, because they were armed to the teeth.

My father was right; when the government fell, the worst of humanity had crawled out from the shadows and taken over. The army I watched wasn't one who brought hope to the survivors; no, it was one who brought death and destruction and served it up piping hot.

I shimmied down the tree so I could head over to a different site that I had found for surveying the town, carefully avoiding leaving any clues that could give me away. Before I could make it more than a few feet, something grabbed me and I swung at it, connecting with flesh to the blow of my small fist.

"Ouch, Lass," Lachlan groaned, and I gasped before I threw myself into his arms.

"Lachlan," I whispered as I started rambling on about what had happened, and where Jaeden was, with the enemies.

"Oh aye, why ya ken I came back?" he whispered against my ear, making no move to release me. "Caught up tae another pack 'o wolves, said some crazy mon was leading a blasted army 'o cannibals. Figured I'd get back here, Cian dinna agree, but he came around."

"They have Raphael on stage, getting ready to carve him up like the others," I whispered past the lump in my throat.

"Last I heard, Jaeden stabbed ye, lass." Lachlan's tone promised retribution for that.

"I pulled away from him and his girls. That one is on Shamus, not Jaeden," I whispered as I moved back to get a better look at Lachlan. He looked starved, but other than that, he looked well. "And you?"

"Sore, but alive."

"That's good news; I have to figure out how to get them out of Hells-ville, and I don't think you can help," I said.

"Nae, don't ye be kenning that ye are going in there, Emma, no fucking way, lass," he barked, his eyes wide as he shook his head.

"They are using silver bullets, Lach, they're the ones who shot you—and worse, they are *eating* humans, and now vampires!" I growled. "I'm killing them, all of them. They have to be stopped. We need a plan, or something. I can't let them do this to anyone else."

"The woman in the woods, the poor wee lass was their victim?" he asked.

"Those assholes were probably part of this group, maybe a hunting party. By the way, how did you know about that?" I asked, shocked since he'd been away from me.

"Ye were nae alone, Emma, I would nae allow it, ya ken it. I promised Addy I'd bring ye home tae her in one piece, I plan tae keep my word."

"I could have used your watcher's help a couple of times over the past few days. Besides that, you could have told me, or hell, let me know," I griped. I hadn't even known they'd followed me. Was anyone *not* following me?

"Hard tae do in my other form, Emma, but ye should've kenned better, aye?" he laughed as he hugged me again. "I should have been here sooner, but we been aboot the woods, listening. I may nae be able tae help ye oot, but I can create a diversion."

"I'm listening," I smiled.

"Ye still can nae do this alone," he argued.

"Lachlan, I'd rather die fighting than leave Jaeden and some of the others to be gnawed on," I argued.

"Ye are a stubborn thing, ye ken that, right?"

"I do, but I have grenades, and I'm pretty badass when under stress, which, if I do this right, my powers should kick in." I hoped. There was no guarantee that they would even work. Other than the better hearing, advanced eyesight, and other sensory things, no other power had worked lately. Not even when I'd fought Jaeden. I'd done nothing but yank myself away from him, impaling myself on a sharp branch. Yeah, my self-confidence was shit.

"What's your plan?" he asked as his eyes seemed to be inspecting me, taking inventory, looking for wounds. I was beginning to get used to it. Between him and Jaeden, I was constantly being checked for wounds or weaknesses.

"There's one way into the compound. It looks like a town to the casual eye, but they've set up barbwire and razor wire around it. The only way in is on the main street, and they've got guards on every rooftop. I'd need to look harmless, because if they think I'm there to get the vampires out, I'm dead or I'll end up as dessert, which doesn't seem to have a very long life expectancy, either, with those assholes. I figure if I walk in looking harmless, I can catch them off guard, throw some grenades, and take cover. I've scouted every position I could around the town that I could safely manage to. They set up car hoods on the inside of the front gates for cover. If I can get to them, I can take a defensive position."

"And when ye run oot of bullets, what then?" His eyes filled with uncertainty. I knew he wouldn't stop me; he was like me, and he'd go out fighting before he let someone he loved die in a horrible fashion as they intended to do with the vampires.

"I'm hoping the adrenaline will kick in, my powers will come online, and I'll be able to stop time. Once that happens," I said. *If it happened.* "I'll have the advantage.

If not, I'm fucked. But I'm pretty sure my stalker wants me alive. He knows how to stop time, and I'm hoping he's close enough to save me if I need it. So I go in with weapons hidden." Betting on my stalker was really risky, considering he hadn't shown when I was injured at the vampire camp, or in the cannibal camp. Either he wasn't close by, or he didn't feel I was in mortal danger in either situation. No matter what, counting on him was a huge gamble.

"Ouch, nae, lass, ye need tae go find something sexy, ya ken? You get more of an advantage if they think with their cock before their brains. Best armor in the world for a woman is something sexy. Something short and provocative," he said with a wide grin.

"Uh, and just where the hell am I supposed to find that?" I asked, and watched as a smile spread across his face. "I just had to ask, didn't I?"

He laughed, pulling me to my feet. I followed him through the woods, and winced when a nightclub came into view. A freaking strip club? We were a good two miles from the camp, or town…whatever the Clarkston Army called their little encampment, I called it hell. How Lachlan knew this place was here was something I didn't want to find out.

I pushed the door open, and made my way slowly into the dark club, stiffening as the scent of stale and sour beer hit my nose. It reeked; half-empty glasses of beer that looked as if something was growing in them littered the top of the bar and most of the tables.

Towards the back was a door labeled 'dancers', which Lachlan had headed for. Once we entered the room, he pulled open a curtain, allowing light in. I turned in a small circle, saying a silent thank you that there were no dead bodies.

"Look at this," he said, holding up a pair of thong panties.

"Not wearing anyone else's underwear, eww," I stated with a cringe.

He laughed and shrugged, tossing them back to the little vanity. Next, he held up a small, barely-there schoolgirl miniskirt and eyed me. I grabbed it, held it around my waist and tried to hand it back to him.

"It will fit, Emma, without the pants and holsters with guns in your waistband," he said with a soft frown. "It's sexy, and I'm nae thinking that they would be wishing ye dead in that thing. Nae, they'd be tae busy wishing other things."

"I need my weapons," I argued.

"Ye do, but ye can hide them in your new pack," he said as he held up a pink Hello Kitty backpack that made my eyes bug out. "You'll be tae cute and sexy tae be suspect, lass," he chuckled at my death stare as his eyes searched through the room until he found a small black tank top that opened on both sides and was split open. Next, he grabbed a few items from the vanity and wiggled his finger for me to turn around so he could push them into my bag. "And a mirror, because I can nae do make-up, lass," he commented, pushing more shit into my pack. "Okay, let's go see what the lads found."

Several hours later I was dressed in thigh highs that were thicker than normal nylons, which would be held up with skull and cross bone garters once I figured out how they worked. The skirt exposed the globes of my bottom, and I'd slipped my boots back on. They held more daggers, which I would need. I'd pulled on the top Lachlan had brought, and fitted it with a black bra. I touched my shorter hair, wishing it was long enough to hide this outfit.

"Damn," Cian whispered, his eyes hot with unbridled lust as he took me in. "That will do the job, Emma. Who knew this was hiding behind all that camouflage?"

"Ha-ha," I sniped, not laughing as my nerves began to get the better of me.

"Lass, you look…you look tae good tae send tae those monsters," Lachlan groaned, his eyes slowly moving down the length of me to my boots, as a smile curved his lips. "Heels might be better."

"Heels would be better for them, not me. I'd break my neck trying to fight in heels," I mumbled as I fumbled with the attachment from the nylon to the skirt. How strippers managed this, I didn't know, but kudos to them, because I was having a hell of a time even trying to figure out how everything attached correctly.

"Let me," Lachlan offered. His hands trembled as

he skimmed my flesh with his fingers. "They attach by slipping the nylon onto the metal, and closing it, like this." He hooked the nylon into the loop and locked it down before he pressed a soft kiss to the back of my leg, sending a tremor through me. "In another life, sweet lass," he mumbled as he stood up and looked down at me. "You'd have been mine."

"In another life, you'd still chase after anything that would give up and bend over for you, wolf."

"Ahh, but the lass who catches the wolf's heart, she has it always," he murmured as he pressed another kiss to my ear. "Until we mark our life-mate, our nature is to rut, to mate with any who can carry our seed."

"And mine isn't," I replied, placing my hand to his cheek and meeting his green eyes. "Which is why you and I would never work out." I tapped his cheek softly. "We do, however, work well as a team, my wolf, so let's do this. Soon it will be too dark for this outfit to cause much of a stir."

"Emma, if ye can nae save them…" Lachlan started, but I shushed him.

"I'm saving them. There's no 'or else' scenario where I walk away without them," I ground out as I pulled on my pack, and tested how easily I could draw the guns when the need arose. I grabbed two grenades and held them in my hands as I looked at the wolves. "If this goes badly, you go back to the Ark. Promise me. Addy will need you. You won't be able to save me, and I am pretty sure that Sentinel will come for me and finish whatever it is that he's planning to do. If he comes before I can get the vamps free, you finish these assholes. All of them. They can't live."

"Did he come tae you again?" he asked, and I gave him a quick and dirty rundown of what had happened in his absence. He whistled beneath his breath and shook his head.

"He called you his *mate*?" Cian asked.

"He did, but I have no idea what the hell it means. He invaded the camp and left dozens of roses on me while I was sleeping, his way of showing me that he could get to me at any time and at any place. Whatever happens, he'll probably show up, and if he takes me, I'll figure out a way to get away from him. So I have no intention of dying in that town if I can't get them out."

"Good tae ken, but do nae expect me tae sit here if ye are in trouble, Emma," Lachlan argued.

I turned to Cian, who nodded, knowing that if it came to it, he'd make sure Lachlan didn't die trying to save me. I started my long trek to the town, alone.

"Emma, be careful, lass," Cian said, his eyes smiling as he took in the ridiculous outfit.

"Thank you." I turned to give him a smile, only to catch his eyes on my ass. "Eyes on the prize, wolf," I laughed, but he didn't look away.

I started walking faster, hating the fact that I had no real plan, other than gain access and start chaos, which should give me enough of an adrenaline rush to kick my Sentinel powers into gear. It was suicide, and I could already feel my heart beginning to hammer as the adrenaline surged through my veins. No matter what had happened between me and Jaeden, he and the others didn't deserve what these sick assholes were doing.

"Don't do this, Emma," the voice whispered in my head urgently.

"Come and get me, Asshole." I almost felt triumphant; he was close, so this crazy-ass plan might just work.

"I said stop!" he ordered, but I ignored him with a slight twist of my lips and a quick mental shake. I walked closer to the main entrance of the town, and I was now within view of the soldiers who trained their guns on me.

"Make me," I taunted with a smile on my lips, and a sway to my hips that I shouldn't be able to pull off, not with the current mission I was on, walking right into cannibal territory. Right towards certain death.

Chapter ELEVEN

The guards let me get closer than I thought I would get before they halted my progress a few yards away from the gate. They were armed to the teeth, and trained their guns on me. I smiled nervously; my arms were crossed behind my head, in each palm a grenade hidden, the rings threaded through my fingers decoratively and at the ready.

"Don't shoot her," a man warned, his eyes on the tiny skirt I wore, and the thigh highs that made me appear sexier and less threatening. "Fuck me, look at the legs on her," he crooned, moving closer, his beady eyes feasting on the thin wisp of material that kept him from seeing the panties I wore. "Get Jason, he's going to want to ride this little bitch first."

"Keep your hands behind your head," one of the other guards shouted, his nervousness showing in his tone. "Search the area and find out if she's alone!" he yelled to another guard, who went rushing out of the gate to see if I was alone or if more people had come with me.

I watched him run by me, his eyes darting to my breasts, and then trailing lower with a hungry look in his eyes. I turned, locating Jaeden up on the stage and slowly moved towards him. I was walking right into the enemy's camp, past the point of no return.

Turquoise eyes rose to mine, and then slowly, with a pained expression, he looked at my exposed body. Blood dripped from a multitude of wounds; huge chunks of flesh had already been carved from his body. Men with guns were moving into the main area, all of them looking me over with the same look a starving man would give a Thanksgiving dinner.

"…And she walked right in willingly?" a big man was asking, and then stopped, looking me over with a covetous look. His brown hair was overly long, but he looked like he was once a prominent businessman, if I could gauge anything by his clean clothing and well-fed appearance. My stomach turned as to why he probably looked so well-fed. "Mine. I want her stripped first; make sure she's not carrying weapons."

I smiled, wiggling my hips for him at the same moment that Jolene walked out of the same building he'd just come out of.

"Kill her!" she screeched upon laying eyes on me, and I grimaced as I brought my hands out, pulled the pins, and flung the grenades outwards as if they were bowling balls, making sure they'd roll far enough away from both myself and Jaeden.

Explosions rocked the camp as I dove for cover, reaching into the pouches of my bag for the hidden guns. Bullets hit the hoods of the cars that they'd used to build a crude inner fence with. I didn't move. I palmed the gun with one hand, another grenade with the other as my heart thumped painfully against my chest. Still, nothing happened. I couldn't freeze time, couldn't move from the hail of bullets that hit the hood of the car I hid behind. I was trapped, and could hear the chaos of people screaming from the cages that housed them, as the armed townsfolk shouted loudly over their prisoners' voices to kill me. Guess my outfit wasn't enough to outweigh the fact that I'd just blown a lot of their armed guards up. I could hear screams of pain, rage, and more.

I crouched to a hunched position and looked on either side of me, noting the guards couldn't see where I had taken cover. I sent a silent prayer to the heavens and rolled away from safety, into the fray. I aimed, shot, and killed men who charged at me with their ungainly movements; bodies hit the ground as I rolled to my feet, ignoring the fact that all guns were aimed at me.

I watched the man they called Jason stand up; I took careful aim and fired at least a full round into his body, but he still remained standing…immortal? I didn't have time to figure it out, because he charged at me. Jason, the leader, wasn't quite human. He let loose a howl and launched himself at me, but he never reached me.

Instead, time stood still.

I hadn't done it. I felt nothing, no rush of power, nothing. I looked around the scene, noting the bullets which would have found their mark on my body, as they hovered midair. I exhaled and held a hand to my heart as the Sentinel materialized a few feet from me. He was wearing full armor, black and deadly from the look of it. It covered him from head to toe, as if it had been crafted just for him. His swords were drawn, and as he slowly walked towards me, he removed Jason's head with those swords in a swift scissor movement that looked effortless.

I stepped back, but the Sentinel materialized behind me, and before I could protest, he took me to the ground as the scene came alive again. I groaned against his weight, and his cerulean eyes snapped to mine. My head hurt from where he'd taken me to the ground, and my legs had instinctively wrapped around him in response. My hands gripped his shoulders; his armor was hard, probably bulletproof, and yet it hugged his muscular body perfectly, like a second skin, and, like the tactical gear he wore before, everything but his eyes was covered by the mask he wore.

His eyes rose as he shifted his weight on top of me, bullets continuing to rain down around us, barely missing their target…us. He seemed oblivious to the peril of our situation and still I couldn't find my words. Speech was just an alien concept at this moment. My heart was beating wildly, and my body was in a state of shock, as if it had become paralyzed. I couldn't move to shield myself from the volley of bullets. He turned his head, looking at where my legs had wrapped around him in an automatic response. His gloved hand slid down to touch the outside of my thigh, and he growled as he found a scratch where a bullet had skimmed my flesh, barely missing me.

He turned those cold eyes back to me, and I tried to force my brain to remember how to feed my lips words. One of the gunmen stepped closer and the Sentinel rolled us, snatching the gun from the ground where I'd dropped it, and took aim as he shot the man moving towards us. The Sentinel didn't move from my body. He didn't allow me to get up, as if he was protecting me, using his body as a shield. As if he was sheltering me from harm.

The moment my body began to work again, I rolled him over without warning; pulling guns from where I'd hidden them in the pouches of my bag, and took aim as I sat straddling his waist. I felt his hands move to my hips as he watched me kill more men who moved in to end our lives. His eyes were hooded when I chanced a peek down at him; his gloved thumbs slid over my exposed midsection as I fired at those who were stupid enough to get too close to us. I'd planned on taking on a lot of the townsfolk in the assault. I hadn't anticipated an army hiding in those houses and outbuildings. Perhaps I should have given more credence to the whole 'Clarkston Army' thing.

They were flooding the area, guns blazing even though they seemed to miss us with every shot. I'd emptied the clip and was rolled beneath the Sentinel instantly. He got to his knees, with me clinging to him as he watched me. His hands reached for his swords and I watched as his swords spun and danced in the air, slicing through bullets; fragments exploded like glitter shot through a cannon. It was as if he could see the bullets even though their velocity was beyond anything he should have been able to see. I slid down his body, and turned until my back was against his chest, pulling out more magazines for the guns as I did so.

"Stay with me," he warned huskily; he moved us with inhuman speed. One minute I'd been touching the ground, and in the next he'd materialized in the middle of the mob of soldiers, swinging his blades deftly. He was trained for war, and damn good at killing.

I ducked away from him, leaving him in the fray as I made my way to where Jaeden had been riddled with bullets. He'd lost more blood than I'd thought, and as I made my way to free him, arms grabbed me and yanked me back hard. I hit the Sentinel's chest painfully, and more bullets zipped past us.

I struggled against him, needing to get Jaeden down from the wooden post that held him up, making him a target.

"Let me go!" I shouted as time froze and his eyes turned angry.

"I'm not here to save your lover, Emma," he snapped.

"No one asked you to; I'll do it myself!" I yelled, fighting to get away from him. His grip was like an iron noose; the more I struggled, the harder it was to get free. He twisted my arm, yanking it behind my back painfully, and then his hand slipped behind my back, yanking grenades from my pack, and pulling the pins as he threw them into the mob of soldiers, turning us just in time to miss being hit by the shrapnel from the blast.

"Stay down," he ordered as he pushed me to the ground.

As if. I pulled my bag off and dug through it, looking for anything I had left to use against this guy. No more grenades, and I'd dropped my guns when he'd grabbed me before I'd tried to free Jaeden. I had nothing. I watched him systematically kill the men who remained alive, and then as he was strolling back towards me, time started up, people screamed from cages, and he ignored everything but me.

I got to my feet and took a defensive stance as he watched me. There was no way I was allowing him to take me, or hurt Jaeden. I kicked out when he got closer, watching him easily deflect it. His eyes slid down the length of me hungrily as I struck out with my fist, once again finding his armor as the pain tore through my hand. I stepped back, and turned to run as I caught sight of Lachlan and the other wolves rushing towards me.

No. He'd kill them; he would kill them all! He was a Sentinel, one who, much like my mother, killed humans. Like me. Hadn't I just done the same thing? Everything I knew about my kind said that we're supposed to *protect* humans. It was impossible to know if he'd allow them to live, or if he would slaughter them all.

I turned back to him and shook my head as I watched him pull his swords once more. My eyes turned to the raised stage where Jaeden showed no signs of life, to the cages that held humans and vampires alike; men, women, and children who watched us with wild eyes.

"No," I pleaded, sensing he was preparing to slaughter my friends. "Take me, leave them alone!" I screamed, my heart constricting at the idea of losing the people who'd helped me; they were my friends. "You want me, not them!"

Cerulean eyes turned to me as if he was deciding what to do with me. After what felt like hours of silence, he slid his wicked looking swords back into their scabbards and grabbed me painfully. I heard Lachlan and his men shouting, but it was muted over the sound of our labored breathing. The Sentinel growled as he pulled me tightly against his body and peered over my head as the wolves charged our location. I turned my head, looking at Lachlan, whose green eyes were wild as he tried to reach me in time, and then the world started to change around me.

"Save Jaeden!" I screamed, forcing the words out as the world shifted around me.

He moved us. One moment the ground was littered with bodies, and the next we were in the forest. He moved like the other Sentinels, in bursts of distance at a time. My head swirled, my vision blurred, and then everything went dark.

Chapter Twelve

I awoke in a strange bed. The room's furnishings and decorations looked as if someone spent a lot of time in some high-end furniture stores. My eyes tried to focus, but my head swam from whatever he'd done to me. I ached everywhere, as if I'd been beaten by a gorilla in my dreams. I stood, and instantly sat back down as nausea assaulted me. I could hear voices from somewhere close, but they were unfamiliar, strange.

I scanned my body and saw that I wore the same outfit I had pilfered from the strip club, but my boots were gone. I had a few raw scrapes from the skirmish, but as far as I could tell, I hadn't sustained any bad wounds. I gave myself a mental shake as images of Jaeden's ravaged body flashed through my mind. Had he lived? Had any of them lived? Where the hell was I? Who were the people outside the room?

I crept towards the only light that illuminated this room, and gasped as an elegant bathroom came into view. There was a huge claw-footed tub with a floating sink beside it. The entire sprawl looked like something you'd find in *Lifestyles of the Rich and Famous,* instead of what I was used to, which was *How to Survive an Apocalypse*. There was a huge sheepskin rug on the floor, and a fire crackled merrily in a fireplace that was built inside the wall between the bedroom and bathroom. I shuffled towards the mirror, hating that I had to destroy the serene beauty, but I needed a way to protect myself and my bug-out bag was wherever Lachlan was.

I placed a towel on the counter to muffle the sound, and used one of the bottles that lined the tub to shatter the large oval-shaped mirror. I carefully reached over, grabbed a long piece of glass, and tested it in my hand. It would work.

I slipped from the bathroom and walked towards the other door, noting that whoever was in the other room was now laughing. I moved soundlessly as I slipped further down the long hallway. Huge paintings depicting battle scenes took up most of the wall space. Normally I loved art, but this wasn't the time to stop and admire it. I had to get back to Jaeden and Lach; I had to know what had happened after I'd blacked out.

I rounded the corner, and stopped cold. People milled about, bringing in boxes of food and other things from the front doorway and through a steel door on the other side of this great room that looked very much like the steel door entrance to the Ark. They were laughing as some of the women had stopped what they should have been doing to dig through the boxes the men brought in as, if it was Christmas. I swallowed and started forward to grab one of them to use as a shield until I got the hell out of the house, but my heart started to hammer and, before I'd even made it past the hallway, he was there blocking my path.

His armor shimmered, his cerulean blue jeweled eyes watched me coldly as the people paused and started moving away from me as if they'd done this drill before. I knew the drill myself; I was stranger-danger to these people.

"Inside, now," he growled at them, but they hadn't needed to be told. They stared at me as they shuffled in swift succession towards the thick steel door and disappeared. I was left standing in the front room with him. "Put it down," he demanded, looking at the mirror shard in my hand, and I smiled coldly in answer.

"Let me go, and I won't slit your throat," I offered.

He laughed; the sound of it made my skin prickle as the fine hairs on the back of my neck rose. I stepped forward, and was slammed into the wall so hard my teeth rattled. I hadn't even seen him move. I groaned as my head bounced; plaster shattered and peppered the floor. I braced myself against the wall, as I jumped slightly and wrapped my legs around him as I pushed the glass shard into his throat. The discovery of armor at his neck came too late as my hand dripped blood, the sound sickening as I felt the glass cut my hand so deeply it touched the bones in my fingers. I cried out, my teeth chattered from the pain, and yet I refused to give in. At least not until the sound of glass scraping across bone filled my ears, sending shocks down my spine.

Drip-drip. Drip-drip. I dropped the glass, as his eyes continued to watch me with no emotion. I cradled my hand against my chest and did my best to ignore the burning pain. I tried to slam my face against his, but his elbow shifted and I whimpered as it collided with my face.

"Stop fighting me," he growled, and I opened my rapidly swelling eyes to growl back, but his hands, which held me firmly in place against the wall, became bare as his armored gloves melted away from them. "You're safe here, Emma," he bit out.

"You had no right to take me!" I snapped, as I felt blood sliding from my nose and down my lip, hating every moment of my weakness. I also hated that my words were slurred from pain.

"You invited me to come and get you; you challenged me," he taunted. "I've never been one to turn down a challenge."

"Put me down," I whispered, using my arm to wipe away the blood, which resulted in even more blood being spread around from where my hand was flayed open. It burned like hell. He pressed against me harder, and I felt his mouth against my ear.

"Try to hurt anyone here and I'll show you what hell really looks like, Emma. Much like your shelter, those here are under my protection and I won't hesitate to kill you to protect them."

His breath fanned my flesh, sending a trickle of fear running down my spine. He didn't release me, not even when I struggled against him. I turned my face away from his and felt him push me firmly against the wall, until my lungs burned and his armor bit into my flesh.

"You smell of fear," he mumbled as he finally allowed me to slide down the wall. I started to move away from him, but he captured my wrist and looked down at me through the slits in his armor. His thumb pressed against my open cut, and once I cried out, he released the pressure. "Tell me you understand that my people are off-limits."

"Fuck you!" I snapped, and tried to pull away, but he was immovable. He held me there, his thumb pressed against the wound and tears burned my eyes. I held back the scream that threatened to explode from my lips as his eyes watched me, until I nodded. "Fine!" He released me as if my flesh was fire that burned him. I hit the ground, the pain in my hand and face too much to feel at once.

He kicked the mirror shard away from me and crouched down, resting his arms on his knees; his blue eyes scanned my face as he spoke. "I can make this easy on you, or I can make your time here hell, that choice is yours. You push boundaries, and enforce laws to protect your people from evil and harm, know that I do the same."

"Who the fuck are you?" I demanded.

"Who I am is unimportant; what I can do to you is important," he laughed mirthlessly. He picked me up without warning and before I could blink, I was thrown to the bed I'd left before this entire debacle had happened. I cradled my arm as I sat up, and watched as he entered the bathroom and made a tsking sound with his tongue. "You didn't like the room? Or do you just normally destroy pretty things that were created with you in mind, Emma?" he called out from the other room, his voice floating through the open doorway.

I didn't answer; instead, I looked around the room. The paintings were of skulls made up of flowers that I would have loved to have owned before the virus hit. The vanity had been carved from redwood and had a matching chair and a lighted mirror. Nowadays, that part was useless, but it looked like something from an era long past. A metal hairbrush with metal teeth had been left on the vanity tabletop, with a matching comb that had small sapphire jewels encrusted along the spine.

The lounge chair against the wall was made of sheepskin, and looked as if it belonged on the pages of *Vanity Fair*, just waiting for someone famous to sit on it. I'd looked at one once, but the hefty price tag had given me a quick reality check. A matching sofa was on the other side of the room. The plush bed I sat on was covered in a velvet comforter that felt like heaven.

My attention focused back to the armored figure as he walked back into the room with a first aid kit. He sat beside me and I instantly moved to get away from him, but he dropped the box and pounced. His long fingers captured my wrists, and he pushed his weight down on top of me.

"I'm only trying to help you," he muttered, but I wasn't buying it.

Maybe I was jaded. Maybe I didn't think there were any nice beings left in this world, or maybe, just maybe, being taken to a strange man's house and being an unwilling houseguest had set off every warning bell inside my head.

When I refused to answer him, he laughed and straddled my body without releasing my wrists. The corners of his eyes crinkled, betraying that he smiled beneath the mask he wore. He sat back, releasing my arms and I felt something inside of me spark. As if something was grasping on to every nerve ending, until I couldn't move. Fear erupted, and tears slid from the corners of my eyes unchecked. I couldn't prevent it, couldn't even move.

"What…" My vocal cords froze and I moaned; it was the only sound I could manage. I continued moaning, trying to force words through my throat, but only noise escaped.

"As I said, Emma, who I am is unimportant, but what I can do to you is," he murmured as he sat back, letting his eyes look over my body. Panic sliced through me as the reality of the situation hit me. I couldn't move, and he could. "You're exquisite," he growled, as his armor vanished, but the room was too dark to make out much, other than his hair was dark and his flesh was covered in tattoos. This close I could smell him; masculinity warred with a woodsy scent, which lingered in my nose.

"Sorry about the paralysis," he mused. "I don't want you harming yourself any more than you already have."

I was helpless to do anything other than watch as he backed up, keeping the light at his back to shield his features from me.

"You're not healing as you should," he commented, almost to himself, and I wanted to throw out a sarcastic comment, but couldn't.

No shit I wasn't healing; if he'd have warned me he was both glass and bulletproof, I wouldn't have sliced myself to the bone trying to kill him. He shook his head, and then turned, exiting the room only to return with a bucket a moment later, and he retook his seat beside me on the bed.

He moved with calculated precision, leaning over while managing to mask his features as he washed the wounded hand, which caused a moan of pain to slip past my lips. Movement? How long would this paralyzed state last? Tears erupted as he washed around the wound with the cloth, and I lay there like a log. I hadn't even flinched from the pain, but I'd wanted to.

"You've healed before, so why not now?" he asked absently, as if he was used to asking questions from someone who couldn't answer back…maybe I wasn't his first victim? "This is going to hurt," he warned, and pain rocked through me until I felt nauseated, and blackness tried to claim me. I fought it, not wanting to be both paralyzed and unconscious for this horror show.

I moaned as I fought to overcome the pain and then, just as quickly as it started, it stopped. He sat back, digging through the first aid kit until he had something that looked like a large tube of paste. His eyes seemed to be on mine, but with the dim lighting and the shadows of the room, it was hard to judge if he really was looking at me or not.

He leaned over once more and the sickly sweet smell of whatever was in the tube made my eyes water for an entirely different reason. The contact sent shocks all the way to my spine as he applied the paste-like substance to the wound and held my hand with both of his, applying pressure until the room swam and blackness took me into its sweet, blissful depths.

When I opened my eyes again, it was to find him watching me. My hand burned, but I also felt the air on my body as what he'd done to me when I'd been unconscious slowly became apparent. He'd stripped me out of the bloody clothes I'd been wearing and left me in my panties and bra. I still couldn't move of my own volition, and he watched as panic seized me once more.

"Sorry about that," he whispered, and I heard splashing as he bent over, and then something warm touched my arm. My eyes drifted down to what he was doing, and I realized he was bathing the blood from my flesh. The light from the bathroom made a sound and began to dim until it sizzled out. The generator must be out of gas, and even in the shadows, I could see the slight shake of his head.

If he was like me, he could see me clear as day, and yet I could barely make out his silhouette. Lovely, this must be another one of his funky powers. He pulled a device from his pocket, which illuminated his eyes as he watched me and it gave me a general idea of what he looked like, but not enough to be sure. He had a strong jawline and full lips, which I already knew. His hair was wet; had he showered while I'd been out? It would explain the clean scent that tempted my senses. He smelled clean, the earthy scent of him tingled in my nose as a mixture of fresh dew and early morning sunlight mixed and wafted to me. My head turned a tad and I almost smiled with the small victory.

He watched me and I blinked as a light turned on from the hallway, shielding his features from me even more. He slipped the small device onto the bed and proceeded to wash my arms, and then my face. He paused when it was done. He scooted forward, reached into his pocket, and I heard familiar sounds as the light from the device glinted off of the blade of a switchblade knife that had come to life in his hand.

I moaned and tried to scoot away from the blade, but I was stuck in place. I watched as he leaned over me, slipped his finger through the center of the bra, and flicked the blade using his wrist. My breasts were bare, and if I hadn't imagined it, I'd heard a sharp intake of breath as they'd become exposed.

He leaned his face closer, kissing the center where the skin was red and angry before he sat back up. That simple action I felt to the very center of my being. I swallowed another moan as he reached for the cloth and continued his slow, leisurely washing of my body. I guess he didn't care for his prey to be as dirty as they were helpless.

He didn't speak through the entire process, but every once in a while, he'd make a strangled sound and my eyes would move to his. The innocent brush of flesh was also something I noticed, as if he was doing it on purpose. His fingers would brush against the curves of my ribs, hips, and the globes of my breasts as he washed me slowly.

Heat furled in my belly with each one of those innocent brushes, and it pissed me off. I wasn't supposed to feel anything. Not when I was his unwilling captive. He'd ensured that I was unable to protest, move, or do anything other than watch him as he bathed me. Yet with each touch, heat unfurled; it rushed to the center of my being, and that, too, scared me.

"You enjoy being helpless," he mused; it wasn't a question. He hadn't directed it to be that way, either. I could sense he was smiling, as if he liked having me at his mercy, and well, I guess most men did. "Such a sweet little thing, so fucking helpless," he whispered huskily. I felt the cold blade as it pushed against the silk fabric of the panties, and then the sound of fabric being cut echoed in the room. I moaned as the blade slowly slid across my delicate flesh. The other side gave way as easily as the first, and the cool air hit my naked flesh.

I moaned and turned my head away from him, noting the movement and wondering just how long his freaky Jedi mind trick shit was going to last. He pulled the fabric out and his knuckles skimmed the inside of my thigh, which pulled forth an involuntary whimper as hot tears slid from my eyes. I was naked, exposed, and at my most vulnerable point for the second time in my life.

I wanted to scream, do anything other than just fucking lay there while he raped me. He lifted my leg, pushed in, and placed my knee against his bare chest and he carefully, methodically washed my hip, the curve of my abdomen, and the inside of my thigh. I wasn't sure why I felt aroused, but it shook me to my core. Whatever was happening between us, I wasn't immune to him, and neither was he to me. He repeated the action to the other leg, hip, and then when I'd thought he'd stop, he pushed my legs open and swallowed hard.

His eyes seemed to burn my flesh where he looked me over; the idea of him doing more sent a shiver down my spine. He moved his hand, running his knuckles over my flesh as he watched me. He lowered his mouth as if he planned to taste me. His hot breath fanned my pussy and I moaned as I fought to make my limbs move. He turned his head, kissing the inside of one thigh and then the other, before he slid between them and looked down at me.

Fear spiked as adrenaline rushed through me.

"No," I murmured, finally finding my voice.

"You let him use your body, and you deny me everything," he mumbled. He leaned over me and picked me up carefully. "Don't worry; I have no intention of raping you. That's what *he* would do," he snapped. "Really, Emma, you sleeping with the enemy has caused quite the stir of rumors in our world. Emma, the vampire's whore, his sad little plaything, and such. You're not his whore, though, are you?" His words weren't said hatefully, but more like he was intrigued.

"No," I whimpered, because I couldn't manage more.

"And yet you continue to let him inside of you," he growled. He placed me on the sofa and I sank into it, unable to do anything else. He moved to the bed, pulling off the soiled sheets and blankets. He went to the closet, pulled out new bedding, made the bed up quickly, and then loomed over me, staring down at me possessively. "If you let him have your body again, I'll take his fucking head. I don't share, and I promise you his immortality won't save him from me," he said as he picked my useless body up, shivered with the contact of our flesh, and then placed me on the bed. "Go to sleep; it's late. I have other places to be," he added as he slipped first the sheet over my naked body, and then the blanket. "Sweet dreams, my little fighter," he finished as he turned and left the room.

Chapter Thirteen

When I woke up, I was alone. The light in the room flickered on, as if it had known the moment I woke up. I laid there for a moment, scared to death that whatever he'd done to me was permanent. My fingers moved first, then my hand. I took a deep breath, sat up, and tried to stand, but caught myself before I could fall to the floor. I slid to my knees and rested my upper body on the bed as if I was praying.

Listening, I heard no noise from inside the house, and I wasn't sure if I could hear anything from the bunker that was attached to the house. My heart raced, alerting me that he was close, but a quick check of the room told me he wasn't here. Good thing, too, because I was still naked. At the foot of the bed was a pile of clothing, a towel, and what looked like a black rose. I grabbed the clothes and slowly pulled them towards me, noting my hand looked like it had begun to heal, and the skin was closed with whatever he'd applied to it last night.

I dressed sluggishly and made my way towards the door, crawling until I made it to the wall. I pulled myself up and forced my feet to move. I struggled in this manner until I'd made it down the hallway and into an overly lavish main living area that was more of a great room. The room was decorated in neutral colors, light grays with black accents. The couch was a large L-shaped sectional, with a chaise sofa situated at the end. I tried to push off from the wall, but my feet wouldn't cooperate and I hit the floor hard.

I cried out as my hand hit the flooring, giving way until my face slammed against the hardwood floor. I lifted myself up, only to find a pair of black boots in front of me.

"Go ahead, kick me when I'm down, asshole," I mumbled as I tried to get up. Rough hands lifted me and then carried me to the couch, where he laid me down and stepped back. He was once again decked out in his armor. It bothered me that he'd seen all of me, and yet I'd never gotten a true glimpse of him.

Had it bothered Jaeden this much? He'd always asked me to remove my mask, and yet I'd refused. It wasn't until it had accidentally slipped from my face as I was maneuvering to get the AR-15 out to scope the wolves that had been stalking us that he was able to see what I looked like. Not that I planned to ask the Sentinel to remove his armor; I didn't give a shit what he looked like beneath it.

"It may take a few hours for your body to get back

to normal," he said softly as he moved to the table and grabbed a plate of food. My stomach growled, and I inhaled the divine scent of bacon. My mouth watered and my eyes grew large as he walked towards me with a steaming plate of breakfast. He set it down on the table and watched me as I stared at the juicy strips. "Hungry?" he asked, and I shook my head in denial.

I wasn't hungry; I was famished. My stomach was growling like a lion in a cage, and my mouth was watering. He picked up a piece of crispy bacon and my eyes followed it until he held it in front of my mouth. I didn't want to eat it, but bacon! I hadn't had real, honest to goodness bacon since the first shitty ass days of the virus.

He tapped it against my lips and I looked up, anger pulsing through me. I wasn't a child, yet I could barely freaking move! I opened my mouth, and felt the crispy, savory goodness as he pushed it deep between my lips and then I closed my mouth around his finger. His eyes grew wide, and I smiled. I moaned around the meat in my mouth, forgetting his digit was in there, or that I planned to bite his finger off. The sheer bliss of it undid me. I pulled away from his finger, and heard his sharp intake of breath as I did it.

I chewed the morsel, watching him as his eyes remained glued to my lips until I'd finished. I swallowed, and waited for him to speak, but instead, he just watched me.

It felt like forever until he finally lifted his eyes

and looked at mine. His jaw twitched; a muscle there was hammering as if my action had upset him. I hadn't meant to suck on his finger; I'd totally intended to bite the fucker off, but it would have ruined the taste of bacon, which had undone me.

"Why did you bring me here?" I asked, and his eyes lowered once more to my lips as if he was unable to stop himself.

"You're mine," he stated. "You feel me as surely as I can feel you." He got up and left me watching him as he headed back to the kitchen.

"I am not yours," I mumbled, but I had felt him. I could feel him now. His heart, it beat as quickly as mine.

"You have access to this level; any of the locked doors are off-limits to you. Stay away from the bunker, and don't try to escape. You won't make it far, and you'll be punished if you try," he said offhandedly as he made his way to the refrigerator. I watched him, wondering why he had the useless thing when something like a gun rack would be way more useful. He opened it; the light turned on, and at that point, I noticed the hum of the refrigerator.

He had a freaking working refrigerator? I looked around the house, noticing a lot of other things. He had lights, a lot of them. Most were off, but they had been on last night; at least, they were on until the one in the bathroom went out when the generator ran out of gas. Or did it? The walls weren't walls at all, most were see-through glass, probably bulletproof, but it flooded the room with natural lighting. There was a TV hooked to the wall and a stereo that was set to a time, as if it had never ceased to work when the power grid went down. Maybe it hadn't gotten the memo that we were living in a time when power was scarce?

The front door was steel, same as the door that led into the bunker. There was a small, black box beside it, which blinked green. It was controlled by power. If his grid went down, that door would open. I could escape. I turned my head, noting that several cameras lined the room. They covered every angle of it, faced every doorway. There would be a live feed somewhere in this house, probably in one of the rooms he'd just forbidden me from entering.

I turned, looked at him, and found him studying me.

"The power is solar. The door is made of reinforced steel; the entire house locks down if the power is cut at any point," he offered before pulling out what looked like freshly made orange juice.

"Smart, but every safe house has an exit," I stated.

"If it was in fact a safe house, but I assure you it is not. Think of it more like how a panic room is built. It's made to keep those inside, inside," he mused as he began rummaging through the cupboards.

"What do you want with me?" I asked with my tone sharper than I'd intended, but really, I wasn't here willingly. He knew it.

"I'm going to make you mine, and from there, we will see what happens," he commented as if he'd just told me it was about to rain and I might want an umbrella before wandering outside.

"Can you hold your breath while you wait?" I asked sweetly.

"I can hold my breath for a very long time—and you will succumb to it, it's inevitable," he said confidently.

"Why am I really here? You could have raped me and been done with it, so why bring me here?" I said, and yeah, I sounded jaded. I was.

"Because you belong to me, you are my other half. It's as simple as that," he replied and walked towards me. I stood up, and stared at him.

"You can't own another human being," I stated.

"You're not human, Emma," he said with a soft tone. "You knew that much, you knew it the moment you woke up after you jumped from the cliff."

How the hell did he know about that?

"You need to let me go, now. I'll never stop fighting you. I'm not interested in you, nor do I clean up well. I bite and I have fleas," I rambled. "I'm not a stray you just bring home and decide you can keep."

"Sit down and sheath your claws," he demanded as he held out a glass of orange juice. He was tall, really tall. He was over six foot, give or take a few inches, but there really was no taking them away. His armor was sleek, mold to a well-defined body; I'd caught glances of his sleek muscles last night, and him? He'd caught an eyeful of everything I had to offer.

"I told you, I bite. Open the damn door, and we can forget you took me."

"That's not going to happen. Ever," he growled.

"Oh, it is. One way or another, I assure you that I am leaving. It's not up for negotiation. You left my friends in a really bad place, and I have something that I have to do."

"Retrieve the pawn from his mother? What makes you think he even wants you to save him?" he asked nonchalantly.

"Grayson isn't a pawn; he's my brother. I raised him, and that bitch? Not our mother. She may have given birth, but she means no more to me than the shit I stepped in last week. I raised him. When he got hurt? I took care of him. He's my world, so this?" I flicked my hand back and forth between us. "It won't work. It's not you; it's me. I'm all messed up, mommy issues. So open the motherfucking door, now," I demanded.

"I said sit down," he growled, and stepped closer after he'd placed the glass down. His armor obstructed any chance of me attacking him. I backed up; my knees hit the couch and buckled. Once I was down, he crouched between my legs, pushing them open as his eyes remained glued to mine. "You're not in charge here, Emma. I am. There is no way out, not unless I agree to it happening. It's in your best interest to keep me happy, and maybe I'll help you find out what you are. Show you what you can become. We know you're fucking clueless, we know you fucked Jaeden because you had no one there to help you so you used what you could for protection. I know and I understand, but it ends here. You are mine. You were created for me, and you're here because you belong to me. Not him. You won't be rushing back into his arms. That part of your life is over. It's time to become what you truly are. You were created to help our race, to lure the evil ones in to the slaughter. You think he wants you? He doesn't. He wants what you will become. The one thing he can never have: Life. You are a Guardian of Life, or will be soon, and he's the undead. He craves you because he can never have you. I know, I understand why he craves you because it's the same reason I desire and crave you." His words were full of anger and bitterness as he stood up, turned, and left me staring at his back as he walked away.

"You're a vampire?" I asked, and watched as he stiffened, shook his head, and moved towards the door. Once there, he shielded the panel with his body. I heard the panel chirp and the door unlocked. He slipped through and the door closed with a finality that seemed to take the air in the room with it.

Chapter Fourteen

Hours seemed to pass, although it probably was only minutes, as I contemplated his bizarre words and tried to figure a way to get back to Jaeden and back on the road to find my brother. Not knowing where the hell this place was made any sort of planning incomplete. Sentinels traveled ridiculously fast, so I could be hundreds of miles from where he took me. I stood up, happy to feel the strength in my legs returning, and removed the cold plate, which was now empty of bacon, and made my way towards the door. Once there, I pushed in a few codes until it blinked red. I looked around the room, and went to the kitchen and pulled out a knife. I walked back to the door, slid the knife into the box, and pulled it open.

I stared at the mess of wires and tried to remember everything my dad had told me about what to cross, and what not to. I remembered dick. I crossed a few and something started buzzing, and then, all at once, alarms and sirens started screaming. The metal casings that had hung from the ceiling by the window walls slammed down, locking into place. A noise coming from the door indicated a secondary set of locks sliding into place; the sound of them driving home in the reinforced steel was like they were piercing my heart, sealing me in.

An alarm began to bleat annoyingly; the lights dimmed, blinked, and turned red as they continued to blink. Panic mode. The entire fucking house had just locked down and gone into panic mode. My eyes searched for the cameras, which followed every step I took. I walked to one of the windows and tested the metal frame. It wasn't budging. I picked up one of the chairs and threw it at the glass. It bounced. The cameras turned again, following me as I moved to another part of the house.

At the end of the hallway, there was a door with another panel. The door had huge steel bars on the surface that were in a locked position. His bedroom, maybe? Or maybe the room that the video feed was playing into? I looked up as I heard a new noise, and winced as the sprinklers sputtered to life and water began to rain down.

I looked at the camera in front of me and flipped it off. The white top I was wearing was now see-through. The shorts I wore weren't much better, but it wasn't like he'd given me back my own clothes. I walked back to the main living area, and he was there, standing in the middle of the room with his arms crossed, watching me. His head turned, lowering as he took in the wetness that was me. I moved into the room as if I didn't care;

my heart raced and I wanted to kick his ass, but that wouldn't solve this mess.

"Find a way out yet?" he taunted, his eyes seeming almost purple in the red hue of the room.

"Working on it," I quipped, moving past him. Before I could take two steps, I was picked up and pushed against the wall just as the red lights went out, plunging us into darkness. The alarm stopped, and the only sound was our breathing. I felt flesh, no armor. I used my hands to explore him, the smooth contours of his rock-hard body. It was a big mistake.

His mouth found mine and I groaned as heat flooded my body; his hands released my hips, forcing me to tighten my legs around him. His mouth was hard, and the strangled noise that escaped his lips fed the fire. I pushed my tongue against his, exploring the minty depths of him, and it was all the permission he needed to turn the kiss from hard to demanding. It stirred a storm inside of me, and everything else faded away.

When I finally pulled away, he yanked at my hair, dropping his forehead against mine. I tried to drop my legs, but he held them, his breathing labored. The sound of our need to gain air filled the room. The moment I'd thought he'd finally allow me down, he pushed his erection against my core and I moaned. He was steel against my silk, and his fingers bit into my flesh as he claimed my mouth again.

The kiss lasted forever. Until I thought my lungs

would collapse from lack of air. It wasn't a gentle kiss, no; he kissed me as if his very life depended on it. What the fuck was wrong with me? I pushed at his chest and he laughed coldly.

"You hate that you respond so naturally to me," he murmured into the darkness.

"I do, I despise everything about you," I mumbled.

"Yet you give in so easily? Perhaps he must not mean as much as he thinks he does to you," he growled and I tried to slap him, but his hand was faster, and I had been aiming via sound. My body slid down his, his own proof of desire resting against my belly.

"Go to hell," I bit out as I tried to leave the room, only to find one of the smaller tables with my shin. I cried out, bent over and felt him as he pressed against me. He picked me up as I struggled in his arms and walked us to the hallway, where he somehow managed not to hit anything with his shins. Unfortunately.

He stopped in front of the room I had awakened in, opened the door, and pushed through, moving us towards the bed. Once there, he dropped me. It hurt. *Asshole.* I glared up at the darkness where I assumed he was. I turned, crawling to the center of the very wet bed, when I felt it move with his weight.

"What are you doing?" I demanded.

"It's wet, everything is wet," he said, and sounded a little disgruntled.

I laughed, and then I laughed some more until my stomach hurt. It wasn't funny. But the entire place was wet. I lay back on the bed, and waited for the laughter to pass. It did, and then came silent tears.

"Emma," he murmured gently, as if he sensed my unease.

"You're an asshole," I whispered. "You didn't even save them."

"They didn't need me to save them," he replied.

"You don't know that!" I snapped.

"If I told you that they lived, would you stop trying to escape?" he asked.

"Never," I whispered. "I'll never stop."

"Good, because they never left that hellhole," he growled, and a giant sob tore through me as I turned over on the wet bed and cried until I slipped into sleep.

Sometime during the night, he held me; when I awoke the next morning, it was to the smell of him all over me. I glanced around the room and felt the bedding beside me; it was cold, indicating he had been gone for a while. I got out of bed, padded to the bathroom, and looked at the tub. The last time I'd taken a bath had ended badly. I'd ended up doing things to myself while imagining Jaeden. He had a front row seat for the entire thing, and judging by the look on his face, he enjoyed himself immensely.

I moved into the bedroom again, looked at the door handle for a lock…no such luck. Shit, could anything else go wrong? I pushed the vanity in front of the door as a weak safety measure; at least if he tried to move that, I would hear him. I made my way back to the bathroom, looked around and paused. There was no camera in here. There were two in my bedroom, but not any in here. I walked to the tub, turned on the water and placed my hand under it. Cold water…no, warm… hot. Yes! I slunk around the bathroom, finding a few bath bombs, salts and other things which I tossed into the tub. It quickly filled with bubbles. The earthy scent of flowers mixed with the sweet scent of cotton candy, which was actually disgusting once it mixed together, but fuck it, a bath!

I stripped and sank beneath the suds, and groaned as the aches and pains faded away. As I closed my eyes, I realized I could feel that he was still inside the house. He'd seen it all already, so who cared? I relaxed and started singing and rocking out to my own song, which sounded more like a country song than the rock hit I'd been trying to come up with. By the time I was done with my song, even I was thinking, *'What the hell was that shit?'*

Laughter erupted behind me and I glared at the wall. I was so over bathing in this new world. Seriously, did anyone believe in boundaries anymore?

"That's the next big song, don't knock it," I growled, turning to look at him over my shoulder. He was decked out in armor, as per usual. I was beginning to think he was afraid of me, because he never took it off around me, unless it was seriously dark, which gave him the advantage.

"Indeed," he mused as he tilted his head.

"Indeed, asshole. Hand me the towel?" I asked softly. It was across the room, where I'd forgotten about it in my excitement of bathing.

"No, get it yourself," he dared, leaning against the door and crossing his arms.

I glared, lifted a brow, pulled the bucket into the tub that I'd used to wash my hair and lifted it as I stood. His eyes moved down as I smiled, lifted the bucket, and tossed the water right at him. He didn't even see it coming, not until it hit his armor and he looked up. I swallowed, his eyes were filled with heat, and it wasn't anger. It was lust, naked and raw; I-should-have-run-my-ass-in-the-opposite-direction lust. I swallowed and shook my head. He stepped forward, I slipped, almost falling back into the tub before I jumped out, slipped on the water, and righted myself.

He was coming around the tub, so I went the other way. He stalked me, not running, but slowly, methodically hunting me. I'd hoped his armor would shrink, or something! It didn't. I slipped again, and he caught me, picked me up, flung me over his shoulder, and carried me into the bedroom. He tossed me on the bed and stared down at me.

"You keep throwing me on the bed and I'm going

to end up with shaken…baby…are your eyes red?" I gasped as I lost my train of thought. I sat up and looked closer but he blinked, and they returned to the startling blue. "Oh, shit, what the fuck *are* you?"

"Now you're finally thinking about what I am," he seethed as he looked down at my still naked, suds-covered ass. "Soon," he growled, turning to leave me on the still-damp bed.

"Soon what?" I asked, sitting up.

He stopped, turned, and I swear to God I saw him smiling through his armor. He stepped closer and I crab-walked my ass backwards. He stopped, paused, his head tilted and he growled. He shook his head, and then righted it. It made him look inhuman, and sent a shiver racing down my spine.

"You'll be mine soon, in every sense of the word, *mate*," he gritted out softly. Although his tone was cold, his eyes were hot and full of lust.

Chapter FIFTEEN

His words echoed in my ears; my heartbeat always seemed to be on overdrive, but I was learning to live with it. Three days had passed since he'd brought me here. Three days in which I worried about Lachlan and Jaeden. The last image of Jaeden I had gutted me, but I knew if anyone could make it through that ordeal, he could.

He was immortal, and yet he'd been in one hellish state from the cannibals. They'd drugged them; otherwise this mess wouldn't have happened. It just wouldn't have.

I was being held in some lavish prison being hand-fed bacon. I'd watched and observed the little things to try and understand where I was. I had noticed that the people here brought in fresh peppermint and other naturally grown herbs. Outside of a garden or hothouse, herbs such as the ones they'd harvested naturally grew in the forest and, based on the wooded areas surrounding us, they must not have gone far to get these plants.

The toilet swirled counterclockwise, which told me I was still in the Northern Hemisphere. The thickness of the air told me we were at a higher altitude, and the directional flow of the waterfall that the house faced told me I was right.

Last night I'd left my room to stare at the stars, and tried to judge where I was from the constellations, but what they told me couldn't have been right. If they were, I was closer to home than I'd thought. Stars are tricky, though, the higher up you are the clearer they become. Newport is a high altitude; we didn't notice because it's what we were used to, but as soon as an outsider would arrive in town, it was the first thing they'd point out. I was currently higher than Newport's altitude, because I now knew how those outsiders felt. It took a little getting used to, but I was handling it.

I hadn't seen him all day. It was nearing dusk and I'd been left to my own devices. I'd wondered where he went for hours, but came up empty. He hadn't returned with supplies, so that crossed sourcing off my list. No herbs, so he wasn't out picking them. Out torturing other captives? That was possible.

I was lost inside my head, staring at the sunset as the sun began its descent behind the falls and dusk set in. Red and pink hues fanned across the sky, mixing with soft purples and blues. For a brief moment, I forgot where I was, and who I was with. It seemed surreal that, for once, I was looking beyond the horror and finding something beautiful that remained in this world. I had been about to turn away from the window when I caught the image of a shadowy figure a few feet behind me.

The window was reflecting his image, and he wasn't wearing armor. Startling cerulean blue eyes framed with thick black lashes watched me carefully. He had high cheekbones and a strong jawline with a trace of a five o'clock shadow gracing it. His chest was bare, his tattoos startlingly dark against his flesh. I could make out one on his shoulder, a male skeletal figure kissing a sugar skull girl with blonde hair. There were a few other tattoos here and there that I tried to make out in the reflection; one above his ribcage had ancient writing, or maybe a dead language scrawled across it. Either way, I couldn't make out the words. A fallen angel with huge black wings took up most of his side, wrapping around his hip, which drew my eyes to the V-line that descended into his pants. He wasn't as thick as I'd thought he would be, muscle-wise, but he was sleek, well-defined. Water dripped from his hair, still wet from the shower he must have taken before seeking me out. Dark hair clung to the tip of his shoulders, and I watched as a stray droplet slowly slid over the sleek ripple of muscles until it rolled down to the V, and lower.

I wanted to turn around, but somehow I knew if I did, he'd do whatever magic he did to call forth his wicked armor.

"There's a storm coming," he commented, disturbing the silence of the room. "I'd like to walk you through the setup, since I will be out of the house when it arrives."

"Okay," I replied, unsure why I remained still, and

were those butterflies in my stomach? I started to turn, but then stopped as I felt him getting closer. I paused, felt the butterflies follow my lead as his fingertips slowly danced across my shoulders. One hand gripped my neck, with his eyes continuing to remain locked with mine in the tempered glass. His lips touched my neck softly, sending a thrill of sensations over my flesh. His lips brushed against my ear and I swallowed the moan that tried to escape, closing my lips to deny it exit.

"The house is run on solar paneling, similar to what you have at the Ark; only mine is a lot more advanced. The house itself is built of stone in case of any wildfires in the mountains or valley; it's protected. The glass is sealed to prevent flooding; it is also bulletproof. You cannot penetrate it with anything inside the house, so do avoid attempting such an act." His hot breath fanned against my throat and his eyes remained locked with mine as he spoke. "We have three wells; each are monitored and tested daily. The house will automatically run on backup generators in the event of the solar cells being damaged or running out for whatever reason. We are in a locale known for its sun, so the chances of having an issue are fairly remote. We have acres of farmland just beyond that wooded area and inside the bunker below our feet is an area designated to grow plants as well. Sunlamps run from the solar panels grow the plants. I also raided several pharmacies for basic medication that may be needed for the humans. Should they need something else, we can get it. There's a medical ward in the bunker as well; it's set up for over a hundred people should the need arise. It's well stocked with emergency personnel; equipment and life-sustaining machines. We are well equipped to face most storms, or whatever Mother Nature may throw at us. I also have a brig built inside this house, one large and strong enough to hold you, should you try escaping me."

He pulled away, his armor materializing over his flesh, and I turned, looking at him as he watched me. I wasn't sure all those details were for the upcoming storm, or just him wanting me to know that I would never escape this place. After the house locked itself down and went into panic mode the other day, I had pretty much figured that out without his little pep talk.

"There's a backup switch in your room should the power go out. I will be gone for a day, two at most," he continued, his eyes following me as I moved to the couch. "Is there anything you need while I am out?"

"Freedom," I mused, scrunching up my nose. "Glass cutter, or, you know, the code to the door? That would be nifty."

"Any personal items, Emma?" he rephrased.

"No, I don't want or need anything from you. The only thing I need? Is to get out of this pretty prison and back into the real world. I'm not a willing hostage so let's not play like I am," I snapped, tired of feeling like a bird in a cage.

"So you can run back into the arms of your lover?" he seethed; his eyes flashed red, but it was gone as quickly as it had started.

"He's not my lover. I ended it with him," I growled back, my own eyes unable to flash red, but my temper rising. "Besides, who I lay with is none of your damn business," I turned to leave the room.

My hair blew up as if a great gust of wind had entered the room; papers lifted and swirled in the air as they fell to the floor. I slammed hard into his chest and had to throw my hands up to prevent myself from falling at his feet. I stared face-to-face with him, having to raise my eyes to hold his. I was pissed, mostly because whatever the hell was between us had me curious, and when he was around, my body reacted.

"You can either have the freedom of the house I've allowed you, or you can wait for me in my bedroom, in chains. It's your choice. Decide now," he snapped, as his hands pushed my shoulders until I was forced backwards. "I could have killed him, so fucking easily. I chose not to, because you would have hated me for it. He lives because you wish it; he isn't what you think he is. His kind feed upon the human race, they're parasites; ones you were created to rid the world of. Instead of doing so, you took him between your thighs," he snarled, stalking me as I backpedaled against the window. "Your mother is the same, spreading her flesh for any who will further her cause."

"Is that so?" I stammered, unsure why I could face off against vampires, and yet this Sentinel scared the fuck out of me.

"You were created for me and me alone. Not him.

I was too far away when you allowed him to become your lover. I was trying to get back to this continent, while my little phoenix spread her legs willingly and succumbed to *his* charms. I knew what he did; what you did. I could see what happened playing out in my nightmares; was tortured by his hands on your flesh, his cock inside of you. Then he left and I knew you'd rise above it, above him. Yet, the moment he came back, you let him between those silken thighs again. No more. The other day when you took him on the dirty floor of some virus-infected trashcan was the last. I am here now and I claim ownership; I took you from them, so he is no longer an option for you. You deserve so much fucking more than to be taken on some dirty floor, Emma."

"You had dreams of when I was with Jaeden for the first time?" I whispered thickly. I cried out as the cold glass touched my back and his hands flattened on the glass beside my head.

"The first time and each time after that," he whispered coldly, as if he was lost in the memory. "Nightmares, not dreams. I watched him pound your flesh, knowing it was mine to do so with. I watched you fight off the ill-effects of the drugs and still, you gave yourself over to him. I saw it through your eyes, every fucking time you took him. I had been watching you long before that, Emma. I felt you the moment you drew air into your lungs. You were a beautiful baby. You had big blue eyes, hair of sunshine, and life that curled perfectly against your pale complexion. They brought you home on a Sunday; it was pouring rain. As if even the world wept over your beauty and the sadness you'd have to endure in your life. I was there when you took your first steps, unable to stay away as I watched the child that would someday become my bride grow. I stood near you at your mother's funeral, watching as you refused to cry or even shed a tear. You brushed against me, and gasped, as if you felt me too. You may not have known it then, but you sealed your fate that day. You confirmed everything I felt. My heart connected to yours, but you weren't ready for me. You were still a mere child who had so much growing to do before I could bring you into your birthright. I watched you become a woman, believing you'd remain chaste because the idea of any other man touching you felt wrong. You made up excuse after excuse to Addy as to why you wouldn't throw your virtue at the feet of the boys, but the truth was you couldn't. You knew it was special, that it was meant for one man alone: Me. Yet, the moment Jaeden walked in, a supernatural being, you gave in. That racing of your heart right now?" His hand pressed against my chest as his armor disappeared to reveal how he really looked. "Matches mine. Perfectly," he whispered as I gasped at his features. He was fucking gorgeous. He stared down at me as I raised my hand from where it rested on his chest to curve it around his cheek.

His skin was bronzed, beautifully so. I was able to get a better look at his tattoos, and every one of them had been strategically placed to enhance the contours of his body. This man was created to please a woman's eye, yet my hands trembled as I touched him. I brushed my shaking fingers along the writing that was tattooed just below his right pectoral.

"What does this say?" I murmured.

"Life is just a beautiful death." He smiled softly. "Do you like what you see, little one?" he asked, and there was a hint of insecurity in his voice that made my eyes rise to capture his. He'd just dropped a few hefty bombs on me, and I wasn't sure if I believed him or not.

"You're beautiful," I whispered. "Wait…What did I wear to my mother's funeral?"

"A black skirt with a soft velvet top," he whispered, and I shivered. "You wore a coat, one that was too big. Your hair was up, it wasn't perfect, and you never complained about the hair pins that your father had secured the wayward strands with. They hurt you, but you refused to add to his pain during the ceremony." He pushed a few strands of hair away from my face as if he was reenacting what he had witnessed. "They asked your father to speak, but he didn't. He held your hand while he carried Grayson on his hip. He refused to let either one of you far from his sight."

Fact.

"How did I not notice you?" I asked, narrowing my eyes as I dropped my hand.

"You were a mere child, grieving for her mother. You grieved for a mother who wasn't even dead. You knew that at the time, too. You just didn't want to believe it. You removed the necklace and refused to wear it, not because you were angry she'd died. You refused to wear it because it made you see what others couldn't, and it made you feel sure that she hadn't been murdered, that she'd in fact left you and your brother. That's why you took it off and hid it in the floorboards of your room. It showed you that you weren't human."

Okay, that? I'd never told that to another soul. I'd bottled it up, thinking it was my childish anger. I'd told myself the lie of being angry for her dying and leaving us so often, that eventually, I'd believed it. The truth was that necklace had done shit to me, made me see things in the shadows, like my mother across the street when we'd been at the park. She'd watched us, and I tried to chase after her. It had been two days after she'd been killed and the day before her funeral. My father had chased after me, and he patiently tried to convince me that I'd imagined it all in my grief, but I knew I hadn't. She'd been there, watching me and Grayson on the playground that day. I knew it as surely as I knew the sky was blue.

It was the last time I'd seen her until she'd turned up with my father and Grayson, and ordered her people to shoot me.

"You've rarely been alone, Emma, and until just before the virus hit, I was near you every chance I got. I was in Europe when they released the virus and I watched as millions died and could do nothing as I tried to get back to the States, back to you. Oceans are one thing I can't navigate. It took close to a year to find a few survivors who had a bit of nautical skill and were desperate enough for the hope of a better life that they were willing to help me cross the ocean. While you were protecting your people inside the Ark, and escaping filth by jumping off that damn cliff, Jaeden tried in his own way to help you. It's why I don't hate him, because while everyone else watched you sink, he threw you a lifeline. He's not innocent either; he's aware of Shamus's plans. Shamus isn't there for the little bit of blood your people can offer, Emma; he's there to build an endless supply of it. He plans to use the few men he's allowed in to impregnate the women inside your shelter to create the next generation. Once it's begun, he'll bring in the elders and he'll become one himself. It's his endgame, it always was. It's why he commissioned your father to build the Ark."

"How do you know all of that?" I demanded; I was getting defensive, but then, I had a damn good reason to be. This Sentinel had been at my mother's funeral. He'd known the moment I'd drawn air into my lungs as I was born, what the fuck!?

"Which answer would you prefer? That I have been watching you, or because you were created for me," he answered enigmatically, his lips quirked into a wicked smile. "It is the way our kind is made. We are created to recognize one another. We are designed to see the world through each other's eyes. When you stop fighting yourself and look to the quiet place inside your soul and search your heart, you will know that what I say is true, and you will stop fighting me and a different world will be opened to you. I've given you much to think over in my absence, but I must take my leave. Sleep well, and don't do anything to anger me in my absence."

I took a deep breath, blinked, and shook off the mesmerizing words. "I don't plan on being here when you return," I said as blandly as I could. I didn't, but hey, I was being honest. It didn't matter how hot he was, didn't matter if he was supposed to be my mate; nothing mattered but getting back to my group and making sure they were alive, and then moving on to find my brother.

Chapter Sixteen

The first day he was gone I spent looking for a way to escape the prison I found myself in. The house was lavish; high ceilings gave a sense of airiness, and the walls had ancient weapons securely affixed to them along with huge portraits of battle scenes. One had a knight on a black horse, facing off against another on a brown horse. Death waited patiently, mounted on a pale horse near the fighting warriors, watching to see which of the warriors he would claim. The other paintings were of similar scenes, but in them all, Death stood in the distance, or close to the artist's eye. He was never missing from any of the scenes. Whoever the artist was, he seemed obsessed with the idealistic warrior he portrayed Death to be. In none of the artwork was Death holding the traditional scythe, or wearing black robes. Death was a warrior in all of the scenes.

The second day, I started going crazy. I'd never been one to sit still, and the virus hadn't changed that. I needed to be out there, searching for my brother. I paced in front of the glass wall, my eyes always straying to see beyond the cliffs that I faced. The promised storm hadn't arrived, and I wondered if it would as I looked upon the tranquil view.

The waterfalls were beautiful; the house was built to face them so those inside could indulge in the calm serenity they offered. I'd always been obsessed with waterfalls and the calmness they gave me. These would be loud outside the house, but the glass was probably soundproof as well as shatterproof.

The sun was setting and the moon was beginning to rise over the falls, which was a breathtaking sight. It was a full moon, which meant Lachlan and his pack wouldn't have as much control over their shifting tonight, and I wondered where they were. I wasn't sure if what mystery man said was true, and if they'd ever made it out of that horrible place of death, or if they'd died there. Not knowing what happened to them was eating me alive. I had enough to worry about with Grayson, but now I had others out there who I wasn't sure if they were alive or hurt and if they needed me.

My mind wandered to the shelter. Addy was probably going crazy without my normal check-ins. Were they doing well? Had they refilled the storage from what we'd depleted during winter? Had they been out sourcing more locations? The train cars were empty, which meant they'd need to venture into more towns nearby. That was a dangerous job; were they taking precautions, sending the immortals instead of those who could be easily killed?

I expelled a long sigh, hating that I couldn't do anything to stop my thoughts from moving back to the man who held me here against my will. His kisses made my brain turn off, and my libido replaced it. I didn't feel that need to pull away from him, and that bothered me. I missed Jaeden, but his kisses had never made me react as this man's did. Jaeden was heat, scorching me to my bones, but this guy? He undid me. His touches sent me over the edge, and his kisses? They caressed and set fire to my soul. They felt right. It scared the shit out of me. Where was my control?

It was as if we were linked, connected somehow, or something far worse. He kept saying I was created for him, but what the hell did that even mean? He was a puzzle; one I wasn't sure I wanted to play with. He held knowledge that I needed, though.

The Sentinel had told me that he would teach me how to use and control my powers. He knew about my brother, but seemed dismissive about him, so I wondered if he would actually help me find my brother if I asked. I didn't know this guy, and so far, trusting other people hadn't worked out too well, and the only one I could count on was myself. That left me with only one remaining option that was logical, so, as I sat idle inside the house all day, I started formulating a plan.

I would seduce him. I could gain his trust and I could get away from him in the process. He wasn't planning on just letting me go, and desperate times often called for desperate measures. My father had once told me that being a girl would be both good and bad during an apocalypse. To always use my brains, and learn the enemy. If I couldn't outwit him, seduce him. Lull my captor into thinking I was with him willingly, and then once I had his trust, run the fuck away. I'd told my dad that I couldn't do that. I wasn't built that way. Pain sliced through me at the memory and I shook it off. I hadn't known what he'd meant back then, but I did now. You did what you had to in order to survive, no matter what.

I could do it. It couldn't be too hard, right? I shook my head, and returned to the bedroom and dug through the drawers until I found a shirt, and a comfortable pair of pajama pants. I slipped the shirt on, struggling to figure out the straps, then giving up on it, only to pick out another that was the exact same style.

I held it up, wondering how the heck it went on, and then fought with it for a moment more before I got it to where it seemed like it should fit. I pulled on the soft lounge pants and made my way back to the kitchen.

I cut up a few different types of cheeses and meats and added a sleeve of crackers, grabbed a bottle of wine and a glass, and headed towards the couch. A few trips more, and I had quite the spread set up. I eyed the TV, then the cameras around the room. I saluted one of the cameras with my glass of wine and took a long sip, popped a few pieces of meat into my mouth and moaned around the succulent juice that seemed to explode in my mouth. The food here was definitely a plus.

I poured more wine, trying to remember the last time that I'd indulged like this. Memories of the day I'd sat with Addy watching the news replayed through my mind. It was a day I thought I'd never forget, and I'd been right. It had changed everything. While so much had changed since then, it had been one of the times that I immediately remembered when I thought of us being together.

I stood and swayed on my feet as I made my way towards the entertainment stand, sinking to my knees as I adjusted the shirt that had moved to reveal my nipples. The traitorous bastard wouldn't stay on right. I adjusted it, pulling it back over my breasts. I reached into the DVD section, pulling out a few old movies and smiling as I ran my finger over the first Harry Potter movie.

It had always been one of my favorite books, and the movies were pretty damn amazing, if not perfectly matching the books. I turned on the flat panel television and pulled the DVD carefully from the package as I fumbled with the buttons. I pushed it in without paying attention and picked up the remote as I moved back to the couch.

The TV turned on with static, and I smiled. Unlike the Ark, he was pushing enough watts to be able to use a TV with a DVD/Blu-ray player. He probably had an Xbox One somewhere inside this place too. Grayson would have been in heaven here.

I pushed 'play' on the Blu-ray player, poured more wine, and sat back, waiting for the movie to start. I'd just shoved a tower of meat, cheese, and crackers into my mouth when moaning erupted from the surround sound. I coughed violently and almost choked to death.

My first thought was to run to the TV and turn the thing off. Although I'd like to say I did, curiosity won out, and I didn't. I tilted my head as a woman dropped her knees open as a man slowly licked her flesh. I swallowed hard. The food in my mouth felt dry, hard to swallow as my eyes followed that tongue as it lavished the woman who was moaning overly loud.

I picked up the wine and sipped it, returned it to the coffee table and looked around the room. None of the cameras were trained on the television, which was a relief. I turned back to the couple, watching as her own fingers played with her nipples as he licked her. The man stood up, positioned her leg over his shoulder, and pushed a seriously too big dick into her. It was pretty obvious why he'd been chosen for his role. He wasn't good-looking, but damn, he needed a concealed weapons permit for that thing!

My head tilted, a soft moan left my own lips as he started to move. Yeah, I was excited. I was so engrossed in what they were doing that I didn't notice anything else.

It wasn't until I felt the sensation of being watched, prickling the hair on my nape, that I turned to my left, and found the Sentinel watching me. My shirt had slipped again, and his eyes were on my very hard nipples, which were exposed. I tried to think of an explanation, but nothing plausible seemed to explain the situation. Heat fused my cheeks as a blush spread across them. I sat there, frozen as his eyes scorched my flesh as they slowly moved over it.

Yeah, so that happened.

He found me with my top askew, breasts exposed, head tilted, watching porn. My mouth was doing a wonderful 'fish out of water' impression, and I had nothing. I couldn't very well say that it wasn't what it looked like, because it was exactly what it looked like. He swallowed hard, his Adam's apple bobbing as his eyes slowly caressed their way up my body and finally focused on mine.

He'd said days, hadn't he? It hadn't been days.

I unlocked my gaze from his, leaned over, grabbed the wine, and drank deeply. Hadn't I been planning to seduce him anyway? I had been. Might as well make the most out of this disaster, right?

"Wine?" I choked out hoarsely. My voice came out throaty, more seductive than I'd planned for it to. He didn't speak, but he sat on the couch next to me, closer than I'd thought he would, and his leg brushed against mine. It was enough to make the nerves in my body strain, and the butterflies took flight. I leaned over again, feeling the weight of his stare as I poured him a glass of wine. I leaned back and extended my hand to offer the wine to him. He took it, and our fingers brushed against each other, sending sparks through my system.

The couple on the screen was reaching the climax of the scene and the room was filled with the sounds of her screams and moans, mixed with the sound of flesh hitting flesh.

I was watching porn with my abductor…so, yeah, that happened too…

"Emma," he started, as I chewed my lip, and after a brief hesitation, I turned to look at him.

"I still don't know your name," I blurted out, and he paused, narrowing his eyes at me before he turned back to the movie and polished off his glass, then held it out for more. I leaned over without thinking, and my top gave way, exposing my breast once again. His eyes left the screen, locked onto my puckered nipple, and he swallowed so hard it was audible. "It was supposed to be Harry Potter," I blurted again. "The top won't stay on."

"It's on backwards," he rasped, and I blushed. "The shirt, it's on backwards."

"Of course it is," I whispered.

"Take it off," he murmured, and my eyes locked with his.

"What?" I squeaked. That sealed it. I was the worst seductress in the history of all mankind.

"I'll show you how it is supposed to go on if you take it off," he replied.

Oh boy.

I slowly lifted the top and sat there, trembling as a new couple started up on the screen. I turned to my abductor and wasn't prepared for the heat in his gaze, or the fire that ignited as he pushed me flat on the sofa, spilling the wine I held onto the floor. I swallowed, noticing his chest was magnificent. He watched me, his eyes slowly roaming over my flesh. His fingers touched me, and I closed my eyes.

I could do this. It was my plan, right? Seduce him, get into his good graces, get him to lower his guard, and I'd be gone before he even realized it. I opened my eyes as I felt the tremble of his fingers as he slowly ran the tips over the globes of my breasts.

"So fucking soft," he murmured, his mouth lowering until it hovered over the heated tip, and his tongue darted out, tasting my nipple. I groaned as pleasure swept through me, as blisteringly hot as molten lava. He sucked one tip between his teeth, nipping at one then the other. His hands trembled as they continued to trace soft circles upon my naked flesh. I was so absorbed by his mouth and the effect it was having on me, that I hadn't even realized his other hand had dipped into the lounge pants I wore.

His fingers found my wet flesh and stroked it slowly, leisurely. I arched my back, spreading my legs for his smoldering touch. His finger pushed inside me, and I cried out; his mouth captured mine, smothering the cries that continued even after his tongue found mine.

It wasn't like the lightning of Jaeden's touch, it was

so much more. I felt him to my soul. As if he held the key to it, and was slowly opening it to test its depths. His kiss was gentle, and yet there was an urgency to it that drove me wild. Like if he didn't continue, he'd wither and die. My lungs burned, and I didn't care. Another finger pushed inside and I felt myself teetering on the edge of a cliff. His thumb rubbed against my clitoris, and when his mouth pulled away, his eyes locked with mine as he turned his head to get a better view of my messed-up hair, my heavy-lidded stare.

He moved his free hand and cupped my face as his thumb trailed over the edge of my bottom lip. He only did it for a moment before he yanked the lounge pants off, as if they were made of some cheap, flimsy fabric, revealing the silk panties I wore. His head lowered until his mouth was close to my stomach, his tongue slowly darting out to taste my skin before he reached his hand out and brought his wine glass over to dribble just enough into my navel to lick it out.

I shivered as a million sensations hit me at once. My legs were parted as his fingers continued to work my pussy over until I danced on the edge of climax, and he held me prisoner there. The coolness of the wine on my heated flesh sent tiny bumps racing over my skin as he continued to kiss his way down my body until his hot breath fanned my wetness.

Was I really going to go through with this? Oh boy…

His fingers left my heat and his tongue licked it from one side to the other in a slow, torturous move that pulled a moan from deep inside of me. He continued doing it until my head thrashed against the couch, moving from side to side as my nails dug into his hair, holding him where I needed him. He laughed against my flesh and I pleaded for him to end the pain, to end the heat that threatened to consume me.

"You enjoy my touch," he said as he captured my hands and shoved them down onto my stomach. "Gods, you taste like heaven, Emma," he whispered as he rained kisses down over my needy flesh.

This was insane! I didn't even know his fucking name. Not that it mattered; I didn't need to know it to escape from him. I felt his fingers push back inside of me and I tried to recall who I was with, but it didn't help. Bodies don't care about things like names, or if it's wrong. That's the brain's job. But mine wasn't functioning. It was misfiring, not computing facts. His mouth sucked on my clit and I cried out, saying things that didn't make sense. I didn't care. I was so close that my body was trembling, shaking with the need for release, to the point that it actually hurt.

"Please," I whispered, begging him to send me over the edge. He pulled up, started moving, and I paused, as I foggily realized where I was and who I was with. "I can't do this, not yet," I mumbled as I slowly pulled up my panties and my eyes slowly drifted down his chest to where his bulge strained against the loose jeans he wore. They hung just below his hips, exposing a dark patch of hair that led into Blissville. "Can we talk?" I felt a trickle of sweat as it beaded at the base of my neck and slowly meandered down my back.

"He is in your mind, is he not?" he asked, his head tilted to the side, and those tranquil blue eyes burned my soul, as if they could see past what I wanted him to see, straight into the part I didn't want him to know of me.

"*He's* not here," I pointed out. "It's just you and me, but I don't even know what to call you."

"Names don't matter," he growled, and his hand lifted, his fingers pinching my nipple and pulling on the delicate flesh. I whimpered, and my head rolled back as he continued to apply pressure until it danced between pain and pleasure and lingered on total bliss. "You fucked him on a dirty floor of a cabin and yet you won't accept me?" he snapped, and I knew he wasn't pleased with me stopping him. "You're mine, what else matters?"

"Names might not matter to you, but they do to me. Jaeden has nothing to do with this. I'm not here willingly; you say you know me, you've watched me, so you do know that I just don't fall into bed with anyone. You may know me, but I know nothing about you. That's why I stopped this!" I argued.

"You want to talk, let's talk," he growled as he roughly pulled the shirt around my head and shoulders, crossing what I had thought were the shoulder straps over my head, and crisscrossing them as he tugged the shirt in place to where it opened to reveal my navel. I'd been way off on the shirt; what I had thought were the sides were the front and back. I wasn't into fashion, and shirts that took an effort to guess how they fit hadn't ever been in my father's or my price range. "Ask the questions burning your tongue, little phoenix," he demanded.

"I don't know where to start," I admitted.

"Did you like being his whore?" His tone was sharp enough to wound as he ran his fingers through his hair. I raised my hand, intending to slap his beautiful face, but he caught it effortlessly and twisted it. "It's a valid question. You followed him around like one of his blood whores. You may not have provided blood, but you gave him something much more precious."

"I'm not a whore," I growled back, not bothering to show him the pain he was causing with his twisting of my arm. "I was never his whore. I didn't sleep with Jaeden because I had to; I did it because I wanted him."

"He's your enemy, our enemy, and yet you continued to part that sweet flesh and let him use you. Doesn't it bother you that he uses you to his own end?"

"He didn't use me," I argued. "The last time we were together, *I* used him."

"On a dirty floor," he added.

"I didn't care what or where the floor was," I whispered guiltily. "I just wanted to forget what I had done."

"I felt it," he rasped, his voice raw; his eyes were cold and emotionless.

"What?" I asked, thinking I'd heard him wrong, or misunderstood.

"I felt the moment you climaxed around his cock, Emma. I watched you together through your eyes," he snapped coldly. "Like a nightmare unfolding in vivid color."

"I don't believe you," I mumbled. He had made mention of nightmares of Jaeden and I together, and he had arrived at the house and tried to kill Jaeden, like he was having some sort of jealous fit, but how was this possible?

"I feel you just like you feel me. When I'm near, your heart lets you know. Mine does the same," he replied softly. "Imagine what it would feel like for you if I found release with someone else, Emma. It's ugly, that much I assure you. The pain of it when we are near one another is excruciating. At least when you were in Newport, the distance allowed me to only see you with him through the connection we share, but the last time? I wasn't so lucky."

"Nothing," I snapped. "I would feel fucking nothing. Whatever you think is between us? It's not. If you think you have some sick connection to me? Sever it," I hissed. "I don't want it or you."

I stood to leave, but he pushed me down hard. My teeth rattled and he loomed over me. Towering over me where I was seated on the couch.

"The only way to sever it is for one of us to die, and neither of us can be killed easily," he growled, his eyes glowing a crimson red color. "Go to bed before I do something we both regret."

~~*

I bathed, washing his scent from my body, and yet his touch was seared into my flesh. His scent lingered on my skin, and it was making it hard to sleep. Eventually, my brain turned off and sleep took hold. It didn't last long, though. Dreams of his heated kisses and feather-soft fingertips took control.

In the dream, his words played on repeat. How he'd felt it, and then it got really weird. Instead of me and Jaeden alone in the cabin, it was me, Jaeden, and my abductor. They were kissing me, touching my flesh until I was crazed from it. One moved behind me while the other slid his pants down and pushed me to my knees. I took him inside my mouth, which one, I wasn't sure. Both were doing unspeakable things to my senses. A cock pushed deeper into my mouth, almost touching my throat as the other entered me from behind. I cried out around the one in my mouth as I felt the other growing inside of me until pain ripped through me.

I cried and begged around the cock in my mouth for

him to release me, but merciless hands held my head firmly where it was, while laughter filled the cabin and tears blinded me. I shook my head, but the dick in my mouth was growing as well, and I was trapped. Impaled from both, the pain was never ending, and it was tearing me apart while they laughed, enjoying my blood and pain.

Heat burned me; my body ached, arched, and a moan slipped from my lips as I opened my eyes, pulling out of the nightmare. I kicked off the blankets, fighting past the remnants of the dream. I didn't feel as if I was out of it. I kicked the blankets off the bed, too sensitive to be covered or touched by anything. I sat up, ripping at the thin nightgown I wore until it was in tatters on the floor. I lay back, struggling to bring my body back under control. My breathing was labored, causing me to become lightheaded as I smoothed my hands down over my curves, trying to figure out what was wrong with me. I felt like I was in the throes of passion. My pussy was soaking wet; I could feel it as my arousal wet the skin between my legs. My nipples were hard as rocks, and my body was thrashing against the sheets.

Panic engulfed me as my eyes searched the room frantically. What the fuck was happening to me? My body wasn't my own, I didn't have control. It hurt. The ache in my belly was excruciating, but the one between my legs felt like my nightmare. It felt like I was being ripped apart. I could feel the painful arousal as it threatened to rip through me. I was crying, moaning, and screaming, and then it let loose. It tore through me and my limbs went stiff, my body gyrated and trembled as pain pushed through the pleasure, and I almost passed out. It wasn't an orgasm, no; it was a sharp ache between my legs, as if I'd been denied the real thing. A sob escaped my lips as sweat covered my entire body. I rolled into a ball on my side and cried, and then it hit me, what he'd said.

He'd *felt* it. I was smart enough to put it together. He'd just fucked someone, making sure I knew exactly what he'd felt. But how? This was insane. No one could feel another person having sex, no one!

The ache between my thighs was brutal; the sick feeling in the pit of my stomach was growing still, long after the pain abated. I rolled over, spent from the nightmare and whatever had just happened to me. I fumbled to my knees, trying to get up from the bed, but it was useless. I felt as if I'd been beaten up, and violated in the process. I was in the middle of moving to the edge of the bed so I could make it to the bathroom and wash the nightmare off of me, when the door opened, and he leaned against it, looking at me with a knowing smirk. His feet and chest were bare; his hair was messy. He shoved his hands into the pockets of the jeans he wore and watched me as I struggled to pull myself together.

"Now you know how it feels for me when you are with him," he whispered as his eyes moved over my sweat-covered body.

"Get out," I whispered back weakly. What the fuck was that? How the hell had I felt him with someone else? I felt everything. I had felt his excitement during the beginning of it, and the buildup as he'd headed towards the finish line. That was where it ended, though. There'd been no pleasure past that point, only horrifying pain. He'd done this on purpose, because he'd wanted me to feel what he had. He'd taken another to his bed just to prove his point. Asshole. I hated him.

Chapter SEVENTEEN

The next morning, I sat on the couch in a pair of lounge pants with a snug black tank top covering my body. I felt horrible; so horrible that I hadn't eaten a thing since last night. I was lost in my head, and riddled with guilt at what I'd allowed to happen without even knowing his name. I'd planned on seduction, but that wasn't what had happened. He'd taken control and I'd allowed it. He'd been in full control of me while I'd been mesmerized by his touch.

Then the nightmare had played out. I'd enjoyed having both of them inside of me. I'd never considered a ménage until that dream. I wasn't the girl who'd ever entertained that type of situation; it was too far out of my comfort zone, which was why I'd never thought about it. Sure, Addy had filled me in on her adventures; I'd called her dirty names and then we'd both laughed. But I wasn't Addy. I felt everything too deeply to ever consider doing something like that.

I wasn't sure what the hell I was doing anymore. Everything was upside down, and I was losing control. I did feel guilty about moving on, but I had ended it with Jaeden. What had happened between us when I'd left the group had been the final straw between us... it had left me broken; I'd severed the proverbial limb. The only way to deal with an infection is to cut it out. It didn't mean I didn't love him, because I did. It just wasn't the same type of love anymore.

Whatever had been happening to us had forced us to drift apart, and while I wasn't fully to blame, I knew that I hadn't helped the situation, either. Jaeden was a soldier, he followed orders. I'd known that from the beginning, and I hadn't expected him to change. Of course, I hadn't expected to fall in love with him, either. I hadn't expected him to stick around. Life was short these days, and tomorrow wasn't even remotely predictable anymore.

I'd done my best to live by the rules of the old world, but the more I tried, the more I figured out how impossible it was. I wanted to protect those in the Ark, and I still did, but we had changed a lot of the ways my father had done things, because we'd evolved. Jaeden and I weren't any different. I evolved into something else, a Sentinel. He was still a warrior, controlled by his elders. He'd changed, though, to be more of what I needed him to be, but only to a point. Unfortunately, I needed more than he was able to give.

I lifted my eyes as I watched my abductor, who I had decided could keep the moniker of 'Asshole' after last night, as he walked into the kitchen and pulled a carafe of orange juice out of the refrigerator. He ran his hand through his hair as he poured it into a juice glass, keeping his back to me in the process. I considered leaving, but I wasn't weak. I'd known what I was doing last night. I'd mentally prepared myself for what I was going to do, and even if the role had been modified, I needed to remain firm and true to the plan.

He turned, rested his arms on the counter and looked me dead in the eye. We stared at each other; the Sentinel, like he was about ready to kick me out, which hell, fine with me. I, however, was shooting daggers his way. He'd hurt me, bad. He'd been making a point, but I was pretty sure there were other ways of getting his point across.

He downed the orange juice in a single swallow and moved into the room I was in, walking past the steel door which abruptly swung open, surprising us both. A man burst into the room, looked at me, then at the Sentinel.

"Azrael, we have incoming," the man said breathlessly as he held out a picture that showed trucks moving down a road. "Twenty minutes tops and they'll be at the door," he explained.

"Lock it down." Azrael looked at me with warning in his eyes. "Stay with him and do not fucking try anything," he growled, pointing to the man as he strolled in the direction of the front door. I moved swiftly, heading with him to the door. He stopped so abruptly that I ran into his back. "Don't do this," he warned.

"I can help," I offered, even though I had no intention of doing so. He'd be busy with whoever was out there, and I could run in the opposite direction.

"Indeed," he mused, looking over my head. "If Emma tries to escape, shoot her. In the head," he ordered.

"I hate you," I muttered as my anger spiked. Shoot me in the head? Asshole.

"Azrael?" the man questioned.

"It's a direct order; if she tries anything, shoot her. She'll live through it."

And just like that, he was gone.

I watched the door close and turned to the man, extending my hand, but he jumped back and looked at it like I was poisonous.

"I'm Emma," I said as I brought my hand back, and watched as he relaxed. "Who are those people, the ones headed here?"

"John, and those guys are probably some assholes who want to take the house and bunker for their own," he replied. "I need to lock it down and I really don't want to shoot you, so please, ma'am, don't try to escape."

"I'm not going to," I answered as I shook my head with annoyance. "I've already searched for a way out, but the only one I know of so far is through that door, which is on lockdown, so tell me how to help you."

I didn't want to be stuck here, but I also knew how bad people in large groups could be. I had no delusions that it was my group coming to save me. They wouldn't be so bold as to come by road in trucks; those had been abandoned long ago. No, my group would sneak up and Azrael's would never see them coming.

"I need to lock it down into panic mode," he said, and I tilted my head.

"What about Azrael, out there, alone? What if he gets hurt?" I questioned.

"Ma'am, he don't get hurt." His English sounded like he was from the backwoods. "He's immortal, a God. He's the best warrior I ever did see. He saved us all," he whispered, with blind faith in his eyes.

"He's not a God," I stated as my eyebrow rose with my skepticism, and wondered what the fuck he was giving these guys to drink. I started to move, but rapid gunfire outside the house drew my attention. So much for them being soundproof windows. We both moved towards the window. John's math sucked; they'd made it here long before his twenty-minute timer was up.

Azrael was in full body armor, his swords drawn, and his armor was deflecting a barrage of bullets. They ricocheted off his armor, hitting the windowed walls, and bounced as well. I flinched when one hit the glass right where I was standing. John stood awkwardly, like he wasn't sure if he wanted to scream, cry, or run back to the bunker. I was betting he was about to do all three.

"Where's the panic button for the bunker?" I asked, but he shook his head as a tank pulled up in the yard.

"They'll get in…if they get in they're going to kill us all!" he cried, turned, and ran back to the bunker as I screamed for him to stop.

"Shit!" I growled as I ran to the panel leading to the bunker and started pushing buttons. Nothing happened, and the sound of the tank as it moved into position made my stomach roll. A fucking tank, seriously? How the hell had they found this place? My eyes swept the room for a panic button or panel that I may have missed before. Last time I'd cut wires on the panel to the front door, which I wasn't sure I should do this time. I turned and looked at Azrael, who was a blur, zigzagging between trees and trucks, his inhuman speed helping as he killed those closest to the house.

I made my way to the glass and started pounding on it. If he died, I'd be stuck in here until someone from the bunker below could let me out. If that tank hit the glass, yeah, I could escape, but I wasn't going to leave his people to die either. He turned mid-slice and looked at me, then his eyes seemed to sweep the glass walls that separated him and our attackers from the room I stood in. He moved so fast my eyes could barely follow him, as he stopped short in front of the window and peered in, shielding his eyes to look for John.

"He's gone!" I shouted, pointing at the bunker door.

"Where's the panic button?" I asked, and then screamed as a man in tactical armor raced towards him. My heart leapt to my throat and I watched as a sword pushed through the armor Azrael wore, hitting the glass.

Fuck! I blanched as he turned, sword still sticking out from his side, and ran the man through with his own blades as if the man was nothing more than an annoyance. He pulled the offending sword out and dropped it to the ground without even stopping or flinching. He turned, pointed at a wall, and I turned my head, located the button and rushed towards it. The long barrel of the tank swiveled as it zeroed in on its target; that much we both could see, and if they shot it…we'd all be in a really bad place. Judging by the way the bodies were falling, Azrael was working his way through the remaining men to get to the tank, and, seeing that it hadn't fired yet, they must not have used it very often and they were probably trying to figure out all the controls.

I slammed my hand down on the button and watched as the red lights began blinking and sirens began blaring as the door to the bunker locked down. Azrael's eyes met mine, and he nodded with a jerk of his chin as he jumped to the top of the tank and ripped the hatch off. Men scattered, dispersing into the woods as he took control of the tank. It was all I saw before the metal shutters for the windows closed, and the only lights inside the house were flashing red ones.

I sat on the couch and pulled my legs up, wondering if those people could find this location, why hadn't Jaeden and Lachlan? Lachlan could track scents, and

Jaeden was a tracker. They didn't come, though, and it had been days. It made me wonder if they hadn't escaped, and by choosing to try and free Jaeden, if I'd condemned Lachlan to the same fate.

I rested my head on the couch and must have dozed off, because I awoke to the sensation of being carried. When I opened my eyes, it was to find Azrael carrying me down the hallway leading to the bedrooms. I wrapped my hands around his neck, noting the way he stiffened when I did it.

"Are they gone?" I asked, enjoying the heat his body offered.

"They're dead," he replied. "None escaped to tell anyone else where this place is."

It was cold, but I understood it. I would have done the same if a bunch of people had arrived at the Ark with the intention of invading or trying to take over, or hurt those in my care. The world was a scary place right now, and only those who were strong enough to make the hard choices would survive in it. That hadn't been an easy lesson to learn.

"You don't approve?" he asked as he sat on the bed, cradling me in his lap. His arms tightened, and I wondered about it. He had people here, but I hadn't seen him without his armor around them. Only with me did he remove it.

"I hate that this world is so cold that you have to do what you did to ensure the safety of those you protect,"

I replied softly as I shifted my position on his lap. He winced, and my mind rushed back to the fact that he'd been stabbed. "You're hurt." I struggled to get off his lap. I moved into the bathroom and returned with a cloth and a small bucket filled with warm water. "Take it off."

"It's already healing on its own," he mumbled as he watched me warily.

"Let me help you. You need to make sure that it doesn't become infected," I replied, not caring if he wanted help or not. I watched as he stared at me, but I wasn't backing down. After a moment he removed his shirt and laid back.

I ran my fingers over the torn flesh, noting that his skin was indeed healing. There were little flecks of silver around the wound, so I dipped the cloth into the water and wrung it out before I gently slid it over the wound. He tensed as the cloth cleaned the wound, but he made no sound as I washed away the debris. My fingertips touched his flesh, and he closed his eyes; before I knew what I was doing, I'd bent over and kissed the seductive V of his hips.

He sat up so fast that I ended up half in his lap, half on the floor as he caught me when I tried to back up. He pulled me onto his lap, and my heartrate shot up, and my eyes widened as I cried out in surprise, but he didn't kiss me. He just held me there, his forehead dropped against mine and we sat there, motionless together.

"You play with fire, woman," he whispered after a

few moments had passed in silence. His forehead lifted and he kissed the side of my throat as I held onto the curve of his neck. I swallowed a moan, but the sound of it vibrated through me. His lips found mine and instead of pulling away, I kissed him first. He rolled us onto the bed, with me beneath him, and kissed me gently. My legs wrapped around his waist and I gave in to temptation for a few moments. The tense situation had made it harder to resist him. I needed a few moments to know that I wasn't alone. It was a weakness, but it was one I'd own up to. He pulled away from me and looked down with a soft smile.

"Maybe I should get stabbed more often if it leads to this," he teased, and I smiled. I giggled nervously, and his eyes watched me as the slow trickle of a tear slipped from my eye. "You were afraid for me today?"

"A little, but more so for the humans," I admitted. "I didn't know how to send the bunker into lockdown, you left that part out of your briefing; that asshole John freaked out and lost his shit when he saw the tank and ran back into the bunker without locking it down first."

He leaned down and kissed me again until my toes curled. He rolled off of me, and lay on his back on the bed beside me. "You did well today, Emma. You could have caused problems, but you chose to help us. Thank you for that," he said softly. "They each have a purpose."

"They?" I asked.

"Everyone inside the bunkers," he explained.

"They're engineers, farmers, gunsmiths, soldiers, medical professionals. I handpicked them, brought them here with their families, and protect them. They follow the rules; they get to live. We even found some leather crafters, blacksmiths, and electricians."

I sat up and looked down at him. "You're planning to rebuild?" There was a master list my father had; most of those occupations had been included in who he was looking for to rebuild and get the grid back up and running in Newport. It was the ideal location. It had its own dam; the grid was small because the town itself was small. "You built an Ark, but instead of animals, you collected people who were needed to rebuild the grid and make a functional society."

He smiled. "You're quick, Emma. Not many could do the math and find that equation so quickly. To answer the question, yes, I'm collecting people who are needed to rebuild cities."

"And you said bunkers. As in plural," I whispered.

His grin faltered but his eyes continued to smile. "Did I? I don't recall," he mumbled as his eyes closed and I lay back down beside him.

"If you rebuild a town, people will try to take it by force," I mused. "Like they tried to do to this place," I continued as I snuggled into his warmth and he wrapped his arms around me. "It's the light. They must have seen it from far away, didn't they?" He nodded, but his eyes remained closed. "It would be a beacon, but they made it here with a tank. So somewhere close is a main road." His eyes opened and turned cold. "We're in a valley, so they must have seen it from above. They found the road and followed it here," I swallowed.

So why hadn't Jaeden and Lachlan done the same? I swallowed harder; my eyes burned as I turned on my side, facing away from him as I put all the pieces together. They weren't coming for me. Either they'd been slaughtered, or they'd left me to my fate.

Chapter Eighteen

I woke up cradled in his arms. His scent filled my senses. I breathed it in and nestled my head against his chest. I went back to sleep, feeling protected, and for once, I didn't feel as if the weight of the world clung to my shoulders. I'd never felt this with Jaeden, but then again his priorities had never been mine. Yeah, I'd felt protected for the most part, but I hadn't felt as if I could allow my guard to drop around him. My relationship with Jaeden had been turbulent and rough, even the sex. It had been hot, to the point of burning my flesh, but he'd never allowed me to believe that I was more important than his orders.

I felt Azrael move and I lifted my head to look at him, trying for my best glare since I had no intention of cuddling. I'd enjoyed it, but that was beside the point.

"Morning, beautiful," he murmured huskily.

"Morning." My reply sounded shorter and crankier

than I expected it to, as I started to sit up. There are a lot of things I'm ready for in the morning. Things like coffee, reports, headcounts, and daily chore lists. Finding myself rolled beneath a hot as fuck man wasn't one of them. Neither was the fact that his dick was hard, and pressed against me exactly where I needed and wanted it buried. "Azrael," I whispered. His head lifted, as he stared at me intensely.

"Say it again," he swallowed.

"Say what?" I asked, and then it dawned on me. "Azrael?"

He closed his eyes, lowered his lips to the hollow of my neck, and kissed it softly. His fingers lifted my shirt and the rough tips skimmed across my flesh. I moaned, which only encouraged him as he continued his slow seduction. My hands found his wide shoulders, and I held him to me; I wanted more, needed it, even. I needed him like I needed air in my lungs. His hand slipped into my lounge pants, and I moaned as his lips found mine, taking the noise inside his hungry mouth. He touched my pussy, and found it wet and ready for him.

He nudged my legs apart, and pushed a finger deep into the heated depths. Another filled me and I lifted my hips as his mouth took control of mine, plunging his tongue in to take control of that, along with the control he was taking of my body. Sweat beaded at the base of my spine as the orgasm threatened to send me cascading over a cliff. The moment I thought I was about to fall over, he stopped; his breathing was as labored as my own.

"Tell me to go," he whispered as he withdrew his hand and held his body above mine. "Tell me you don't want this thing that's between us, and to leave your bed."

I didn't want to. I wanted to pull him closer and investigate whatever this thing between us was. I wanted him to take me over the cliff, and hold me while I fell into the depths below. I wanted the painful ache he created to go away, to be replaced with the sated feeling you got after vigorous, rough sex.

"Go," I whispered reluctantly, and he rolled from the bed as I bit my lip to keep from calling him back. His back was muscled, his obliques defined; the thick cords of muscle in his sides were exposed from where his pants rode low on his hips, and I wanted to explore them with my fingers and tongue. I was thankful he'd stopped, because I wasn't sure if I would have, but it physically hurt to watch him leave the room.

Once he was out of sight, I let the air expel from my lungs as I sat up and I punched the pillows in frustration. I sucked at seduction. That much was clear to me. The idea of allowing him to go all the way with me sat like a rock in my stomach. I waited a while before even attempting to move from the bed. One stroke and I'd go over that cliff he'd left me teetering on.

I stood up, stretched a bit, and listened as people milled around the front of the house. It didn't sound like there was any happy chatter, but then again, after what happened yesterday, I was sure there were a few bodies to be burned, not to mention a wrecked tank that probably needed to be relocated. Oddly enough, I didn't feel bad about the men who'd attacked us and lost their lives. I dressed in soft jeans and a cashmere baby blue pullover.

After wrapping my hair into a ponytail, I made my way into the main living area just in time to see Azrael as he stepped closer to John. It was the first time I had seen him around others without armor as he spoke loudly, emphasizing John's abandonment of his post. I understood it; John had run like a bitch to the safety of the bunker. If the house had fallen to the men outside, he would have been to blame for those assholes getting into the bunker. I stood silently, watching it play out and secretly admiring how Azrael looked in a black Henley with the sleeves pushed up, and a pair of jeans that hung low on his hips.

John was shaking his head, swinging his arms in wild movements as he protested and tried to defend his actions. I almost snorted at one point, as he'd almost made it sound as if I'd told him to go. The fact that he thought I was a Goddess to Azrael's supposed Godhood almost made me snicker.

John turned to Azrael, and grabbed Azrael's forearm, as if to drive his point home, but cried out as everyone else took a big step backwards. A collective gasp spread across the group. John screamed as he hugged himself around his waist and coughed violently. My heart sped up, and nausea rose to the back of my throat as what was happening played out.

I watched from the hallway as John gasped, spit blood, and screamed as if he was being torn apart from the inside out. I screamed a warning as black spider veins webbed over his face. Every pair of eyes in the room—other than John's, whose eyes seeped blood—looked at me. I stepped back, turned, and ran back to the bedroom, because what the fuck!

I started piling furniture against the door. I heard a knock and pushed the couch against the door, then the vanity, and then, of course, the wall art, because every pound counted. I saw Azrael rip the hatch of a tank off yesterday like it was a cap of a soda bottle; how much easier would it be for him to get through my pathetic barricade? I paced the room; my mind raced and yet John continued to scream in pain. The sound echoed through the house. They were all watching him die! What sick fucking freak reality had I just entered into? I felt like I was in an episode of the Twilight Zone.

I hadn't waited around to see what happened, because hello, a motherfucking virus wiped out most of the world. Were they out of their ever-loving minds? They weren't afraid? They didn't seem to be afraid.

"Emma," Azrael called from the other side of the door.

Even though his tone was calm, I jumped, turned towards the door, and felt my stomach flip. John had touched him, and then John had spewed blood, everywhere! He'd touched Azrael and started to die! You couldn't do that in reality, and yet, *he* had! Did he knowingly allow John to touch him, knowing he'd die? No. It had moved faster than any disease I'd ever seen, and we'd seen a lot of it while watching the cameras my father installed. We'd watched the CDC bring people in, and days later they were dead. They carried them out and burned them near another set of cameras that had been installed just outside of Newport.

Days. Not minutes. John had gone silent, which my guess was that his silence meant he'd died. He'd gone from healthy to the end stage of the virus in less than five minutes.

The door knob turned and I watched it, biting my nails as I tried to do the math for what the fuck had just happened. Many of the inhabitants of the bunker had been crowded in a circle around Azrael and John, watching silently as he'd writhed in agony and died. Sick as fuck motherfuckers.

Who willingly watched another human die, and didn't even try to help him? Better question, how the fuck had Azrael done it? The door moved and I continued pacing, ignoring it. I was trapped. Sure, I could hide in the bathroom, but he'd probably only knock down that door too, like some sort of sexy Hulk. Pictures fell, crashed to the floor and shattered. I heard him cussing, but just laughed nervously. I had just turned towards the door when he shouldered it, and everything crashed in front of me. I turned on my heel, ignoring him as I resumed pacing.

"Emma, look at me," he demanded, but I ignored him. My brain wasn't processing what my eyes had told me. That was probably because it was impossible, and yet, according to my eyes, it had happened. "Emma!" he snapped and grabbed my arm but I screamed and pulled it away from him. He recoiled as if I'd hit him.

I calmed my breathing and shook my head. "Not fucking possible," I whispered. "It's just not. It can't be, right?" I chewed my lip until I tasted blood. I was trembling, freezing. I felt as if I was going into shock. "You can't just touch someone and kill them."

"Emma, sit down," he urged, and I pulled away from him, yet again.

"Don't touch me," I cried, and backed up against the wall. I'd seen some strange shit since the virus started and spread, but this? This was among the few things that my brain wouldn't compute. It was listed right under finding a half-eaten woman in a tent. At least then my anger had worked, and I'd fixed it. Finding healthy people killed or slaughtered, I'd dealt with that too, but this? How the hell was I supposed to accept it?

"When they arrive at the bunker, the first thing they are told is not to touch me. Ever," he said, his voice soft and full of regret as he sat on the bed. "The armor isn't necessarily to protect me; it's to protect them."

"What the hell are you talking about?"

"Emma, sit down for a minute," he ordered, and I crossed my arms, looked at him with a chilling glare that dared him to try and demand anything from me. "Anyone I touch dies."

My stomach flipped, my heart raced and I shook my head. Impossible. He'd touched…no one since I'd met him, no one but me. I shook my head.

"Impossible; you touch me, a lot."

"Yes," he nodded slightly, his elbows resting on his knees as he leaned over, watching me. "I can touch you." A thought struck me as if it were lightning.

"So when you said you kissed me because you wanted to see if I survived…" I stammered out, a note of horror in my voice.

"I had to be sure it was still true, Emma," he said softly. "That you were the one promised to me so long ago."

"Bullshit," I snapped.

"The fact that I can touch only you should tell you that you belong to me," he growled as he stood up and moved towards me. I backed up until I was against the wall, but the moment he moved to cage me in, I spun and worked my way away from him. "Fine, sit in here and stew, Emma. I have to dispose of what is left of John. When I return, we will finish this. I have to leave tonight, and I'll not do so until I know that you are aware of what I am."

"You're Death, so go, fly free fucker," I snapped. "I'll be here like a caged fucking pet when you get back. Lord knows you can't keep me here without locking the doors."

He stiffened, turned cold eyes on me and paused, expelled a shaky breath and shook his head. "If I let you go, they'd catch you. They'd torture you, and in the end, you'd do whatever she wanted you to; you're not strong enough to fight her control."

"Who?" I asked.

He smiled grimly, bowed, and left the room.

Chapter Nineteen

My words had angered him, but I didn't regret them one little bit. He was holding me here against my will, and yeah, I enjoyed his touch, but I wasn't some pet he could keep caged. At least, that's what it felt like. I entered the main living area, and my eyes darted to the locked door as they always did. It was my reminder to myself that I was being held here. I was so used to it being locked that I didn't realize something was different until the wind that ruffled my hair and tickled my flesh drew my eyes back to it.

The door was open. I looked around the room, noting each of the cameras pointed at the entrance. I didn't hesitate, I fucking ran. Barefoot, half-dressed, wearing nothing more than a pair of short shorts, a camisole top, and no weapons, I ran. I flew over the grass as if it burned my feet, running over it until I burst into the woods and stopped.

Too fucking easy.

He hadn't made a mistake yet…

I turned, looked at the house, and watched as he stepped out from the doorway. He wore a pair of jeans and nothing else. He tilted his head, watching me. He wanted me to run? He looked like a predator as he stood by the door. His eyes narrowed, his nostrils flared, and he tipped his head, ever so slightly, like a cougar does before it gives chase to its unfortunate prey.

Fuck it.

I turned and took off, running through the thick brush, cutting my feet and my arms as I protected my face against the thick branches. I broke free from the woods and paused. I looked around; my lungs burned, my feet hurt, but the adrenaline rushing through me numbed it all. I turned left, and found an open meadow with a bubbling spring running through it. To the right was the edge of a cliff. I ran towards it, wondering how far of a drop it was. The cliff dropped down into jagged rocks, preventing entrance to the valley, while making it impossible to leave it from this side as well. The other side was sheer cliff walls that went up at least a few hundred feet.

I turned to the spring, and slowed down as I made my way towards it. I must have miscalculated when I ran. This way was hopeless if I wanted to escape him. I knelt beside the spring and lifted my eyes to the stars. They were beautiful, and the entire scene was surreal. I sat down at the edge, dipped my feet into the water, and found it warm. A natural hot spring? It felt heavenly against the soles of my sore feet.

I felt him before I saw him, but he didn't rush in and force me back to the house; instead he walked over, bent down, and looked at me.

"Feel better?" he asked.

"No. You should have let me go. I don't want to be around you and your bullshit." I couldn't even look at him, so I tried very hard to look at my toes.

He laughed and sat down, closer to me. "Not quite what I was expecting. Please, tell me why you think I'm full of bullshit?"

"For starters, you slept with someone else. You told me I was created for you. That you couldn't touch anyone else, and then you slept with them. After that, you killed John, so there has to be a way to turn it off if you slept with someone else," I blurted out before I could stop myself.

"Did I? Or did I give you a taste of what I felt when you lay with Jaeden?" he countered.

"I felt it!" I snapped, turning to look at him. He looked worried, and yet strangely at ease.

"I know; I know exactly how it feels. However, I was never with anyone else. It was a bit of a trick; those kinds of sensations aren't easy to project, and no, I didn't touch anyone else. I can't turn it off, ever," he murmured sheepishly as he looked at his hands. "I haven't had sex with anyone since I became a Guardian of Death. Killing those who pleasure me isn't something I seek out. I don't know how the connection works; it is more complex than the connection I have with other Sentinels and I never had a chance to speak to the other Guardians about how it works before everything went to shit. I only know that you alone can survive my touch. I know that you were created for me, the rest? It doesn't really matter to me. I've watched you for a very long time. I watched you fall down only to get back up every time, stronger than you were before. I watched you sneak off to a spring just like this one. It's why I picked this location. Well, it is a strategic location, of course, that, and the stars, and waterfall. It had everything you loved. I am not sure if you ever told anyone else about the stars, but I could feel it as you stared up at them. It was the same with the waterfalls when you'd pass them while training with your father. You'd pause, pretend everything was normal for a moment, and then you'd slip back into warrior mode. You're a phoenix, but you already know that."

"How is it you watched me without me knowing?" I asked, needing to know how I could have missed seeing him.

"You knew; your heart would race, but you didn't listen to what it was trying to tell you. You weren't ready, and maybe you're still not ready, but I am. I've waited lifetimes for the one I'd be able to touch. Before you hate me for what I've done, consider what you would do to be able to feel the touch of another human being. I know we're not exactly human, Emma, but we start out that way. We have the same needs, the same desires, and we need human contact. In taking you, I have saved Jaeden from what you will become, as well. You're a Guardian of Life, and he's technically undead. Consider what that would mean for him."

He stood up and turned to leave me alone beside the water, and I stopped him.

"Wait," I whispered. "Stay with me, please."

I wasn't sure why I didn't want to be alone, but I didn't. I also couldn't weed through the information, or the little bombs he'd just dropped on me, if he left. I watched as he turned slowly, looking at me as if he wasn't sure he wanted to remain in my company.

"Or go," I said. "How do you know I was created for you? I was born, just like everyone else in this world. So how do you know that I alone was created for you?" I swallowed as he slowly sat beside me, slid his feet into the spring, and flexed his toes in the water.

"Because out of everyone else in this world, it's you alone who my touch doesn't kill," he stated. "I'm not sure why you arrived when you did, but here you are."

"You said you were at my mother's funeral. Why were you there?" I countered, my hackles rising with just how wrong it was for him to have been there. He'd been shadowing me during one of the most turbulent days of my life.

"I told you that until the virus struck, I tried to be

near you every chance I got," he murmured with a small smile.

"You mentioned something about seeing me the day I was born?" I asked, and he tipped his head to the side as he considered the past.

"I had actually been following you since before you were born; not that I knew I was following you at the time," he admitted with a small chuckle. "To understand what is going on, I think I need to go back a little bit. You and I are part of a prophecy. Death and Life Guardians are only born when the world needs us the most. Death Guardians are born when there is too much of an upswing in the immortal population for the current Sentinels to handle, and Life Guardians are born when a catastrophic event happens that humans may not recover from without our help. Divine intervention, if you will. We are always in mated pairs, sort of what humans refer to as soulmates, just waiting for the bond to be completed. Even though we may be born at different times, we always find each other. I was born in the Sentinel temple that's located between Bristol and Bath, and I was raised as one of them. When the time came for my trial, the markings for the Guardian of Death appeared and my training to be one of the next Death Guardians began. Not only was I to protect humans from immortals, I was to be a judge and executioner for our own people if the situation warrants it. Much of what I was taught had been passed down from previous Guardians, and most of it was hard to believe. Yes, there was another Death Guardian at the time, but he's at the temple outside of Rome and let's just say that we weren't really able to correspond very well back then."

He gave me a wry little smile. "Yes, we can be killed; it's next to impossible, but it has happened. One flaw with the teachings is they were an indicator of what was coming; they just weren't clear about *when* things would happen. Although the markings indicated I would be a Guardian of Death, I didn't know that my powers wouldn't manifest fully until they were truly needed, and it lulled me into a false sense that it would never happen," he said sadly. I leaned my head against his shoulder as he continued.

"The teachings indicated that the only one I wouldn't kill with my touch was a Guardian of Life; my counterpart; my mate. Since the only Guardian of Life at the time was already mated, I was going to have a very long wait until there would be another being that I wouldn't kill with my touch, and the knowledge that the birth of my mate wouldn't happen until the world would be trying to recover from a catastrophic event was troubling."

Azrael tucked me into his side and caressed my hair, lost in his story. "Centuries passed, and disturbing rumors of immortals and a group of Sentinels working together against the mortals we were supposed to protect began surfacing. One of the Sentinels that was rumored to be working against our purpose was based in Newport. I was only supposed to observe and not interfere, at least, not until we discovered how many players were plotting together. So I watched your mother, and on the day she gave birth to you, I followed them to the hospital, hoping that one or more of her partners would come there to check on her. I was in the room next to hers when you were born. Your first breath filled me with something I can't really explain. I can say that for the first time in centuries, I felt emotions. Before you were born, I felt lost. Unsure of where I was supposed to be, but your first cry…it woke me up as if I'd been sleeping most of my life. I felt this intense need to follow your cries, to protect you. I waited for your mother to walk the hallway, but instead of following her as I should have, I slipped into the room and found you. You were this little screaming, red creature. I feared your screaming would bring one of the nurses in to check on you; even *I* knew babies are not to be left unattended in a hospital. The moment our eyes met, you stopped howling. I am one of the things our people fear the most, and here was this tiny little blue-eyed creature looking up at me with curiosity. No fear, no hate as many others do, but instead, you looked up at me as if you felt the connection as well. They say that our eyes are the portal to our souls and on that day, I believed it for the very first time. Yours allowed me to glimpse the woman who you would become. I saw this woman, one who protected her people against all odds. So there I stood, exposed to my enemies, unable to look away from the prettiest blue eyes I'd ever seen." He gave me a tight smile.

"I am Death, yet you looked up at me as if you knew I was your mate. As if our souls recognized each other. At the time, I wasn't sure what to believe, but since the moment you drew air into your lungs, I've been unable to stay away from you. I wasn't sure that you were going to be a Guardian then; we weren't at war, and there was no real threat. You have to understand, the last Guardian of Life was born at a temple outside of Constantinople during some pretty extreme weather events in the sixth century. They were the precursor to a plague that wound up wiping out something like twenty-five million people in a little more than a year, and there was nothing like that going on when I first saw you. Not to mention, you weren't born in a temple as the rest of us were."

"What happened to that Guardian of Life?"

"The worst possible thing ever," he grinned. "Lailah is blissfully mated to Adriel, the Guardian of Death who is based outside Rome." He chuckled at me, and I punched him in the arm and rolled my eyes.

"Anyway, your mother knew I was getting close to what she was up to, so she faked her own death. I attended the funeral, figuring that Trina's narcissistic ways would make her attend her own funeral. She didn't show, not even to check on you. I stood beside you, watching this fierce little thing fight through her emotions. I felt your anger, the betrayal, but more, I felt that you knew she wasn't dead. You only cried once, and you pushed the emotions down and boxed them away. You felt her, but you were uncertain how or why you knew she was alive. I stood inches away from you while you stood proudly beside your father. You brushed up against me, and I feared my touch would kill you. It was the first time I'd ever been afraid since I'd become immortal. Yet you just turned, looked into my eyes, and smiled with this life inside of you that drew me in. It's when I knew you were my mate and that the teachings had to be flawed if you existed now. I had to leave you for a while, to discover what ploy your mother was making, but you were never truly alone. When you went through puberty, I began to be able to catch glimpses of your life through your eyes; more details would happen in dreams. It's how I first watched you with Jaeden. I tried to separate it so that I wasn't trespassing, but if I was sleeping when you were together, it became my nightmares, which weren't dreams at all."

"I'm not sure how to process that, since I've felt alone for a long time. Now I find out that you were always there? Since I was born?" I questioned.

"Longer, if you consider the time I spent watching your mother while you were in her womb," he said offhandedly as he stood and dusted off his jeans, extending his hand for me. I accepted it, smelling the storm in the evening air. "A storm approaches."

"I can smell it." I dusted myself as well, and felt like I was grieving the loss of the beauty and fresh air as we started towards the house. I'd made it a few yards before he picked me up. "I can walk, my feet work."

"They're already sore from running through the woods. You weigh next to nothing; it's not a hardship to carry your slight weight."

"Wow, you really know the way to a woman's heart," I grumbled.

"I could drop you on your ass," he laughed, and I turned to look up at him, my laughter dying in my throat. His eyes were smiling, right along with his mouth, and he was fucking beautiful. I hadn't seen him like this; this carefree smiling version of him disarmed me. I stared at him, as if seeing him for the first time. "Girl, you keep looking at me like that and…" Thunder exploded in the sky, shaking the ground and cutting him off.

"How many women have you been with?" I asked, sallying forth into foreign territory. His inability to touch anyone else had piqued my curiosity.

"Many; I started out as a human, remember?" He looked up at the sky, as if he was judging how long it would take for the storm to reach us. "Unlike you, I knew what I was supposed to become. Don't worry, I promise you that I am very skilled in the bedroom."

"So what was it like?" I asked.

"Fucking?" He smirked as he carried me through the woods. I hadn't noticed just how far I'd run until I was being carried back.

"No, knowing you'd be unable to touch another person," I clarified.

"When I first found out what I was going to be, I didn't believe it," he chuckled, even though we were about to get drenched from the fast-moving storm. "I just spent a lot of time in beds, not fully understanding what I would become. When I'd given up on the idea that I would actually be a Death Guardian, it happened.

I wasn't given warning, I just changed," he said, lost in thought.

Something passed over his face before he concealed it, and I wondered if he'd hurt someone he'd cared about when he'd discovered his touch was poison. I leaned up and kissed him before I'd even thought about it. He released me, letting my feet touch the ground as he deepened the kiss, his hands wrapped around my waist, holding me in place. The sky let loose, and rain pelted us as we ignored it. He lifted me up, kissing me as we made our way towards the house. His hands tugged at my shirt and I considered letting him do it, but the thought of doing it without first speaking with Jaeden stopped me. I pulled away from his kiss and shook my head.

"You can't just be hot and then cold, Emma," he growled. I knew he was frustrated, because I was, too. I wanted him, and it scared the shit out of me.

"I just can't do this with you!" I shouted over the rain. It hadn't come out right. He made my brain turn off with his addictive kisses, and then I ended up saying things horribly wrong.

"Why? Because Jaeden's so fucking faithful to you, is that it? He's a fucking monster! Do you know how he's spent his time? He hasn't even fucking started looking for you! He's spent this entire time feeding and fucking," he growled. "If it was me and you'd been taken from me, I'd never stop looking. I'd tear this world apart to find you!"

"You're lying!" I shouted back, and he smiled coldly as he grabbed me roughly. I felt the world spin around us and I held on to him as if he would somehow anchor me. One minute we were in the woods, and then towns and cities passed by as we stopped, only to be propelled forward again swiftly.

When he finally stopped moving, I gasped. We were standing in the same place where he'd taken me from. He'd stopped teleporting us, or whatever the hell it was that he did when he moved so fast, but what I saw made my world spin much faster than he ever could. The streets seemed to be bathed in blood. The cages that had once been full of victims held nothing but corpses. As if they'd opened them only to bring their victims out to slaughter them before returning the lifeless bodies back to their prisons. Shamus was leaning over a girl who couldn't be more than twelve or so, and he was still feeding from the corpse even though she'd long ago expired from blood loss.

My stomach rolled and nausea swirled viciously inside of it. I turned, finding Lachlan and his men camped close by, trying to ignore the macabre debauchery of the vampires.

"Emma?" Lachlan called out, as if we had startled them, but Lachlan didn't move. No one did.

I looked at the ground, watching a river of blood as it flowed in pools and down the sides of the road. As if the rain had followed us here, and was cleansing the earth from the bloodbath. Only, it hadn't followed us here. There was no rain; it was blood from the bodies that littered the sidewalk.

"Emma," Jaeden's voice pulled me from the horror show, and I looked at him.

He was drenched in blood. His shirt was covered in both dried and freshly spilled blood. A woman screamed from the tent he'd just left, and crawled out with her throat exposed, naked. She had a deep gash in it, and even I could see she was bleeding to death slowly.

I stepped back as he took his first step towards me. I shook my head. This wasn't right. Azrael had taken me from this place days ago, and Jaeden hadn't even tried to find me? He was supposed to love me! Why hadn't he come? Why hadn't he even tried?

The woman stretched her hand towards me, and I gagged as her blood flowed to meet with the other blood that pooled beside the tent he'd been in. How many other bodies were inside that tent?

"I told you she'd be back," Astrid snapped. "Oh look, she brought fresh meat," she chimed in as she noticed Azrael in his armor behind me.

A loud slurping noise pulled my eyes back to a feral Shamus, who smiled around his mouthful of teenager. Lachlan said my name again, and I shook my head; it was all wrong. Lachlan was my friend and he hadn't tried to find me, either. More people started coming out of tents, all covered in blood. I stepped back.

"Emma, come to me, now," Jaeden ordered with his hand reaching to me, but it was covered in blood. Just like the rest of him.

"You didn't come," I whispered. "You didn't even try?"

"Emma…" he called softly, but I turned away from him, burying my face against Azrael's armor.

"Take me home," I cried, wrapping my arms around him, letting his warmth seep into my frozen soul. They hadn't even tried to look for me.

I'd been missing for days, and while I hadn't expected them to save me, I had expected my friends to at least look for me. They could have made some effort. I would have if it had been one of them. I was in my current predicament because I had risked myself to free them.

The world faded away, and with it, the pain of what I'd been forced to face. No one had looked for me, because feeding and murdering those people had been more important to them than I was. Jaeden hadn't even bothered to try.

Chapter Twenty

When the earth finally stopped spinning, I realized we were back at Azrael's home. Unsteadily, I stepped away from Azrael and spun around to face him. He smiled coldly, and all I wanted to do was smack the smugness off his face. I raised my hand as tears started to slide down my cheeks, and slapped him.

"You knew!" I slapped him again, and he grabbed my arms and pulled me close. A sob ripped from my chest and I shook with anger, pain, and the worst of all, denial.

"If I had told you what they were up to, you'd have called me a liar. I had to show you. You have to understand what they truly are," he murmured against my hair.

"I hate you!" I sobbed, trembling and shaking as pain and anger pulsed through me. He picked me up and carried me through the door, kicking it closed behind him, and moved with me to the couch, where he held me until I couldn't cry anymore. I was a mess, and when I turned towards him and tried to kiss him, he stopped me. He stood up, dropping me on the couch.

"I'm not your fallback, Emma. I'm not your second fucking choice. You hurt; you want to get back at him. I get it, but no matter how much I want you, I'm not your fucking rebound. When I take you, it will be because you've accepted what we are, not because your ego or your heart is hurting. I'm willing to wait for you to come to terms with it, to get over the pain he's put you through. I can wait, even if it takes you centuries to figure shit out. You need someone to hold you, fine; I'll do it. I'm not the guy you can slip and fall on my dick, then hate me because you regret what we did in the morning. Go to bed. You need to sleep; you look like hell."

He left the room, and I tilted my head. Yeah, I obviously had a sign on my back that said 'kick me'. I leaned back and screamed. I hated this place; I hated him for being right. I hated Jaeden for being what he was. He killed that woman, I was sure of it. Hell, he may have killed most of them! I was an idiot. I hated myself most of all for being weak. I was stronger than this!

I just wanted to find Grayson and go home, to go back to thinking I was human before I'd stepped into this mess of immortals. I wanted the world back to normal, and if what Azrael said was true, I wished he had done his damn job. I wished he'd had enough information in time and just finished my mother, so that my father would still be alive and Grayson would be home, safe.

I missed Addy and the day-to-day shit the Ark took to run. I missed my world, the one I'd lived in before I'd met Jaeden.

I closed my eyes as I was picked up and carried into the bedroom. He loomed over me, and shook his head, as if he was trying to figure something out.

"I'm sorry for taking you there like that. Like I said, it wasn't something that I could just tell you. You wouldn't have believed me and all that would have happened is you would have hated me." His voice was gentle and laced with remorse. "He's healing; blood is the only way he can do it. He's a fucking parasite. It doesn't change what I said in the other room; if you need me to do something…" He scratched his neck and frowned. "Like hold you, I will. I'll be whatever you need me to be. Just not a second choice or the one you use to get over him. I don't want to be something you regret. I've waited too long for you to have you regret anything with me."

I nodded. "Will you stay with me? Just until I fall asleep…or whatever," I whispered as I wiped away the tears. "I just don't want to be alone right now."

"Scoot over," he ordered softly, removing his shirt to reveal his chiseled chest and washboard abs. I crawled further onto the bed and turned towards the heat his body offered as he lay next to me. "You're a bed hog,

Emma," he grunted, as he pushed me onto my side and pulled me against himself.

"Do you miss it?" I whispered.

"Do I miss what?" he asked.

"Touching people," I murmured as I snuggled closer into his arms. "Like this."

"I don't think I've ever held anyone else quite like this." His hand rubbed lightly, soothingly along my arm. "When I first found out about what I would be, I didn't really think about how much it would bother me. After my full powers came in, I think I missed the simple things the most. Things like having to worry about my proximity to other people and fearing that the most casual of touches would kill them, or not being able to comfort a soldier as he died on the battlefield; if I touched them, they would die in more pain than they already were in. Eventually I formed armor, a solid manifestation of what most Sentinels project. I've tweaked and modified it over the years to what it is now. It prevents innocents from dying, but it also prevents me from ever feeling human flesh. Until you." I could feel his breath across my ear, and the tone of his voice was gentle and reassuring in the darkness.

I nodded and shifted to get a little more comfortable.

"Emma, I'm not a fucking saint," he groaned in a deep rumble that sent shivers racing down my spine. "Keep moving that ass and we'll both regret shit come morning."

"Noted," I quipped softly. His arms wrapped around me and his lips touched my neck.

"I'm an asshole for showing you that. I regretted it the moment we entered that camp. I haven't had to care about people's feelings for a very long time."

"I wanted to kill them," I admitted into the dark room. "All of them, and I knew he was healing; he was really bad off when you took me. I could see the huge chunks they'd taken out of his body; but earlier, the feelings I had, it was like I had never seen what those assholes had done to him. I had this sick urge to kill them all, and Lachlan wasn't even a part of it. His pack doesn't feed from humans."

"It wasn't because of what he'd done. It was because of what he is. It doesn't make you a bad person for wanting to avenge those who had been needlessly slaughtered. Your job is to preserve life, mine is to take it. You felt the need to save them even though they were dead. I felt the need to help the vampires in the slaughter. It's who we are. It takes a lot of control to not indulge in needless bloodshed. I've had centuries to learn control. You, on the other hand, have not. There is so much you still need to learn about our race."

"The people you collected, why did you save them?" I asked.

"Because our job isn't just to save them, it's to help them continue to thrive. Humans tend to take each other out more than other creatures do. We've helped them rebuild before; the black plague was one such instance. At the time, it struck down most of the world's population."

"Most of the population?" I questioned.

"Records of it weren't well-kept, so most humans don't know exactly how many died. They estimate it was close to a third of the world's population that died of it over a ten-year period. The numbers were higher than the historians estimated and it went on longer than they thought, not to mention, the plague kept cropping back up. We control history, therefore whatever spin we want to put on the situation, the humans will believe it. Those who were hidden from the plague rebuilt, but they didn't do it alone. Of course, back then information was easier to control. They didn't have cell phones or media. They got word from those who survived in other locations…which was us, sending false hope."

"False hope is mean," I commented.

"False hope is better than no hope. Humans need hope to survive tragic events. The plague struck down people in staggering numbers. By the time we were able to intervene and get in front of it, not as many had survived as historians thought. We have been with the humans since the beginning of time, though, so those who were with us bred more humans, and their children and so forth. When the world is in trouble, we repair and redirect it, little phoenix. This is just a snippet of what you would have learned as a child had your mother taught you as was her responsibility."

"I'm kinda glad she ditched me. If she hadn't, I may have been someone else. I'm glad my father raised me and Grayson. It made us who we are. He taught us to help those who couldn't help themselves," I replied, feeling unsure if I wanted to know more of what he had to teach me. I wasn't sure I was ready to know it.

"She wasn't always as she is now. She was once a respected Sentinel, one who would move mountains to help this world. Your mother is very old, but somewhere along the way, she changed. She became greedy for power, wealth, and then she decided she wanted to control the world as she thinks Sentinels should. It wasn't what we were created for. We're watchers; when humans are in trouble, we intervene and help. They're God's favored children. We were created to protect them. Sometimes even from themselves. They're still a young race, and youth tends to be resilient."

"Why save them? Why not let them just work it out on their own?" I asked.

"Because they're unable to thrive through a virus such as the one your mother helped release on them," he murmured against my ear. "Too many were lost and the monstrous few are systematically enslaving or snuffing out those that remain."

"You knew what she could potentially do, so why didn't you just kill her?"

"Because I had no proof of what she would do," he supplied. "I can't judge someone based off of rumors alone, or what they might do."

"You could have prevented this from ever happening. I wish you would have killed the bitch."

"You're too smart to believe that," he whispered. "There was only one thing I was sure of, Emma; that you'd be mine. I was close to being lawless when I looked into your eyes. I'd gone to Newport willing to kill a pregnant woman and her unborn child if I found any sign of her guilt. The moment I looked into your eyes, I felt how wrong killing you would have been. You intrigued me, and I'd like to say fate intervened, but I'm not sure fate cares about me that much. I know you saved me that day, because killing you would have taken me further than I'd gone before. I've killed thousands of people, but never a baby."

"I wasn't worth the world," I said thickly.

"To me, you were," he mused. "I haven't seen anything that tells me that killing your mother in a preemptive strike would have stopped what happened. It wasn't just her who turned on our people. If I'd have taken her out, someone else would have just taken her place. There were a lot of conspirators within the immortal community. Following leads and tracking exactly what was going on was what led me to Europe. I was too late and was there when the virus was released. They were always one step ahead with their plan, with nothing tangible that could be proven, and that is something that I will always regret. I will never regret waiting for you, though, even at the cost of the world."

Chapter Twenty-One

I puttered around the house, uncertain of what to do with myself. I'd watched all of the Harry Potter movies—the real ones this time—but my mind kept going back to seeing Jaeden and Lachlan. I still felt that sick twisting in my gut as I considered how they hadn't even looked for me. If it was one of them, I'd have looked. I'd have fought my way to them, and yet they'd remained in that town, indulging in debauchery. It stung.

I thought I meant more to them, but maybe there was a bigger reason they hadn't. Azrael admitted Jaeden was healing, which I knew was true. He'd looked worn out, but then he'd also been inside a tent with a naked woman that he probably wound up killing in his bloodlust. That took energy, right? The idea of him with anyone else wasn't what hurt. Although we were done, finished, ended, I still would have searched to the end of the world to save him. He, on the other hand, hadn't even moved a mile and that was the core of what hurt the most.

I was sure that a lot of Jaeden's actions had to do with Shamus being in charge, and I suspected he would have put a stop to Jaeden even attempting to find me. I knew Jaeden was a soldier; I knew he would follow whatever his orders were. In my girlish dreams, though, I was supposed to matter more to him. I didn't. In the end, he'd always follow orders.

I stood at the window, watching as the rain cleansed the earth. I wrapped my arms around myself and considered my next move. I still intended to seduce Azrael, gain my freedom, and continue on my way to free Grayson. I no longer planned on finding Jaeden and taking him and Lachlan with me anymore.

I'd never intended to let them get close to the Sentinels anyway. Now that I knew more about the Sentinels, and had seen Azrael in combat, I knew the vampires and wolves would be cut down in nothing flat, and it wasn't something I could watch play out. Trina wanted me for whatever reason, so I'd trade myself for Grayson. I'd figure the rest out from there. She wanted me because of what she thought I was, but it didn't mean she'd get to use me as she wanted to. She seemed just as surprised as the rest of her baddie Sentinels that I was a Guardian, which meant a lot more to them than it did to me. All I was sure of was I could get away from her, head back to the Ark, and we'd continue to live our lives. I'd planned that from the beginning. After I got Grayson back to the Ark, I'd figure out where she was holding Lachlan's father and Jaeden's sire, and figure out how to get them out.

It was flawed, but it was the only real option I could see. Sentinels could easily kill vampires; I wasn't willing to let Jaeden die, not even if he was acting under orders. I'd protect him from himself if need be. Lachlan too, they would both end up hurt, or worse, dead.

I pulled the door of the fridge open and looked inside, finding fresh meat, veggies and a few other things to make a roast. It had been forever since I'd cooked, which I used to love to do. Dad hadn't been the best cook. When I was younger, we'd eaten mostly burned or microwaved meals, more than I'd like to admit. He had tried; the man just couldn't cook to save his life.

I rummaged through the cupboards as a plan percolated in my head. I pulled out herbs, spices, and beef broth, then luckily found a pot which would fit all of the ingredients. I set to work on making a romantic dinner for two, one that was fit for seduction.

Once the meal was on the stove simmering, I made my way to the bedroom and opened the closet. I gawked at the fine clothing and shoes. The closet had been filled with dresses and stuff that looked like it would have cost an arm and leg.

I ran my fingers over the delicate fabrics and frowned. I had never been one to dress up. I was never what you would call a girly-girl, much to Addy's frustration, nor did getting dressed up figure into my father's prepper-plans. After pulling out several dresses, I settled on a black T-shirt dress with slits up the sides. I matched it with a pair of thigh high socks with thin lines that accentuated the curves of my thighs, and slipped on a pair of soft ballet flats. Now that my hair had quickly grown out again to its original length, I decided to wear it up to show off the V-line of the back of the dress. It was sexy while not being obvious that I'd done it on purpose.

I sat in front of the vanity and stared at my reflection. I'd never spent much time worrying about my appearance since the doors to the Ark closed; I figured seduction should include a little gloss. It would draw his eyes to my mouth, which is what I wanted, right?

I dug through the drawers and found expensive brands of make-up, along with a box of jewelry. I pulled out a delicate silver chain, probably the least expensive piece in the collection, but the most beautiful trinket in my opinion. It had an infinity symbol charm dangling from it, which matched the marks on my wrists. I secured it around my neck, then applied eyeshadow and liner sparingly, along with mascara and finished with a red gloss. I stared at the woman who looked back at me. I looked sexy. I stood up and spun around, admiring my reflection. It had been so long since I'd cared what I looked like that it felt awkward. I felt like an imposter, but I had a mission to succeed in, which was seduction. And right now, I fit that role.

I exited the room and made my way to the dining room table, and found long elegant candles with silver holders that I set in the middle of the table to flood the room in candlelight once they were lit. I placed the dishes at the head of the long, wooden table and then the silverware. A few more trips and the table was finally set for dinner, and the roast was simmering on the range top. I placed a bottle of pinot noir in a grand brasserie champagne bowl, filled it with ice, and placed the wine glasses in the freezer for them to chill, and then padded over to the couch to wait.

My nerves were going crazy, the idea of seducing him wasn't one that sat well with me, but I had to get out of here and back to looking for Grayson. It didn't matter if Azrael was the nicest person left on this planet, I had to find and save my brother.

I got up from the couch to pace and then eyed the stereo. Music couldn't hurt, and maybe it would calm the storm building inside of me. *I Want to Know What Love* Is by Foreigner started up when I selected 'Seduction List' from the iPod in the stereo dock. I sat back down on the couch and closed my eyes until the rapid beating of my heart told me Azrael was close.

I quickly made my way to the kitchen island and rested my hands on it, wondering if I had enough balls to go through with this. I wasn't sure what worried me more, that I felt excited at the idea of being with him, or that I felt safer knowing he was home. I heard him as he stepped into the room, as I removed the roast from the stovetop and headed towards the table with it.

"You cooked," he commented, and I nodded, hoping to God I didn't drop it with the way my hands were trembling. I placed it on the table, moved the roast from the pan along with selected vegetables to the serving plate, and took the pan to the sink.

I turned and smiled, finding him covered in mud and watching me with wide eyes. I swallowed hard; this man even looked good in mud. I was *so* screwed. Wasn't that what I was aiming for? My eyes drifted to his muddy feet and he shuffled them, as if he wasn't sure what to say.

"You're beautiful," he murmured thickly.

"You're covered in mud," I replied, and he blinked and looked down at his feet.

"I'll go change for…dinner. It smells really good, Emma," he said sheepishly as he scratched the back of his neck and watched me.

"Thanks." I wondered why this was so awkward. We were both awkward at the moment. He looked as if he didn't know how to react to someone doing something nice for him.

He walked out of the room, and I let the breath I just realized I was holding go with a shaky whoosh. This wasn't going to be as easy as I'd thought. I lit the candles and sat at the table, waiting for him; when he returned, he was dressed in a black V-neck T-shirt, with jeans and slippers, along with a masculine version of the necklace I wore, only his had a small omega symbol charm. He looked at me as if he intended to turn around and go change again, but then shoved his hands in his pockets and shrugged.

"I'm not used to having company," he explained softly.

"You look great," I whispered and smiled nervously. His eyes darted to my lips, and I self-consciously chewed on my bottom one. What the fuck was wrong with me? Why was I so nervous? Why was *he* so nervous? "I shouldn't have cooked, it's weird, right?" I babbled as I started to stand up, but his hand touched my shoulder, stopping me.

"It's not weird," he rasped thickly. "It's nice." He fumbled with his words, like he didn't know what to say. "I don't mean it's nice…I haven't had anyone eat with me in a very long time. Actually, no one really does anything with me. I'm not very good with people anymore; a little bit rusty on my social skills. I guess having Death over for dinner isn't something many people would wish to do."

"You're good with me," I blurted, and then regretted it as his eyes turned heavy, and his smile lifted on one side.

"You're different," he replied as he sat down and looked over the meal. "I didn't know you could cook."

"I used to cook for Grayson and Dad, mostly when Dad was busy with the shelter." I wasn't sure why I was opening up to him, but the idea of getting to know him actually excited me. "He used to fall asleep at the shelter, and I'd have to take him dinner. Some days he didn't even come home or show up for conferences at the school. I guess I just kind of took over and filled the role when he became obsessed with prepping the Ark."

"He probably felt it through you, the end coming. It's likely that Shamus used compulsion on him to hurry the process. Had I taken a closer look at what was happening in your life at the time, I might have stepped in a bit sooner. Like I said, I tried to check in on you every chance I got—but between tracking what your mother was doing and being busy with our bunkers, I didn't pay much attention to what was driving your father, and just assumed he was sensing what was going to happen because of you. Almost twenty years ago, we broke ground on our own bunkers and began scouting for potential candidates who would be needed for rebuilding society. They all knew where to go in the case of a catastrophic event, so when the virus hit, the candidates who survived brought their families, or what remained of their families, to the nearest bunker."

"So you knew?" I asked.

"The other Guardians and I knew something was coming, just not what or when it would hit. The other Sentinels sensed it to a lesser degree, but they knew too. Our role is to police the immortals; to be sure they do not kill too many humans or step out of the shadows. It's not our only role. We also help the humans regrow when the need arises. As I said before, we rebuild this world and wipe away the history of what our part was that we played within it," he said as he piled his plate with slices of roast. "You felt it, the pull; the need to save the people. You felt the need to protect life. You took action because you are a leader. As am I. The others need one or both Guardians to follow. To lead them. What happened this time is a global threat, rather than a regional or continental one, so logically we would be intended to lead this side of the world and Adriel and Lailah would be expected to lead on that side," he said before he shoved a forkful of meat into his mouth and chewed.

I did the same, and chewed, and chewed, and chewed. I swallowed the dry meat and looked at him as he choked it down, and used his water to hide it from me. He took another bite, smiled weakly, and I shook my head.

"It's horrible," I laughed nervously.

"It really is," he agreed as he downed more water. "Who taught you to cook?"

"Apparently not Martha Stewart," I murmured sheepishly as I chewed my bottom lip. The vegetables were raw, still hard, and not even halfway cooked through. I frowned at the spread, because it looked great. It tasted like shit. He took another bite and I winced as the sound of raw potatoes being chewed filled the room. "Stop eating it, it's bad. They're not even cooked."

He laughed and watched me as he continued to chew the raw vegetables. I blushed and scrunched up my nose. At least the meat wasn't raw, but how I'd managed to get the meat dry, and yet the vegetables undercooked, was beyond me.

"I have to say; it's the best meal anyone has cooked for me in a very long time." How he could say that with a smile on his face after the awful meal puzzled me.

"That's sad, because I'm not sure we should even feed it to animals. They may keel over from it," I replied. "How about wine on the sofa?" I cringed with how stupid I sounded.

"That sounds like seduction, and very tempting," he replied. "Alas, I have other obligations to tend to." He looked over the outfit I wore as I stood. "Very tempting," he whispered huskily. And just like that, he left me standing in the dining room, alone, with a bottle of wine and a crappy meal. Yeah, some seductress I was.

Chapter Twenty-Two

I'd been unable to sleep, so a noise coming from the main living area was a welcome distraction. I'd spent the last few hours going over everything that Azrael had disclosed to me, and sorting through my own feelings. I also had to consider the reality that Jaeden and Lachlan weren't going to be storming in to rescue me; I'd been left to my own devices, and I was once again on my own. I padded down the hallway to the main living area, dressed in a soft baby blue camisole and matching shorts that had lace on the bottom of them.

"Azrael?" I whispered sleepily. He had been looking outside with his back to me, but once he turned towards me, my mouth quirked into a soft smile.

"You're still up?" he remarked, and I nodded at the stupid question. I hadn't been able to sleep, mostly because of sorting through all the shit in my head. He frowned, and I felt as if something was off. My stomach flipped, and I felt as if someone had torn my insides out, only they weren't my emotions. They were his.

I wasn't sure how I knew it, but I did.

"Is everything okay?" I asked, stepping closer to him as he watched me come closer until I stood right in front of him. "Are you hurt?" I ran my hand over his arm as I looked for any injuries. He must have been back for a while, as he was freshly showered and wearing a long-sleeved Henley and jeans.

"I'm fine," he murmured as he dropped a gentle kiss to my forehead. I wondered how it would feel to never touch someone else without killing them. His hands drifted down my shoulders, sending tiny bumps over my flesh. I wanted to wipe away the pain I felt, because if it wasn't mine, it had to be his.

I lifted my lips and claimed his, gently at first; my tongue pushed past his lips and found his in an ageless dance. His hands lowered to my hips, and I tried to move closer. One minute I was standing, and before I knew what I'd done, I jumped up and wrapped my legs around him. His hands cradled my face as if he was afraid I'd disappear, which wasn't a possibility.

He started to stride towards the hall, and I didn't stop him. I deepened the kiss, and struggled to get his shirt up and over his head. It wasn't as easy as it should have been, since I wasn't ready to stop kissing him. He pulled away as he pushed me against the wall. He pulled his shirt up and off, then mine was off and flying across the hallway as he claimed my lips in a toe-curling kiss that left me boneless.

"I swear, if you stop this now, Emma, I won't be able to do as you ask," he warned, but I was past that point. There was no going back. I wanted him. It was that simple. I wanted this man more than I'd ever wanted anything else in my life. I wasn't sure why, I only knew I wanted him so much that it hurt me. It terrified me, but none of that mattered as long as he was touching me. It was like finding home after being lost in the woods for weeks.

"Don't stop," I breathed against his mouth as he pushed open a different bedroom door and soft lights automatically lit, creating a romantic atmosphere. I looked up as he kissed my neck, and discovered the solar system had been recreated on the ceiling in tiny white lights. He had Venus and other constellations depicted in perfect detail. I slid down his body, and yanked at the button and zipper of his pants, which he helped me remove. I slid to the floor, taking his cock between my lips, and watched as his eyes grew large and round as a pained moan exploded from his lips.

"Jesus," he groaned as he watched me try to take more of him into my mouth. I was clumsy at best, but he didn't seem to care or notice. He rocked his hips and then withdrew as I fought to keep him where he was. "Emma, I'm holding on by a thread, and you're about to snap it."

"So," I whispered as I stood up, hooking my fingers in the waistband of my shorts as I slid them down and stepped out of them. He scrubbed his face with his hands, and shook his head.

"You're so beautiful," he murmured before he pulled me close and claimed my lips as I lifted myself and straddled his hips. I felt his cock pulsing against my entrance, seeking to plunge into the wetness he'd inspired, but he didn't. He just kissed me as his hands explored the curves of my ass. He walked us towards the bed, and when I tried to push his rock-hard cock inside, he withheld. How the fuck! He hadn't had sex in, like, forever—give or take a few centuries? Why wasn't he giving me what I needed? "You're mine, now," he growled as he sat me on the bed and pushed my legs apart.

His head slowly lowered to my pussy, his mouth dropping sweet kisses to the sensitive flesh inside my thighs as he slowly worked my body. His fingers pushed inside and I cried out at the intrusion, right up until his tongue slowly licked it from the top to the center. I trembled as he slowly licked, sucked, and teased a massive storm that threatened to explode inside of me.

"I need you," I whimpered, and he laughed against the delicate flesh. I rocked my hips, desperately trying to encourage him to enter my body. He held my stomach down, preventing me from moving as he slowly, torturously licked my heated flesh.

"You taste like heaven and you move like sin, woman," he whispered hoarsely. "I can't wait to hear you screaming my name while I ride your body."

"And you can, just get in me!" I urged. I was out of my mind with the need to come. Nothing in my life had ever made me feel like this. I felt like if he didn't connect with me, I'd die. I was trembling and shivering like a drug addict chasing my next high. There was something primal happening, something that tugged at the back of my mind, but I didn't know what it was, nor did I care. He parted my legs as he moved up, pushing the head of his cock into my tight sheath. "Yes!" I screamed, trying to hurry him the fuck up. What the fuck was wrong with me?

"No going back," he warned. "I can feel it, our souls connecting. You're mine, Emma, swear it to me."

"I swear," I gasped, and felt something connecting, igniting as he pushed himself inside. I screamed, and my body exploded violently. I held on to him as I felt myself fragment; pieces of me seemed to be reaching for the constellations on the ceiling. His face loomed over mine and I watched thin, lacy, glimmering black lines appear on his face and fanned out across his arms as white ones spread across my own. They mingled, danced and frolicked together as he continued to thrust inside of me. His entrance was painful; he stretched my body further than ever before. Tears slid from my eyes as I sobbed and pain rocked through me, but it wasn't from him. It was from inside of me. I somehow knew that my soul was opening for his, allowing him to see the pieces of me no one else had. I looked into his eyes as he strained over me. His eyes were obsidian, peppered with glowing red, like the stories told of demons of old. For a moment, I swore I saw huge black wings on his back, but once I looked into his eyes, I was lost.

He hadn't been lying; from the moment I was born, his life had revolved around mine. He'd watched me, loved me from afar, and he'd held back even though it caused him suffering. He'd known I was with Jaeden, and he'd let me choose that path instead of forcing his will on me.

I tried to pull away, to let his secrets remain his own, but I wasn't sure how to. I felt my body shattering again, shudders from another orgasm that ripped through me, and his followed it a moment later. As our racing hearts slowed and our bodies cooled, I realized we were bound together, as if some hand of fate had locked us together.

When he finally tore his eyes from mine, he lifted me. I was trapped on his cock; his hands were the only thing making my body work as he used my hips to guide me over his swollen cock. Being with him terrified me, but more than that, I knew I belonged with him. Everything in my life had driven me to him, even before I was born.

"Emma," he whispered against my forehead and I moaned his name as he sucked my neck softly, letting his blunt teeth nip at the flesh. "I'm so fucked, I want you so fucking bad," he muttered hoarsely, driving me onto his shaft harder and harder until I screamed his name as I exploded again, milking his cock as he came with me. "Not done," he growled as he pushed me flat on the bed, and I got a closer view of the huge black wings behind him.

"You drink too much Red Bull?" I mumbled, wondering if I was hallucinating.

He laughed, and closed those beautiful wings over me. He pulled my legs up and entered me hard; I cried out as the air left my lungs in a whooshing sound, and his hands captured mine, the black and white lights beneath our skin reaching for the other, meeting at the tips of our fingers as our eyes locked together.

"I have lived my entire life knowing that death would never experience life unless I found you, and here we are," he whispered. "My soul and yours, locked together, little phoenix," he murmured through each thrust.

"You make it sound as if we were fated in the stars?" I grinned wickedly with a thickness that made my voice all seductress, and a little Emma.

"Fate's a fickle bitch, sometimes we have to give her a push and show her what is right. I was afraid you'd reject me, because you're pure, perfect and so fucking beautiful. Now you're mine, there's no changing it," he whispered as he leaned over and kissed me.

He flipped me over onto my stomach, and pushed my legs apart, lifting my ass, and nudged his cock against my opening. He slapped my ass and I cried out; my hand instinctively moved to rub my ass, but he captured both of my hands in one of his, holding them against my back as his other hand threaded through my hair.

"Scream for me, Emma," he rasped as he thrust

into my core, as he pulled my hair and kissed my neck softly. The contrast was overwhelming. Gentle kisses and complete domination. He was in control, while reminding me that I was safe. It undid me. My toes curled, and I detonated, screaming incoherent words as my entire body was covered in tiny bumps and shattered with multiple orgasms that left me a quivering mess of pleasure.

"Again, Emma," he demanded, and it continued until we exploded again into a heap of limbs and both of us gasping for air. "Don't take this the wrong way, but I've never been so fucked in my entire life."

I laughed, and laughed some more until we were both laughing. "That was…wow. That was fucking scary."

"We mated, Emma, our souls are now connected; more so than they've ever been before."

"You should have told me that," I whispered.

"Would it have changed your mind?" he questioned, and I *felt* his insecurity. He had a vulnerability that left me feeling as if it was my own.

"No, but it would have warned me that shit would get seriously crazy during it. At one point, I thought I saw wings behind you."

He laughed.

"I'm not yanking your dick," I giggled.

"No, not now, but feel free to do so." He pushed his already hard cock against my thigh.

"The black and white—things?" I asked as I took his cock in my hand and stroked it, watching as he shuddered from the slow, sensual strokes.

"Souls, we're the only ones of our kind that connect on that level," he whispered.

"So, that was our souls?" I asked.

"Yes, you might say it was a physical representation of them," he murmured as he rolled on top of me and thrust inside. "Fair warning, little one; I have centuries to make up for, and you will get no sleep this night." His husky laughter swept through me, wrapping around me as he growled deep in his throat.

I cried out, meeting him thrust for thrust as he took me until the sun began to rise the next morning. This man was insatiable, and very capable of carrying out his threat. He'd continued until I was nothing more than a boneless mess, and even then, he took what he needed as I held on to him, allowing him everything he needed from me, and more.

Chapter Twenty-Three

I awoke sore, my body one solid ache. I smiled like a cat who'd indulged in a little too much cream. I sat up, slowly, taking in his room for the first time. I paused, blinked, and blinked again to rid the sleep from my eyes. Nope, still there.

Thousands of pictures of me decorated the walls of his room from floor to ceiling. Most of them looked to be from before the virus hit, but a few were more recent. One was even from the battle where we'd fought the rogue wolves. Someone had taken it right before the battle had begun.

"Gunpowder and lace," he mused from where he'd awoken to watch me gawk at his walls. "That's one of my favorites. It's the day you rose. You stopped hiding and took control. You also reminded me why men shouldn't allow women onto the battlefield."

"And why's that?" I asked, getting heated at his

sexist opinion.

"Because the combination is a very strong aphrodisiac," he murmured against my ear as his fingers slowly danced upon my skin.

The tips of his fingers controlled me more than any restraint ever could have. It was as if his fingers knew exactly where to touch, and when, to entice my center. I craved his presence, not necessarily the sex, but being able to sit beside him, to feel him there. I'd never felt that way with Jaeden, and that I did with Azrael frightened me. I liked the idea of doing mundane things together. Just sitting together felt magical, and the idea of leaving it behind caused a tightening in my chest that I couldn't explain. When I was with him, hours felt like seconds, but the moment he left, time stretched on endlessly.

He rolled me beneath him slowly, giving me enough time to change my mind. His lips found mine in a slow, tantalizing kiss. His teeth pulled on my lip and I spread my legs, giving him access to what he sought.

"You're a little gunpowder and lace, Emma. So soft and yet once that fuse is lit, you light up," he whispered huskily. He nudged against my pussy and pushed inside. When he was buried in my depths, he lifted his body up and looked down at me with a look I couldn't understand. His feelings, though, I felt them. They created warmth inside of me that made my entire body quiver and tremble. "I didn't just fall in love with you, Emma. I've always loved you. From the moment I saw you, I felt you were the one for me. That one day we'd be together because, for me, there would be nobody else. I walked into this with my eyes wide open and my heart even more so. I chose to take every step beside you, even when you weren't aware of it. I believe in fate and destiny, but even without them, I'd still choose you over anyone else. I know you don't feel the same yet, but I've had a lot longer to understand everything about you, starting with your beauty all the way to your flaws. I know you still love Jaeden, I can feel it. I'm not asking you to love me right now, but I'm asking you to try and love me a little, too."

I swallowed tears and shook my head. This wasn't the time or place to discuss this. I didn't love Jaeden as I had, and I was beginning to think it was because of Azrael and the fact that I didn't feel as if I had to always be on guard with him. Things between Jaeden and me had changed; they'd started to the moment he'd walked away and left me broken.

"I'm afraid to love you," I replied honestly with a slight tremble to my tone. "I'm afraid you'll break me into teeny-tiny pieces, and I'm not strong enough to handle it."

"I can't hurt you without hurting myself," he said softly, with a gentle smile. "I can't betray you, and I won't ever let you down like he did," he promised, and I felt the truth in his words. "I've spent centuries looking for the one woman I could hold, and be with; do you really think I wouldn't move mountains to get to you, and do anything to keep you?" He began to thrust himself into me, slowly. Deliberately.

"Azrael," I whispered roughly, but he covered my mouth with his, stopping anything else I might have been about to say in the process. I felt his need to please me. I felt his insecurity, which only turned me on more.

I kissed him back harder, which ignited a need in him that made his motions faster, harder, and before I knew what was happening, I was screaming and clinging to his massive body as I yelled his name on repeat, like a scratched record.

"That's it, give it to me, I want all of you," he murmured as he lifted me against his chest, in a half kneeling, half seated position which pushed him even deeper into me. He used my hips as I clung to his muscled shoulders, driving his cock deep into my depths.

I felt his pleasure building. I opened up my mind to feel even more of the connection we shared. It was as if my own orgasm was growing but inside of him. I lifted my limp head to watch as his muscles clenched, tightened, and he roared his own release. I exploded again, as if our orgasms had been linked. He undid me.

This creature that had so much arrogant confidence and self-control came undone. And, in moments like these when he was unguarded, I was able to see that he had insecurities that endeared him to me. Where Jaeden had held back a part of himself from me, Azrael gave me everything. Where Jaeden had always wanted control, Azrael had it naturally. A single touch made me bend to him, and he didn't force it, didn't ask for it.

"I wish we could stay like this," he rumbled against my ear. "We need to present you to our people." He caressed my back and shoulders gently. "As greedy as I am to keep you all to myself, it's time you met some of them."

Wait up, go back. I had people, and didn't need any more people, per se.

"Sentinels?" I asked, knowing he wasn't referring to the people in the bunkers.

"Yes, but you have nothing to worry about. They're going to adore you. You are everything our kind stands for. If they can accept me, Emma, you have nothing to worry about."

"Other than them knowing that I was sleeping with the enemy and that my mother is a crazy bitch? That one Sentinel I met didn't seem very happy with me." I pointed out as he watched my walls slam up. I wasn't much of a people person. I'd never been good with them before the world went to shit, and my people skills hadn't improved since.

"I'll be with you every step of the way," he whispered as he lay down beside me and smiled as he wound a strand of my hair around his finger. "If you don't put on clothes soon, we'll never leave this bed, ever," he warned and I laughed, turning to look into his seductive eyes.

"We could just forget the world," I replied, knowing I never could. The thought was nice, but I needed to find Grayson, and I had to get home to Addy before she ended up birthing puppies without supervision.

"There is a pack and suitable travel clothing waiting for you in your room; once you are ready, we will head out," he informed me as he got out of bed and headed into the other room. I watched his firm backside until he was out of sight. I rose from the bed, enjoying the ache he'd created throughout the night.

I milled about his room (yes, I was snooping), finding a few familiar things. Like a couple of my missing panties that I'd brushed off before, thinking Jaeden had done it. I also found my senior portrait that had been taken off my dresser. He also had the one from the wall, the one where I'd been in the meadow. I frowned, and figured I'd ask him about his sticky fingers later.

I showered and dressed in jeans that hung low on my hips, with a belt to keep them from sliding down. Next, I picked a white tank top and found weapon harnesses similar to what I normally wore—only better—laid out on the bed. I slipped them on and snapped the fully-loaded weapons into my holsters. One thing I had to acknowledge, the man knew his weaponry. I looked a wild mix between country girl, and apocalyptic fashion queen. I snorted, because that was something that should never go together. Apocalypse and fashion queen. I turned, slipping my boots on, and wiggled my toes in the familiar leather boots. I shoved the rest of the ammo, weapons and some practical clothes that were suitable for travel into the new sturdy pack that he'd left out for me.

"Might want to put your hair up for the ride," he commented from where he leaned against the doorframe in a black V-neck T-shirt with loose fitting jeans and leather boots. I liked him out of his armor, but I really liked him out of his clothes.

"Why?"

"Ducati; you're on the back. I want to feel your arms around me for a while," he replied with a wicked smile.

"And where are we going?" I countered.

"Provo." His eyes held mine meaningfully before he turned, and left me with my heart in my throat.

"Wait, come back here!" I shouted, already chasing after him as I struggled to pull the heavy pack on my back. I caught up to him and turned him around. "My mother was following a route to Provo. Not to mention that we had a lead that those Sentinels who were in cahoots with her were there."

"They are not with your mother, never have been. They've been looking for her. As soon as we were able to prove what she'd done, she was marked for death. Hayden had been hunting for traces of her and her conspirators when he discovered you. After that, he shadowed you on and off for a few weeks before you met him to see how loyal you might be to her and if you were part of her conspiracy. Your loyalty to those who fought with you was the only thing we questioned after that."

"Hayden, huh? How's his arm?" I smirked, knowing Raphael had managed to shoot him with an arrow in the shoulder.

"He's healed," he mumbled as we stopped at the door to the bunker, and asked me to wait for a moment.

I stood there, considering the irony that he was taking me right where I wanted to go. I ran towards the door without waiting for him and was gazing out the glass when he pulled up in front of the house. His Ducati was a work of art. The sight of Azrael on it made my ovaries physically hurt. His arms were bare, and I could see the omega glyphs branded on the inside of his forearms that were similar to the infinity glyphs on mine. His shirt did little to hide them, and he looked good enough to eat.

He straightened the bike, stood up, and looked at me with his hand extended. I swallowed, and smiled as I made my way to him. I missed my Ducati, but it was home, safe. I hadn't wanted to bring it since we hadn't expected to be on foot for most of the trip and the terrain was shit.

"You know, you're faster than the bike is," I teased. "Are you getting lazy in your old age?"

"Sometimes I like to enjoy the trip, smartass," he laughed and smirked as he placed his hands on the bars. "Hold on tight," he said as he slid his helmet on and I followed his lead. We may be immortal, but head wounds hurt like a bitch.

I wrapped my arms around him, placed my feet on the pegs, and inhaled his heavenly male scent. He turned his head, smiled and clicked a button and music began to play inside the helmets. I so needed one of these back home. Luke Bryan's *Kick the Dust Up* surrounded my senses and I smiled. I could do the country thing. I'd grown up in a town that thrived on it.

He hit the gas, and we were off; the smile wasn't leaving my lips anytime soon. I liked this. Holding on to him, letting him drive, all of it. Just a few minutes into it and I was rocking with the beat. Yeah, I could get used to this, which, for me, was dangerous.

After a few hours and a couple stops, we were entering the outskirts of Provo. It was a humid day, and the city was greener and lusher than I remembered seeing in pictures. It reminded me of home, only a lot bigger. No cars lined the streets; no bodies littered it, either. Someone had spent a lot of time cleaning it up.

Azrael killed the music and I turned, sensing the same thing he had once my senses weren't muted by the music's beat. My heart spiked, and everything inside of me said to run. I looked behind us just in time to catch the flash from a muzzle.

"Go!" I shouted, but he hadn't needed me to tell him. His armor had already materialized around his body as if from thin air, and he pushed his motorcycle helmet off as his armored one materialized around his head.

"Get in front of me," he ordered as we hit bumps,

caught air, and bullets whizzed by.

Get in front of him? I felt a burning sensation in my arm and frowned as blood became visible. I struggled to ignore it, as I slowly wormed my way around him, but with the shots ringing out, it wasn't easy. One moment I was clinging to his side, and the next he'd somehow managed to help me slip around. I wrapped my legs around his waist, pulled the guns from their holsters, and searched the trees.

"How bad are you hit?" he demanded.

"Grazed; I'll live," I replied, and watched as a four-wheeler caught air as it burst from the woods. I aimed both guns, shooting to the left, knowing they would hit the same bump we just had.

Not going to lie. Riding like this with Azrael and feeling him against my delicate parts? Hot. As. Fuck. Deadly, but I felt bulletproof with him and his armor protecting me. I reached up and removed my helmet to make it easier to see, and watched as his eyes slowly drifted down to meet mine.

"Hold on," he warned as he turned left, and we made our way through the brush. His Ducati had the same wide tires as mine. He easily and expertly navigated us through the branches and back trails until a large gate loomed in the distance. "Tighter," he growled at the same moment he caught air.

I was holding on to him, but gravity isn't kind. The bike flipped off a jump, and we went airborne. I was screaming as other people came into view. This was going to suck, because we'd jumped a hill, a gate, and now we were falling to the freaking ground.

Right before we would have crashed onto the pavement, time stood still. I watched as Azrael bounced, stood, and turned, plucking me out of the air. He'd fucking frozen *me*! He wasn't even hurt from falling to the ground? He walked without a limp. Perfectly.

"Told you, Emma, I'll never let you fall or let you down," he mused with a sexy grin. I smiled up at him and released the breath I'd been holding. I turned, finding about a hundred or so pairs of eyes staring at us.

So much for making a normal entrance.

I'd made it to the stronghold in Provo Utah, but it hadn't been with the people I'd intended to. I was here, with my people.

Chapter Twenty-Four

I stared in awe at the sheer magnitude of the temple. They'd created a stronghold, one that stood proudly against the backdrop of the mountains that it was nestled in. People had stopped what they'd been doing when we'd jumped the bike over the gates, but now they put their heads down, waiting for something or someone to say something.

My vision was going gray; people's images blurred, revealing their status as they waited. I held on to Azrael, as if he was my anchor. A group of people made their way through the crowd towards us. One familiar, as his image shimmered to reveal the Knight. The once cold blue eyes were now warmer, and his skin looked bronzed instead of the olive color he'd had when I'd met him on the field in the middle of the rogue battle. His head tilted, as if he was trying to gauge my response to him. He pushed his long brown hair from his face as they closed the distance to stand in front of us.

"Azrael, I see you have finally claimed your woman," he mused, his smile warm and affectionate. It was a huge change from the last time. He'd called me the vampire's whore. He'd also been willing to fight me then; not so much now.

"Hayden, this is Emma. Emma, this is Hayden, your Knight," Azrael whispered the last against my ear. "Maude, Kayden, and Hayden are brothers and sister sired from the same parents. Kayden and Hayden are twins, but Kayden tends to be a bit more circumspect than his brother."

"We've met," I informed Azrael.

"Indeed, we have. I do apologize for the way I behaved the last time. I was sure you'd chosen to side with your mother. I mean, based on how it looked, you were balls deep with the enemy," he grinned, the pun not lost on me.

"Hayden, she's a Guardian of Life and deserves respect," Azrael growled, his eyes holding warning with each word. "Why hasn't the area been secured?" He swiftly changed the subject.

"Trina is growing bolder," Kayden offered. "Dagan is closer than we expected as well. It's probably because you have her daughter," he said, his cold blue eyes shifting to me. "It seems as though they are willing to sacrifice much to secure her capture."

"They won't get her," Azrael replied. "Where is Katie?"

"She's…busy. There have been a few developments while you were otherwise detained," Hayden advised. "She's below; if you'd like, I can escort Emma to her chambers while you see to Katie. I'm sure she'll be excited to know that you have returned, Azrael."

I wanted to grab onto Azrael and beg him not to leave me. The eyes were on us; all of them. I felt uncomfortable here, as if I was an outsider who didn't belong. They all knew of my mother, what she was and what she'd done to the world. I understood the ones who watched me with mistrust. I was the daughter of enemy number one.

Azrael must have felt my unease, because he pulled me closer and whispered against my ear. His hot breath fanned my flesh, causing a ripple of need to pulse through me.

"You're safe here, Emma. They will not judge you based off the actions of your mother. They are aware that you were never a part of it, not willingly. Hayden will show you the room; bathe and I'll be there as soon as I can be. I have much to show you," he chuckled wickedly; the sound of it caused the hairs on my neck to rise in awareness.

"Okay," I replied as I stepped closer to Hayden, who nodded.

I watched as Azrael walked away from me with the others. He looked as if he fit in here, even though his armor was securely in place. His tall frame towered over most of the others in the crowd as they parted to allow him through.

"You're just full of surprises, *Guardian*," Hayden commented, pulling my attention back to him.

"What's that supposed to mean?" I was on guard now that I was on my own in the strange temple.

"First your vampire lover, and now Azrael." He looked back at me as he led the way. "You've been with him, right?" he asked.

"That's personal," I muttered as I started to follow him as the crowd stared at me. "They're staring at me."

"No, they're staring at a Guardian of Life who just walked in holding hands with a Guardian of Death. You understand that no one expected another Guardian of Life yet, right?" he asked, giving me a mischievous smile.

"I don't know what you're talking about," I said guardedly. Azrael had said something to that effect, but I wasn't sure where Hayden was going with this line of thought.

"Guardians of Life aren't supposed to arrive until the world is ready to be mended, and yet here you are in the midst of chaos. I came back from the battle and told all what I had seen. No one but Azrael believed that you had become a Guardian. To him, you were a gift. To the rest of us, you're a problem. Your birth is from questionable parentage; you weren't born in a Sentinel temple, nor were you raised as one of us, so you are ignorant of our ways and your function. A Guardian of Life is supposed to be a gentle soul that values life, and yet I know you have taken it. Azrael is not wrong in wanting you, but I wonder just what it is about you that draw so many men to you. The wolf, he's in love with you. He has been for some time. He hides it well, but he'd die for you. The vampire, he's fucking smitten by you, and yet conflicted because of the rules he lives by. Azrael, well, he's simple. He can't touch anyone else. Even so, he was drawn to you before he knew it."

"Azrael said it's because I'm Life," I answered softly. "That Jaeden is drawn to me because I am life and he is sort of the undead. He craves what he can never have. Azrael said it's the same for him. Lachlan would love a stick if it could get him off. Lachlan is a rare breed as well. He has loyalty, which he gives to those who earn it. I'm not sure he loves me in the way you're thinking. He'd die for me, yes, but then again, I'd die for him, too. That's not love. It's family. We've become close; we care that the other survives."

"Back to the question that started this," he replied, ignoring my reasoning. "Have you fucked Azrael?"

"Back to the answer," I snapped. "It's still none of your damn business." I turned to look at him.

"So you have," he mused. "And his seed didn't poison you?"

"Seed? I'm not a flower, and we didn't pollinate."

He laughed. "You're on birth control, yes?"

"Yes," I replied. I'd been on it since I'd pilfered it from the clinic. I was due for another shot soon. Every three months, like clockwork, I'd give myself that damn Depo-shot. Not that I needed to worry with Jaeden; his seeds weren't planting any flowers. I took it for my peace of mind alone.

"Good, because no one really knows what would happen should you and Azrael create a life. The other pairs never conceived, so no one is sure if that is by choice or design," he said cryptically.

"I would guess that in nine months after we planted the seeds in the garden, that we'd have a baby. Afterwards we'd become sleep-deprived, go insane for the first year, and then run our asses off keeping up with the baby for the next eighteen years. Just a guess," I stated as we arrived in front of a set of very tall doors.

"If you were human, yes," Hayden laughed. "You're not, Emma. Keep this in mind: You can have Jaeden's child. You are a Guardian of Life; you bring back that which is dying. You can heal. He is infected with the virus of vampirism, but should you be with him when you've fully become Life, he'd no longer be vampire. He'd be human. Judging from your face, Azrael forgot to mention what would happen should you run back to your lover after you come into all of your powers. It is our guess, but considering what you are, its probability is high."

"No, he must have left that part out of it," I replied crisply. Why would he have left that part out? It was huge! I could potentially turn vampires mortal. What if I'd run back to Jaeden and done so? Had he knowingly left that spicy tidbit out in case I would run back to him? Wait. No, he had tried to tell me; I just hadn't understood what he meant at the time.

"Your new rooms, my lady," Hayden announced, pushing the doors open.

"Wow," I said with a low whistle. The room was huge. It was decorated in a country-chic theme that included sheepskin rugs, with soft blue and white accents. The bed was huge, with a fancy wrought iron metal frame that had a canopy which was draped with soft sheer curtains to match the room's soothing colors. There was a couch against one wall, which faced the front gates of the temple and looked over the courtyard.

"You like it?" he asked, watching me carefully.

"It's gorgeous," I acknowledged.

"I'm glad. The bath is through there." He pointed at an open door. "The tub has heated jets and all. Luckily this place was in the middle of being refurbished when the world went to hell. We've updated a few things, but Azrael insisted this room be fit for a queen. There are Mongolian-lab stools in the bathroom and on the balcony. I do ask that you stay away from the windows until Azrael returns, as the people who shot at you have yet to be contained. There's fresh clothing in the drawers, all in the sizes Azrael had us obtain."

"He stole my undies. That's how he knew my size," I whispered while crinkling my nose.

Hayden coughed and laughed nervously. "Actually, I was the one who stole them and a few other items from your room. When Azrael made his way back here, he confiscated them from me along with some pictures I had taken when I was following you," Hayden said ruefully, and I wondered how that confrontation went down. "How was I to know that he'd known you were there and he was biding his time? He's a strategist. If he wasn't, he'd have just ridden into your town the day the world started to crumble and taken you. It's what I would have done had I known you were going to be mine. Azrael, though, he's got the patience of a fucking saint."

I meandered around the room picking things up and examining them before putting them back down. He'd had more than one room created for me. The house he'd first taken me to had mirrored this room. Both locations had simple luxuries that made it more comfortable, and yet were simple things. Like the sheepskin couches.

"Do you plan on watching me shower?" I asked as I turned to look at Hayden.

"Only if my lady wishes it," he quipped as his eyes slowly drifted down my body. "I'm yours, Emma. I was born to serve you. I am your protector, your knight. If you move, I move. If you ask me to do *anything*, I do it. The knight protects the queen," he smirked boyishly. "Or in this case, Guardian."

"Well, I don't need protection and I sure as hell don't need you to assist me in bathing."

"I'm just a boy, standing here, hoping to the Gods you need help getting naked, my lady," he groaned with a smile on his face.

"Oh…hmmm, maybe I do need help," I offered, smiling as Azrael stepped from the shadows behind Hayden.

"Oh, you do?" he asked, his eyes smiling. I frowned, and he paused. "Azrael is standing behind me, isn't he?" he laughed. "Well, can't blame me for trying. I'm sure your lord and master will see to all your needs now. I bid you goodnight, my lady," he grinned, and gave me a mock bow before he turned to Azrael and held up his hands. "Had to try, just making sure she's faithful to my lord."

"Get out, Hayden," he growled, and then shook his head at the guy's audacity.

I watched Hayden give me thumbs up before he fled from the room. I stood there, staring at Azrael as my emotions warred inside of me.

"I could have killed Jaeden," I whispered as I chewed on my lip.

"Had you run back to him, I would have killed him.

It wouldn't have mattered what he was at that point," he explained. "You haven't bathed." He stepped further into the room before he closed the door.

"Hayden was a chatty-Cathy," I offered.

"He's infatuated with you. I don't blame him for that. You'd have to be a monk or made of stone not to see your beauty, Emma. He's neither of those."

"Did the meeting go well?" I asked, wondering why the hell I was so suddenly nervous about being alone with Azrael.

"Take off your clothes," he ordered. The way he looked at me felt like he was undressing me before I even had a chance to take them off.

Chapter Twenty-Five

I leaned against Azrael as he washed my hair. I was in heaven, and at the same time, my emotions were all over the place. He'd told me absolutely nothing about what required his immediate attention when we'd arrived here. When I asked him about it, he ignored the question, and instead started pulling my clothes off, stripping me bare as he walked me backwards into the bathroom.

Once there, he'd stripped as well. He poured richly scented bath salts into the tub, his eyes trained on what he was doing instead of me standing awkwardly behind him. This man gave me butterflies. My emotions became a mess of nervous energy around him, but more than that, he simply undid me. He climbed into the tub, extended his hand, and helped me in, as if I was some delicate flower.

"You know, you keep spoiling me and it's going to be hard to go home," I whispered, realizing my mistake when he stiffened behind me.

"Your home is with me now," he replied, his hands moving around to encircle my waist as he kissed my ear. "You're mine. You go where I go; I go where you go."

"Azrael, my people depend on me. At some point, I have to go back to the Ark. I need to speak to Addy. She's probably really worried about me."

"Addy is enjoying Liam; she's fine without you." His voice was soothing, as if he was trying to comfort me. "Tonight, it's just us. Leave out all the rest, Emma."

I turned to look at him, finding him smiling as his hands slipped between my legs. Oh shit. I felt his cock growing hard against my derrière. He turned me around until I was facing him and then lifted me up so that I was sitting in his lap.

"I want you," he stated, his eyes growing heavy as lust filled them. "Tonight, I'm going to enjoy you the way I have always wanted to. Tonight, I show you what it's really like to be with me. Last time I was careful with you because I didn't want to scare or hurt you. It's been a very long time for me, and I didn't want to shock you. There's so much that has changed, and so much I want to try with you."

I swallowed down the moan that was caused from his words, mixed with the sensations of my pussy rubbing over his cock in the warm water.

"What exactly do you want to do to me?" I whispered

huskily. Considering how wild our first night together was, I couldn't even think of what else he could do to me if that was his idea of going easy on me.

"Everything," he growled as his mouth crushed against mine.

His kiss was hungry, as if he was starving and couldn't get enough. His hands rocked my hips against his velvety length until I thought I would come from that alone. The moment I got close to the brink, he lifted me up with him as he stood. Water went everywhere; tiny tendrils raced down his chest, and before I could stop myself, I was kissing them, catching them with my tongue as he groaned.

He set me on the bed carefully, like a treasured jewel, and I watched as he stood back, his fist working his massive cock. "Spread your legs," he whispered huskily.

I did, and his eyes slid to my heat and turned red. They glowed with an emotion I couldn't place, but then he snapped out of his haze and his eyes rose to hold mine.

"You're so beautiful," he murmured as he climbed onto the bed, and scooted my body until I was situated to his liking. He reached over me, pulling down a length of the sheer material that had adorned the bed, and used it to capture my hands. I felt a rush of panic as he secured them to the wrought iron frame. "Scared?" he asked, sitting back to look down the length of my exposed body.

"A little," I replied honestly, unable to hide the quiver in my voice. I watched as his lips broke into a roguish grin, as he lowered his mouth to capture the peak of my nipple, which he nipped at. A moan erupted from my lungs before I even knew it was coming. He let his teeth graze my flesh softly, before his eyes focused on mine.

"I'm going to enjoy this." He reached up for yet another length of fabric, and I shivered as he lifted my head and covered my eyes before he kissed me. I swallowed as he pulled away, fully intending to ask him what he was thinking, but the velvet tip of his cock pushed against my lips.

I opened for him, knowing I wouldn't fit all of him in my mouth, but I worked the tip and sensitive flesh with my tongue and lips the best I could, since I was trapped in this position. His fingers found my heat and slowly worked my flesh as I moaned and made crazy noises with his cock securely in my mouth. I was about to come when his fingers stopped, and he slapped my pussy hard enough that I cried out in wonder. He used my surprise to push his dick in further. It slammed against the back of my throat as his hand slapped my pussy again. He withdrew a little, and his fingers softly caressed the stinging skin.

"You enjoy it rough," he mused as he rocked his hips, filling my mouth as he pleasured himself. His fingers felt like heaven against the sore flesh; one tantalizing finger slid teasingly into my molten depths. There was no denying that I liked it. I was soaking wet, he had the proof of it there for his greedy eyes to see, if he was looking at it. I struggled to take more of him, crying out with frustration as he withdrew from both my mouth and pussy.

His hot breath fanned my flesh as he placed soft kisses against my skin. He kissed my neck, then the swell of my breasts as he kissed and licked a slow, lazy trail down my belly, until his mouth hovered over my pussy. I lifted my hips, expecting him to do what I wanted, but he didn't. Instead, he kissed the inside of my thighs, slowly making his way to my calves and then my ankles. It was torture; beautiful, painful agony. I felt as if I was in physical pain, needing him to take me.

I whispered his name repeatedly, but he ignored my pleas for mercy. He spread my legs, pushing them open as he slowly moved between them. His cock pushed against my opening, slowly sliding over it until I was panting and lifting my hips off the bed to increase the contact. He stopped, backed away, and then his mouth kissed and licked around my opening, never once touching the flesh I needed him to.

"You're killing me," I whimpered, and he laughed huskily.

"Fucking is easy," he mused. "Making you beg for something you desire while you squirm; that's something I've dreamed of since you became a woman,

Emma. It's so much better than I had envisioned it," he groaned as his mouth went back to work, kissing around my heated flesh. "You smell of heaven, so wet with the need to be fucked. If I could keep you like this forever, I would," he whispered hoarsely.

His fingers parted my flesh and held it there, exposing my secrets to his eyes. His tongue slowly worked my pussy from the front to the back, and I cried out as the storm in my belly began to unfurl and shoot towards my pussy.

"Azrael," I whimpered, as he ignored my plea yet again.

"Mmm, so wet, so fucking good. Out of everything I missed when I lost the ability to touch, it was the taste of a woman when she was in need. I could taste you for eternity and never tire of it, sweet girl," he groaned as he moved his mouth in a frenzied motion over my flesh. His fingers pushed inside and I lost all control.

I shattered. My back bowed, and my legs clamped around his head, holding him in place. His free hand reached up, pinching one nipple and then the other as he continued pushing his fingers to a silent tempo as his mouth sucked and kissed my pussy. I was floating, or dying. I didn't care. It didn't matter. I was in heaven, and he'd taken me there.

He pulled away and I screamed for him, the loss of him too much to bear. His mouth touched mine as he pushed inside my body. He kissed me with fervor, an urgency that matched my own as he filled my body until it was painful to take anymore. He tore his mouth from mine and lifted my legs, rocking my hips until I took what he gave me.

"Jesus, woman, you undo me," he roared, as he pulled out only to lunge in again. He rested my feet on his shoulders, and I struggled against the delicate material as I tried to free my hands to touch him. I couldn't see, couldn't touch him. He only allowed me to feel what he wanted, and it was too much. I lifted my hips, giving him more depth as he rocked and worked his hips.

Once he'd worked me into another storm, he stopped, causing me to growl at the loss of his cock. I tried sitting up, but he merely laughed at my sad attempt. He turned me over onto my stomach, parted my legs with his knees, and then pushed his fingers deep inside my pussy as he lifted my stomach with his other hand.

"You're wet, Emma," he announced, like it was some sort of surprise.

"You think?" I asked, turning my head in the direction where I knew him to be. His hand came down hard on my ass, and I moaned.

"Jesus," he mused as he lowered his mouth and licked my pussy around where his fingers continued to work me over. He pulled his mouth away and I moaned, over his slow seduction and ready for the next orgasms. My body was tight; it was like a guitar string, ready to be played and he was toying with me as he primed and tuned it.

"Just do it…ow!" I screamed as he bit my ass. "You did not just bite my ass!" I yelled out as he did it again, and then he kissed it gently. "No kissing my ass!"

He laughed.

I turned to glare at him, but unfortunately, it had little impact since my eyes were still covered. He pulled away; his hands grasped my hips as he nudged my legs apart again. One left my hip to slowly glide up my back to touch the back of my head. I was just about to ask what he planned to do, when he thrust inside me and pulled my hair at the same time.

"Oh God, yes!" I screamed as he started to move with precise, punishing thrusts that had me meeting him, teetering on the brink of orgasm. I didn't hold back; I gave him everything I had. I screamed his name, praised his cock, and felt everything he did as he rode me. Fuck beast mode; this man was the God of sex. His cock touched that special spot. The spot that most men spend their entire life trying to find, and he went there with ease.

I exploded violently over and over again until the orgasms turned to pain, and still, I begged for more. My body was a mess of nerves and they were all being touched at once. He didn't stop, even when I'd stopped moving. He was hard, unforgiving, and aggressive as he took me. He'd come at any moment, or so I told myself on repeat.

He didn't. He flipped me onto my side and lifted my leg until it was in a painful position, then surged forward. I bucked against him screaming as I climaxed yet again. Tears filled my eyes as I whispered things to him until I felt him tense and shout as his cock jerked inside of me, and he finally rested his head against my breasts.

"I love you too, Emma," he whispered, and I blinked. Oh. Fuck.

"Did I say that?" I whispered, my throat on fire from emotions he'd created by saying it.

"No, I feel it. I feel it as surely as I feel you when your orgasm rushes through you. Your emotions are no longer hidden from me. You don't have to say it, I feel it. I'm guessing you fell in love when I bit your perky ass," he teased lightly as sweat beaded against my skin.

I laughed. "I am a sucker for an ass biter, but no, I don't know if I love you. I don't even really know you," I admitted, feeling his fingers as he removed the blindfold to reveal the tears in my eyes.

"I feel it, just like I know it is hurting you to hear me say it," he murmured as he leaned over my sweat-drenched body to untie my hands. "I know you love him still," he whispered. "I can wait for you to know it. I can wait until you're ready to let me love you. I don't expect you to forget him. I know he's a part of you. It's how you are built. You don't let go easily, but neither do I. I've known we were meant to be together for a long time. You've just learned of it, so I can be patient with you."

"It scares me," I replied honestly. "It's terrifying to feel so much this soon. I feel everything from you, shit, you came and I felt it. I felt your need to unleash your aggression on me, too. I wanted it, all of it. I wanted to be the one who took it from you. I'm not one who goes into anything blindly, and yet I'm willing to with you, and that scares the shit out of me."

"You need to be in control," he murmured gently.

"Always," I agreed. "I have to be, or people die. Even before the virus hit, I had to have control. I had to be the parent for Grayson."

"You're barely old enough to be a parent, Emma. Grayson isn't here, so you shouldn't feel bad about letting go. You wanted me to be rough; you wanted to lose control, and yet you fought it. You fought your own needs because even though you think you're giving me everything, you continue to hold a sliver of yourself away. The piece of you that thinks that, if you let anyone else see that you may have a weakness, they will use it to crush you. I won't let that happen. You're my soul, little phoenix. We're in this together. You and me. Got me?" he whispered.

"It's just not that easy."

"It is, you just have to let it all go. As Sentinels we don't control everything, it's just not possible. You'll find a way to live without having to control everything."

Chapter Twenty-Six

I'd slept like the dead. Azrael had wrapped me in his heat, curling my body close to his as I succumbed to sleep. I'd felt cherished, safely curled in his arms. The man unraveled me, terrified me, and wrung out every sexual desire all at once. He disarmed me and left me confused. Azrael made me confused about my feelings, myself, and my sense of purpose. I'd planned to escape him and yet, somewhere along the way, I'd stopped trying to. I still intended to go home, that much was a given, but the thought of leaving him physically hurt me. If I could get him to help me find Grayson, I'd have an actual chance of doing it without trading myself for him.

From the moment Grayson was taken, I knew I would most likely have to trade myself for him. I wasn't an idiot; after seeing the way Hayden outmaneuvered me so easily during the battle with the wolves, I knew none of us could fight Trina and her group of Sentinels until I was trained. They most likely would have slaughtered us. I'd been desperate and naïve to think it would have worked, but now I had Azrael in my corner.

I sat on the bed as I brushed my hair, unraveling the inner turmoil that I'd struggled with for so long. I wasn't in love with Jaeden as much as I thought I was. Too much had happened to go back to what we'd been. There wasn't any way to salvage our relationship, and it broke my heart to let him go, but in a way, it was a kindness. If Azrael hadn't come for me, eventually I would have caved and let Jaeden back into my heart, and eventually Shamus, his maker, or the elders would have given some stupid order that would have taken him away from me again. Or, if Hayden was right, when all of my powers eventually manifested, I would have turned him mortal. Either scenario would have made one or both of us bitter, and I hated to even think about how that would have played out.

A knock sounded at the door, and then it swung open to reveal Hayden. He looked as if he hadn't slept at all last night.

"Emma, Azrael sent me to get you. He said you'd want to know that we've captured Dagan."

"What?" I asked. My heart sped up, and my stomach dropped.

"We captured Dagan and a couple of Trina's followers, but there's something you should know," Hayden's voice was soft, a contrast to the tenseness of his body as he folded his arms across his chest. "They're infected, and the symptoms look a lot like Pacers flu."

"Sentinels are immortal." I was really confused, because I still grasped little about what I was. What we were.

"Indeed, but he's sick nonetheless."

I was up and heading out the door. "Take me to him, he knows where Grayson is."

"Emma, he hasn't got long to live, if the virus he has is anything like the one the humans had. They're holding them in the courtyard; I'll take you to Azrael."

I followed him, and I could hear the others chattering excitedly about the capture as if it was a good thing. I, on the other hand, had a sick feeling in my stomach that wouldn't let up. Trina had gushed with pride when she'd told me Dagan was my father, so why would she allow him to get captured? Was she close? Was Grayson?

"Faster," I urged, needing to get to Dagan and question him. We were in the courtyard within moments and once there, I felt like my heart and stomach dropped. Dagan was sick, very sick. He had bloody tears running from his eyes, along with a steady flow of blood oozing from his nose. I looked around the full courtyard and shook my head. "This is wrong."

"It's all wrong," Hayden agreed as my eyes locked with Azrael's; I knew he could sense my overwhelming panic as it rushed through me.

Trina wasn't just a disgraced Sentinel; she was a scientist, and she worked with some of the world's most elite scientists. She'd gathered her followers before the virus, and together, they'd created the very virus that had killed most of the human race off within weeks. They'd created a perfect killer, one that would lift her up to where she wanted to be: queen of this world.

"They're like a Trojan horse," I whispered as the implications of what I was seeing whirled through my mind, as others gathered closer to where Azrael stood just inches away from Dagan. "Azrael," I cried as he lifted his hand to wipe at a trickle of blood that slid from his nose.

I ran forward, needing to know he'd be okay. He was death personified; he couldn't die, right? I rushed to him, but he held up his hand as his armor covered him protectively, as if he was trying to protect me from himself.

"No, I can help you," I cried.

"Stay away, Emma. I won't die, but the rest…" He let his words trail off as the complications of the reality of the situation hit him. "*Shit.*"

Others were watching us, and I noticed a few of the Sentinels—they must have been the ones who captured Dagan—also had blood trickling from their noses. Trina had found a way to kill Sentinels; she'd done the impossible. I wondered if the humans had only been an experiment in her plot, or had she needed them weakened as well?

"Why?" I demanded of Dagan, who watched me coldly. "Why kill your own people? She wasn't happy killing off the humans, so now she's willing to kill us all?" I screamed.

"Not all, just him. You weren't supposed to be here, Emmalyn. You're supposed to be with that horde of monsters you tramp around with."

"Where is she? She left you here to die! Where's Grayson?" I demanded, letting my emotions connect with Azrael's, sensing that somehow he was purging the virus from his system. His heart was steady; his breathing was labored, but I focused on his heart.

"Stupid girl," Dagan hissed. "She didn't need him," he laughed darkly; spittle ran down his lips. "He was nothing more than a pawn, meant to be used for the greater good. He played his part beautifully. After we left you in Priest River, we met up at the Albeni Falls Dam, and the human scientist with us gave Grayson the first dose of the new virus. It killed him, and he came back, as Sentinels do. Unfortunately, he did not become a strong Knight as Trina thought he would. He was given another dose, and this time, sweet Emma, the little bastard died. I guess neither of her children turned out how she thought they would," he laughed coldly.

My heart dropped, and I had to force myself not to rush forward or scream at him. I couldn't let him see how much his words were tearing me apart. Everything inside of me was demanding I do one or the other.

"You're lying. I know she wouldn't kill him. Not without getting me first!"

"Did you really think she'd keep him alive? He was weak, killing him was a kindness. She'd planned to catch you sooner, but you just can't stop yourself from falling in with the wrong men."

"Grayson isn't dead!" I screamed, the anger inside of me unraveling.

"No? His corpse is still inside the dam, right outside the shitty little place you love so much. We made sure he wasn't coming back before we left him there. Couldn't have him interfering with what Trina has planned for you. We finally have a way to control the Sentinels; nothing will stop us now. Not even Death himself."

"Kill him," I growled as someone gasped, and a woman beside me collapsed to the ground. "Azrael, kill him, please!" I pleaded through the tears blinding my vision.

I could see Azrael studying me carefully; when he didn't move fast enough, I lunged, only to have him catch me and hold me tightly as I struggled to get to Dagan.

"If you spill his blood, more than is already leaking from every orifice, you could make matters worse," he whispered against my ear as I struggled to get free. "He is goading you; he wants you to end his suffering. She left him here to die; look at him," Azrael demanded. "He knows he has outlived his usefulness to her and we are his only hope of a quick death."

Dagan did look like he wanted us to end his suffering, but I wanted to slaughter him. I wanted to rip him apart for even saying my brother was dead without proof.

"Grayson isn't dead," I repeated, more to myself.

"He's dead, Emmalyn, I assure you it's true," Dagan taunted. "He died screaming your name. Begging for you to save him, but you were too busy, weren't you, Emma? You were too busy bedding down with your enemy while your sweet baby brother begged for you to save him. His death was painful; Trina wouldn't allow us to end it prematurely, and so we watched. It took him hours to perish, where were you? He screamed for you."

I struggled in Azrael's arms to get to Dagan, but he held me back and whispered soft words to calm me. I was barely keeping it together. I wanted to kill Dagan. I wanted to cut his tongue out to keep him from saying anything else.

"Kill him, please," I begged. "Azrael, kill him!"

I was released, Azrael vanished, and Death stood before Dagan. He was dressed in Azrael's clothing, and thick black lines now slid down and expanded across his exposed flesh; glyphs pulsed and slithered over his skin. Red eyes the color of freshly spilled blood looked at me.

"You're sure you want this?" he asked, and I nodded without hesitation. He reached out, his hands touched Dagan's cheeks, and a scream ripped through the courtyard, loud, terrifying, and final. Dagan slumped over, and his body jerked; tremors pulsed through him until he was at last still. His remains decomposed at a rapid rate and left nothing but a skeleton and a smattering of ash. Azrael turned towards me and stepped closer, as one of the women screamed behind him.

The virus was spreading.

"Did I…?" I whispered, unable to finish my thoughts. I'd wanted vengeance so much that I'd begged for it. Had I just killed everyone?

"No, it's airborne." Azrael's features returned to his normal handsome self. "You're out of time, beautiful," he growled, moving until he stood in front of me. "Clear your mind, and listen to me very carefully, Emma. I took his life for you, now you return the favor. Save our people," he murmured. His eyes filled with pain and something that scared me, *trust*.

"You're not sick," I pointed out. I felt nausea as it rushed through me. "How is that possible? I saw the blood."

"Trina doesn't know enough about Guardians to make an effective virus against us; no one does," he stated, his eyes turning red as he watched me. "We are running out of time. Focus on me. You're the only one who can save them. I am able to kill and purge the live virus from my body. I can't do the same to them without killing them in a worse fashion than the virus could. There has to be a way for you to take the virus from them. You just have to figure out how to do it."

"Azrael," I whispered, terrified. I had no idea how it worked, or if I could even do it. "I don't know how to do it," I choked out through trembling lips.

"Clear your mind and stop doubting yourself," he said softly, as more cries erupted.

I looked around as people watched us, some already sick with the virus. They'd walked the virus right through the front gates, and now everyone was dying.

"Azrael, I can't do this," I pleaded. I had no fucking idea what he expected. I had no idea how to control my powers, or even what they were.

"Do you trust me, Emma?" he asked as he pulled out a dagger.

"Are you going to stab me?" I asked, already backing away from him.

"Yes," he said grimly, as he bowed his head and pulled his shirt up and away from his body. Black ethereal wings expanded, and his crimson eyes watched me. He totally looked the part of the Angel of Death in this form. "I'm going to kick-start your powers the only way that I can think of. If we don't, they're dead. Do you trust me, Emma? Say you trust me, because we're out of time, little phoenix."

"I don't have wings," I whispered, not sure he was playing with a full deck. Maybe I'd misjudged him. Maybe I was as crazy as he was, but not enough to think I would grow wings.

"You're a Guardian of Life, Emma, you have wings."

"You drunk?" I asked, backing away from him. "I really don't have wings."

"Hayden, catch her and hold her down," Azrael ordered. His armor formed around him, and his wings folded back and lay neatly tucked against his armor as he got closer to me.

I turned to run, but Hayden caught me. "Sorry about this, Emma," he said sheepishly. "Remember, it's for a good cause, yeah?"

"Let me go!" I screamed, as I struggled to get away from him. "Don't let him cut me; I don't have any fucking wings. I'm not a chicken!"

I was pushed to the ground as I struggled to get free; my face was shoved into the dirt and I felt the blade cut through the flimsy material of the shirt I wore as he exposed my spine. His fingers probed my back until they found a ridge just above my shoulder blades that I wasn't even aware was there.

"Azrael, no!" I sobbed, as I felt the blade touch my flesh and sliced. The second cut sent me over the edge. Something inside of me snapped. I growled; white light filled my vision and then I was up. Hayden was thrown to the ground, his mouth wide open as I spun on Azrael and the blade he wielded. "Don't. Cut. Me. Fucker!" I screamed, the sound echoing through the courtyard as I felt my fingers flexing as I prepared to fight him. I slashed at him with my hand, watching as it tore through his armor. I looked down, finding claws where my fingers had been. I hissed, my eyes locked with his as I lunged forward, only to be caught by him as he vanished and appeared behind me. His arms wrapped around me, pain and feathers erupting as I screamed.

"You have beautiful wings, love," he whispered gently. "Fuck, Emma, you're fierce."

"I'm going to tear you apart!" I snapped.

"No, Life, you're going to do what you were created for. You're going to save their lives. You're going to save our people." He released me and I exhaled, planning on ripping his dick off to repay the pain he'd just put me through. Instead, I was lost in the sea of faces that needed me.

I could see the sickness inside of them. It was crystal-clear. I could see the mutated virus spreading through their bodies, killing live tissue and cells. It was literally eating them from the inside out. I opened my mouth to reply to Azrael to tell him to go to hell, but no words came out. Instead, I felt my body jerk and I could see my hands glowing; I could feel the sensation of my entire body glowing and burning. Light burst from my eyes and mouth, engulfing everyone in the courtyard and blinding me; everyone began to scream. The screaming was horrifying and terrible. I covered my ears as blackness filled my vision. Pain erupted inside of me, and before I could ask Azrael to end it, to end me, everything went dark and numb.

Chapter Twenty-Seven

I woke up pressed against something hard and warm. I struggled to open my eyes, only to find them caked with something that refused to allow them to open. Pain filled my head, and I groaned as hands softly smoothed my hair away from my face.

"You're safe, sweet girl," Azrael's voice filled my ears.

"I'm blind," I moaned. I felt something wet and warm being pressed against my eyes.

"There's dried blood on your eyes, I'm cleaning you now," he explained.

"What happened?" I asked. The last thing I remembered was blinding light, and screaming.

"You took the virus, and it ran its course," he elaborated. "It was most…unpleasant."

Most *unpleasant*?

"Am I contagious?" I asked, wondering what the hell I'd really done. He was sugarcoating something.

"I am sure you are," he replied.

Okay, so maybe he wasn't sugarcoating it.

"You asked me to take the virus from them, and I did. Now you're telling me I'm contagious? Like a walking plague?"

"It will pass," he promised.

I coughed and wiped my mouth with my arm as he worked on clearing the dried blood from my eyes. I didn't feel sick. In fact, I felt great. Tired, but other than that, not sick. As the blood was gently wiped away and I was finally able to open my eyes, I saw Azrael; his clothes, face and hands were splattered with blood.

"Are you hurt?" I asked, my voice raw and rough.

"It's not my blood, Emma." His voice was soft as his eyes carefully watched me.

"Did you take a hatchet to someone?" I countered. It was a lot of blood. It looked like he'd either stood in front of something that had an arterial blood splatter, or someone who…shit. "It's mine. You didn't leave me while I was sick?"

"I wasn't going to leave you when you were in pain," he admitted as he continued to wash the blood from my face.

In this moment, I loved his stupidity and his inability to leave me. I laughed, and shook my head. I'd bled all over him. He was splattered in it, and looked like a serial killer.

"You look like you slaughtered a village and then bathed in their blood," I laughed, the sound throaty and a little sadistic.

"You kept crying my name," he whispered as he kissed my forehead, ignoring the fact that I was covered in blood and God knew what else. I was a mess.

"You sure I wasn't begging for death? Like, kill me?" I giggled.

"You called me by name, not by what I am." He picked me up carefully. "Let's get you cleaned off, shall we?"

"Grayson," I whispered as tears filled my eyes and my stomach dropped to the floor. "Oh my God, what if he is there? What if she killed him?"

"We will go check once you are no longer contagious," he offered. I looked around the room, noting that we were sealed in. They'd erected a hazmat room. Thick red plastic covered the walls, the floors, and tape had been patched around anywhere air could escape.

"We have to kill her," I whispered. "She can't

continue to do this to people."

"By sending Dagan in, she's done nothing more than confirm her guilt with the virus against the humans. She won't go down without a fight, Emma. She'll take as many as she can down with her. I'm not sure we can afford to meet her head-on until you're ready to counteract the virus she's turned into a weapon. You've been out of it for days," he said.

"Days?" I tried to figure out how that was even possible. I hadn't been down for days. Hours maybe, but days?

"You have been fighting the virus; your body may be able to contain it, but you still had to live through it. I'm not sure how your power works, but when I give death, it's simple. It's as easy as breathing. You're different. Messy. Just like life." He smiled.

"Thanks." I laughed nervously.

"That's not what I meant," he amended. "I figured you'd be immune against it, and able to nullify it. You didn't. You took their sickness from them. They were in different stages of the virus when light exploded from you. The others started screaming as the light engulfed them; it was like the light pulled the virus out of them as it receded back to you," Azrael explained as he arranged me comfortably on a chair then started the bathwater. "You disappeared from my senses. I thought I was losing you. I tried to stop whatever was happening, but you were incoherent and then, one by one, they started to rise with no symptoms. So yes, it was messy. After the last Sentinel rose, you started exhibiting signs of the virus. I took you from the courtyard and we sealed off this room. You whispered my name through the worst of the pain, crying out for me if I left your side. So, other than a brief period where I had to take care of some business, I stayed, I held you as your body exhibited each phase of the virus."

"That couldn't have been easy," I mumbled, wondering why he hadn't just left me to rot. If it had been anything like the virus that had swept through the humans, it started with thick black lines that looked like spider webs; after that, the fever ravaged the brain, and blood would escape from the body through every orifice it could. The body would tremble, shake, and, eventually, death would take over.

"You seemed immune to most of the pain," he acknowledged.

"I meant for you," I countered. "It couldn't have been easy for you to hold me through it."

"It wasn't, but I wasn't about to leave you alone through it. I'm not going anywhere, Emma," he said gently, as he helped me to stand and remove the blood-spattered clothing. "It looks like your mother made the virus that killed the humans into a weaponized version of the plague so she could target Sentinels. I'm guessing she doesn't even have a cure for it. Luckily, we have you."

"No one died?" I asked.

"Trina's people that were taken with Dagan survived because of you. I interrogated them and killed them. We couldn't afford for any of them to escape and get close enough to communicate with your mother to let her know that we had survived. We need the element of surprise if we are going to win this war."

"I don't blame you for killing them," I admitted. "I hadn't even thought about them communicating with her. I guess it's time you teach me to be like you, Azrael. I can't just go into this fight blindly. You can train me, so that when I need them, I know how to use my powers, right?" I asked, as he hooked his fingers through my panties and pulled them off.

"Most of your abilities can't be learned traditionally." He held his hand out and helped me into the tub that was sweetly scented with lavender. "I can teach you to fight, and what triggers mine. Anger, fear, anything that pulls enough emotion from you can trigger your abilities. You just have to find that trigger and pull it."

"Do you think they killed Grayson to trigger me?" I asked as a sob built inside of me. Dagan said she wanted my humanity gone. Without Grayson, I wasn't sure I would be able to hold on to it. I was losing the battle; this world wasn't making it easy to hang on to much of who I had been before the virus.

"I hope not, but Trina doesn't value life, Emma. She values power, and he had very little. If I wanted to kill what little of you was left, what I thought kept you holding onto humanity, I would have killed him, too. As you said, you raised him. He is and will always be your anchor, but he's also a weakness. Any enemy would have chosen to use him against you."

"I'm not sure I want to go on if he isn't here," I whispered through the constriction of my throat as tears threatened to choke me. "I hate not knowing where he is. It kills me to even imagine a world where he isn't in it."

He crushed me against his chest and held me as I pulled my emotions together and brought them under control. He held me until I pulled away; his beautiful eyes searched mine and then he released me to sink down in the tub. He didn't join me. Instead, he knelt beside the tub and leaned against it.

"We will figure out what they've done with the boy, and we'll go to the Ark before we leave for the Olympian peninsula. According to one of the men I interrogated, your mother is most likely there with some of her scientists. I know about Jaeden's maker, and Lachlan's sire. You shouldn't allow yourself to believe that they're savable. I'm pretty sure she's either killed them, or turned them into mindless beings by now. She's cold, it's how I feared you might become, but you're not cold at all, little phoenix," he smirked, splashing me with water.

"If she'd stayed, I fear I would have been like her," I admitted. "I think her leaving was the best thing that ever happened to me, even though at the time I felt otherwise. I don't remember all of it, but I think you're right. I think deep down I'd always thought she was still out there. Like I could feel it, but didn't understand it at the time."

"You were young," he mused, his eyes lingering on mine before they drifted to the murky water. "Clean up; we need to prepare to make our way north."

"When?" I asked, trying to hide the tremble in my tone. Going home felt weird, as if it was empty. I'd expected to return with Grayson. It was supposed to be a victorious celebration, but instead, I was returning to see if his corpse was there, at the dam.

I was terrified of returning without Grayson or the others who I had started out with. I wanted to know though, needed to know if I'd failed him. I couldn't keep running into things blindly, because it wasn't working. I kept pushing only to get pushed back. There was only one way to know the truth.

"I need to see to a few things, but we should be able to start towards the Ark tomorrow morning. You need to eat, and you could use a little rest as well. There were also a few things that came to light when I questioned Dagan's people. You and I need to be on the same page before we leave this place, Emma. We'll talk more after you've rested."

"I'm not tired," I lied. I was starting to feel as if I'd been hit by a train. Every nerve in my entire body was on fire, and the lump in my throat was growing. My stomach wouldn't release the sick feeling, or the tension of not knowing if Grayson was alive or dead. "Did they say anything else about Grayson?" I asked barely above a whisper, heart in my throat.

"No, they had no knowledge of where he was or what happened to him," he replied as he brought his hand up to cup my cheek. "We will find him, I promise you that."

"You stabbed me," I accused, wondering why I didn't mind it so much after the fact. I mean, he'd held me through the virus and hadn't let go while it had run its course.

"I did, because I had to jumpstart your transition into obtaining your powers," he replied, his eyes slowly looking me over.

"I have wings," I murmured, even though they weren't out right now. In fact, I'd felt them more than saw them before. I had fucking wings!

"Beautiful wings," he affirmed. "Now rest."

Chapter Twenty-Eight

I'd thought coming home would be good, exciting. It wasn't; now it was terrifying. Azrael had kept his word, and we were here. We'd passed through the City of Priest River, followed Highway 2 towards Oldtown, and now stood in the parking lot for the dam complex, squinting against the early afternoon sun. I should have been optimistic; Dagan was shallow, and he'd wanted me to kill him. He'd wanted us to end his suffering, so he would have said or done anything to make it happen. He could have been lying about what they'd done to Grayson. I was grasping at straws, I knew it, but this was my baby brother. I'd pick any other scenario than the one that ended with him being dead.

A big part of that was because, if he was in there, if he was dead, it meant I'd failed him. I was afraid that knowing he was gone would wreck me. I'd been so blind in my rage over Trina taking him that I'd never even stopped to consider that she may have killed him. I'd run blindly into the fray, never stopping to consider the *what-ifs*. In my head, there had been no other alternative, but reality wasn't as black and white.

I noticed the riot of flowers that covered the ground in front of the main entrance to the dam. Not even they could hide the scent of death that lingered in the air. There were a thousand reasons that it could smell like this, and I tried to dredge up every single one of them to hide from one little fact: It could be Grayson rotting somewhere inside the dam complex. I was getting good at making excuses.

Moss grew from the cracks of the cement, making it look as vacant and abandoned as I felt inside. The big double doors of the powerhouse were closed, but they didn't hide the smell of decay. There were broken windows where the ground rose to become part of the wall, as if they'd sustained damage in one of the many storms we'd had. There could be a worker inside, dead; maybe he'd failed to get out or had tried to stay? It could be anyone else, as long as it wasn't Grayson.

Anyone else.

"Emma." Azrael's voice broke into my thoughts; his fingers brushed against mine as he watched me. He'd been silent up until now. He was allowing me to work through my shit alone. I'd told him what I feared most. That if Grayson was dead, I'd fall and I wasn't sure I'd ever get back up. "You're not defined by how you fall. Everyone falls at some time or another. You're defined by how you rise. Every phoenix has to burn before it can rise from the ashes. It's why they are a symbol of strength and hope."

"If I go in there and it's him, that's it. I can't pretend he's out there alive somewhere. He'll be gone, and with him, my hope of saving him. It's final. I just need a few more minutes," I replied as I closed my eyes, feeling the wind pick up, my hair rustling in the breeze. "Just a few more minutes of this, please," I whispered through tears that threatened to choke me with emotion.

"I'll freeze time if you need more of it, Emma," he offered, his fingers continuing to brush lightly against mine. "We can stand here all day if it's what you need."

I stepped closer to the doors on legs that threatened to give out. My feet felt weighted to the ground; the vice grip that seemed to have my heart in its grasp tightened. My breath came in small bursts as I struggled to inhale, my lungs stiffening as pain took control. One foot in front of the other, until I was at the doors. I opened them slowly, listening as metal clicked, released, and then I was inside.

No sun illuminated this place. It was wet, dark and chilling to my senses. Azrael turned on a lantern, then another, as he took control of everything I couldn't manage. I was grateful that he could feel my needs, because I couldn't verbalize anything that would make sense. I was numb with the realization that Grayson could possibly be in here. I thought I had seen them take Grayson to an underground lab in one of the three visions I'd had so long ago; now, I realized that it could just as easily have been the bowels of a dam that they'd brought him to. That flash of clarity hammered home the reality that this was probably the place he'd been. It was too much. It was like going to the morgue to identify a loved one, but there was no doctor to break the news, no one there to pull the sheet off and write down that it was the wrong person. No one to explain what happened, or why death had occurred.

We slowly walked through the main reception area and through the doors that took us deep inside the powerhouse. Our steps echoed eerily as we made our way down the long hallway, and we passed numerous darkened rooms and peered through the glass walls, I guessed that these offices had once belonged to the administrative staff of the dam.

Before we could reach the end of the walkway that led to the spillway complex, I stopped dead in my tracks.

My world stopped.

It collapsed on me.

Air left my lungs in a solid scream as I took in what was before me.

My legs gave out and I hit the ground as I closed my eyes against what was behind the floor-to-ceiling glass that separated the walkway from the huge control room of the powerhouse.

Grayson. Dead. My baby brother was, in fact, dead.

Instinctively I knew it was him, and he was dead.

Crumpled against a corner of the room was his small body. Isolated and alone. His arms hung above what remained of his corpse. Animals must have gotten into the powerhouse to nest and gnawed on him, but even with the damage, I knew it was him. A sob exploded from my lips and I opened my eyes. My head shook, denial was on my tongue, and I wanted to say it wasn't him; that it wasn't the only family I had left in this world who rotted inside this forgotten tomb.

"No, no God, please," I begged. I'd done everything I could to protect people, and this was how I was repaid? Why? He was just a child! "Oh, baby, no, get up!" I sobbed brokenly as tears fell unchecked to the cold cement floor. I screamed, my hands rose to my hair and I screamed at how unfair life was. I needed this to not be real. I needed him to open his eyes and assure me that he wasn't dead. He was lifeless, in pieces! I moved closer, scooting on my hands and knees, and then stopped again, screaming until the sound reverberated around the room.

"No, no, no, this isn't right. I was supposed to save you!" I cried. My eyes took in the boots I'd sourced for him, the ripped up, ruined coat that was supposed to keep him warm, keep him from getting sick. I sobbed until no more tears would come, my body trembling with disbelief. My mind refused to process what my eyes told it to be true.

"Please, no," I begged as hate and anger tore through me. *I could bring him back*. The thought hit me like a ton of bricks and I was up, shucking my pack as I prepared to do the unthinkable. Strong arms wrapped around me, and I fought against them. "No, I have to! I have to bring him back!"

"He's already dead, Emma," Azrael whispered. "You have to be careful of how your powers are used. A Guardian of Life can save those who are dying; however, a Guardian shouldn't bring the dead back to life. To reanimate them," he explained softly. "If you tried to give him life, it wouldn't be your Grayson anymore. He's been dead for a long time. He'd be mindless, and nothing like the boy you knew and loved. He'd be little better than a zombie. You wouldn't want that. You have to let him go," he replied, kissing my forehead as the tears continued to fall, as if he could wash away the pain that was killing me.

"No, I need him!"

"You need to let him go so he can find peace," he argued gently. "I'll go find something so that we can take him to the Ark, don't try to bring him back. It won't work; at least not the way you want it to."

Once Azrael was gone, I sat beside Grayson and whispered, pleading for him to return to me. "I need you, Grayson. I need you to get up and stay with me. I can't do this without you. I need you, and you need me. Please, don't leave me," I begged as tears raced down my cheeks. "I can't be strong without you. I failed you. I fail everyone I love; I'm so sorry, baby. I'm so sorry I couldn't get to you," I cried. I wrapped my arms around my knees, as I felt my shirt rip up the back as my wings expanded. I'd never really felt them before. The first time they'd released, I'd passed out and they were gone when I woke up. Now, I didn't care. They were worthless. What good was it to have some power that wouldn't bring back the one person I wanted it to?

Of everyone who deserved to be saved, didn't Grayson also deserve it? He was just a child. He hadn't even begun to experience life yet. Now, he never would.

Eventually, the tears stopped. The pain didn't seem like it was going to leave anytime soon. I felt as if I was dying from the inside out. My heart squeezed with pain, as though someone had ripped my ribcage apart and held my heart, squeezing it with every beat.

I couldn't even pretend it wasn't him. It was. His hair, what hadn't decomposed, was scattered on the floor or still attached to his remains. The clothing, the boots, I'd gotten them for him. The necklace that cut into his corpse, also something I'd gotten for him. He'd smiled so big when I'd brought those flag-covered dog tags home for him.

The rustling of plastic and movement caught my attention, and I turned my eyes to Azrael, who had returned with a body bag and sheets of thick plastic.

"No," I whispered through the constriction of my throat. "No, he won't be able to breathe."

I heard the nonsensical words coming out of my mouth, but I didn't care. I couldn't imagine putting him in there. It was plastic. This was Grayson. This was my brother! I stood up and shook my head as my vision blurred through the tears. I wasn't going to allow him to wrap that plastic around him. Not my baby brother. Not the kid I'd raised, the one who I kissed goodnight when Dad wasn't around to do it. The one I'd rocked to sleep when I was barely big enough to hold him in my lap. He'd saved me; given me a purpose when I'd been buried in grief when we'd thought our mother was dead. He'd kept me centered, and made me want to be a better person. Now I was just supposed to wrap him in plastic and bury him in the cold ground?

"Azrael, I can't do this. I can't bury him. I can't; he's my brother. I have to find out how to bring him back. There has to be a way. I can't put him in the ground. I can't do it. I just can't," I babbled as my breathing labored and stars erupted behind my eyes as I started to hyperventilate.

Azrael dropped the bags and rushed to my side, holding me as my knees buckled. He caught me against his chest and whispered against my ear.

"Inhale through your nose and out through your mouth, Emma. I know it hurts, trust me, I know. You're going to be okay, not today, not tomorrow, but one day you'll be able to breathe again. The pain won't get easier, but you'll learn to live with it. Right now, you need to focus on what has to be done. You have to bury him, because your father would want Grayson beside him. I know, because I'm inside of you. I can feel what you need to do and you're not alone. Right now isn't the time to fall apart. We need to give him a proper burial;

he's waited this long for you to find him, and now you need to be strong for just a little while longer. Let's take him home, sweet girl, together. After that, you can fall apart and I'll be there to pick up the pieces."

"Oh, God, Addy," I whispered through a sob.

"She's waiting for you to bring him home," he murmured as he stepped back and looked at me. "You're the strongest woman I've ever met, Emma. You can do this. Not because you want to, but because you have to."

"I can't," I sobbed. "I can't pick up the pieces," I choked out brokenly. I couldn't touch what was left of Grayson. I just couldn't do it.

"I'll do it," he offered, moving past me and kneeling in front of Grayson. He picked each piece up with gentle care, as if it wasn't the broken remains of my brother, but just an amputated limb he planned to put back on with surgical precision. Once he had everything in the proper place, he wrapped the thick plastic around the body to hold it together. I stood, sobbing as Azrael took care of Grayson's remains, and more of my heart was shredded.

He'd done it for me. I couldn't have loved him more if he'd brought my brother back to life. He'd handled my brother with love because *he* loved *me*. Azrael unzipped the black body bag, placed Grayson inside of it, and turned to look up at me.

"I know you don't believe me right now, Emma, but it gets easier. I'm not going to lie and tell you that the pain goes away, because it doesn't. You just adapt and learn to live with it better. Sometimes when you least expect it, that pain will consume you. Someday, though, you'll be able to think about him without it feeling as if a knife is ripping you apart, I promise."

"Azrael, how do I even take him home? They're expecting him to be alive; it's going to hurt everyone. Addy, she lost everyone. How do I tell her that I failed, or that I can't stop this from happening to them all? Every time I take a step forward, I get pushed five steps back. I can't promise them that they're safe anymore, it's a lie. Everything I touch or love dies, like I'm cursed!"

"Emma, that is life," he urged. "This is what happens. People die every day, sometimes tragically so. This was beyond your control, and there wasn't anything you could have done that could have been more than you already did. Please don't second-guess this. Look at what you've accomplished. You've managed to save people where others would just as soon destroy them. You have taken lives, yes, but you've saved more than most people have. You can face them because you're their leader. You were human when you saved them. Human, fighting against immortals, and yet you didn't stop until they were safe. You've faced an alpha pack of rogue werewolves, and you won. No one expected you to win, yet you refused to fail. That's what makes you beautiful, not what is out here for everyone to see, but what's in here." He tapped my heart. "I didn't fall in love with you just because you're beautiful, Emma. I fell in love with you because you fight against the odds no matter how high they are, to protect those you love. Because, when those you love are in danger, you don't look before you leap. You're selfless, and you let your heart guide you, which, in this world, is pretty fucking rare. I fell in love with a little phoenix that burned to ashes, and rose up a fierce warrior who doesn't give a shit about what others do or that the world is dying around her, she chooses to continue fighting for the underdog. So how will you face your people? Like the little girl who has protected them since the moment they entered her world. You'll face them with your heart on your sleeve and head held high because it's who your father taught you to be. A good man in a storm, Emmalyn," he said evenly as he moved to where I stood, shoulders slumped in defeat. "You can't be defeated. You can't let her win. Use that anger; use what she did to help me take the bitch down. You can't save Grayson, but you can save those who still need to be saved from your mother."

"I want her dead," I replied, straightening my spine, even though the only thing I wanted to do right now was crumble and not get up again. I wanted to crawl in that bag and die beside Grayson. I didn't want to live in a world where he ceased to exist. I wanted to take the easy way out, but I wouldn't. Azrael was right. I would help him kill my mother, and take out anyone who got in my fucking way.

"Use it. It's your trigger," he murmured, his lips brushing against my forehead as he turned, bent down and picked up my baby brother. "Let's get to the Ark before it gets dark outside."

We walked the better part of three miles in silence.

Me needing the silence to ponder exactly how I would face my people and deliver the news of my worst failure to date, and him knowing I needed it. Once we entered the clearing for the Ark, I stalled as people sounded alarms to alert the others to our presence.

Guns were drawn and aimed at us until Liam and Addy were alerted, as word spread that I'd come home. Once she rushed from the shelter, she paused; her eyes darted to the black body bag and back to me. How was I supposed to do this? How could I tell her that I'd failed and Grayson was dead? How could I crush her world and allow her to feel this earth-shattering pain that I couldn't even handle?

Her beautiful eyes filled with confusion and her shoulders slumped as she slowly made her way closer. How was I supposed to convince her that Grayson was dead when I didn't even want to believe it myself? I wished this entire thing was nothing more than a nightmare, one that I could wake up from and have Azrael kiss the phantom pain away.

"Emma," Addy's voice trembled, her eyes shifting from me to the bag and back again. Liam moved into my vision and I blinked back tears, watching as he sniffed the air. His smile faltered and turned to a sad frown as he and his heightened senses put truth to the identity of the occupant of the bag. Others began to flow out of the Ark as the word of my homecoming made its way through it. Their excitement was short-lived as the importance of the small wrapped body began to register in their minds.

Tears swam in my eyes as I watched Addy shake her head as realization hit her. There was only one body I'd bring home to bury. One person I wouldn't leave behind.

"No, no, it has to be wrong," she whispered through tears. "He's just a kid. She wouldn't do that, she's his mother." Her hand covered her trembling lips and I couldn't stop the sob that left my lungs as I made my way to her and hugged her against me. Everything I'd been holding in broke free, as if some dam opened up and the tears I'd thought I'd cried out let loose and proved me wrong.

We stood there, crying together. Others moved closer to us, hushed whispers sounded, but we ignored them as others started to cry silently with us. I could see Maggie; her gentle gray eyes swam with tears as she shook her head. I held my hand out, and she rushed forward; others who had loved Grayson did the same. I didn't have to tell them he was dead, it was written on my face, in the tears I cried. In the defeat that marked me like nothing else could have.

I'd failed my brother, and I had to own it. I had to make it right. That emptiness was draining me, the little part of me that had once been bright because he'd been there slowly extinguished, and darkness took its place. My eyes swam with tears, blurred with them, but even through them, I locked eyes with turquoise ones in the distance that stared back. I blinked as I blearily realized Jaeden was here, at the Ark, and I wondered when he'd returned. Was it just the vampires, or did the wolves return with him?

"I'm so sorry, Emma," Addy whispered as she sobbed. "I'm so sorry."

"Me too. I couldn't save him, Addy. He was dead before I even left to try."

"Where did ye find him?" Lachlan asked, as he smoothed the stray hair from my face. I closed my eyes briefly, relieved that Lachlan was here too. No matter what had happened, I missed him.

"At the dam," I choked out as a tear slid down my cheek. "She killed him before she even left town."

"He needs to be buried," Azrael spoke softly, causing all eyes to turn in his direction. "He deserves to be given proper rites."

"Is he the one who took ye, lass?" Lachlan asked. I could understand why Lachlan asked who he was; Lachlan had never gotten a good look at Azrael and at the moment, Azrael was wearing a leather jacket, jeans, T-shirt, and thin leather gloves to reduce the chance of anyone brushing against him. Azrael and I had decided on the way to the Ark that it would be better for us to minimize what the immortals knew about what we were, and what we could do.

"No, he's the one who saved me," I whispered as I clung to Addy like a lifeline. Really, he had. He'd saved me from myself, because I'd been slowly losing myself and going numb, and somehow, he'd breathed life back into me.

Chapter Twenty-Nine

Grayson was buried the following day. We'd asked those who hadn't known him in life to remain in the shelter while we said our goodbyes under the old oak tree. There were a lot of new faces, and those were in addition to the men and their families from the National Guard unit I'd met in the mountains a few weeks ago.

I stood beside the pastor, a nice man who had also found his way to the Ark and become part of the community. I listened dully as he droned on about the world we now found ourselves stuck in. It wasn't a nice place. It wasn't somewhere you wanted a child to live or grow up in, yet his overall message was still one of hope despite the odds we faced.

I stood holding hands with Addy, while Azrael stood behind me at a safe distance from accidentally bumping into anyone. Shamus, Jaeden, and Astrid stood across from me, watching me. Jaeden had given me space, which I was grateful for. I had been avoiding him and

Lachlan since we arrived the day before, because I just wasn't ready to address what I had witnessed in that hellish town, and Jaeden hadn't pressed the issue. Yet. Shamus, on the other hand, had demanded I come to his room and speak with him immediately following the funeral.

Yeah, like I was going to jump up and follow his orders.

I'd ignored everyone except Addy, needing to be close to the one person I had left in this world who really knew me. She understood the pain I was going through; shared it, even. I hated battering her heart even more when I explained that I couldn't stay here. I'd filled her in on Trina's new virus, one she'd weaponized against immortals.

I wouldn't chance Trina bringing it here to use on my people. Azrael had agreed that a few days here wouldn't hurt us, that we had people out looking and watching for any sign of her and her group of fallen Sentinels.

Shamus had to be dealt with as well; he couldn't be allowed to use my Ark, my father's life work, to grow an entire colony for his selfish use. After the debacle at the town, they must have made their way back here rather than continue the search for their maker and Lachlan's father. They certainly hadn't gone looking for me, and oddly enough, I was okay with that now. Azrael had been right; I wasn't defeated and I was damn sure I wouldn't be. I had refused to lie down and die beside Grayson. I had people who needed and depended on me keeping my chin up and my eyes on the prize.

Azrael had agreed to train me and felt that it would go faster now that I had found a trigger through Grayson. I wasn't sure how it would help, but he'd promised to start training me tomorrow. I wanted to rush it, to get back in shape and train to take my mother and whatever supporters she had down. I was numb, I'd gone from denial, to numb, which everyone thought was a bad thing.

Maybe they thought that eventually, I'd explode. That my emotions would all flip on and everything would hit me at once. It was possible. Hell, anything was these days. Addy and I agreed to live every day as if it was our last.

She'd held me last night, and I'd held on to her. I'd cried and she had as well; all the while we'd been watched by Azrael, Liam, Lachlan and Jaeden. We hadn't given a shit who witnessed it, or that they were watching us as we literally lost our shit. We'd whispered, we'd sobbed, then we'd sat up, wiped away the tears, and dressed to bury Grayson.

That was life now. You cried, you figured out how to go on again, and you kept going.

There was one thing I knew without a doubt that I had to do, which was get my mother. She had to be stopped at all costs. She was a murderer of children and families of this world. She had to be taken down before she could hurt anyone else. Before anyone else could suffer the way my family had.

After the service, I left to go to my old house. I needed to be where I had happy memories of my family. It was the last place we'd all been together before the world turned into a dark, gloomy place that chewed you up and spit you out.

I didn't need to see Azrael to know he'd followed me here; I could sense him as surely as I could feel my arm was attached to my body. He'd been giving me space, which I could sense bothered him, but he remained firm on allowing me to grieve in my own way. Everyone grieved differently; that was something I'd learned the hard way.

Cat had adopted Sarah to grieve over her own child, and in doing so, had grown to love the sweet toddler who had learned to giggle since I'd been gone. Others clung on to those they still had, while some shut down and mentally checked out. I wasn't sure if what I was doing was actually grieving.

I entered the house and made a direct path to Grayson's room. I stood in front of his door, wondering if it would smell like it had when he'd lived here. Normally, it had stunk of socks, or dirty laundry. God, I'd yelled at him to clean his room so many times. Coming home after my internship was a pain in the ass.

He'd never picked up after himself, always needed to be nagged to do so. One time I'd even threatened to take his charger cords, which had only made him scream about how much he hated me and wanted his mom back. It had hurt. I'd wanted to be his sister, but at the same time, our father had mentally begun to check out as he'd rushed the last things for the shelter to be functional. I'd stepped up to the plate, knowing that in a small town, rumors would begin to swirl. CPS would end up at the front door, and we'd end up going through the same shit again, so I'd done it all.

I'd cooked the dinners, done the laundry, and complained the entire time because it wasn't my job. I'd give anything to go back to that time. I'd love to go back to that time of doing every mundane freaking chore, just to see them again. To catch the glimpses of them as they rushed here or there, or on my way out to work. I'd endure those kids who made fun of the prepper's daughter willingly, meeting them with a smile as they did it.

I pushed the door open and closed my eyes as the wind pushed into the room. The windows were shattered; the neighbor's tree had landed on the house, smashing out Grayson's bedroom windows. The musky scent of mildew assaulted my senses, and I frowned. So much for the smell of dirty socks mixed with old food left in dishes. His computer was still on his desk, the chair had been knocked over, and the closet was open.

My eyes searched out every detail, knowing someone had been in here. Someone had gone through his room, why? Dagan or one of Trina's other lackeys? It pissed me off. They had violated and murdered my family, and for what? To get to me? To use me to get

Death? I'd give them death.

I progressed deeper into the room, the glass from the window crunched beneath my boots. The lace curtains blew from the wind as it raced through the room and down the open hallway. I looked around his small room and in a single moment of clarity, I knew what I had to do.

I made the bed, righted the chair, and cleaned the room. Once it was perfect, I walked out to the garage, pulled out the gas can and went back inside the house to Grayson's room. I poured gas on the bed, the computer, everything, while moving impassively through the house until, once again, I stood outside staring at it.

I pulled a matchbox from my pocket and stared at it. We burn the dead; it's what my father taught us. I had to burn this place down, because it was dead. It was a structure, and it felt like a piece of me. You remove the rotting parts of you. You cut them off, surgically or however you can to survive. I struck the match on the box, and dropped it.

The flame of the match hit the ground, igniting the gas as it rushed towards the house. Grayson hadn't died alone. A huge part of me died with him, in a way. No one who had lived in that structure was alive. No one. That naïve girl who used to live here, she was gone. The one who'd done her best to be what her family needed had failed them. She'd thought she could save everyone, but it was impossible to save them all. I'd evolved. I was no longer the weak girl, but someone who would do her best to keep those who depended on her alive.

In order to be that person, I had to let go of the past. I had to let go of the things I couldn't change and focus on the things I could. I couldn't save the world. I was one girl; even immortal, I couldn't save them. It was impossible, and while I wanted to, I had to deal with reality. There was me before I lost Grayson, and after. Me after him, well, I was going to live in the now, with the others who'd known the truth all along.

I'd refused to believe it. I'd refused to acknowledge that I might be fighting a losing battle. It had cost me Grayson. I wouldn't let those rose-colored glasses touch my nose again. I had to get hard, to be hard; I had to be cold to live in this world because the fact was; it wasn't the one we had loved. This new world wanted us dead, and to survive, we'd have to be as cold and dark as the world around us was.

I turned, and found Azrael staring at my crackling house. He knew what it symbolized. He felt it, and as he ambled towards me, I smiled at him. On my own, I couldn't save the world, but with him, my odds just got a lot better. Maybe it wasn't a losing battle. As if he sensed I needed him, he sped up; the dull shine of his leather jacket reflected the glowing flames.

"My sweet little phoenix," he mumbled, his eyes searching mine as his own smile spread across his generous mouth. "You're ready," he murmured as his thumb came up and trailed my bottom lip. "I must admit, the idea of training you turns me on, Emma. I won't be easy on you." His voice was husky, as his eyes burned with naked intensity in their cerulean depths.

"I didn't ask you to be," I replied easily, as glass exploded from the attic window. I turned, looking at the house as I melted against him. "They'll be watching us," I whispered.

"I'm counting on it," he mused. His hands cupped my face as his lips met mine in a toe-curling kiss that connected to my center and stirred the need that only he could create in my soul.

"Azrael, we can't let her hurt anyone else. We have to stop her. You can't go easy on me, because she won't. She will throw everything she has at us and we must be ready. The entire world needs us to win."

"Damn, Emma, no pressure?" he laughed, kissing me as he picked me up. The fire created a glow that lit up the dusk of night, lighting his features in the shadows. "I need to be with you, now, because tomorrow, you may not like me."

"I'll still like you," I murmured. "There's a cabin in the woods, though…one I've never taken anyone to…" My hair rustled. The world blurred and rushed past us. I really had to learn to move and travel like the Sentinels did.

Chapter Thirty

Apparently, Azrael already had somewhere else picked out. The house was one of the more secluded ones in the mountains. It didn't have any power, but was illuminated from the many candles that he'd lit. As he would light each taper, his eyes would watch me every few moments as I wandered about the cabin. I leaned over and picked up yet another red rose.

"You planned this?" I asked, noting the wood stacked by the stove.

"If I say yes, then it's premeditated seduction," he smiled.

"There are fresh roses and rose petals scattered all over the floor, and wood stacked in the shed, along with candles, that are, get this…*rose* scented. The cabin looks like it belonged to a logger," I pointed out, picking up a magazine that had an AR-15 with skulls painted on it. "Or a serious hunter who loves guns," I smirked playfully.

"Or someone who didn't want to be found," he offered, not bothering to elaborate as he finished lighting the candles. "What do you think?" I studied him carefully as I sensed his nervous energy.

"I think this place is yours," I whispered, looking at it through new eyes. It was secluded. *Very* secluded. No one would come up here, as there were no roads, only trails for ATV's.

"What makes you think that?" He folded his arms over his chest as he looked at me through hooded eyes, heavy with lust.

"The sheepskin bedding, for one. It's the same as you had on your bed. There's also a sword mounted to the wall above the bed, which unless I'm wrong, looks like the ones you carry."

"You figured me out, Emma," he smiled. "It's mine," he admitted. "I built it shortly after you were born. I would use it when I came to town to watch over you."

"So what happens now?" I asked, flirting with him. I was nervous, but so was he. He oozed confidence, and yet there was a part of him that worried that he'd lose me and I loved that. I loved that he cared enough to worry.

"Now? Hmmm…I think you'll need to remember that I like you, because I'm about to fuck you like I don't," he chuckled, his eyes lowering to the black silk dress I'd worn for Grayson's funeral. "You gave a piece of yourself to Jaeden, and I want it. I want that piece of you. You're mine now; I am asking for you to give it to me. I want nothing between us, no holding back, Emma. It's just you and me, and there's nothing standing between us." His voice was low and sultry, which curled my toes with both excitement and unease.

"You have me," I replied, feeling that little piece of me as I instinctively tramped it down, trying to keep it hidden. I wasn't some sex goddess; I was insecure, and yeah, I hid pieces of me like a two-year old hid puzzle pieces around the house.

I wasn't sure how to draw that part of myself out because I wasn't even sure what it was. I'd watched other people change to be whatever the guy they were into liked, but I'd never done that. What you saw was exactly what you got with me.

I was a little crazy, a little insecure, and thought I was passingly pretty, nothing more. I wasn't some great mystery or had some hidden talent. At least not in comparison to his experiences, growing up as a Sentinel and all.

"It's not that, Emma." He reached down and removed his shirt, slowly pulling it over his head. "You hold back, like you're afraid to let go. Let go for me," he ordered, his voice firm and full of confidence as he reached low and pulled the dress up over my head. It left me standing in my panties and bra. He picked me up and my legs wrapped around his waist as he walked me to the bed. The entire place consisted of one main room, a fireplace, and a bathroom.

He tossed me onto the bed and followed me down, claiming my lips hungrily as he captured my hands above my head. He growled hungrily, low in his throat, the sound reverberating in his chest and tickling my lips. I felt his cock, hard, ready and straining against his pants to get out. He ground it against my soft mound, pulling away as he watched my eyes turn heavy with lust.

"Don't look away from me," he urged as he sat up and maneuvered himself between my legs. He pulled a knife from the table next to the bed, flicking it open so the blade was exposed. "And don't move," he warned as he put the blunt edge against my skin. The cold metal made me flinch as he used it to slice through the sheer material of the lacy bra I wore. "Good girl," he crooned, his eyes locking with mine as he continued to run the blunt edge of the knife over my skin. "It scares you, doesn't it?" he whispered, his eyes moving to watch the blade as it caressed my flesh.

"Yes," I replied honestly, which caused his eyes to rise and meet mine. "You scare me, Azrael."

"You scare me too." He lowered his mouth to one nipple, rolling it between his teeth, grazing the flesh before he pulled away. "You make me feel again, and sometimes the emotions are too much. The way you kiss me, it makes me think that I am redeemable, no matter what I've done, or will do." He rained soft kisses against my flesh as his words made it pebble in awareness of the mixture of heat and pleasure it created.

I smiled at him, but the knife turned; the blade touched the flesh inside my thigh, and I swallowed hard. He trailed it down the inside of my thigh and back up, never cutting the flesh, never hurting me. When he finally dropped it beside us on the bed, I saw blood on the palm of his hand from where he'd been holding it.

"You cut yourself?" I tried to sit up, only to find myself pushed back against the soft sheepskin blankets.

"I'd cut myself a thousand times before I would let anything hurt you," he replied, moving to unzip his pants, revealing his cock, which jutted forward, proud and thick. "My intention isn't to hurt you, ever. But you, you have a wild side and I plan to enjoy the fuck out of it."

"Is that so?" I wondered exactly what he thought we were about to do.

"So," he mused, his eyes lighting with excitement. "He's not happy." Azrael's eyes darted towards the door.

"He?" I asked, confused, as I tried to grab the blankets and cover myself.

"Jaeden," he chuckled; his eyes watched me carefully. "I overheard he was going to be leaving soon and it didn't sound as if he was very happy with the way things stand right now."

I swallowed. I owed Jaeden a talk. I knew that, but I didn't owe him more than that. I didn't want Azrael to stop. I wanted the numbness that sex would bring. I wanted my mind to stop thinking about how I'd found my brother, or that he wasn't ever going to smile at me again.

"We can stop," he offered, his eyes watching me for any reaction.

"No, we can't," I assured him. No way in hell.

He smiled, and lowered himself on the bed, parting my legs as his lips followed the trail the knife had taken. He kissed me, his tongue darted out every once in a while, licking and teasing me, causing my breath to hitch and catch as he worked his way towards the one spot where I needed him the most.

He didn't touch it, didn't allow me to do so either as he captured my hands when I tried. He pushed them against my stomach as he pressed his mouth against my pussy, which was still covered by my panties. He blew hot air against it, watching my eyes as I moaned. He was fucking hot; his eyes told me he had nowhere else he'd rather be, or anything else he'd rather be doing. His tongue moved, flicked my sensitive flesh at the apex, and for the briefest of moments, released my hands long enough for him to rip the flimsy material to expose my state of readiness.

I bucked my hips on instinct, and he laughed, the sound making my flesh break out in bumps. He wanted control; well, he could have it if he gave me what I wanted.

"Leave your hands above your head and don't move them," he growled hungrily; his mouth chose that moment to lick and suck against my flesh. I didn't listen. Instead, my hands flew to his hair, grasping it to hold him against my pussy. He laughed coldly, shifting away from my heat to sit up and look down at me. "Bad girl," he teased as he leaned over to kiss my forehead, his hand rose as if in slow motion, only to descend with blurring speed and slap the delicate flesh. The gentleness and punishment together was erotic, and did more to my senses than anything else could have. My hips bucked and rolled in reaction; it stung. He smiled wolfishly, the kind that said he'd enjoyed hurting me. "Now be a good girl and don't make me withhold from you what we both need," he urged. "Hands up above your head, eyes on me." He smiled roguishly. "Understand?"

"And if I like being punished?" I countered, knowing I was playing with fire, but damn, sometimes I liked being burned.

"Then I may have to rethink the best way to punish you." He dropped his lips to the side of my labia, kissing the area while leaving my pussy neglected, and yet it still turned me on. His lips were liquid fire, his tongue the igniter switch. He pushed his finger inside, and then another, the sensation creating a new heat that burned from within. He crooked them, and made a 'come here' motion that hit me in all the right ways. His tongue flicked the hood of my clitoris and I moaned and almost closed my eyes, but somchow managed to keep them on him.

He was smooth, his pressure was just enough. His mouth wasn't too much too fast. Instead, it was doing everything right. There was no rushing, and he slowly devoured me until I thought I was going to combust, but the moment my orgasm got close and teetered on the edge, he shifted again, parting my legs before he rocked his thick cock against my entrance. All the while, never breaking eye contact; instead, he used my reaction to gauge everything he did.

If I moaned, he continued, if my reaction dimmed, he did something else. He lifted my legs, spreading them further apart than I'd had them, and continued feeding me the tip of his cock, only to pull out when the sensation became too much temptation. If I tried to take control, he backed away, watching me as I whined and rocked my hips in welcome for him.

I was going to die if he didn't do something soon. Death by teasing.

"Azrael," I whispered throatily, wondering whose voice had just escaped from my lungs.

"Emma," he crooned, watching me. "Oh, you thought I was just going to fuck you? That's sweet," he laughed, the sound sending a multitude of sensations over my flesh. His wings exploded from his back, sending black feathers floating in the air. "I'm going to fucking wreck you, just like you did to me."

He backed up, flipped me over and pushed me down until my face was against the mattress, and then he pushed his knee and fingers into my back until a scream erupted from my lungs, and my own wings burst from my back and expanded. The moment they did, he backed up and kneeled on the mattress as his fingers touched the wings, sending a shock of pleasure through my body, searing me all the way to my soul.

"Wings are delicate until they are fully formed. They will always be sensitive, erotically so if touched right."

"That hurt," I mumbled, wondering if I'd bit off more than I could chew. This man was more than a mouthful.

"Mmm, but you like pain," he growled, right before his hand slapped my ass, and then lifted my hips. "Remember, so far, every time I've fucked you, I've held back. No more. This time it's bare flesh, and souls," he growled, parting my legs as he gripped my hips. He lunged forward and I cried out; he hadn't stretched me, and my body wasn't prepared, not fully. He pulled out, and then pushed back into my body mercilessly as he continued to stroke the…well…whatever the fuck was between my wings that felt like he was kissing it instead of touching it. I was screaming; the sensation of his cock thrusting inside of me and that delicate bone being stroked at the same time was too much. I lost my shit. I struggled to roll out from under him, turned, and lifted my leg as he laughed, deep, sultry as he used it to his advantage. He adjusted me, stretching my legs into the most painful position ever, and fucked me until my eyes closed and my body detonated, milking his cock as the orgasm rushed through me.

He rolled us, forcing me to be on top of him and I glared down as my wings flexed and readjusted to the movement.

"That wasn't nice," I hissed, wondering what the hell had just happened. I'd gone blind as I came, because the only thing I'd seen was my body on the bed looking hot as hell as I screamed my head off.

"It was fucking beautiful," he argued. "Ride my dick, Emma," he demanded, and I frowned.

"Mmm, are you giving me orders or control?" I smiled as I began to rock my hips, and he released a contented groan. I planned to rock his world, and when he tried to sit up, I slammed him back down hard. He tried it a few more times, but I refused to allow him to get up. I smiled victoriously, right up until he grabbed my waist and threw me onto the bed, following me as he thrust inside of my heat, capturing my hands and driving his cock in hard, punishing me for taking control, or what little control he'd offered me. His hands refused to leave mine, even when he tensed and released his own orgasm; he stayed with me, continuing to take what I gave and even more. I cried out as the next one rushed through me in blissful waves, and then he smiled, turning me onto my stomach as he nudged my legs apart, slapping my ass until I raised it high enough for him to enter me. His hands grabbed my hips, entering me hard, without mercy, and then one hand moved to my hair, which he pulled roughly. His mouth found mine, uncaring that it bent me into a weird, painful position as he used hard, painful thrusts to fuck me.

"I have control, Emma. I always have control," he scoffed, his eyes burning red as he watched me explode again.

Chapter Thirty-One

I rubbed my ass, growled and turned angry eyes on Azrael, who was smiling. He'd thrown me into the air and, like the other times, I'd landed flat on my ass. He hadn't been joking when he'd promised he wouldn't take it easy on me.

"Focus, use the pain and anger," he urged as he returned to his position in the clearing.

I got back into the fighting stance he had shown me just in time for him to move faster than my eyes could track him, only to end up flat on the ground with another bruise to my ego and ass.

"This isn't working!" I growled in frustration, my anger simmering as I tried to get over constantly being knocked on my ass while dealing with the bomb Addy had dropped on me this morning when we had arrived back at the Ark.

"Clear your pretty little head, Emma, stop worrying about it. It can't be changed," he muttered as he closed in on me, his bare torso a welcome distraction. It didn't help that so many people were outside, watching us.

"He got her pregnant," I grumbled.

"She's happy, they're happy. It's not a problem you can fix, and she doesn't want you to." His eyes narrowed as he studied me for a few moments before he smiled grimly. "You fucking failed with everything you set out to do, didn't you?" he sneered. "Grayson is dead, and you let it happen."

His sudden verbal attack was so shocking, I exploded, my hands pushed him, moving air and displacing molecules as time stood still, and he went sailing across the field. I didn't stop. I attacked, moving as fast as he had, displacing time and space as I landed close to him, only for him to reappear across the field.

"You failed to save him," he taunted, and I screamed. Tears blinded my vision and I wanted to hurt him in the worst possible way. I wanted to place the dagger at my hip in the spot where his cold heart should have been. "Come and get me," he challenged and I moved again, same speed, slamming into him and taking him down with cold, calculated precision.

He rolled me over, capturing my hands as I went for my dagger and smiled down with an irritatingly beautiful smile. I bucked at him, freezing time as I howled for him to get off of me. I saw red; his words had hit home and it fucking hurt.

"Emma, meet your trigger; it's your heart," he whispered, his eyes locking with mine before he vanished.

"That was a low blow," I snapped, standing up and realizing he'd done it. He'd triggered me, and it had worked. I didn't want to think of Grayson, because the pain was a raw wound that seeped, and refused to close.

"It worked, didn't it? You froze time, and you 'ported across the clearing without me having to do it for you."

"Ported?"

"Yeah, short for apport or apportare, take your pick." He grinned. "The way Sentinels move…the way time seems to stop for us."

I looked around us, noting that everyone was still frozen in place. I exhaled, released the anger, and slowly they came to life. I'd done it! I jumped up and down as my eyes locked with Jaeden, who had no idea what I had done.

No one did. They only saw us when I failed to move, or when I landed flat on my very sore derrière. I smiled and shook my head. I was evolving. Slowly, very slowly, but it was progress. I looked over at Liam, who was leaning close to Addy, whispering something in her ear as his hand lovingly stroked her flat belly.

Fucker.

"Not your problem," Azrael murmured against my ear. "You see that smile?" His hand slipped against mine as his fingers slowly touched me, caressing me. "They are in love. Would you make her regret being so happy just because you don't like the situation?" he asked softly.

"No, but he's not human. He already broke her heart once. What happens if he decides he doesn't want the baby? What happens if she has it and something goes horribly wrong?"

"Stop what-if-*ing* everything. They're happy now; you and her both chose to live in the now. She is. You're not. Stop trying to control everything and let it go, for once in your life, just let go," he murmured.

I punched him, froze time, and he sailed across the field before he'd even realized I'd done anything. Let *that* shit go, asshole. I smiled as he brought his hand up to his nose and grinned at me. One second I was smiling, staring at him, and the next I was on my ass, and he was still across the field. I blinked, frowned, and shook my head.

"How the hell?" I whispered. He'd struck so fast that it appeared, even to me, that he hadn't moved. Yet, here I was, flat on my ass. He did it again, and I had to stop myself from blinking; his wings had expanded, and he was moving in slow motion. I stood up, moving my arm back, and the moment he got close enough, I let it fly at his nose. I hit him, hard.

"Jesus," he groaned as he backpedaled in surprise, righted himself, and laughed. "Good girl."

I bit my lip and smiled. "Wings," I whispered, watching as his wings seemed to be absorbed back into his body. Up until now, we'd been careful to keep most of our abilities to ourselves. We had eyes on us, a lot of them.

"That's good for today," he said after he'd shaken off the hit. "You're getting faster, but you need to learn how to do it without me having to rip your heart out. I hate doing it."

"It works." My eyes focused on Addy, who was staring at me. "I should talk to her," I whispered. "She thinks I hate that she's with him. I owe her an explanation, and it's time I spoke to Jaeden, alone."

"No," he growled, his eyes glowing red with anger.

"Azrael, I owe him an explanation and I need the closure as much as he does right now. Living in the now means I have to say goodbye. I have to tell him to move on so that I can move forward with whatever this thing between me and you is. So, you're going to need to trust me."

"I trust you; it's him I don't trust," he admitted. "There's also the fact that you're Life, and he isn't exactly breathing."

"What does that even mean?" I asked as he frowned and looked away.

"You'll figure it out; I need to go source for boots anyway. You put a hole in my favorite pair yesterday. I know you feel bad about leaving him. He can find someone else, though, I can't," he whispered as he shoved his hands into his pockets. "He'll love again; he's already proven that with you. Without you, my life is sterile, cold, and black and white. You're my color. You're my warmth, and I don't want to give that up. I won't give that up. I know I sound like an asshole, but would you give up the world for him? Would he give up the world for you? I'd do it in a heartbeat for you. I'm a selfish prick, yet I can live with that."

I frowned and raised my eyes to his. "No, I wouldn't," I answered honestly. "I'd give up a lot of things for him, though, but I don't think you're one of them." I watched him carefully as he smiled.

"You rock my world, Emma," he murmured as he froze time to kiss me. My toes curled as his lips touched mine in a gentle kiss, one that made me feel like I really was his world. That was the thing that made me want him. He made me feel beautiful, and I wasn't afraid of him shirking his duties for me, or ending up dead because some group of old-as-fuck assholes decreed it.

Jaeden wasn't free to choose me. He would always do as the vampire elders told him to, not just because he was compelled to, but because his very life depended on it. If they told him to leave, he would. He held back from me and while I knew it, and had known it, I didn't want to face up to how much it bothered me. I'd been content to ignore it and I'd settled, which, looking back now, had been okay for a time. Now? Now I needed someone who didn't have to run off when I needed them at my side.

"I'd say something witty, but you have a big enough head," I replied, stepping away from him as he unfroze the world around us.

"You make it big with all the screaming for God when I take you, Emma," he chuckled.

"His name is easier to remember when my eyes cross and my toes curl," I joked, smiling as I turned to head to Addy.

Once I reached her, Liam moved away, and I sat beside her at the picnic table someone had stolen from the local park to place outside the shelter.

"He knows he will have to put this back, right? Stealing a table from a park is like a felony, or something," I stated.

"Sure," she quipped as she gave me a sideways look. "I'm sure that state troopers are going to be here any minute to arrest him." She leaned close to me conspiratorially. "You're happy with him," she whispered, which was ridiculous because every ear in the place could hear us.

"I am," I replied softly as I turned to really look at

her. She wasn't glowing, but she had been smiling until I'd sat down beside her. "Liam makes you happy, too."

"He does," she responded carefully. "I know it bothers you, but he's changed since you guys left."

"We weren't gone that long," I pointed out.

"Long enough," she countered with an impish grin. "He told me you weren't happy, that he could smell it on you."

"You deserve better." She deserved the world. This was my best friend, my family by choice. "You deserve the world, and he can't give you it."

"I deserve to be happy, and he makes me happy," she argued.

"You deserve security and to know you're the only woman he will ever set his paws on," I continued.

"He knows I'll neuter his ass if he so much as looks at another woman," she growled.

"You deserve to smile and be cherished." I glanced at her from the side of my eye as she frowned.

"He cherishes me and he does make me smile, Emma. He's brilliant, too; the guy is smart as all get out. He makes me belly laugh, and you know how hard that is to do. He even gave me a back rub the other day because my lower back was killing me. He helps me, and he challenges me and I love him!"

"Then marry him," I ordered softly, watching as her mouth dropped open.

"I can't do that," she argued.

"Why not?" I turned to look at her with a frown.

"Because you don't approve, and you're the only family I have left. I want you more than I want him. There, I said it." Tears clouded her eyes.

"Why can't you have us both?" I raised an eyebrow at her emotional outburst.

"Because you don't approve," she whispered.

"Who said I didn't? Liam? Because he caught a whiff of something, and used his doggie senses instead of asking questions. Perhaps talking to me?" I mused. "He needs to work on being human." I shook my head. "He sucks at it."

"I don't understand," she squeaked through a hiccup.

"Nothing changes us being family, Addy. I chose you as my sister the moment I met you. We've lost everything and everyone we love. You think I'd keep you from being happy? I want you happy, and I don't care who it's with. I don't think he's good enough for you, but then again, I'm pretty sure no one would ever be good enough for you if you left it up to me to decide. No one is ever good enough for someone you love as much as I love you. You're having his baby, nothing can change that, but this world needs some order to the chaos, so marry him. We can't control the world, but we can keep some semblance of normalcy in *our* world, and find some happy, yeah?"

She threw herself at me and hugged me as she cried. Liam watched from the tree he leaned against with a soft smile and a firm nod, letting me know he'd listened to the entire exchange.

"Besides, Addy, if he breaks your heart, I can break his head," I added, winking at Liam.

"You could, couldn't you?" she laughed nervously.

"In a fucking heartbeat," I smiled.

"I'm glad you're back," she whispered as she watched Liam. "Lachlan's been trying to get you alone so he can speak to you, by the way."

"Has he?" I asked, wondering what the wolf wanted to talk about. I'd been so lost in my head that I hadn't given a thought to what everyone else was feeling. "Where is he?"

"Behind ye, lass." His wicked Scottish brogue brought a smile to my lips.

"Lachlan," I sighed, and closed my eyes as I turned to look at him. I'd missed him more than I thought I would, and I had avoided this conversation long enough. "You wanted to talk?" I asked.

"Aye, I wanted tae ken what happened tae ye, lass."

He nodded to Addy as she stood up and dusted off her dress.

"I have things to get done, I'll see you later." She hugged me tightly and trotted over to Liam as Lachlan sat beside me.

I had a feeling guilt was chewing at him for not coming to find me. My voice was even as I held his hand and looked into his green eyes. "He pulled me out of there…out of that hellhole." I swallowed hard as I looked back on everything that had happened since Azrael pulled me out of that shitty place. "I learned about what I am. I got to know him, and I even met some Sentinels that weren't trying to kill me," I laughed a little. "You know, it's a real mind fuck to live my life for this long and then find out there is a whole other part of me that I never knew existed. The night that we came back and I saw…" Lachlan placed two fingers against my lips, and tried to shush me so I wouldn't finish that line of thought, but I pulled back and rambled on. "I just want you to know that I'm not disappointed with you, at least not anymore. I know you had a good reason for not leaving and I'm not mad at you."

"Nae, ye would nae be, would ye, lass?" He smirked. "I kenned ye were in trouble, but we couldn't get o' scent, or find o' single trace of you. I figured ye would get back tae us, but when ye didn't, aye, I started tae worry aboot ye. I wanted tae come searching for ye, but it was nae that easy, ye ken," he explained softly; the guilt in his voice tugged at my heartstrings. "So I stayed and sent Cian oot and aboot tae look for signs of ye, but there was nothing. It was nae good there, Jaeden was in bad shape, and I wasn't sure the daft arse would make it for a bit. Then the bloodlust took hold, and I was nae sure I wanted tae stick aboot, but I could nae leave him like that. He's an asshole, ye ken, but nae one deserves tae go through what he had. I kenned ye would want me tae save him if anything happened tae ye, so I made sure he lived. In case ye dinna ken, we got the wee ones oot before the vampires sacked the place. That town paid the price for what they did tae the vampires; their wrath was something terrible tae see." He nodded knowingly at me. "Ye saw the last of it before ye disappeared. I am sorry, lass. I should have done more tae find ye."

"You wouldn't have been able to. Azrael isn't quite like us; the way he views things and his priorities are really different than what I'm used to. He's always a few steps ahead; he's smart. He didn't hurt me, either, and I think I'm supposed to be with him. It just feels right. He knows my flaws and he still wants me. I can feel him on a deeper level, but more than that, Lachlan, he makes me think that there's a future. He makes me laugh. He's unlike anyone else I've ever met, and I know you feel guilty because you didn't come. I forgive you. You're my friend, and I know if you could have come to save me, you would have."

"Without a moment of hesitation," he confirmed. I leaned my head against his shoulder and gave him a chaste peck on the cheek.

"You did what I would have wanted you to do, even if at the time I sort of lost track of that. When he took me, I had no idea if you all were dead or alive, and the not knowing had me a little freaked out," I said with a shake of my head as he moved from the table to stand in front of me. "You're a good man, Lachlan, and I'm glad we met."

"Aye, lass, even if I was nae sure if I wanted tae kill or spank your wee sexy arse when we first met," he laughed. "I need tae check in on the wee ones; I promised one a bar o' chocolate if she learned tae hopscotch."

I laughed and watched as he walked away. We were going to be okay.

Chapter Thirty-Two

I sat at the table long after Lachlan had gone inside. Although I was happy that Lachlan and I were all good, and Addy and I had cleared the air about the baby, my heart was still hurting, knowing that while Addy thought everything was fine, it wasn't. Liam was a born wolf, not a turned one. He was immortal. She was mortal. Eventually, she'd age and he'd remain the same unless he bit her, and werewolf bites came with a lot of risk.

"Emma," Jaeden murmured as he sat close to me.

"Jaeden." I turned to give him a sad smile. My eyes drifted to Astrid, who stood less than a stone's throw away from us, listening.

"Can we talk?" His turquoise eyes searched mine as I sat staring at him. At that moment I knew that I still loved him; that hadn't changed. I just couldn't be with him, and that hadn't changed either.

"Of course we can," I replied, watching him as I turned, and gave him my full attention. "As soon as Shamus and Astrid stop listening to everything I say, of course," I amended.

He smiled and tilted his head playfully. "We can talk in your bedroom."

"Or in a meeting room," I countered carefully. I stood, held out my hand, and watched as he took it, taking control as he pulled me behind him. I knew Shamus would be listening no matter where we were. He was old, old enough that his senses were heightened more than any other vampire here.

Once we were in the meeting room, he pulled me into his arms and I allowed it. I felt my body react, but unlike the way it came alive with Azrael, now it only sparked with Jaeden. I was sure we could have great sex; that had never been one of our problems. Timing, however, was never on our side. I stood on my tiptoes and kissed his cheek chastely before pulling away from him to sit in a chair.

"It's really over, isn't it?" His eyes searched mine for the answer and found it before I could put words to his question.

"Look, I love you, I do, but sometimes what seems written in the stars is actually written in lust. We are toxic together. You and I? We burn too hot and then we turn to ice; you have a lot of baggage, and I have more issues than Vogue. Too much shit has happened and, while you have rules to follow, I don't. I lost my brother, and I can't for the life of me understand why it happened," I admitted.

"Emma, you can't try to make sense of something so senseless. Evil doesn't follow rules, or codes of conduct. Your mother, she's the worst kind of evil because she doesn't live by any code that you or I recognize. She's fed by greed. Grayson's death? That's not on you. You can't carry that burden."

"It's on me because, had I been where I was supposed to be, he'd still be here. I can own up to that. If I had been here, he wouldn't have been able to be lured away," I whispered as tears clouded my vision. "I don't blame you for what happened. But I can't allow myself to be who I am with you. With you, I let my guard down, I fuck up. The stakes aren't just some trivial thing anymore, it's people's lives. Then there's the fact that Shamus and Astrid keep coming between us. I know you have feelings for her, and it is okay to. You have a past together. I know that. Shamus, however… he pushed me away from you, and you allowed it to happen. Then there's the elders. If they called you right now and ordered you to run, you'd run. That's okay too. We don't live in the same world. Well, we do, but you dance to a different beat than I do, and I have to learn to walk before I can dance, ya know what I mean?"

"That makes no sense," he grumbled as he ran his fingers through his hair.

"I'm saying that I have to let you go. I will always

love you, Jaeden, always, but sometimes the world doesn't care what we want, it gives us what we need." I swallowed the sob that threatened to break free at saying the words.

"I can send Astrid away," he replied, his eyes watching my pulse.

"But you won't," I retorted. "You won't because it's not what Shamus wants. You are an amazing soldier, and I get that you have a duty to your people. I'm okay with that. Shamus is the one you take orders from, Jaeden, not the other way around. He is the one in control, and I'm not sure you understand the implications of that. He switched the birth control in this place. They're all on sugar pills, a placebo. Five women are pregnant, including my best friend. He's willing to risk their lives to feed his people." I noted he didn't flinch or show any emotion over the news.

"You knew, Jaeden," I gasped breathlessly. "You knew what he did, and you didn't say anything to me. You knew I wouldn't like it and I would fight against it. It's not a lie, but a deliberate omission. Your loyalty isn't to me, and I don't feel like we're on the same side anymore. I hate it, but I can't change it, and it wouldn't be fair of me to ask you to switch sides as your life could be the payment should you do so."

"I suspected it, but no, I wasn't told it was happening. This setup was planned a long time ago, to replenish the population so that we had a continuous source of blood. It was a request from the elders." His mouth tightened with each word that came out. "You're wrong, though, we are on the same side. I've always been on your side."

"Careful, Jaeden," I warned. "Treason against your own people isn't something I want to see you charged with. Shamus is just outside that door; he can't help himself. He has to know everything that goes on between us." I could hear his breathing; I'd studied it in the last few days. I was learning everything I could about my enemy and all his twisted quirks.

"He knows I follow the elders' orders and always have. He and I don't always see eye-to-eye on things, but the elders have the final say in everything," Jaeden shrugged, obviously not surprised that Shamus was listening. "It doesn't change the fact that I want you. I'll always want you and I'm willing to fight him to get you back."

"Don't waste your time, Jaeden," I whispered. "We gave it a good try. It didn't work out, and we both know that no matter how much we want it to be otherwise, it would never work out. I'm not going to say that it was you or me, because it wasn't. We did well together, but the timing was all wrong. You'll always be my first love, and you have a place inside of me that no one else can touch, ever," I whispered.

"Emma," he growled as he stood and pushed the table away from me. "I'm not going to just stand by while he gets the girl. I'm a fucking Viking! I take what I want, and right now, it's you."

"I wouldn't do that," Azrael warned as he pushed away from the door, where he'd just appeared.

"The fuck you say," Jaeden snapped; his fangs extended and his eyes turned red with hunger.

"Go ahead, kiss her," Azrael replied, undisturbed by Jaeden's transformation. "You might get lucky, you might not. It's a crapshoot right now while her powers are still emerging. You might want to know what she is before you take what you think it is that you want from her. I am a Guardian of Death, Emma is a Guardian of Life; anything I touch…dies. I'll let you add up what will eventually happen if you keep trying to touch her, or she touches you," he mused.

"Hayden was telling the truth?" I whispered. Azrael shifted his attention from Jaeden to me.

"He told you, and you didn't believe him? Hell, I tried to tell you, but you must have not wanted to hear what I was saying. You're a Guardian of Life. Remember what I told you about my powers when they emerged? One day, everything was normal, the following day someone dear to me touched me and they died. There will come a time soon, where he will touch you, or try to kiss you and he'll be back on a solid food diet. Is he willing to throw his immortality away for you? I asked you earlier, is he willing to give up his world for you?"

I shook with the knowledge of why he'd asked the question after training. He meant it; Jaeden wouldn't pick me, because he'd become mortal. Shit.

"Elaborate," Jaeden growled.

"Vampirism is a type of virus; Emma is a cure for diseases, viruses, and can prevent death if she can get to the person prior to rigor setting in. You fit two of the criteria, so go ahead. Keep touching her if you're willing to give it all up for her." Azrael's expression seemed so calm and clinical. However, I could tell how he was fighting against himself. He told me before that he would kill Jaeden if he touched me again.

I trembled with the idea of what might have happened. What if my powers kicked in while we were traveling? What could have happened if Azrael hadn't taken me?

"What about Lachlan and the wolves? What if I touch them?" The wolves were also infected with a type of virus that allowed them to shift; if I messed with that, Liam would never let me near Addy's baby.

Azrael shook his head. "From what I was told, you would be able to touch born wolves like Lachlan without changing them. Rogue wolves are pretty well-fucked. You are their proverbial version of screwed, without the fun stuff."

I glanced at the open door of the meeting room, and the people who were gathered and frozen in place in front of it. How the hell?

"What did you do?" I asked, wondering how everyone else was frozen except Jaeden.

"He was part of the discussion and it is pertinent to him," Azrael explained patiently.

"So, I can't touch her anymore?" Jaeden's face looked pained.

"It's a risk. Her powers could mature at any time. She's evolving, slowly. At the moment, she doesn't cure through touch," he admitted.

"But eventually she'll be able to." Jaeden studied me contemplatively, as if he was weighing his options. "How do I know this isn't just bullshit? You seem to think she's yours," he ground out.

"She has always been mine," Azrael stated firmly. "We are a mated pair. That is how our kind is created. You had her for a time, while I was detained. I came for her and I will not let her go. One thing I know about Emma is, she wouldn't forgive me if I didn't warn you what would happen if you tried to convince her to remain with you."

"No," I interrupted before this could go any further. I wouldn't give Jaeden the option of the wrong choice. "I would hate myself, and I wouldn't age. You would. Think of it as if I remained mortal and you immortal. I'm not watching you die. I can't lose anyone else. You don't get to decide this," I growled, my hands trembling with frustration. No way in hell was I allowing Jaeden's lips or any part of him close to mine.

"I love you," Jaeden whispered. "Not enough to change who I am." He gave me a look filled with longing and regret before he turned and left me in the room alone with Azrael.

"You have no right to look happy!" I shouted. "Damn you! I could have killed him."

"You wouldn't have killed him. Your powers don't work that way," he murmured, his eyes watching me carefully. "Besides, you wouldn't have kissed him. Your soul is locked to mine. You may have wanted to kiss him, but I would have stopped it before it got that far. I wouldn't have let you hurt him because it would have hurt you more. Not that I wouldn't want the man who took what is mine gone, but I'm bigger than that. That doesn't mean I like it, Emma. It doesn't mean I have to like him either. I can't blame him for wanting to keep you. You're very addictive."

Chapter Thirty-Three

I walked down the aisle of the store we were currently sourcing from. Sears was a hell of a find, one that we weren't walking away from until we had gotten everything we needed out from the building. The barred security gates had been pulled down and locked to prevent looters from taking whatever they wanted, however locked gates weren't a deterrent to a Sentinel. That much was for sure.

"Load the generators first," I instructed. "We need them, and then clothes." Jaeden and Lachlan were looking for semi-trucks with trailers while the others cleared the streets to get them through. "Load up the truck and the SUVs while we wait," I ordered. We'd stayed away from the downtown area before, since we'd assumed it would have been the first area looted. This time, we went all-out and had stolen a 26' U-Haul truck on our way into Spokane. It would hold a ton of stuff, but there was a lot we needed to take back.

I was pretty sure the guys had planned this trip to get my mind off Grayson, but being in the mall reminded me of him. I'd spent a lot of time in North Town Mall, sourcing the comic book stores and clothing outlets to find him specific things he'd preferred. I swallowed the pain, noting that yesterday had been a little easier than today had been. Azrael had been right, sometimes it was easier, and then sometimes I couldn't catch my breath because the pain hurt so badly.

I'd sensed Cayla following me, and ignored her for the most part. Nery was popping in and out, watching me, which sent chills down my spine as I wasn't sure if they were Shamus's eyes and ears when I was outside of the shelter. I wasn't sure what was up with the pair, but they seemed scarce on most days, as if they were afraid of being too close to the Ark.

I also had Addy to consider now; her condition made it hard to leave her in charge of the Ark. While I knew she was strong enough, I worried about the stress it caused, because the day-to-day task of running the place was hard on anyone. Liam had stepped up; he'd asked her to marry him and that satisfied some of my worry, but there was still the fact that she was having a baby and shit could go sideways with that, even when civilization and working hospitals with doctors in them still existed. Nowadays, the risks were a lot higher.

I was looking for baby stuff, unsure what she would want or need, and being lost in my head wasn't helping either of our situations. I rounded a corner and was shoved against the wall. Cerulean blue eyes smiled at me with heated lust in their depths.

"Sloppy, Emma, I could have killed you," Azrael murmured as he kissed my forehead gently. "You have to stop that."

"Stop what?" I whispered, chewing my lip to stop the sting of tears.

"Carrying the weight of the world on your shoulders," he replied, kissing away one of the tears that escaped.

"I worry, it's what I do," I replied with a shrug as I tried to pull my head out of the mush I'd been wading through.

"She's not going to die, you won't allow it. Women have been having babies since the dawn of time. You're not alone, and that's what's really bothering you the most right now. Look around you; look at the people you draw to you. They're good people. Grayson was blood; your father wasn't. He was family by choice, as are your people," he assured me, his lips slowly kissing the side of my neck until the butterflies took note and fluttered.

"Azrael, you aren't supposed to be able to read my mind. It's annoying," I grumbled.

"It's easy when you're projecting everything you are thinking," he said. He smiled against my flesh and pulled back, nodding when the pain eased a bit as the emotions faded.

"Failure hurts, and I think that's what makes losing Grayson ten times worse. Knowing that I failed him and that, when I do fail, it cost someone their life. I won't fail Addy. I can't. Now, stop kissing me so I can find baby stuff. My brain stops working when you use those voodoo lips on me."

"Like this?" he teased as he kissed my collarbone and nipped at it.

"Mmhm," I agreed. "I'm pretty sure my father would be irate if he could see me running around with you. We've broken almost all of his rules for staying hidden and safe," I replied.

"Lucky for him his daughter became stronger, and is immortal. I'm not sure he considered that before he came up with those rules. Besides, you have an army of immortals watching your back, and one addicted to watching your ass," he murmured as he finally claimed my lips and gave me a kiss that sent heat rushing through me.

"Azrael," I groaned as he bit softly into my bottom lip and pulled at it gently before he released it to smile, revealing Colgate-white teeth and a perfect boyish grin that made the butterflies flutter faster. "You make it impossible to get anything done; you know that, right?" I teased.

"Baby stuff," he replied offhandedly. "That's what we're looking for, right? Let's find Addy some baby stuff so you can be selected as godmother."

"It's important," I emphasized. It was very important to me. I had to prove to her that I was happy about her baby. I really had to stop calling it a puppy, though. Although Lachlan had laughed about it, he told me that Liam was upset about the puppy comments. I'd joked around about that with Addy before I'd left the Ark to find Grayson, but now it was happening for real.

Lachlan had explained that the baby would be human, appear human, act human, and be as weak as one until the child was about sixteen, when the first shift would usually occur. The child would be a born wolf, and since Lachlan and Liam were blood brothers, the child would be considered royalty in their world. He'd explained about their hierarchy, but it had been hard to follow when my mind kept going back to pretty much everything that could go wrong with Addy.

"Very important; you go look down those aisles and I'll take these ones," he said with mock-seriousness, and handed me a flashlight, since my way included going down into the lower level, which was pitch black. Even though Sentinels could see at night as well as they did in the daylight, that area was like a black hole down there and it never hurt to be a little cautious.

I trotted down the stairs, turned on the flashlight and, before my eyes could adjust, bumped into Cayla. She giggled as I dropped the flashlight and I grabbed onto her to stop myself from falling. She smiled sadly, and I pulled away.

"Jesus, you scared me," I laughed breathlessly as

she nodded and I picked up the flashlight. I frowned when she just watched me with a look of hopeless desperation. "Everything okay?" I asked, and turned to find Nery illuminated by the flashlight, a frown on his ghostly features. "Hey, you guys okay, what's up?" I asked again, and watched as Cayla's frown deepened.

"I'm so sorry, Emma," she whispered before she grabbed me, yanked on my arm and bit down into my forearm, hard. I struggled against her, and it only gave her more leverage to get her fangs into me like some sort of multicolored terrier.

"Cayla, what the fuck!" I screamed, feeling her draw my blood from the wound she'd made. She released my arm and backed away, not stopping to close the torn, shredded flesh as she looked at me sadly.

"It was this, or death," she whispered as she tilted her head and slumped against the wall.

"What are you talking about?" I growled as I held my bleeding arm against my chest.

"What happened?" Lachlan asked as he came down the steps two at a time.

"She bit me," I said with a confused frown. Why the fuck would she bite me? That was insane, even for her.

"It's okay." Nery's voice was soothing, and I could feel him patting me on the back like a child as Cayla smiled and blood started to trickle from her nose.

"Oh my God," I whispered. I'd killed her. Well, technically I was bringing her back to life, or my blood was. "Cayla, what did you do?" My question came out as a plea as I began shaking, physically shaking with fear that this was going to go way wrong on us. My luck sucked, it went from bad luck to 'you're fucked' kinda luck. There was no good luck in me.

"Couldn't do it anymore," she wheezed. "Couldn't go on or do as Master wanted anymore, so I chose this," she coughed out; blood slid from her lips and dripped on her jacket as she dropped to her knees and it began oozing out of her eyes and ears.

"Get Jaeden," I yelled with a tremble in my voice. I tore my eyes from Cayla to look at Lachlan. "Go get Jaeden, now," I roared as Azrael started down the stairs to where we were at. He turned, armored up, and vanished. I pulled Cayla into my lap and stroked her hair away from her face. She'd dyed it red with sapphire blue highlights this time. "What were you thinking?" I sobbed, knowing she'd been through hell as a human, and she'd suffered a serious head wound when Shamus had found her. She'd always been a little out there, but this took the cake.

"You're safe now, don't worry, okay? I know what I am doing," she coughed, and raised her eyes towards the stairs, where Jaeden stood looking down at us.

His turquoise eyes darted between me and Cayla, and then noted my torn and bloody forearm that Cayla had savagely gnawed on. I swallowed the guilt and eyed him, knowing I'd beg and plead for her life. He could change her back; if anyone could do it, Jaeden could.

"Jaeden, please," I whispered, knowing he'd hear me. I watched as he ran his fingers through his hair as he made his way slowly down the stairs.

"What happened?" he snarled, turquoise eyes looking at me accusingly, or maybe that was my guilt talking.

"She touched me, and then she bit my arm," I explained, holding up my arm which had since stopped bleeding as badly as it started to heal.

"She belongs to Shamus, we will call him," he announced, but Cayla shook her head with what little strength she had left, and gave Jaeden a pleading look.

"You," she begged as blood trickled from her lips. "Please, not him."

"Cayla," he murmured as he watched her. "Shamus is in charge."

"Not for long," she sighed cryptically. "What goes against must be righted, and what is right is never wrong…" She smiled, blood covering her teeth as her eyes flashed red before becoming vacant.

"If you plan to bring her back, do it soon," Azrael advised, his eyes searching Jaeden's face. "Unless you're afraid of becoming mortal because she carries Emma's blood now?"

"I'm not afraid of her blood. I'm afraid that Cayla may not be changeable. It took Shamus almost a year to do it the first time," Jaeden replied, his tone clipped and angry as he stared down at us.

"I'd change the lass tae a wolf, but I ken she'd be unable tae control it if she is nae present in her mind." Lachlan's green eyes watched as more blood poured from her lips as I held her to me. "If ye turn mortal, mon, I'll change ye tae a wolf," he offered as he rubbed the back of his neck, and Jaeden chuckled.

"And what's Nery got to say about all of this?" Jaeden asked, his eyes searching mine as he asked about the ghost they'd always assumed Cayla had made up.

"Nery?" I asked, but as I looked around, he wasn't anywhere to be seen. "He's gone." I froze as I felt the icy coolness of Nery's lips as he whispered in my ear.

"I told her to do this, Sentinel. You were her only hope to be released from Shamus. He has abused her since he first found her; horrible abuse that you can only imagine in the darkest of your nightmares. It didn't take a year to turn her. He played with her for almost a year in the house I died in. He gave her the head wound and turned her because she was dying and he is possessive of his toys. Shamus can't keep her; he isn't what you think he is. You freed her, Sentinel. Now she will have a new master."

"Jaeden," I expelled a shuddering breath with what I was about to ask him. He had to follow Shamus's orders, and this could put him directly in that vampire's crosshairs. "You have to trust me in this; you have to change her right away, and Shamus can't know about it," I pleaded. "You have to become her master."

"Emma, I can't. It's just not done in our world. It is the same as stealing," Jaeden reasoned.

"Shamus is abusing her, has been for years. Which is worse? Stealing, or abusing a girl until she *wants* to die?" I cried.

"You're certain of this?" Jaeden demanded as I nodded.

"Nery just explained what's been happening and why she did this. Please, Jaeden," I begged. "You have to help her."

Jaeden sighed heavily as he reached down, and picked up Cayla's slight weight. "I may be gone for a few days; she'll need a quiet place to change," he said quietly.

"Fourth floor of the bunker is a good place, it's used only for the water purification system," I replied. "Use the back entry, the one I showed you. The code is 1665. The back elevator can be used without dimming the lights from using the power, but only if you go straight down and don't stop at any other floors."

"If Shamus discovers her…"

"We tell him she accidentally brushed up against

me," I mumbled. "We tell him it was a mistake, and that we moved quickly to save her life." I stared at him, watching as he swallowed hard. "If you turn mortal, we will figure out how to change you back as well. I won't allow anything to hurt you, Jaeden, ever." I meant it. Shamus wouldn't touch him for this. I'd kill Shamus first, even if I had to hold him down and force my blood down his throat, then stab his nasty little heart as he became mortal.

"I appreciate the gesture." He nodded as he turned to leave.

"Lachlan, have the men load up the trucks. I want everything we can fit loaded and out of this place as soon as possible. Have them empty out the tools and more important stuff first. I'd also like the entire baby-area packed up. It's possible we may have more people pregnant than we know of at the shelter. Best to get it all," I mused. "I'll leave everyone with you; make sure they know what things to grab. Azrael will go with me, and we'll hit up the Army Surplus over on Division Street. My father hid a stockpile of the MREs in the attic, so they should still be there. It's gated and locked up tight like this place, or was the last time we were here together."

"God speed, Emma," Lachlan said, kissing my cheek before he turned, winked at Azrael, and started issuing orders to those who'd come this way during the commotion.

I turned, looked at the baby department, and

grabbed a giraffe stuffed animal off the shelf. I looked at it and frowned. It wasn't the crib or nursery set that I'd intended to get for Addy, but the situation with Cayla changed everything. I had no more time for sourcing baby stuff today. I needed to get back to the Ark and make sure Jaeden and Cayla remained hidden from Shamus so that Jaeden could save Cayla from what she'd done, and hopefully save her from Shamus.

"Addy will love it," Azrael murmured, his eyes watching me as I frowned and turned to look at him.

"She'd love a nursery more. I saw her going through some catalogues yesterday that were like two years old," I mused.

"She loves you. She knows you love her. You're sisters. Tell her how you feel, and that you'll go to war to protect her and her unborn child. Just be yourself."

"Let's go. By the way, you really suck at pep talks," I replied, pushing the giraffe into my bag before I swung it on my back.

Chapter Thirty-Four

We hadn't been able to get the SUV we'd driven down here in through the cars that blocked the street on Division, so we'd left it covered with a tarp before starting out towards the Army Surplus store. We had left our jackets back at the SUV as the temperature outside was getting a lot hotter than it had been in the mall, and I was starting to regret not changing into a tank top before we left the car.

It was silent; no one was about, which was nice. We didn't have to worry about being attacked, because we could hear anything within about a quarter of a mile moving. Nothing with a beating heart was close to us, not even a wild animal.

"You're adapting to using your senses quickly," Azrael commented with a touch of pride in his tone.

"I have a good teacher," I replied absently as I trotted up the steps of the Army Surplus store behind

Azrael. He wrenched the door open and cocked his head to one side as he listened for any disturbances. I hung back a little, still reeling from what Cayla had done, and praying that Jaeden would be able to fix her without Shamus finding out. At least not right away.

"That you do," he agreed as he motioned for me to go ahead of him into the store.

I took two steps and stopped. I turned as I tilted my head, listening. Something had changed. "Do you feel that?" I asked, as gunfire ripped through the quiet day and blood splattered my face. "Oh my God," I gasped and cried out as I caught Azrael. He'd been shot!

"Wait…for…" he mumbled, blood dripping from his lips as he dropped his head to rest against my shoulder, and his body sagged and went limp and heavy in my arms as I collapsed under his weight.

"No, no, no, get up," I begged. As more shots rang out, sharp pain tore through my shoulder as I tried to hold on to his lax form. I felt warm, thick liquid flowing over my hand that was holding on to his back. He'd been shot in the back of the head! I wasn't sure if we could come back from that. "No," I pleaded, as another shot tore through Azrael's chest as I struggled to get to my knees, and felt the next three bullets as they ripped into my chest.

Blood gurgled in my throat as I tried to get words out. I could feel my lungs struggling to work, and my eyes grew heavy as I leaned against Azrael. I tried to send my senses out, but I couldn't feel him. Panic started to sink in, desperation to keep him with me. A sob bubbled up, but my lungs were ceasing to work and I felt as if my heart had been shredded.

"Isn't this sweet?" Shamus's voice asked coldly. My eyes rose up to find him and Astrid both staring down at me. A malevolent smile quirked at the corners of Shamus's mouth as he raised a handgun, pulled back on the slide, and emptied the clip into Azrael's chest, then kicked his lifeless body as I struggled to try to defend him. "Grab her; she'll heal in just a little bit. Him on the other hand…" Shamus's words trailed off. "Do yourselves a favor and don't touch him with bare hands, just in case. Use gloves when you move the body. They said they wanted proof, so whatever you do, don't damage his face so they can identify him," he directed, as his men moved in to roughly grab me.

I was losing consciousness, but my last thought was of Azrael. He wasn't supposed to be able to die easily, so what had happened?

"Remind me to thank Trina for her helpful insight on how to get rid of this trash. I never would have guessed that you can kill a Sentinel this way. I thought for sure we were going to have to decapitate him, but the chances of getting close enough to take his head were next to nil…I still might take it, but they were pretty specific that they wanted him as intact as possible," Shamus mused as he kicked Azrael's body again. "You on the other hand, Emma, you I have been looking forward to having for a very long time now. You'll scream so prettily for me, won't you?" he asked, his smile cold and malevolent.

"Kill…you," I whispered, or tried to. Blood oozed from my lips as the blissfulness of unconsciousness took hold of my mind.

~~*

Drip-drip.

I groaned as I forced my eyes to open past the pain to get my bearings. My chest and shoulder were on fire, alerting me to the fact that I hadn't healed very much since I had been out. The dim light that flooded through the dust-covered windows in the room I was in told me it was late afternoon, which confirmed that only a few hours, at most, had passed.

I tilted my head back and squinted at the leather cuffs on my wrists that were attached to chains that suspended me from the ceiling, my feet barely touching the floor. I tested the chains, finding them firm and more than adequate to support my weight. That one small exercise had me gasping and coughing up blood. Son of a bitch, it burned like hellfire in my chest. I looked down, and saw blood crusted to the shirt I'd worn. I'd been sloppy, foregoing the Kevlar for comfort and speed, and since I'd had an army out sourcing with me, I didn't think I was going to need it.

I forced my eyes to remain open as they tried to close on me. I could make out beds in the room beyond this one, maybe a hospital? It didn't smell of death, so it wouldn't be one of the large hospitals. Maybe Eastern State Hospital, the hospital for the mentally ill…*fucking* hell.

I could smell the coppery scent of blood, but I wasn't sure if it was mine or someone else's. I could hear noises, but I couldn't make out where they were coming from.

I closed my eyes, sending out everything I had to search for Azrael, knowing he was here somewhere. He had to be. He couldn't be dead. Azrael had said we were near impossible to kill, but he'd been shot in the head. In the head! I remembered back at his house, he had told John to shoot me in the head, like it was something I could come back from. But if we could, why didn't he get up? What the hell had they used to shoot us with? The back of his head looked like it had been torn apart, from what little I could see. Hot tears built behind my eyes as I swallowed the urge to scream and cry. If he was dead, I'd have to mourn him after I got away from Shamus.

The others would have noted that we hadn't come back by now, so they were probably out looking for us. I'd made sure Lachlan knew where we were going; he knew my scent, and he would see mine and Azrael's blood splattered all over the entryway of the surplus store.

"It wakes," Astrid mused, her tone snide, which matched the ugly smile on her otherwise beautiful face. "How I've waited for this day, sweet Emma," she hissed. I felt weak, really weak. I wasn't healing fast enough to prevent her from hurting me yet, and I knew she wanted to in the worst way. "Shamus has some very perverse needs. Some of them, I assure you, will be to die for," she laughed. A chill snaked up my spine at her words. "Poor, sweet Emma, the stupid little slut that every man wants," she crooned. She poked me with her sharp fingernail, making me wince. "Why is that? What's so special about you? You're nothing," she seethed. "I am royalty, and his wife!" She slapped me, and my head snapped back; my eyes glazed over and blood dripped from my nose. I hadn't made a fucking sound. I wouldn't give her that satisfaction no matter how bad off I was. "Shamus says your blood is different, maybe I should taste it and see what it is about it that draws men to you?"

"Go ahead, Astrid, taste me," I whispered through cracked lips that burned and hurt. My tongue was heavy; it felt like I'd licked sandpaper.

"Think I won't?" she hissed, moving closer as she raised her hand and slapped me once more. My head flew back from the force of the blow, and I laughed.

"You hit like a little bitch," I smirked. I dropped my head as I tried to look at the snide witch, blood dripped from where she'd reopened a wound on my lip, and I licked it, letting her see it. Hoping it would tempt her. One taste and this bitch would be mortal, and I couldn't think of anyone else who deserved to be weak and exploited as she did. She deserved to feel helpless and vulnerable like those she preyed upon.

"Astrid, enough," Shamus warned as he loomed just outside the doorway. I hadn't even heard him approach the room, which told me I wasn't paying attention. I had to find a way out of this mess quickly. "Return to the Ark, and let the others know it's almost time," he instructed.

"I want to be a part of this," she whined, her bottom lip pushed out in a little frown as she turned to pout at Shamus. "I want to watch you take her, and hurt her over and over, like we did to Cayla a few days ago. I love it when you hurt them; when you use things on them."

I wanted to throw up. Use things? Fuck me? Oh hell no.

"We did have fun with her, didn't we?" Shamus smiled at my reaction as if he was feeding from my fears. "She took all of my men between her slender white thighs, and we took turns experimenting with different…items. Forcing them inside of her while she begged us to stop." He walked closer to me, his red eyes filled with lust and a sickness I'd never noticed before. "We stretched her so much that I feared she'd rip apart, and unfortunately we had to stop. She hadn't fed enough to heal properly, but you, Emma, you heal without feeding, don't you?" he mused. "My men can't wait for their turn with you. I told your mother you wouldn't be harmed too much, but she didn't seem to mind us having fun with you. In fact, she preferred you weak and a little broken."

"My mother?" I asked, fighting against the panic that was sinking in no matter how much I tried to push it away.

"You are so gullible, Emma. You think I found your father by chance? Because he was searching the internet with keywords? I was led to him by someone who understood what an asset I would become in this war. Trina told me where to find your father, and how exactly to convince him to do as I needed him to. Yes, I compelled him to increase his desire to build the Ark, of course. Time was of the essence. I gave him the plans for the Ark, knowing he'd build it for me, because he couldn't say no. Trina assured me that it would be mine when she took you. You, however, were more trouble than she thought you would be."

Shamus casually paced in a circle around me, and I had to close my eyes to keep from getting dizzy. "I knew the end was coming because I helped your mother from the very beginning. I gave her our maker, knowing that he was the strongest of the elders and would be the most challenging to overthrow. Mahar was the oldest living vampire, and only a Sentinel would be able to bring him down. It freed me and all of his progeny from his control, not that they knew it," he chuckled darkly. "And since I was the first vampire he sired, I naturally took over, becoming father to all of the children he created."

He grabbed my chin in his hand, making my eyes pop back open as he forced me to look at him while he gloated. "Trina promised me the world, and so far, she's delivered it perfectly. The only thing she has asked me for in return was you and a Sentinel going by either the name of Adriel or Azrael; which by the way, thank you so much for bringing him with you when you returned." His voice dripped with sarcasm as he patted my cheek. "I should thank you for saving the others and bringing them to the shelter, as you provided me with an endless food supply that I'll enjoy for centuries to come, but since you didn't do it with the knowledge that you were helping me, I won't. Instead, I'll show you my thanks for that by taking it from your flesh."

Shamus ran his hands over my breasts and moved closer to murmur in my ear. "The first taste I had of you only fueled a need and obsession to have you. I should thank Jaeden, really; he gave me the first taste of your blood." His hands slid down to my inseam and he cupped me intimately with one hand, as if remembering and savoring what he had done. "He is responsible for this need I have to break you. I've been forced to watch your little love story play out, but eventually, I had to drive a wedge between you so that I could finally take my turn. And, well, your mother didn't care for you taking him as a lover. She's obsessed with Knights, whatever that means. I'm obsessed with breaking pretty little things," he announced, his confidence mounting with each little bomb he threw at me. "Once I found out you had a Sentinel following you, I had to slow our push to Provo down even more so we could get him too. I had a feeling she would be willing to wait a little longer for you if he panned out to be the Sentinel she was looking for."

"So all this time, you were really just taking me to her…" I rasped. "Did Jaeden know?"

"Of course not; I told him about the Sentinels in Provo. He thought we were going to raid them so we could get your brother. Once he believed that, he fell in with my plans quite nicely."

"Too bad the Clarkston Army had dinner plans for you, huh?" I wheezed and watched his face darken at the jab to his oversight in his grand plan.

Shamus pulled a dagger from its sheath at his waist as Astrid moaned, as if the sight of the blade turned her on. I shrank back, fighting the bubbling scream that threatened to rip from me as he pushed the blade against my shirt, cutting through the material like butter. He nicked my skin, his eyes glowing as he watched the cut open; those horrible eyes rose to mine as I choked down a sob, refusing to give him what he wanted. The blade went deeper, sliding a path from the bullet wounds in my chest to my navel, and yet I still refused to allow any sound to leave my lungs.

It burned; the blade sliced through my flesh easily. He didn't drink from my blood though, and I needed him to.

"Taste me, Shamus," I groaned, my eyes heavy from the pain as I mentally sent the pain into a box inside my head. Burying it. "You know you want to."

"We've got a long time to play together, Emma. I'm in no rush to taste you. Astrid, bring me the corpse," he ordered offhandedly. "I promised your mother I'd catch you both. Pity, she said he would have to die and that we would have to do it fast before we took you. I was sure he'd be more sport than he was. I do love torturing proud men; they scream and beg the loudest. They scream even louder when they're forced to witness the torture of their woman, though. I hate that I had to forgo it. Perhaps letting you see him again will give me the screams I want."

I watched as Astrid, who now wore thick black gloves, dragged Azrael's corpse into the room. Emotions rushed through me; despair tore me apart. Not him. Not when we'd just found each other. He'd said we were hard to kill, near impossible, but yet he was dead. I couldn't hear his pulse, couldn't sense his soul, and that almost broke me. I fought the burning tears in my eyes as I watched Shamus put on gloves similar to the ones Astrid wore, and then gripped Azrael's hair to show me his lifeless eyes. I closed my eyes against the sight.

"You see, my sweet, not coming back; not coming to save you," Shamus taunted and then chuckled as if this was one of the funniest things he'd ever seen.

I opened my eyes again, struggling with the chains only to feel my strength fading as Shamus's voice filled the room. Azrael was motionless and lifeless. My eyes locked on to him, ignoring Shamus and the way he watched me as I processed the truth of what I was seeing. Azrael was fucking dead. Shamus briefly rolled Azrael so I could see what had been done to him. His hair was a sticky wet mess of blood with bits of pieces of brain matter and bone caked in it. I struggled not to lose my shit as Shamus rolled Azrael back so I could see his face.

Azrael's eyes…his eyes were the worst part of it. They were coated in a glaze, death's glaze. Sightless, unmoving eyes stared blankly. I sent my powers in search of any sign of life, but found nothing. Why? Why did the world keep taking from me? Why him? I failed to keep the sob at bay as Shamus slammed Azrael's head on the cool tiles of the floor. He whispered something to Astrid, who smirked, and looked at me with venom in his eyes.

I swallowed the nausea, wishing I could just curl up beside him and give up for once. I wouldn't, though. I couldn't. It wasn't in me to give up.

"No," I whispered as I shook my head. This wasn't supposed to happen; if he came back, he'd need to be whole, right? Could he heal with the back of his head missing?

No, Azrael was dead…and I was about to be tortured for fun, for Shamus's sick, perverted pleasure. He'd been working with my mother this entire time, and I'd missed that tiny piece of information somewhere. That one piece had led me here, to this situation, because I'd never even taken a moment to think that part through.

The vampires wouldn't have known the end was coming unless they'd been tipped off.

My mother had orchestrated it all. Right from the bunker to the virus, and she'd been ahead of me every step of the way. Why hadn't I stopped to ask the one question I should have? How was she ahead of me every time? Because she had eyes inside the bunker, she had eyes on me.

I'd thought losing Grayson had been the last straw, but I was wrong. She wouldn't stop taking people away from me, ever. She'd never stop until I stopped her for good.

Chapter Thirty-Five

I watched as they dragged Azrael's body out of the room. I hung there, feeling useless and helpless. I wondered where they had taken him and what they were doing to his body now. Shamus returned with a satisfied look on his face as he slowly removed the gloves as he made his way back to me. He enjoyed inflicting pain on others, but he didn't strike me as the kind to take it well.

"You disappoint," Shamus said as he made a clucking noise and shook a finger at me. "I thought you would show more distress about your dead lover. Perhaps I misjudged the situation. At least you now know he won't be coming to your rescue." He chuckled as if he was pleased with the way everything was working out. I guess I couldn't blame him; he had bested Death, and if my mother told him what I was, he now held Life in his hands. I had a feeling that she needed Azrael out of the way, and was more than happy to share enough about him so the vampires could catch him. From what Shamus had disclosed, she needed me, so she probably hadn't shared what she knew about the Guardian of Life. Hell, the mere fact that I turned out to be a Guardian had appeared to surprise her, and seemed to please her more than if I had been a Knight, as she'd originally wanted.

I turned my eyes away from the doorway that they had taken Azrael's corpse through, and watched Shamus as he set out an assortment of knives and other sharp implements. He was talking, but I wasn't listening to his stupid monologue anymore. I was listening to those outside the room, trying to figure out exactly where I was.

They kept saying that no one would find us, which meant we were probably out at Eastern State Hospital. This place had been cleaned up; it looked like someone had been working hard to make it that way, and my money was on Shamus. He and some of his guys had disappeared several times since I'd been back at the Ark, and with their speed it wouldn't be hard for them to cover several miles in a short time.

It smelled of solvent and cleaner. I could hear at least fifteen people moving around inside the building, and a few weren't here by choice. One woman was screaming, while someone else was laughing. They spoke openly about the Sentinels that were alerted to the news of my capture and were on their way.

Shamus hadn't been lying about being in cahoots with my mother. They were excited about what was coming. They talked about killing the rest of the elders, forming new laws, and taking out any who opposed them. One talked about killing Jaeden and his men, like they'd already decided to end their lives I wasn't going to let them do it.

I had to get free, kill them all and get home. I wanted to break down, cry for Azrael and allow the pain to take me, but first I had to be sure my people were safe, that this threat no longer loomed over their heads. My first priority was to get away; my second was to kill them all, no matter the cost. And last but not least, I had to get home and warn them, since some of Shamus's people were still inside with them.

"Go to the Ark," Shamus ordered Astrid, and I wondered if she would do as he'd told her to this time. Both of them were ignoring me. I wasn't considered a threat since I was in chains and vulnerable. Only, I could feel how weak the chains were; sense that while he pretended to not fear me, he did. They all did. They should.

They'd taken a piece of my soul, and I was going to collect a piece of theirs in return. I was done playing around.

He pushed the remains of my shirt and bra off of my shoulders, and I began to feel a familiar itch above my shoulder blades and along my spine. I tilted my head as I heard a door open and close, and knew Astrid was being a good little dog and rushing back to the Ark as she'd been told. By now they had to know I was missing.

"Should I cut you open and then allow the men to use

you, Emma?" Shamus asked, his words sliced through my mind. "Or, should I allow them to use you and then cut you open? Decisions, decisions," he continued with glee.

I turned my head and looked at him, really looked at him. His hair was greasy, his teeth yellowed from his lack of hygiene. He'd hidden it from us, showing us what we'd wanted to see in him. He wasn't beautiful as I'd first assumed; no, if you looked beyond the façade, you could see the monster lurking in the depths of his soul. He was cold, and had an ugliness to him that was bone-deep. Cayla had tried to warn me, but she'd been tied to him; she'd freed herself by drinking my blood. Smart, she was very smart, which he took for granted, assuming she was damaged.

He'd taken that girl from one abusive life and given her an even worse one, and acted like she owed him for it. She'd taken control back from him. Nery was perceptive; he'd been able to predict things and, for Cayla's sake, I was so happy that he had told her how she could save herself. Having Jaeden change her was risky for both of them. Especially because the vampires all thought she was damaged, and the elders would have destroyed her if she hadn't been tied to another vampire.

"Bitch," Shamus bellowed, raising his hand and slicing through my face with a scalpel. I felt the searing agony as it ripped through the skin of my cheek. I stifled a scream as pain burned through me, and slowly, carefully, turned to look at him through a smile. At least I think it was a smile; my cheek was flayed open, and skin gaped uselessly. "I asked you a question," he smiled back as he admired his work. "I think I should let my men have you first," he taunted.

"I think you should die. Now," I whispered coldly. My wings unfurled and I wrapped my hands around the chains and yanked with all of my strength, pulling until the wooden beam in the ceiling gave way and the hook came undone. I swung it towards Shamus; the hook and chains caught him in the face, tearing flesh with the sheer force I used to slam the chains against him.

He cried out as he placed his hands on the torn skin and vanished. I screamed in frustration that he'd disappeared like a coward before I could give him the ass-kicking he richly deserved. I was slower than I had planned to be, but my limbs were numb from the position I'd been in for hours. I moved through the door, refusing to look at anything except the first vampire who waited for me just outside the door.

He held a sword; his red eyes greedily looked at my breasts and then the blood that seeped from the wounds on my face, chest, and abdomen. He hefted the heavy blade and prepared to swing it, but I was faster. I used the chains as weapons, hitting him with the metal as if they were whips. The blade made a sharp sound as it cut through the chain, severing it into two separate pieces still held by each of my wrists. I pulled them back swiftly, and swung them out again, wrapping both around his neck. I pulled him close, watching as his mouth gasped for much-needed air.

"You were born mortal, and you will die mortal," I whispered as I wiped the blood that still flowed from my face with my fingers and dragged it across his tongue. He tasted it and then yanked back, as others moved forward, watching as he lunged towards me for more of my blood. Before I could stop them, they attacked, biting my flesh to get my blood. Azrael had told me that when my powers completely emerged, that my blood would more than likely smell like an aphrodisiac to vampires, making it difficult for them to ignore it.

I cried out as they latched on painfully, sucking greedily until it hit them. I waited until the last one had drunk and pulled away from me as they coughed and gasped for air. My wings expanded, and I used them to shield my naked breasts as I watched them change, painfully and slowly. Some screamed, some cried and pleaded. None of them understood what my blood was doing to them.

I looked around the room, seeing a lot of women that had been chained to beds and most had bite marks all over their bodies. They'd used this place for Shamus's sick perversions. On the far side of the room, crumpled against the wall, I saw the body of the man I loved, broken and discarded like trash. I stood up, rising on my shaking legs, and moved towards the first woman. She shrank away from me, but her eyes were large, blue, and curious as she took in my wings.

"Are you an angel?" she whispered, tears flowing down her ravaged cheeks.

"I can save you," I replied. "I can save you all," I sniffed back a sob as the memory of the ravaged woman from the cannibals came rushing back with enough pain that I doubled over with it. If my powers had emerged then, if I had known what I was, there was a good chance that I could have saved her. "Do you want to be saved?" I asked, because some of these women were in pretty bad shape from what the vampires had done.

"We do, but what they did to us…" one whispered, and I turned to her, noting her eyes were *gone*. I didn't know if I could fix that, but I'd do my best. So far, my blood seemed to be a cure, I moved away from the women, finding the tools Shamus had been planning to torture me with, and sliced through the palm of my hand. I held it over a bowl, and made my way back to the women.

"I know you're not going to like it, but you need to drink this. It will help you and then we will get out of here, and away from this place. I have a bunker, and you will be safe there," I said as I helped free them from chains that were similar to what I had been held with, and helped one after another to drink a few sips each of my blood. They didn't question it, they trusted me. This would be a lot easier if my powers were fully emerged and I could just touch them and heal them.

I heard something moving behind me, as the women started to cry out in horror. I turned and watched as Azrael sat up. While Shamus was toying with me, Azrael must have been healing with immense speed. He turned his head slowly, and his vivid blue eyes found me. He exhaled, and his wings shot out wide as he stood.

"Emma," he mumbled as I rushed towards him, and we hit the ground hard as I threw myself into his arms. I couldn't stop the sob that exploded from my lips, or the tears that fell in relief as he wrapped his own arms around me, his armor covering his body as the women moved in closer to us. "Did they hurt you?" he asked worriedly, his hands searching my body for any sign that Shamus had assaulted me. His fingers gently caressed the wounds on my face and chest where they had literally shredded my heart, along with the bite wounds that were all over my body. His eyes looked like they were full of pain and I sensed he was hurting because he wasn't able to protect me from what happened.

"No, but he's working with my mother. We have to get out of here, now," I informed him with urgency in my tone.

"I heard a lot of what Shamus said," he whispered as his eyes searched mine. "Some of it was fractured as I healed. It feels like it took hours."

"It did. I was afraid I lost you," I said through the tears. "You can't leave me, ever. It felt like I was splintered, like a part of me was just gone."

"I was gone, briefly. I told you, sweet girl, hard to kill."

"He said Trina told him how to kill you," I snuffled, and he smiled as he wiped my tears away.

"Yes, I am sure that whatever that type of bullet was, a shot to the back of the head would kill the average Sentinel. Lucky for you, there's nothing average about me. It took me down, but it couldn't keep me there. I told you, Trina doesn't know enough about me. You made friends?" he asked, looking at the women who had gathered around us. "Where are Shamus and Astrid?" he questioned before kissing me hard. His arms tightened around me, and I groaned as my chest wounds opened up again. "You are hurt," he chided. His body moved away from mine, and he looked around until he spied something and strode to one of the carts where he pulled out bandages and medical tape.

"Flesh wounds," I lied. "They're healing, and we have to go; whatever Shamus is planning includes the Ark. We have to get there now. I can't lose any more people." He shut me up as he pushed me down and swiftly bandaged the wounds for me like I was a child, at one point smacking my hand out of the way when he thought I was interfering with his ministrations.

"That should hold until you heal enough on your own." He patted the bandage on my chest gently and then helped me up.

The women who had crowded around us stepped back to give us some space and I saw movement at the other end of the room. "Azrael, we're going to have to kill those ones," I said with a nod in the direction of the vampires who were now mortal. "They were all part of Shamus's sick plans and helped him torture these women. If Shamus gets his nasty hands on them again, he will turn them back." I remembered his and Hayden's words about the Guardians of Death and Life, and realized that Azrael and I were meant to work together as a team. I never truly trusted another person enough to really consider myself as part of a team. This would take some getting used to. "I mean, could you take care of them?" I smiled. "Please?"

"As my lady wishes it," he smirked playfully. "It shall be done." He pulled his gloves off and touched the people I had indicated that, up until twenty minutes ago, had been vampires. After he'd finished with the last one, and his hands were once again covered in gloves, he turned to me and smiled weakly. "Let's find a car and get home."

Outside was a van, and once we'd tested it to be sure it worked, we loaded the women up and headed off in the direction of home. My heart was in my throat as I worried if we would make it in time to save everyone.

"We have a big problem," I mused after I'd relayed everything that Shamus had disclosed to me that Azrael may not have heard as he healed.

"And that is?" he asked. His blue eyes met mine, and I felt hot tears prickle behind my eyes as I looked at the face I never thought I would see again.

"My father was under compulsion when he built the Ark, which means it's not safe. We can't stay there. Shamus could have told him anything and he would have done it unknowingly, like the codes. He could have the override code, and it's one that can't be reset. If you try to reset it, my father put in a failsafe that poisons the water and the air supply. He added that in case it was ever taken over by force."

"So Shamus can get inside the Ark at any time with the codes?" he clarified.

"Exactly, we can't lock him out. I'm the only one who is supposed to have the override code besides my dad, and if I was Shamus, I would have asked him what it was. I would have made sure I had all the codes to gain control of the place. I mean, he planned to take control from the beginning, so it makes sense." I frowned as I realized that he hid this from Jaeden and used the lockdown of the Ark to get Jaeden to find me. The bastard probably figured that I didn't have the guts to really leave the main group. The entire time, Shamus was just letting me have the illusion that I was going to Provo of my own free will to get my brother. In reality, he was manipulating every situation he could, like some sort of demented puppet master, to keep me as a prisoner until he was ready to hand me over to my mother.

"I have a place your people can go; it's secure and secluded. It's also got a medical facility, which your people will need with the pregnancies. I made it with you in mind." He gave me a small smile.

"The same house where you took me?" I asked, my heart kicking up a notch with hope.

"No, that place was so I could get to know you better

alone, without the others around. That was designed to keep you in, just in case; this one was for our future. If we had one," he said sheepishly. "It had been almost two years since I had last seen you. I wasn't sure who you would be, or if you'd accept me and, honestly, I wasn't sure I would let you leave if you chose to."

"That's the sweetest thing anyone has ever said to me," I said sarcastically with a hand over my heart.

"Sleep, smartass, you need to heal. Your face looks like hell," he smirked, and winced when I glared at him.

"See, you just know all the ways to give me the feels, don't ya?" I replied as I moved to lay my head in his lap, enjoying the way he groaned when I did it. "Now I'm going to bleed all over you, and you're going to like it."

"Indeed," he smiled down at me, the love in his eyes taking my breath away as the emotions warred inside of me.

I loved him; it was that simple. I wasn't sure when it had happened, but the idea of losing him had torn me apart. Seeing his dead body had torn something inside of me to pieces, and I never wanted to feel that kind of pain again. Ever.

Chapter Thirty-Six

The Ark was silent, no movement from inside or outside as we slowly approached it. We had stopped along the way to clean up and find supplies. Clothing for me and the rest of the women was our first priority. Now, my goal was to get inside, get Addy safe, and rip Astrid's head off. As we got closer, I noted a few who I knew to be included in Shamus's group, but what surprised me were their shadows. Jaeden's men were close by, their eyes watching me as I made my way to the door.

"Bjorn," I acknowledged, watching as he nodded but kept silent. I knew something was off, it was in the way Bjorn stood, and his stance was ready to lunge if the need arose.

The question was who were they watching, me or them? I moved inside the first set of doors. My eyes searched for Jaeden and found him as I walked right in, because I owned the place, at least, I did for the time being.

"Lachlan," I whispered, barely above a breath as the wolf turned to look at me. My face was washed, but the healing damage was still visible and I didn't need words for him to understand what I needed.

His green eyes turned, located Liam and, before I had to ask, Addy was being pushed back into a room, the door locked as Astrid strode into the reception area where we were gathered. She didn't have the brains to figure out that everyone else had stopped moving as my face came into view, or that it was quiet enough to hear a pin drop.

"No, find him and make sure Shamus has what he needs," she snapped at some poor sap that was too busy watching her boobs bounce with every step she took. She paused; her eyes darted to Jaeden's and followed them to where I stood.

"Where is he?" Astrid demanded, her eyes filling with hatred as she noticed we were unscathed and I had a very much alive and breathing Azrael standing next to me. "Where is Shamus!? Attack them!" she screeched, and a few vampires lunged, while others, Jaeden's crew, watched.

"He's a traitor! To you and every vampire in this place," I yelled, focusing on Jaeden's eyes as Azrael countered each attack from the vampires. "He handed your maker over to my mother to gain his power when she killed him, he told me so," I shouted to be heard over the fighting as Jaeden moved towards me, anger radiating from him.

"She's lying, Jaeden baby. You know Shamus wouldn't do that!" Astrid cried. Big fat alligator tears rolled down her flawless cheeks. "He is law; he wouldn't have harmed him! He's his master; he was trying to save him."

"You lying bitch, why don't you tell him about what you two did with Cayla? How you helped to torment her while his men took their turns hurting her! Why don't you tell him that?"

"She's insane, I would never," she hissed. "Shamus was called away by the elders, and I was told to protect this place from her, because she is evil! She's on their side now. She plans to kill us all!"

"He's away with the elders? Did Shamus leave to meet them before or after he told me how Jaeden allowed him to taste me?" I sneered.

Jaeden blanched, and his eyes held mine with a look of apology. Then he lunged, and grabbed Astrid as Azrael moved to intercept her shadow, the Arabian Moor who she always had close to her.

"This is for our child, sweet wife," Jaeden growled as he reached up and twisted her neck, and then literally threw her towards me. "Make her mortal, Emma. Bjorn, kill the others. Any who follow under Shamus die," he shouted, and the chaos erupted as vampires fought each other, and werewolves protected the mortals by creating a wall between them and the chaos.

I stood, watching the fight as if it was playing out

in slow motion. This was my world, these were my people, and Jaeden was fighting *for* me. He'd believed me over Astrid, which tore me apart inside. I loved him; no matter how this ended, I'd always love him. Too much had happened to pretend things would ever be right again. If we'd loved each other enough to begin with, nothing would have been able to tear us apart. But it had, and we'd given it our best shot. It just hadn't been enough.

I brought my palm to Astrid's motionless form and used a blade to reopen the earlier cut, pressing it against her lips until the blood dripped inside. My eyes rose to Jaeden's and I wanted to ask him if he was sure, but the look in his eyes told me that was a pointless question.

"Shamus is involved with my mother. He's been with her from the start. It's why he found my father to build the Ark. We can't stay here. Shamus has the master codes; he could get inside and hurt the humans at any time he chose to. I won't take chances with their lives, so we need to leave." I pulled on Jaeden's sleeve. "Come with me. Come with us."

"If what you say is true, then Shamus will make a move to kill the elders. I can't leave them to that fate. Without them, there is no order or code to my people. So go, protect your people. Protect *our* people, Emma. I'll find you again. I promise."

"Jaeden," I pleaded as I pulled my hand away from him. "I need you."

"No, Emma, you don't need me anymore. I love you. I'm still *in* love with you. I can't watch you be with someone else, so you're going to let me go. We're going to part ways, because I can't be around you and not touch you. So let me go," he said softly, as he leaned over and stroked my healing cheek with a finger before he pulled away as he remembered that just touching me might turn him mortal at any time. "Don't ever think you're not worth fighting for, because you are. If I thought I could have you, I would fight with everything I had to keep you. But he's right; I won't turn mortal for you because I'm needed right now, and well, I couldn't be with you even if we both wanted it. Cayla needs to go with you. She's healing and went through most of the change easily in only a few hours. She didn't wake with hunger, but she's a little more…special." He smiled. "She told me you'd be coming and that you would speak the truth. She needs you. Promise me you'll look after her. Promise me you'll take care of her so that I can do what I have to without worrying about her."

"I promise," I said, knowing I'd do my best for her. She'd been through hell; she deserved a real shot at life. "Jaeden, I wish…" He pushed a finger against my lips before yanking it away as if it was on fire, and looked at me with a smirk.

"Don't," he said, his smirk deepening. "I wouldn't change a moment of being with you, and I knew I'd have to leave. I'm an asshole, because I knew I would. I knew it wouldn't last, but I couldn't stop myself from the moment I tasted you. Hell, from the first moment I saw you, I knew I'd have you and that you'd break my heart. I knew and I took a chance, and sometimes that's just how it works. You love him; I can see it in the way you look at him, so I know you'll be okay." He smiled as he stepped back, away from me. "I don't want to know where you're going, because if the elders demand to know, I need to be able to say that I have no idea where you are. So we'll go, and one day, I'll find you. Besides, sweet girl, I can't help but touch you and we all know how that will end." He smiled sadly, and pulled out his sword and met my eyes. "We can't afford for her to find another vampire to sire her. So, for my child, and what she has done to you and her own people, it is better that she not wake another day," he growled, letting the sword fly as he severed Astrid's head from her body. Blood splattered my face, Jaeden's face, and anyone else close enough to be caught in it. "She can't be forgiven for her sins, as she refused to acknowledge them as sins." Jaeden nodded to Azrael, who removed a glove and touched her face, and then her body. Astrid's head and body decomposed rapidly until all that remained was a skeleton and some ashes that scattered on the floor.

I stood, looking around at the bodies of Shamus's people, who Jaeden's men had easily dispatched. I turned, finding Azrael watching me carefully, knowing he was feeling the sense of closure I'd gotten from talking to Jaeden. I smiled at him, right before I moved into his arms and rested my head against him before I announced that we were leaving Newport for now.

~~*

I stood outside the Ark, watching as explosive charges were mounted and set inside, and the last few items we needed were carried out by the wolves. Addy stood beside me, her hand clasped in mine as we watched them work.

"You sure this is the only way?" she asked.

"If I thought we could stay, I'd stay," I said, turning to look at her. She was glowing; her complexion was radiant, and her eyes sparkled. She'd finally found her pregnancy glow. "It's just a place, and you're my family. Wherever you are is my home now. I have to keep you safe because my mother is hell-bent on taking everything I love away from me, and I can't let her have you. So yes, I'm sure this is the only way. Shamus built this place, everything we thought my father did was him. He built this place while under compulsion, and that means it isn't safe. So, we'll go somewhere that is. You're having a baby, so that means it's time to stop thinking of just ourselves and plan for the future. Grayson wouldn't want me to hold on to a building, and neither would my father. It's just a building. So, you thinking of names yet?" I asked, changing the subject to something that was safer. My eyes prickled with tears at the idea of the Ark being destroyed, because it had played a huge part of my life, and knowing how it had truly come to be tainted it.

"Grayson, if that's okay with you," she said with a frown. "Liam says he'll have a human name, but he'll also get a wolf name."

"Or her, it could be a girl," I said.

"Liam says that it's very rare to have a female cub. He says it's something in the genetic make-up or something like that."

"Did he say it was impossible?" I asked as the men exited the Ark. My heart leapt into my throat, and I fought tears.

"No," she whispered as tears slid down her cheeks.

"Then he could be wrong," I sniffled.

"It's just a building," she cried as she hugged me.

"It's only a building," I repeated.

"So why does it hurt so fucking bad?" she blabbered.

"I don't know," I choked out. "It's not worth crying over."

"No, no because it's just a building." She exploded in tears with me.

We hugged each other, holding on to what little of our world we had left. Each other. We'd been through hell, and while it may be only a building, it was a part of us no matter how much we lied to each other about it.

"You want to tell them it's ready?" Azrael whispered.

"Ouch, nay, mon, ye can do it," Lachlan groaned.

"Emma," Azrael murmured, his fingers reassuring on my shoulder as I struggled to regain composure. "We have to go; we have a long drive."

I turned, looking at the people who stood behind us. A Sentinel, vampires, and werewolves stood shoulder to shoulder with the humans as we prepared to embark on a new adventure. I blinked away the tears and nodded to Liam, who waited for Addy to take her away from the blast site. Cars and trucks were loaded up, along with a few buses Lachlan had pilfered from the school district. I exhaled a shaky breath and folded myself against Azrael.

"It hurts," I admitted. "It's the last thing standing that belonged to my family."

"We don't have to destroy it," he said.

"If we don't, Shamus will probably claim it and use it to torture people in there. I can't let him have it. It may sound childish, but if I can't have it, neither can he. I'm ready," I said.

"You sure?" he countered, sensing the turmoil inside of me.

"I'm entrusting you with our lives, Azrael. So are you sure you can do this? Are you sure you want me enough to take this on? I'm not an easy person to deal with. I have major trust issues, and mommy issues. I normally lose my shit and have anxiety attacks at least twenty times on a good day. Are you sure you can handle me?"

"I've seen you at your worst, and I wouldn't take the best without being able to love you at your worst. I don't care if you snore, or throw shit at my head when you're pissed, as long as you kiss it better afterwards," he whispered, his lips fanning my ear. "We'll wait for them to go, and then you and I will do this together," he said. "We'll meet up with them at Ark II later; first, I have somewhere I want to show you," he continued.

"Oh yeah?" I asked, smirking at him with tears in my eyes.

"Definitely," he assured me.

We waited for the last bus to leave and once we were at a safe distance, he handed me the detonator switch. I took a mental picture of the Ark, and closed my eyes as I pressed the button, felt the earth rock from the concussion of the explosion. When I opened my eyes, there was a hole where the Ark had been. I turned, and looked at Azrael, who watched me carefully.

"I'll build you an exact replica if you want," he said softly.

"I love you for offering to do it, but I don't need it, thank you. What I need is for you to take the pain away. Right now. Take me somewhere and take it away," I whispered, and before I could inhale his scent, we were moving.

I let him hold me as he 'ported us to the clearing where the SUV waited for us. He liked it, touching me, and after centuries of touching no one else, I understood his need for contact, to touch me when he could. Frequently, I would catch his hand barely touching mine, and that little whisper of contact gave him so much comfort that I felt it in his soul.

"Emma," he groaned as he pushed me against a nearby tree and started to remove the skirt I wore.

"No talking," I said. I bent down and removed my panties, right before he reached behind my thighs and lifted me up, pushing my back against the tree. He claimed my mouth in a soul-searching kiss that curled my toes as he fought for domination that I refused to give him easily. He fumbled with his pants, and I decided I couldn't wait and gripped his shirt, lifting it over his head as I balanced on his knee and the tree to undo his pants. My hands found his cock, and I groaned as my hand worked the silky flesh until he growled.

"I want this, now," I whined with need.

"Do you? I want to taste you, so maybe you'll just have to wait," he whispered, as he lifted me until my legs rested on his shoulders, my back was braced against the tree, and he was kissing the flesh between my legs greedily. "You taste like I'm about to fuck you," he groaned, his eyes holding mine as his nose pushed against my clitoris.

"Do I?" I asked. My hands captured his hair, and I pushed him back to where I needed him, balancing to be sure I didn't fall and land on my ass. He'd lifted me higher as if I weighed nothing, and yeah, I probably had sap in my hair, but who the hell really cared? This was hot as fuck! How many women could say yeah, he picked me up and ate my pussy while I climbed a tree? I giggled and his eyes narrowed, he pushed his fingers inside until I moaned and threw my head back, slamming it against the tree, hard. "Jesus, I see stars," I laughed.

"God, I fucking love you, woman," he groaned as he brought me down and pushed me onto his cock.

"Oh damn, that hurts," I groaned, wondering how pain and pleasure could meet each other so perfectly. "So good," I moaned while he used my hips to guide into me and worked our bodies until we both were trembling and hanging on by a thread. "Let it go, Azrael," I whispered as I felt him holding back. "I'm not porcelain, I won't break."

He dropped to his knees, taking me with him as his hand reached up to thread his fingers through my hair, wrenching my head down as he claimed my mouth hungrily. His cock hammered my pussy until I shattered, kaleidoscopic lights exploding behind my eyes. I could feel him to my soul, and when his release came, he cried out for me and I kissed him, raining soft kisses over his beautiful face.

Chapter Thirty-Seven

"It's ten times better," Addy insisted, raising an eyebrow at me and my lie.

"Okay, so what if it is; you don't have to be so damn happy about it!" I argued defensively.

I eyed the crib Liam had found, and the one that I had found. Mine was missing a few pieces, and his was built perfectly. These things were a bitch to build. I frowned at his mattress and smiled victoriously.

"However, his mattress really sucks," I announced. Addy eyed it, and frowned.

"It does, and it's dirty," she agreed.

"So use my mattress, and his crib," I grinned triumphantly. Okay, I could compromise…a little.

"What's wrong with a little dirt?" Liam asked, and I smiled at him with a twinkle of mischief in my eyes.

Yeah, I knew her better than him.

"It is dirt. My baby is not sleeping in dirt. Ever. It's just not happening." She placed both hands on her hips to signal it was end of discussion.

"I'm going to leave now," I sang as I turned to leave the room.

"Addy," Liam said. "Don't you have something to ask Emma?"

"Oh, right," Addy giggled as she rocked on her heels. "So Emma, as you know, we are having a baby."

"Oh my God, no way! I thought the crib was for Liam?" I smiled.

"Mmm, you sure she's the one?" he asked, kissing Addy's cheek and touching the giant diamond that rested on her left hand. Yeah, he'd married her, finally. I was waiting for the topic of mating marks to come up, and that was going to open a whole new set of challenges for us. If he bit her, she would go through the change. If my best friend survived the change, she would not be a born wolf, and I would have to be very, very careful as to how I hugged her—that is, if Liam would ever allow for me to hug her again. Yeah, it was going to be tough to get my mind around it all, but it was a thought for another day. Live for now and all that.

"She's the only one, Liam. Now, stop acting like children," she groaned. "Emma, you're the baby's godmother, period. I don't care if you say no, because you're the only one I trust with my child. Lachlan is the godfather, but you don't have to be, like, together to be the godparents."

"It's about time. I was wondering who I would have to kill to get that position," I huffed.

"Like anyone else would take your place, bitch?" she asked.

"That isn't happening, skank," I replied, kissing her cheek. "I'd be honored to be the godmother. Plus, I was already planning on spoiling the shit out of him, assuming it is a boy, and feeding him sugar while we watch horror movies, so no one else would have been able to handle the job. Now, if you'll excuse me, I have to go and figure out what the plan is to kill my mother and catch her little snake, Shamus." I winked and left them in the nursery that was attached to their suite.

Azrael had taken us to Montana, where he'd commissioned a huge bunker in the Mission Mountains about fifteen years ago that was close to a quaint little town and wasn't too far from the Flathead Indian Reservation. It wasn't Newport, but it felt a lot like home. I was learning that sometimes it wasn't the place that made it home, but the people who you surrounded yourself with instead, that made it so. The bunker was impenetrable and I wasn't a prisoner here. I was his equal or, at least, he treated me as such, and he took in to consideration what I knew, and my thoughts on the war that was brewing. Sentinels now trained the wolves that had joined us, and Cayla was healed and more coherent than she'd ever been before.

"Cayla." I smiled at her as I met her in the hall. "How are you feeling?"

"I'm doing well, my queen," she smirked.

"I'm not a queen," I said with a frown.

"We live in a castle high in the mountains, and you're the mistress here, which makes you the queen and Azrael, the king."

"Is your head wound acting up? Are you well?" I asked, watching her.

"He's doing well and he misses you, but he is glad you are safe and happy, Emma," she interrupted. I hated her topic swings. They made me dizzy. "I can feel him because he's my maker. That's why I had you make me mortal."

"You didn't have me do anything, you bit me," I reminded her. "I'm glad he's well. Shamus is still out there, and until he's dead, no one is safe from his sick, twisted nastiness. There's no place in this world for his kind. What he did to you…he will die for it."

Cayla's hair was blonde now; no colors adorned it, and all the piercings she had were gone. She watched me as I examined her, and then motioned to her face and hair nervously. "I didn't want any reminder of him, and if I wanted to be the person I need to be, to fight beside you, the old me had to die. She was weak; I am not."

Her voice was soft, yet full of resolve.

"She wasn't weak, Cayla. She fought to live against insurmountable odds. She was a brave fighter, but if you need her to be gone to be stronger, I understand. We've all changed a lot since we first met, haven't we?" I asked.

"Some more than others," she smiled. "Hey, Nery and I have a date that I need to get to. I found a box set of *'Friends'* seasons 1 to 10, so we'll be in our room catching up on a lot of TV that we missed. Ya know, just in case you need us." She winked and turned on her heel. "Death comes, because, you know, he wants to come…" She snickered.

I smiled and felt him before I could physically see him. I turned, and watched as he strolled towards me with a wide smile. He took my breath away most days, but on days like today, when the world felt right, he melted me from the inside out. His hair clung to his shoulders, and his armor was gone, leaving his skin bared even though he was surrounded by people.

He was Death, but he'd given up hiding behind his armor all of the time. Most days, he stuck to a uniform of T-shirt, jeans, and gloves, and the others kept a safe distance unless he was wearing the armor. So far, it seemed to work out. Today he'd been meeting with the other groups of Sentinels we'd been gathering together. He'd done something that in Sentinel history had never been attempted. He'd brought our people and immortals together for one cause: To kill the threat to the humans and rebuild their world.

"Emma, you look happy," he said as he kissed me.

"Mmm, so do you," I replied with a bright smile.

"The new group of Sentinels arrived, and await your presence in the courtyard, my queen," he teased with a smirk as I groaned at the title.

"I'm not a queen," I whined. "You told me that Sentinels don't believe in that kind of stuff."

"For the most part, we don't. We do believe in marriage, though." He locked eyes with me and I felt as if my heart was going to jump right out of my chest. I was terrified I hadn't heard him correctly. "Marry me," he murmured as he dropped to one knee and held his hand out towards me, palm up. Laying on his palm was a band of titanium that had little infinity and omega symbols engraved into it.

"Get up," I whispered. "Azrael, get up," I begged.

"No, not until you answer me."

He smiled, and I chewed my bottom lip nervously.

Butterflies fluttered inside my stomach, and I couldn't come up with one reason not to marry him. I loved him, and when I thought I'd lost him, I'd felt despair and a hopelessness that I'd never felt for anyone else. I had no reservations, and I trusted this man with my people, so shouldn't I trust him with my heart?

"Yes," I managed to barely squeak out, and clapping erupted as he rose and picked me up, kissing me as his armor formed around himself as others rushed forward to congratulate us. "Oh my word, you planned this?" I snapped. I felt heat rushing to my cheeks as Lachlan and Addy moved in to hug me. "I hate you all!" I cried as tears fell.

"You deserve it," Addy laughed. "Out of all of us, Ems, you deserve to be happy. So yes, he planned it. We helped. Tomorrow might be world war three, but today, today is for us. It's our world; we're going to make it a world worth living in." She kissed my cheek as she backed up for Lachlan to move in.

"Lass, ye deserve it, congratulations, beautiful girl," he growled, kissing my cheek. "I kenned it would nae be the wolf who married ye, or the undead. Ye deserved a Knight, and ye have him now, Emma." He hugged me tightly.

"Nery told you Death was coming for you," Cayla laughed. "Nery also says that you'll be happy. You'll never want for anything or be cold, and that we will win this war. There will be losses, but they'll be a small price to pay for victory. That the world is looming on a dark age unlike anything we've ever imagined. But in the darkness, your light will save us, Emma. So say yes, because tomorrow is going to be a bloodbath that won't wash off anytime soon. Enjoy the times of happiness while we have them," she said sadly before she moved away from us and Nery put an arm around her shoulders, pulling her close as they left the impromptu gathering.

"Well that was creepy and scary as hell," Addy said as she turned to me. "She can't really see the future, or Nery, right?" she asked.

I swallowed, because I knew Cayla was just telling everyone what Nery said; he could have told me or Azrael that directly if he wanted to. Nery might be vague when he was relaying his morsels of advice, but if he said this world was about to get rocked, then I planned to enjoy life while we could. I was suddenly very grateful for Azrael's keen mind and the fortress that surrounded us.

"Find that pastor you all adopted," I whispered as I turned to Azrael. "Let's not waste any more time."

No matter what tomorrow brought, we'd be in it together. In the end, it's all that mattered. We were safe, we were together, and every day more people found their way to us. I'd face my mother, but I'd do it on my terms and when I was ready to. I'd do it with those I trusted at my side and protecting my back.

I'd lost Grayson, but he was with me. He would always be a part of me, and that could never be taken from me. He was in my memories, and my heart. Those we lost never left us, not as long as we held onto them.

I turned to Azrael and smiled. "I love you," I whispered.

"I love you, Emma," he replied, his lips touching my forehead and then my heart, sensing where my mind had wandered to. "He's here, with your father and all those we lost. Lost, but never forgotten."

Until Next Time...

About the Author

Amelia Hutchins lives in the beautiful Pacific Northwest with her beautiful family. She's an avid reader and writer of anything Paranormal. She started writing at the age of nine with the help of the huge imagination her Grandmother taught her to use. When not writing a new twisting plot, she can be found on her author page, or running Erotica Book Club where she helps new Indie Authors connect with a growing fan base.

Come by and say hello!

www.facebook.com/authorameliahutchins

www.facebook.com/EroticaBookClub

www.goodreads.com/author/show/7092218.Amelia_Hutchins

Printed in Great Britain
by Amazon

63160792R00248